I0603915

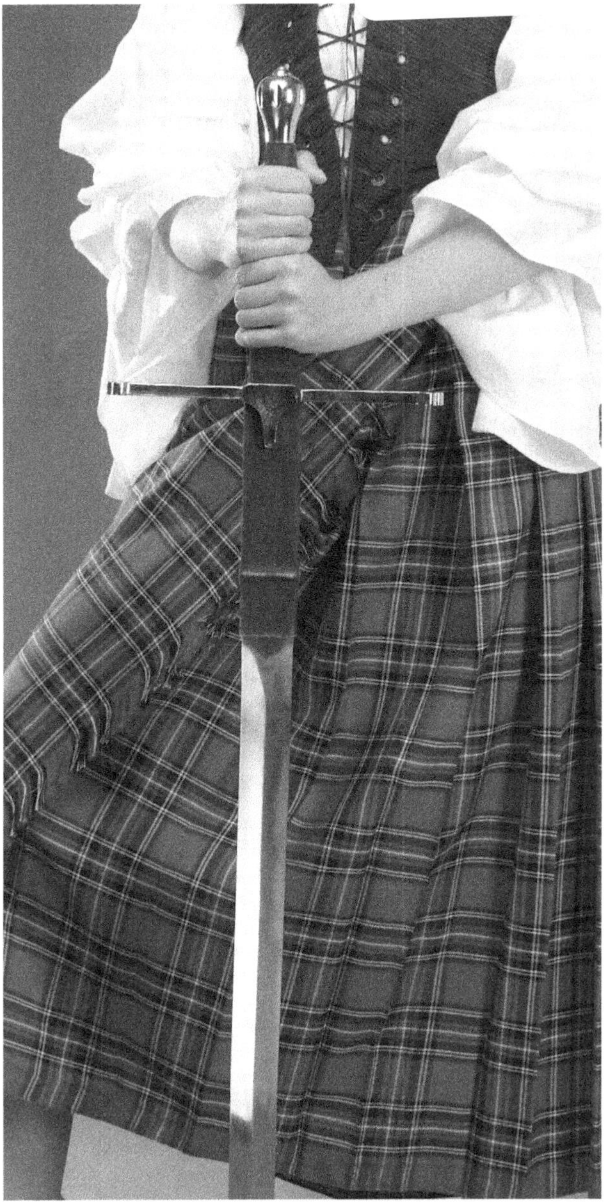

Lord Difficult

Maitland's Rogues

EILEEN PUTMAN

For Alan, Always

Chapter One

London, 1811

"A WOMAN OF MODEST beauty, independent means, and a tireless passion for marital, er, relations." Emmaline hoped her frozen smile projected confidence, not desperation. "I will find just the right bride for you, Mr. Burwell."

"Not too headstrong, mind you, Mrs. Stanhope."

Emmaline looked aghast. "Oh, no. Headstrong is not the thing."

"Her passions must be limited to the marriage bed. I want no intemperate shrew."

"Ugh."

He frowned. "What?"

"Certainly not," she quickly amended, lowering her lashes. The floor, she noticed, had a new crack. Yet another entry for the vermin.

"My work is very demanding," he went on. "I won't stand for a nagging wife. You're certain you are not available?" He stood on her sagging front steps, a speculative gleam in his rather beady eyes.

"I am afraid not." Emmaline's voice filled with

what she hoped was regret. "My heart will always belong to my poor husband, God rest his soul."

"He was lucky to find such a helpmeet." Mr. Burwell tipped his hat. "With your help, I suspect I will be lucky, too. Indeed, you have restored my faith in the future."

He walked toward the street. Emmaline couldn't suppress a surge of elation. The deposit he'd given her would see them through the month.

"Mind the Mail, sir," she called. "The driver never has the courtesy to slow his team. You will wish to cross quickly to avoid his dust."

Mr. Burwell pulled a watch from his waistcoat, which stretched tightly over his ample midsection. "Five o'clock. I didn't realize the day was so far advanced."

"Oh, yes," she replied, with forced cheer. "You can set your watch by the Mail."

And by the bill collectors.

And the drunken sots sleeping on the stoop each morning.

And the stench of cesspits in the night air.

"There's the rent, thank the Lord," muttered a voice at her elbow.

Emmaline turned to her aunt. "Shhh. He will hear."

"Not with the commotion of the Mail," Aunt Heloise replied. "Ruins my afternoon nap."

"When one lives near the Tyburn tollgate, one cannot be particular about noise."

"Or clients." Her aunt studied the man in the street. "If his middle was any larger, he'd not see his shoes. And that scruffy beard—pity the woman who marries him. Her complexion will pay the price. Do you have a prayer of finding him a bride?"

"His requirements are rather stringent," Emmaline conceded. And loathsome. Why had she thought this wretched business would save them?

"Like all of them," her aunt agreed. "The men want doxies, and the women want dukes."

"Unfortunately, I don't know any beautiful, well-fixed women with passionate natures."

"Find him a woman who enjoys the marriage bed, and he won't mind about the other," Aunt Heloise said. "One of the Covent Garden set will take him on, once she sees he's a man of means. In my day, that lot was always on the lookout for the main chance."

"Mr. Burwell is not seeking a prostitute."

"Nonsense. All husbands want their wives to be whores in the bedchamber."

Emmaline sighed. Ever since she'd placed the notice for Harmonious Matrimony Services in the *Times*, they had been deluged with men of the worst sort. "If we don't get more paying clients, we'll have to return to fortune-telling."

"I shouldn't have given away my crystal ball," her aunt said as they stood in the doorway, watching their new client. "Bird in the bush, and all that."

"Bird in the hand."

"Hand, bush—what does it matter? It all boils down to money in the end."

Emmaline couldn't argue. "With Mr. Burwell's

funds, we can afford Dr. Black." None of the other doctors they had consulted could help her aunt's crushing fatigue.

Aunt Heloise patted her shoulder. "It pains me to see you spend your youth on me. In a just world, you'd be married to a prince by now and readying the nursery."

"A prince? You sound like Father. But daydreams don't pay the rent."

"A woman cannot have too many dreams," her aunt said. "By the time she's my age, she'll need every one of them."

"Then let me dream of a cure for you," Emmaline said. "Come. I will make tea. And you can tell me more about the magnificent Mr. Kemble."

"Stepped on everyone's lines," her aunt grumbled. "We loathed him. Did you notice that the door hinges squeak, dear?"

"Candlewax will help," Emmaline said absently.

Mr. Burwell was talking to an elderly woman, apparently giving her directions, for he pointed toward the park, then bowed politely as the woman, her back bent with age, wrapped her voluminous cloak more tightly against the wind.

But after the woman moved on, he remained standing in the road.

"Mr. Burwell," Emmaline called, "the Mail is due any minute—have a care."

Already, the dust cloud that heralded its arrival was in sight. The Mail guard sounded a blast on his tin horn to signal the toll keeper to open the gate.

Mr. Burwell did not budge.

"Lives dangerously, that one," Aunt Heloise observed.

The thundering of hooves and the rumbling of the heavy coach roared nearer. Still, Mr. Burwell did not bestir himself. He wore a pleasant, but strangely empty expression.

Emmaline ran down the steps, nearly tripping as her bad leg tried to buckle. "Mr. Burwell! Sir, you must move this instant!"

He was still smiling when the Royal Mail ran him down.

If George Campbell, the sixth Duke of Argyll, hadn't known beyond doubt that the man behind the desk was his deceased sister's child, he'd be hard pressed to believe it. That Portia could have birthed such a cold creature as Robert Tavish defied comprehension.

The relentlessly recalcitrant Earl of Kent sat at his vast desk, glowering at a scrawny yellow bird. Next to it rested a white bone as big as a man's thigh.

Macabre images came to mind, involving cannibalism and the like. Unthinkable, even for his nephew—no matter that Robert looked but a step removed from the wild. His long hair was not in the current fashion, which favored short at the ears and longer on top so it could be swept into curls approximating some absurd notion of an ancient Roman emperor.

Instead, Robert's sand-colored mane fell to his

shoulders. Occasionally, he pulled it back in an old-style queue.

And while Robert's father had been a fashion peacock given to embarrassingly colorful attire, the son never met a shade of brown that didn't appeal. Now and then, he mustered a drab moss green; otherwise, he seemed determined to sink into mud-colored oblivion.

No oblivion to be had with that unruly hair, though. Or his hard jaw, high forehead, imposing dark brows, and gray eyes the color of unforgiving stone. Even the roaring blaze in the fireplace did not banish the chill he radiated.

If only Portia had seen fit to send him to town years ago to gain polish. But no, she'd taken him off to the wilds of Scotland, and Scotland had produced a beast.

The beast had rebelled. *Shunned family and clan. Refused to embrace his heritage.*

Bringing him back into the fold would be a challenge. Robert rebuffed his every overture. He hadn't so much as glanced up when George showed himself into the study.

Never underestimate a Campbell, however. There was no more politically astute clan. George had set his sights on high office. Already, he had purview over certain War Office matters—his sporadic alliance with Whigs notwithstanding. He was aiming for Privy Council, Chancellor of the Exchequer, and—in time, perhaps—prime minister.

But first, there was the matter of his nephew. Family mattered. Clan, above all. Inveigling Robert was a long game, but George had finally arrived at the perfect plan.

"There has been a death," he began. "Unusual circumstances that fall, as it happens, within your area of expertise."

His nephew's disapproving glare remained fixed on the bird, which was staring back.

"The deceased, William Burwell, was a clerk in the War Office," George continued. "He was under investigation for possible treason."

This statement likewise had no discernible effect.

"Documents have been disappearing," he went on. "Last month, the French obtained schedules for our supply ships to the peninsula. They sank one ship, damaged another."

George paused to allow Robert to commiserate with England's war woes.

He did not.

"We'd been shadowing Burwell, hoping to catch him in the act," George said, more forcefully. "His sudden death was cause for consternation. We are no closer to identifying those behind this treachery."

Those unnerving gray eyes blinked once.

George prided himself on his calm mastery of the vagaries of politics, London weather, and the silly social scene. He rarely spoke intemperately. Nevertheless, his blood boiled.

"The Mail ran him over." He barely restrained himself from shouting. "By all accounts, Burwell stood in its path like a suicidal squirrel."

An appreciative chirp came from the desk.

"Can't you do something about that bird?"

George demanded. "Surely, your cook has a recipe for pigeon pie."

"Canary," his nephew corrected. "Most unsatisfactory in a pie."

The low voice flowed like thick honey—the bitter kind from heather, not the mild stuff from orange blossoms. His mother's voice had been pure and sweet. Robert's left a distinct aftertaste.

With a muttered curse, George pulled a newspaper from his pocket and tossed it onto the desk. "Burwell died outside this woman's establishment. She runs some sort of marriage agency. I've circled her notice."

It read:

Gentlemen desirous of meeting agreeable ladies for marriage are requested to call at Harmonious Matrimony Services, 709 Oxford Street, where a Respectable Widow will assist them in the process of selecting a future mate. A small fee will ensure the happiest of outcomes.

"And this handbill was found in his pocket." George thrust it under Robert's nose. "Seems she also dabbles in fortunes."

Fortunes told, wishes fulfilled, future unveiled. Madame Flora, 709 Oxford Street.

When Robert did not react, George turned the handbill over. On the back was drawn a skeleton in black armor riding a horse, its reins adorned with skull and crossbones.

His nephew blinked. "The Tarot death card."

"Exactly. It's possible she was involved in Burwell's death and possibly his treason."

Robert regarded the drawing thoughtfully.

"She lives with an aunt," George said. "Nothing

criminal in her background, but that death card has unnerved more than one investigator. Some suspect that mesmerism or other occult art caused him to stand in the path of the Mail."

His nephew's mouth curved in what might have been a smile, had he been one to indulge in frivolity. "I know of no occult practice capable of causing a man's feet to stick to the cobblestones as death bears down on him."

"Still, we lack an explanation as to why he didn't save himself."

"Rational explanation lies behind all unusual phenomena."

"We don't have one here," George insisted.

"I tried to enlighten Parliament about this sort of thing years ago. Failed." Robert picked up his pen. "I've a paper to finish, Uncle. What do you desire of me?"

"Visit this woman. Pretend to be a client in need of her matrimonial services. With your background, you'll discern things others might miss."

Robert's pen moved smoothly over the paper. "No."

"Do it for your mother's sake, Robbie. You might prevent someone else falling victim as Portia did."

His nephew looked up, his gaze hard. "You dare invoke her memory for such triviality?"

"It's anything but trivial. With Massena on the run, the peninsula war's at a turning point. We must discover who is behind this nefarious scheme." George took a deep breath. His expression softened. "I honor you for what you tried to do in her name. Just because you failed to convince some quarreling Tories is no reason to—"

"It's every reason," Robert tossed his quill on the desk as the canary fluttered in protest.

Time to shift tactics. "I know you had a difficult boyhood—"

"I am thirty, Uncle. Boyhood's a lifetime behind me."

"Yet I cannot forget that summer Portia brought you to us." Dangerous ground there, but George pressed on: "You were so lost."

Robert's features flattened, until they were empty of all expression. He picked up his quill once more but did not dip it into the inkwell. Instead, he began to move it back and forth.

"The woman's name is Emmaline Stanhope," George said. His eyes tracked the pen's steady tempo.

No response.

The silence lengthened. The pen kept moving.

The bird, meanwhile, had gone still at the edge of his nephew's desk.

In fact, everything seemed to freeze. There was only that slow-moving quill.

Robert's gaze fixed unblinkingly on George.

George's vision shrank to the tip of that quill. A strange heaviness beset him. Time seemed overcome by the same lethargy. His brain felt… scrambled. His legs were lead, his arms paralyzed. Whispered words penetrated the fog that engulfed him.

They ordered him to throw himself into the fire. Deadly flames flared in his mind's eye.

With great effort, George stepped backward. "What are you doing to me?"

"You've done it to yourself, Uncle." Robert rapped his pen sharply on the desk.

The world struggled into focus. It was a moment before George could speak.

"I may have…lost the thread," he said slowly.

"No, you've proven my point," Robert said. "While the mind can be led, it inclines above all to survival. It will triumph over insidious efforts to subvert that instinct. You, for instance, declined to throw yourself on the fire. If your traitor was murdered, it was not by mesmerism."

But George had recovered his senses. "I remain unconvinced. I insist that you investigate Burwell's death and prove me wrong." Spoken firmly, in a tone calculated to brook no argument.

It was a risk. His nephew was not one to be pushed.

Robert regarded him incredulously. "Am I to understand that you wish me to discover whether this Mrs. Stanhope put your suicidal squirrel under a spell?"

George shot him a pained look. "I am aware that sounds slightly ridiculous. Do this for Portia's sake, if nothing else."

Shameless tactic, that. But it had the desired effect.

Robert gave a curt nod. Abruptly, he rose. "Show yourself out, Uncle. I have papers to write.

The beauty of science is that it is not dependent on human foolishness."

His nephew, so pitiful as a child, had grown into the very devil himself. Complete with a familiar, which—freed from its own tiny trance— squawked loudly as George beat a swift retreat.

Chapter Two

"A GENTLEMAN IS DOWNSTAIRS." Aunt Heloise struck a pose in the doorway of Emmaline's bedchamber. "Compelling sort. Claims to be in search of a bride."

Emmaline looked up from her diary. "I hope you told him our services are no longer available."

"I did no such thing. The rent is due."

Emmaline gave a weary sigh. "Poor Mr. Burwell."

"Pity him if you must, but no sane person would stand in the path of a coach and four."

"He gave no sign that his wits were addled," Emmaline said.

"'He dies and makes no sign.'" Aunt Heloise brought her handkerchief to her lips. "You ought to have seen me as Queen Margaret. Although that line was Henry's. Shakespeare gave the best lines to men. He made Margaret a she-wolf because she dared to be ambitious."

Emmaline smiled. "Only because you were not there to inspire him."

"Perhaps. But to the matter at hand: The gentleman's clothes are of good quality but not ostentatious. His hair is not in the usual style—

long and full, almost leonine. Odd sort, though. Doesn't speak much."

"If he lacks manners, that might explain why he needs help finding a wife." Emmaline sighed in resignation. They did need the money. They had returned Mr. Burwell's deposit to a pair of investigators who could give her no clue as to why the man had failed to save himself. They promised to convey the funds to his relatives.

She checked her appearance in the mirror. Men who came to them for matrimonial assistance often misunderstood the services they offered. Thus, precautions had to be taken. Her hair was secured in a tight coil so as not to convey frivolity or worse, lascivious intent.

Her forest green dress—her one serviceable frock—was equally spartan. Its unfashionably high neckline rose nearly to her chin. No flounces or adornments marred its hem.

Moreover, she looked exceedingly grim. Dark circles under her eyes reflected the sleepless nights she'd spent since Mr. Burwell's horrifying death. She turned to her aunt. "Out of respect for the poor man we should drop this venture."

"Respect's a fleeting coin," Aunt Heloise insisted. "Won't pay the rent."

"I cannot force a pleasant countenance and pretend that everything is as usual," Emmaline protested.

Her aunt preened in the mirror and tossed her own, faded copper curls. "Women pretend. It's one of our gifts."

Emmaline mustered her resolve. Perhaps this man would be their salvation.

Or not. Miracles did not walk into one's parlor and await discovery.

Making her way down the narrow stairs, Emmaline fought against her limp. Today required more effort to control it. Perhaps that was due to fatigue. Or the pall that had settled over her since her client's death.

Aunt Heloise was well-suited to pretense. She wasn't.

Emmaline halted outside the parlor and peeked in to see what manner of man awaited.

A gaze—gray as gloom but penetrating as a stiletto—slammed into hers.

She stifled a gasp, though it was too late for stealth. He'd seen her.

The man's large frame took up most of the sofa. It was as if a giant tried to fit on a pin cushion. Even as she tried to grasp an overall image of the man, her eyes fixed on individual parts. His undisciplined long hair put her in mind of a pirate, its color wet sand with a hearty burst of red clay. His face was clean-shaven. Strangely, that made him look more dangerous.

His clothing was brown, like rich earth. The moss green walls she had painted just last week seemed to exist solely to frame him as a force of nature.

Quickly, Emmaline pasted a smile on her face. "Good afternoon, sir. I am Emmaline Stanhope. I hope I haven't kept you waiting."

"You have." He rose, his gaze icy. "Robert Tavish."

He regarded her extended hand as if it were a piece of rotten fish, not that she could blame him. Her hands were red and raw from soap-making. She'd added too much lye, and it left her with burns. But they couldn't afford the gentler, expensive bar soap from Gerrard Street.

She tucked her hand into the folds of her dress. "How may I be of service, sir?"

"Wife. Need one." His deeply resonant voice held a rough undercurrent.

How could such a robust specimen of a man need assistance? His broad shoulders and rugged physique put her in mind of a medieval warrior ready to do battle—with or without a weapon. Indeed, those large hands were weapons enough.

His temperament was suspect, judging by that stern brow, grim mouth, and disregard of complete sentences.

"I should inform you that an unfortunate accident occurred last week," Emmaline began.

One forbidding brow arched.

"A client had the misfortune to be struck by the Mail. Investigators tend to drop by at odd moments. I'm afraid I cannot promise that your association with me would remain confidential."

When his frown deepened, she immediately regretted her candor. Aunt Heloise had the right of it. If he took his business elsewhere, there'd be no paying rent.

Emmaline had no doubt he could afford her fee. Though his clothes were plain, the facing of his coat was silk serge. A woman who had to trim her frocks every year to disguise the wear developed an eye for such details.

"I could meet you elsewhere," she offered, "so that we would not risk observation."

He was silent for so long Emmaline feared she had offended him. Or—heavens!—thought she was suggesting another kind of rendezvous altogether.

"What I meant to say," she added carefully, "is I am aware that those who seek assistance in matrimony may have no wish for that fact to be known."

He scowled at the floor. She turned to see a small black shadow dart around a chair leg.

"Can't abide cats," he growled.

Emmaline scooped up Thomas. "This one has a gentle nature. And people who come to have their fortunes told expect to see a black cat in residence."

"Fortunes?" Uttered with distaste.

"My aunt and I read the Tarot occasionally," she said. "It can be amusing."

"What of those who take your words to heart and ruin their lives?"

His hostility took her aback.

"We do not ruin lives here, Mr. Tavish," Emmaline snapped.

Thomas squirmed in her arms, and she quickly released him. He landed at her visitor's feet and proceeded to rub against his leg.

He stiffened.

No wonder the man's marital prospects

were dim. A man with a perpetually stern countenance and insufficient warmth to abide even so independent a creature as a cat would have difficulty gaining any woman's affections. Emmaline had a fierce urge to send him packing.

Instead, her practical nature won out.

"Perhaps it would be best to go over the terms of my services." She seated herself in the chair, leaving him to stand or sit as he preferred. He remained standing.

"My fee is fifteen pounds." Usually it was far less, but he could afford it. "Half paid on signing our agreement, the rest on your betrothal. If, for some unforeseen reason, marriage doesn't occur, I refund a small sum to be applied to a new search through our agency."

His gaze narrowed.

"I am well-qualified, as I was married myself," Emmaline said, the lie making her throat as dry as dust. "Unfortunately, my husband is deceased."

This revelation usually caused prospective clients to eye her with compassion. Mr. Tavish's stern expression did not change.

"Moreover, I attended Catherine Warwick's School for Young Ladies in Hadley," she continued. Her father had sent her there to gain what a mother would have imparted. "Perhaps you have heard of it? It is known for its education in the womanly arts, such as managing the household, supervising meal preparation, mending…"

Boredom swept Mr. Tavish's features. He still didn't trouble to sit but stood towering over her.

Men such as this irritated her. Their high

regard for their own importance required that they diminish or dismiss other human beings, especially females. Women were expected to accept their disregard without complaint.

A task at which she routinely failed.

Emmaline's temper snapped. "I imagine you'd view Miss Warwick's as beneath your attention. Especially as there's little left but one shabby building and elderly teachers with nowhere else to go."

The stony contempt in that gray gaze might have slipped a notch.

Drat her wayward tongue. She needed to salvage this. Emmaline forced a conciliatory tone. "Suppose we begin with the type of bride you seek."

"The marrying kind."

She fought the urge to box his ears. "What I *meant* was her character, her temperament, that sort of thing. You would, of course, wish her to share your interests."

"I study rocks. I would doubt her sanity if she shared my interests."

"Rocks?"

He reached into his pocket, pulled out some bank notes, and tossed them at her. "I must finish a paper for delivery tonight. Argyll Rooms, eight o'clock. We will talk then."

With that, he gave a cursory bow and strode from the house. The front door's creaking hinges punctuated his departure, mocking her increasingly desperate plight.

To Robert Tavish's growing list of undesirable

qualities, Emmaline added the sin of unbridled arrogance.

She would find him a wife. Then the devil could take him.

⌇

Infinity, Robert thought darkly, might well be measured in cobblestones. Someone, somewhere, was always building roads in the name of progress.

To him, progress meant avoiding the past. But despite the years he'd put behind him, the darkness stalked him still. How like George to dip into his bag of tricks and summon unanswered questions and disturbing memories.

George had in common with centuries of Campbell chiefs the skill of manipulation. Invoking Portia was a low blow. Robert ought to have saved his mother. He didn't. Guilt festered.

And George knew it.

Robert had sent his carriage home, deciding that walking was a better remedy for his mood than a closed vehicle. It was a choice he now regretted. The rows of uneven cobblestones stretched to forever under his feet as late afternoon grew into dusk.

His thoughts were equally unrelenting. Emmaline Stanhope's eyes—startlingly blue, like cornflowers—had not quite disguised her disgust of him when he shunned her cat. Odd how the old fears could be summoned so easily.

No matter. If he had to apologize every time someone took him in disgust, he'd spend eternity in supplication.

Besides, the pinch-faced Mrs. Stanhope seemed to take offense at everything. Life, or perhaps a threadbare widowhood, had given her a flinty nature and sharp edges.

Robert did approve of her frock—plain with no embellishment. She kept her spine straight and her gaze direct, perhaps to inspire trust from clients. More handsome than beautiful, she hadn't fluttered her lashes or deployed other silly feminine strategies, which was a relief. He had no patience for silly women.

If ever he was inclined to seek a wife—God forbid—he'd never hire someone like her for the task. Her ideas were absurd. Why the devil would he wish a wife to share his interests? So they might go digging together? A wife would only get in the way.

Perhaps his uncle's suspicion was correct—that Mrs. Stanhope's marriage brokering, or whatever it was called, served as cover for illicit activities that turned a better profit. If not treason, perhaps the occult. That feline proved nothing, of course. Many people had cats, even black ones.

Nevertheless, signs of trickery were apparent if one knew where to look. Robert hadn't learned them in time to save his mother, but he'd studied them deeply since.

Discovering the dour Mrs. Stanhope's tricks would be an unpleasant use of his time. As unpleasant as the endless cobblestones that with every footstep sounded a question about whether life held much to interest him anymore.

A clatter of wheels punctured his bleak

reverie. The very carriage he'd dismissed at Mrs. Stanhope's cottage rolled to a stop beside him. Gibbons peered out, silently opened the door.

Robert sank gratefully into the squabs. "Remind me to pay you better."

"As you say, my lord." Gibbons regarded him benignly, as if it were perfectly ordinary to rescue his employer from whatever fate awaited a man so foolish as to walk the turnpike at dusk, alone save for his own depressing thoughts.

❧

"It is possible the bone derives from an ancient, as yet unrecognized creature. Size and weight rule out human origin." Mr. Tavish scarcely glanced at his audience as he held up the ghastly bone.

He pointed to a chart. "The New Red Sandstone strata contains the oldest relics, the Chalk strata the most recent."

His baritone was dry and flat, as if he'd intentionally wrung the life out of it. Emmaline detected something in his speech—a slight lingering over a syllable here and there—that added an exotic note. But he seemed determined to wrestle it into drab monotone.

Emmaline felt distinctly out of place in this room of men. She'd brought her walking stick, which made her feel conspicuous, as most women didn't carry them. But most women had no need to walk by themselves at night or fend off the human predators who plied the streets.

Mr. Tavish hadn't even offered to send a conveyance, despite all but decreeing her presence.

But she told herself to stop looking for slights. They needed this client.

From her seat in the back of the room, Emmaline noticed that a few in the audience had dozed off. If she hadn't been so intrigued by Mr. Tavish's transformation from the wildly edgy man in her parlor to this lifeless pedagogue, she might have nodded off, too.

Fortunately, the lavishly decorated room, though not large, offered much to see, like the massive chandelier hanging from a thunderbolt clutched by a gilded eagle. There were other distractions. Laughter filled the corridor beyond the room as scantily attired women passed by to the grand saloon, which served as the ballroom.

Mr. Tavish seemed oblivious to the noise.

"Diligent study will be required to determine the bone's origins," he droned on. "It is my recommendation that the Society undertake new excavations in Cornwall and along the <u>Devon coast,</u> the most promising sites." He massaged the bridge of his nose, as if unburdening himself of such weighty information had given him the headache.

Heaven save the world from such scholars. Her father had been one, and if he had ever come down from his ivory tower to grapple with real life, Emmaline had missed it. His lofty detachment was fed by the adoration of his students, who thought he could do no wrong.

And wasn't that a bitter thought? She wasn't proud that she had envied those students for capturing her father's undivided attention.

Resentment, envy, boredom—this evening was bringing out the worst in her. Emmaline tried to focus on something positive.

Such as Mr. Tavish's appealing superficial qualities. His clothing was understated—dark brown coat, tan trousers, and drab neckcloth. On him, they looked anything but dull.

Rather, they proved a perfect backdrop for showcasing the muscular frame that, with those slashing cheekbones and unruly hair, gave him a look unlike that of any man in the room. Truthfully, it was no chore for her eyes to feast on that.

The more she studied him as he paced the stage with his charts and his bone, the more she realized that while Mr. Tavish was a scholar, he wasn't like her father. He didn't seem to care, for instance, whether the audience hung on his every word. His gaze did not roam around the crowd looking for adoration, making eye contact like a needy performer.

That fascinated her. Most scholars, her father included, loved to show off their brilliance. Mr. Tavish didn't seek affirmation or acolytes.

Yet he had made an important discovery—that ghastly bone.

Why, then, this dry-as-dust delivery?

The man in her parlor had been as restless as a caged bird of prey. But perhaps parlors and stages did not suit him. Perhaps he belonged out in the open, stalking red sandstone and chalk strata with shovels or picks or whatever tools he used.

Almost, Emmaline envied him that freedom. Save for Oxford, she'd never lived anywhere but London, first in her father's house stuffed with papers, and now the shabby cottage she'd been forced to let after selling the house to pay his unexpected and strange debts.

Slowly, methodically, Mr. Tavish neatened his papers into a precise pile, then regarded his audience with a lifeless gaze. It seemed he had finished.

One by one, the men in the audience bestirred themselves as they realized the lecture was over. No women—to their credit—had wasted their evenings by coming. Women had flocked to her father's talks, mostly to flirt with the handsome widower.

Woe betide any woman who undertook a flirtation with Mr. Tavish. As a conversationalist, he was sadly lacking. As a scholar, he seemed intent on stamping the life out of learning. As a prospective groom, he perhaps held possibilities: Some women might be drawn to that savage look. Still, Emmaline would have her work cut out for her finding him a bride.

A smattering of applause spread through the room. Mr. Tavish bowed in acknowledgment. Another man on stage made closing remarks praising his scholarship.

The room emptied, leaving Mr. Tavish to gather his bone and charts. Emmaline made her way to the stage. When he failed to notice her, she cleared her throat discreetly.

"Whatever it is you are peddling, madam, be it arcane theories or your person, I'm not interested." He hadn't even glanced at her.

Emmaline frowned. "I understood this was urgent."

"Nothing exigent about fossils." He wrapped the bone in a swath of linen. "They've lain in repose for millions of years. And will for millions more."

"I beg your pardon?"

"E-x-i-g-e-n-t. Something that requires immediate action. Or was it *'repose'* you did not comprehend? This meeting's for Society members only."

He still hadn't bothered to look at her. As she stood below the stage, looking up at him, he seemed impossibly tall and beyond her reach—in all meanings of the word, the arrogant man.

"I am here at your invitation—nay, demand," she snapped. "I cannot imagine why you have forgotten our appointment, unless the lecture numbed your brain as much as it did mine."

At last, he turned. Annoyance gave way to slow recognition as he looked down at her.

"Mrs.....?" His brow furrowed.

"Stanhope. Emmaline Stanhope."

"Ah." He pointed to the pile of charts, as if that explained his lapse. A gentleman might have apologized for his rudeness, but Mr. Tavish did not.

Emmaline took a deep breath, striving for calm. "Have you decided whether the terms I outlined are acceptable?"

He gave an indifferent shrug. "Need to know more about your customers—"

"Clients," she corrected.

"—the dead one, especially."

"What do you wish to know?"

"Whether hiring you puts me in mortal danger."

Emmaline gritted her teeth. "May we sit, Mr. Tavish?"

She didn't wait for a response but marched up the steps to the stage and sat in a wooden chair vacated by the man who had closed the program. "I keep information about my clients confidential, but in the case of poor Mr. Burwell, I suppose it does not matter. He was in a jolly mood. His last words to me were along the lines of my having restored his faith in the future."

"Ironic."

It was all Emmaline could do not to kick his shins. "How unkind. But I suppose it's useful for me to learn your faults if I am to find you a bride. I will note that your humor tends toward sardonic. *Some* women may find that appealing."

Such candor was unwise, she knew. But she couldn't resist a chance to puncture the arrogance she was certain lay beneath his relentless disregard of her.

Something flared in that gray gaze, then vanished. "What of the grieving fiancée?"

"We had not gotten that far," she said. "I had only obtained a list of his requirements."

"Which were?"

Emmaline bristled. "I don't see why that is your concern."

"Wondered whether you'd satisfied his needs." He gave the last word a slight emphasis, and it lingered in the air between them.

"My business is entirely aboveboard. I hope you do not suggest otherwise." She paused in the event he chose to reassure her that he intended no such insinuations.

Mr. Tavish remained silent.

Abruptly, she rose. Rent money or no, she wouldn't tolerate insult. "If you are looking for an abbess, you had best look elsewhere."

"Abbess?" His brow furrowed.

"A-b-b-e-s-s." Emmaline wrapped her cloak around her and turned to leave. "I doubt you'll find the meaning in Mr. Johnson's dictionary. Perhaps some of the noisy ladies out in the corridor can enlighten you."

He moved to block her way. "Wait."

Emmaline's chin rose. They regarded one another like two fighters in Gentleman Jackson's boxing exhibitions. And yes, she knew more than most women about such events.

"My, ah, requirements for a bride…not something I've thought about," he said.

Why then, had he come to her?

"Intelligence, I suppose," he added. "Aversion to sentiment, disinclination to hysteria."

"Most men wish for brides who are beautiful and passionate," Emmaline said.

"No passion."

Emmaline blinked. "I see."

"You think that odd?"

"Marriage is said to foster the sharing of mutual passions," she said carefully.

"Never met one."

"One what?" she asked.

"A mutual passion. Illusion created by poets. But I defer to your experience. Doubtless you shared such with your husband." His speculative gaze made her face warm.

Emmaline studied him. "Why, exactly, do you wish to wed, Mr. Tavish? In my experience, people marry for passion and companionship on the one hand, money and lineage on the other. In the happiest of marriages these goals coincide."

"I have money. I've no use for pedigree, and passion never serves."

A revelation—the man could muster complete sentences.

"Would you wish for children?" Emmaline asked.

Something flickered in his gaze. "I think not."

Her stomach chose that moment to growl rebelliously.

"I've a biscuit in my pouch," Mr. Tavish said.

There was no denying the obvious.

"I did not have time to eat," Emmaline confessed.

He handed her a small cake. While she ate, he finished packing.

Emmaline's temper improved with food. "So, as I understand your requirements for a bride, she must be smart, practical, even-tempered—"

"More than even-tempered. Phlegmatic. P-h-1-"

"I know how to spell, sir. My education was in no way defective. You want a woman without an ounce of emotion."

He looked surprised. Did he think her vocabulary limited to words of one syllable?

"What of her appearance?" Emmaline asked.

Mr. Tavish stared at her blankly.

"Her *looks*, sir. Some of my clients prefer dark-haired women, some light; some prefer thin women, others ladies with m o r e…fullness."

"Big as a barn or as thin as a rail, just as long as she doesn't get in my way." He pronounced "rail" with a slight trilling of the R. "I have precise habits. Commit them to memory, as my wife must observe them scrupulously."

Emmaline eyed him warily. "My memory is excellent."

"I rise at six, breakfast at seven. Luncheon is flexible—noon, give or take the half hour. I am not to be disturbed when working in my study. I take sherry at dusk, dinner at eight, brandy after. Prefer whisky, but not the English turpentine."

"Sherry at dusk," she murmured, dazed.

"In summer I am in Cornwall for digs. Autumn I prepare a paper on my findings for presentation to the Society. Winter I teach at Oxford."

"And the spring?" she managed. "Is that planned, too, or do you leave it to chance?"

"I leave nothing to chance. Spring is Sussex—wealth of fossils in sandstone. But I'm intrigued by Devon's possibilities, so that may change. You are looking at me strangely."

"It is just that—" Emmaline began.

"Those are my requirements. How soon can you find someone?"

When hell freezes over.

"I may need a few days," she said cautiously.

He picked up his charts and bone. "Time to leave."

Emmaline waited for the arm she assumed would be offered. But Mr. Tavish simply strode off. At length, he turned and frowned. "Coming?"

<hr>

Mrs. Stanhope looked peaked. He'd been tempted to take her arm or offer a steadying hand, but she was a prickly sort who exuded capability and undoubtedly would take offense. Odd that she had a cane; she carried it like an accessory, never once leaning on it.

As they descended the grand staircase, her lips were pursed, her expression strained. Judging by the rigid set of her shoulders, she was consigning him to the devil.

No matter. She might be a traitor, she might be a whore—albeit an educated one—but it was nothing to him. He had agreed to do this for the sake of his deceased mother; nothing else mattered. Certainly not Mrs. Stanhope's sensibilities.

Fashionable peers of the realm escorting provocatively attired women brushed by them. His lecture had coincided with the Cyprian's

Ball—a night of bacchanalia when some of London's most fashionable aristocrats cavorted openly with their light-skirts. Robert was not unfamiliar with Cyprus and its association with Aphrodite, the sexually insatiable goddess of love. But using Greek mythology as excuse for louche behavior was both unoriginal and excessive. One more reason—not that he needed it—to be repulsed by the titled elite.

Robert was learning to bear the nuisance of a title, but Society members and his students knew him simply as Professor, the only title he valued.

Some of the men, he noticed, eyed Mrs. Stanhope speculatively. Though she must have felt their scrutiny, she held her head high amid the tawdry birds of paradise.

Even in her plain frock and worn cloak, she exuded a taut dignity. Her auburn hair was disciplined into a severe coil at her nape. Her simple cloth bonnet lent her an air of innocence that Robert suspected masked a calculating mind.

Had she conspired in Burwell's death? Did evil lurk behind her striking features?

Outside, private carriages were lined up for blocks. Mrs. Stanhope would have to walk some distance to find a hackney. Robert hesitated. Whatever she was, he couldn't abandon her in the crush of leering peers and half-naked women.

"I will help you find a hackney," he said.

"How kind."

Was there an edge in that clipped response? But she merely stared straight ahead.

Robert strode past the carriages—his wasn't

among them, as he'd walked the few blocks from his home—leaving her to follow. But when he reached the corner, he was alone.

Frowning, he turned. Half a block behind, Mrs. Stanhope stood between two disheveled dandies. One of them pulled her into his arms.

She uttered no cry of distress, no plea for rescue.

Instead, she swung her reticule, landing a blow on the man's head. He staggered, then lunged for her, but came away with only her cloak. With a roar, he tossed it into the street.

"Hell," Robert muttered.

The dandies were foxed. There'd be no reasoning with them. Robert secured his bone and charts under his arm and strode toward them.

By the time he reached Mrs. Stanhope, she was readying her reticule for another blow.

"Do stop dallying, madam," Robert ordered.

She eyed him incredulously.

"Is she yours?" one of the men drawled, putting a proprietary hand on her shoulder. "Ours now. Finders, keepers."

Mrs. Stanhope sent a sharp elbow into the man's gut. When he grunted in pain, she swung her reticule again. It connected with his face— but not before he tore at her frock.

"Madam," Robert said in a low voice. "Step aside. I will handle this."

Instead, she caught the ruffian's hand and bit it.

There was nothing for it but to set his priceless bone and charts near her ruined cloak and pray they did not meet the same muddy fate.

Robert's kick caught her assailant in the back.

His next kick sent the man to the ground. He turned to the other dandy in time to see Mrs. Stanhope bring her cane down on the man's shoulders. The culprit wobbled, then fell to his knees.

Robert plucked her cloak from the street. It was dirty and damp, but he tossed it over her shoulders nonetheless. Then he rescued his bone and charts.

He grabbed her hand, and they fled.

Chapter Three

"I AM GRATEFUL FOR your assistance." Emmaline clutched her soggy cloak, unable to resist adding, "Such as it was."

They rode in the well-appointed coach that had mysteriously appeared at the corner of Little Argyle and King streets as they dashed from the scene of the scuffle. It was a welcoming respite—her leg ached, and she had not a prayer of keeping up with Mr. Tavish.

He eyed her with undisguised curiosity. "What do you carry in your reticule?"

"Rocks. I bring them when I am on my own, especially at night." If that made him feel guilty for not sending a carriage to carry her to his dreadful lecture, so be it.

"And the cane—"

"Walking stick," she corrected.

"May I see it?"

She passed it to him. He held it in both hands, weighing it. "Wee bit of lead inside, if I don't miss my guess."

"I've had it modified for my own protection." She hesitated. "Are you Scottish?" That would fit with the subtle difference in his speech she detected earlier.

"Not usually."

He did not elaborate. Instead, he returned her stick and sat stiffly on the seat.

"Do you have any notion where this vehicle is taking us?" Emmaline ventured.

"Yes."

Again, no elaboration. The man was insufferable.

"Are you always rude?" she demanded.

Mr. Tavish glanced at her. "You are angry."

"A brilliant deduction. No wonder you rendered that audience hopelessly inert for one hour and forty-five endless minutes."

He blinked. "Speak your mind, don't you?"

Emmaline knew she had gone too far. "Not always wisely."

"Indeed. You delivered your verdict without a shred of knowledge about my field."

"I apologize." But she wasn't sorry. He was infuriating.

Mr. Tavish studied her. Emmaline was certain he was about to demand his money back.

But he surprised her. "I don't do well in closed carriages."

"How do you mean?"

"Tight spaces trouble me. Conversation is unwelcome."

Emmaline stared at him. "I have never heard of such a thing."

He did not reply. Remoteness settled over him.

Yet he was such a solid physical presence in

the confines of the carriage that Emmaline was acutely aware of him. She picked up the scent of damp leather—his boots? The faint whiff of parchment—his charts. Decay—that bone?

The man was a mystery. It surprised her that he was a scholar. With his size and strength, he didn't seem suitable for a field that had him writing papers at a desk for months.

Up close, he was more imposing than in her parlor. The broad shoulders and hard-muscled thighs made it impossible not to notice his attributes.

Finally, he looked up. Caught her staring.

Mr. Tavish did not play the gentleman and pretend not to notice. Instead, he arched one questioning brow.

Emmaline flushed.

He merely sat back against the squabs and closed his eyes.

⁓

The carriage rolled to a stop before a house, a wholly inadequate word for the *grande dame* that rose above Brook Street like royalty presiding over its lesser neighbors.

Gleaming mullioned windows looked out from the regimented gray stone façade, which ascended multiple stories into the rarefied Mayfair air. Above the arched front door—its polished ink-black set off by two gold door pulls—loomed a ferocious stone elephant.

Head thrown back, trunk curved upward, the wild-eyed creature was frozen in the act of trumpeting his might. Another moment and he'd be charging full tilt through the streets.

Moments later, Emmaline stood in the mansion's foyer, which could have contained their entire world-weary cottage. A marble staircase graced by a gilded banister spiraled upward.

A distinguished-looking man with silver hair joined them, and it was to him Mr. Tavish spoke.

"Gibbons, fetch Mrs. Stanhope a dress."

The man did not by so much as an eyelash betray that he thought this an odd request. With a slightly apologetic air, he studied her. "His lordship's mother was about your size."

Bewildered, Emmaline turned to Mr. Tavish, but he was already striding away, leaving her little choice but to follow.

She did. Past priceless paintings in gold frames, through corridors covered with intricate carpets, past a full-length mirror that reflected a tired, disheveled creature back at her. Past more grandeur than Emmaline had seen in her life, she followed him into a large study.

This, too, was exceptional. The walls were a pea green, with windows on two sides and a majestic carpet of pink and beige. A gold-framed mirror rose over the massive white marble mantel; a carved ram's head jutted out from each of the breakfront's two vertical supports.

Mr. Tavish poured himself a drink from a decanter on a table near a carved rosewood desk. Then he seated himself at the desk in an enormous leather chair that looked more comfortable than anything Emmaline had ever sat on.

She perched carefully on a tapestry-covered chair. "This place—"

"Is an abomination."

Emmaline blinked. "Is…this your home?"

"I take no blame for the folderols. I've been here two months. Plan to leave at the first opportunity."

Her gaze returned to the mantel and fixed on an inlaid panel between the two rams. Carved garlands entwined around an oval cameo of a woman, whose delicate features and softly curved cheeks and lips were surely meant to represent the epitome of feminine beauty.

Her father would have seen the patriarchal metaphor: The female, for all her beauty, was a passive figure; the rams were not. Their protruding, ridged horns and elongated chins conjured male power and arrogance. Mythology's Ares, a volatile and prolific seducer.

Emmaline doubted Mr. Tavish ever thought about metaphors.

"You appear to be quite wealthy," she observed.

"Regrettably."

"Most of London would be happy to accept the burden of your good fortune—"

"Spare me the lecture," he snapped.

She bristled. "Evidently you do not realize how difficult it is for the rest of us to—"

"Mrs. Stanhope."

Emmaline glared at him. *"What?"*

"Evidently *you* do not realize your frock has sustained a mortal injury."

She looked down, only to see that her cloak

had slipped, exposing the front of her torn dress, which gaped scandalously. Hastily, she pulled the cloak around her and prayed for the arrival of the efficient Mr. Gibbons.

At last, he appeared, holding several garments. "These are somewhat out of date, but perhaps they will serve."

Emmaline rose, eager to end the embarrassment of her torn frock.

"I regret we have no maid to attend you, as none are employed here," Mr. Gibbons said as he escorted her out of the room. "There is a small chamber off this corridor that might serve. His lordship used it when he grew too feeble to climb the stairs."

"His lordship?"

Mr. Gibbons hesitated. "The Earl of Kent owned this house. He died earlier this year, as did his older son, his heir."

"I see. Mr. Tavish has only recently purchased the property?"

The man merely inclined his head. "Please ring when you are ready, madam."

The chamber he considered small was larger than her parlor and bedchamber combined. An enormous bed, its heavy mahogany frame ornately carved, occupied the center of the room. A tapestry depicting a picturesque castle with rounded towers hung on the wall.

Emmaline held up the first of the two dresses. The taffeta, in riveting turquoise, was finer than anything she'd ever worn.

It proved such a perfect fit, she didn't even glance at the other.

The room's beveled cheval glass, supported by mahogany feet, confirmed that while the gown was flattering, Emmaline nevertheless looked a fright. Her hair was mussed, her eyes weary, her cheeks flushed. Even so, the gown made her look almost beautiful.

The woman in the mirror frowned. *None of your daydreaming, Em. It's only a dress, and a borrowed one at that. It won't change your circumstances.*

Best to remember her place.

The canary fell down the chimney Monday last. Robert had found it in the hearth, looking dazed and out of sorts. Gibbons unearthed an old bamboo cage and presented it to the bird as if he were visiting royalty. Alas, the bird was not often in it.

Just now, it had swooped down from some high perch—one of the dreadful hunting paintings his father had hung in the study and throughout the house—and landed on his desk.

Robert contemplated the creature, wondering how to coax it back into its cage. He was not good with living things. Bones and rocks were more complacent companions.

When Mrs. Stanhope appeared in the doorway wearing the very opposite of her practical, pedestrian, tantalizingly torn frock, every other thought vanished.

His mother's gown deepened the blue of her

eyes to the color of Cornwall's seas. And while he had avoided staring at her torn frock, now Robert couldn't avert his gaze from the heart-shaped neckline that dipped low enough to expose the rise of her breasts.

"It's a bit much, isn't it?" Embarrassment was written on her features. "I am not accustomed to something so fine."

Robert made some rough, unintelligible sound.

Gibbons, who had followed her into the room, shot him a reproachful look. "We are not accustomed to females, so you must forgive his lord—Mr. Tavish's—lack of tact."

"Gibbons, pour Mrs. Stanhope some sherry," Robert ordered.

"No, thank you." She appeared to notice the bird for the first time. "A canary, is it not?"

"Mr. Tavish is right, madam," Gibbons said gently, pouring her a glass. "Spirits have a way of soothing one's nerves."

When she relented and took a sip, Gibbons nodded his approval.

The man was excessively protective. There was no need for him to keep sending carriages after him, as if he were a child wandering the streets alone. Though admittedly, tonight's conveyance had come at an opportune time. Robert had had no wish to give Mrs. Stanhope more opportunities to fend off thugs.

"The bird is handsome," she said. "You should call him Galahad."

"A bird? Ridiculous."

"No more ridiculous than a man reluctant to ride in a closed carriage." Her smile robbed the words of bite. "You are quite the curmudgeon, aren't you?"

Dear God. Mrs. Stanhope had dimples.

Robert scowled—what else to do when such a woman invaded his household? "What I am is not your concern. You shouldn't have fought those ruffians, by the way. Foolish."

Her gaze narrowed. "Ought I have stood passively and let them do their worst?"

"*I* was there," he pointed out.

"Ah. You wished me to await your rescue." Her chin rose. "I am a practical person, sir. Men do not rescue women like me. Nor do I expect it."

Mrs. Stanhope rose, and Robert couldn't help but notice how the fabric of the dress flowed around her willowy form. Yet she was not fragile—she had wielded that rock-filled reticule with considerable strength.

"Mr. Tavish."

He forced his gaze upward and noticed uneasily that her features had hardened.

"Much about our arrangement does not make sense," she said. "You are a wealthy man. Scores of women would marry you in an instant. Why come to me for assistance?"

A reasonable question. If only George were here to answer. His uncle had polish to sail through any situation—he'd even married his best friend's former wife with no repercussions.

"Not interested in scores of women," he improvised. "I seek an, er, uncommon female."

The dubious glint in her eyes told him she found his explanation lacking.

Robert cleared his throat. "Truth is, I am not accustomed to females. There are none in my home."

"I must point out that I, a female, am in your home."

"Accidentally," he pointed out. "Anyway, I need someone to run the household."

"Mr. Gibbons seems quite capable."

"Gibbons is not a wife."

Mrs. Stanhope was silent for so long that Robert congratulated himself for putting her questions to rest.

That proved premature.

"I'll not be party to inflicting cruelty upon an unsuspecting woman," she said sternly.

He was baffled. "Cruelty?"

"With respect, Mr. Tavish, you seem to be something of a misogynist. For all I know, you would beat a wife or otherwise abuse her."

Robert stiffened. "I have never beaten a woman in my life." *Dangerous subject, that.*

Her gaze held steel. "Nor will I abet perversity."

"Good God, woman. What do you think I am?"

"I don't know. What sort of man has no female servants? Did you abuse them? Did they flee? Perhaps you are a violent libertine, like that French marquis—de Sade, or some such."

He eyed her blankly.

"You mean to make me spell it out, I see," she said. "I have an obligation to make sure you are not given to orgies and beatings and carnal activities with children—"

Robert rose abruptly. How the devil had she heard of such things? Perhaps she was a whore, after all. But the icy anger in her gaze looked like pure righteous indignation.

"I am waiting for an answer, Mr. Tavish."

Damned his uncle for setting him on this course. Robert searched wildly for inspiration.

"The truth," he heard himself say, "is that women do not like me."

Mrs. Stanhope frowned. Her gaze swept the room. "A man with all this?"

"I only lately acquired a fortune. My work leaves me no time for female companionship. And now…" He let his voice trail off, hoping it held a note of sincerity.

"Now?" she prodded.

"I don't know how to, er, court a woman, how to talk to one, how to—"

"We are not a foreign species, Mr. Tavish."

In for a penny, in for a pound. Robert took a deep breath. "Fear making a fool of myself."

There. Women were vastly pleased when a man humbled himself.

"You may be eccentric, sir, but you do not strike me as fearful."

Right. A man of his size and strength surely had few fears. And his loathing of closed spaces was more discomfort than fear. Robert decided to brazen it out. "Nevertheless, there it is."

For a long moment, she seemed to consider.

Then, suddenly, she smiled. "A wealthy

curmudgeon who needs schooling in the ways of wooing a bride. A challenge, but not impossible."

Robert was certain he did not need *schooling*. He might be a little rough around the edges, but no woman had ever complained.

"You cannot imagine how nice it will be to have a wife to supervise your meals, oversee the decorating, handle the social correspondence ..."

Ruin my life. He could manage his own meals. He didn't care about décor. He had no social correspondence. Marriage sounded dreadful. Thank God, this was only a charade.

"Some things a man just can't manage without a woman," Mrs. Stanhope went on. "And if you change your mind about having children, needless to say you will need a wife for that. Come around tomorrow and sign our contract. Already, I have one or two candidates in mind."

"You will warn them about my...lack of skills?"

She eyed him dubiously. "Something tells me you are a quick study."

"Nay, I am quite hopeless."

Mrs. Stanhope beamed. "Leave everything to me. I will find you the perfect bride."

Chapter Four

HIS EYES REVEAL nothing, his words little. He is possessed of rigid habits and loath to relax them. I cannot imagine that any woman would truly please him. He displays no compassion, yet he did come to my aid tonight...

The words Emmaline had written in her diary captured Mr. Tavish exactly. And perhaps one other: unapproachable. In that, he was like many scholars—her father included.

Augustus Perryman Alcott had spoken seven languages. His life's work was translating foreign folk tales for an English audience. Scholars revered him. Publishers sold his translations as children's stories. Emmaline thought some tales too dark for children—in one, a wolf gobbled up a girl's grandmamma. Justice was better served in the tale of Blue Beard, a wealthy cad given to murdering his wives, until his last wife was rescued by her brothers. Emmaline would have preferred the wife save herself, but she supposed the old story reflected its times.

When her father died two years ago, Emmaline set herself to the task of organizing his papers for his final book. He'd done the translations; the manuscript lacked only the fuller commentary he typically provided about their cultural and literary significance. His publisher was eager for the final manuscript.

Perhaps he wouldn't have wanted her to be the final arbiter of his words. In fact, one French story especially troubled her. In it, a selfish prince is turned into an ugly beast. When a woman he imprisons comes to love him in beastly form, he is transformed back into a prince.

Why? Beauty loved him as a beast. Didn't he deserve to be accepted as such? And did only one woman exist for one man, one Beauty for the Beast? Her father surely deserved to find love again after her mother died in childbirth, but that hadn't happened.

Emmaline didn't waste effort hoping that she would find romantic love. She was malformed—not in the way of the story's Beast, exactly, but in ways the world cared about. Her left leg was several inches shorter than her right. She had devised a shoe lift to give her a normal gait, but nothing could mask the ugly scars on that leg from a childhood injury. Fortunately, stockings and long skirts kept those hidden.

Oh, she saw the irony—Beast ought to be accepted with his defects, yet she was unwilling to reveal hers. Not that anyone had asked.

At all events, her plan to assemble her father's last work had come to a lurching halt when she found his finances in worse disarray than his papers.

Her father had kept secrets.

To all appearances, he had lived frugally. Yet he left large debts to tradesmen, tailors, and—most befuddling—an ice sculptor whose usual patrons were wealthy society hostesses. Emmaline wrote to the vendors, asking for patience. They were unmoved. So she had sold his house to settle the debts. When sickness forced Aunt Heloise to retire from the stage, this tiny, rented cottage on the shabby end of Oxford Street was all they could afford. The sewing they took in didn't keep them afloat. Her aunt's health was such that Emmaline couldn't take any post that kept her away for long hours.

It was Aunt Heloise who came up with the idea of telling fortunes. She understood how to make money from fantasy.

"Take Ophelia, dear," her aunt said. "I performed it to raves. I've a girlish way and could have played her for another decade. Even now, at fifty-nine, if my health held…"

"I am certain you were excellent, Aunt, but—"

"The point, dear, is that if you ask people whether they wish to see a young woman spurned by a madman and whine about it endlessly before drowning herself in a pond, most will demur. But throw poetry in the mix, hint at erotic secrets, put her in a diaphanous gown, and they love it. Everyone in my audience had fantasies about that gown, and the woman in it."

Thus had Flora's Fortunes come about. Aunt Heloise played Flora to a fare-thee-well, with her Tarot cards and unerring grasp of the nature of human desire. Emmaline copied handbills to slip under doors and nail to street posts.

But the days when Aunt Heloise took to her bed came more often. They consulted doctors when they could afford it, with widely varied results. One predicted she'd not live to see Michaelmas. When September came and went, they saw another who claimed a tonic of bitters and pine bark would cure her. It had not.

The idea for Harmonious Matrimony came to Emmaline one night as she worked to organize her father's papers, wondering why the women in those stories were often married against their wishes to men they never would have chosen.

What if ordinary women—those without wealth and, like Emmaline, beyond the first blush of youth—could choose? They had no access to the Marriage Mart, which aimed to preserve the aristocracy by matching titled men with well-bred debutantes. But what if those ordinary women were presented with a crop of eligible men already scrutinized by an agency?

First, she had to find clients. Emmaline canvassed churches, sewing groups, and markets. Some women were interested but couldn't pay for such a service. Others thought the entire endeavor unseemly. In short, her idea proved utterly unworkable.

Aunt Heloise had persuaded her to focus instead on bringing in male clients.

"It's men who have the money in this world, and they've no patience for courting. Guarantee them a painless way to find a wife, and they'll flock to our door."

Their notice in the *Times* did indeed bring several dozen men to their door. Most misunderstood the services being offered. Emmaline had to invent a deceased husband to depress unwanted advances on the grounds she was mired in grief.

When Mr. Burwell appeared, she was so relieved that he truly wanted a wife, she hadn't minded that his requirements for a bride were crass.

After tonight's disastrous events, Mr. Gibbons had driven her home in that very fine carriage. She felt like Cinderella in the lovely taffeta gown. But the only thing princely about the unsettling Mr. Tavish was his wealth.

Emmaline set her diary aside and exchanged the beautiful blue dress for her serviceable night-rail, riven with holes she'd not yet mended. As she slid into her lumpy bed, she felt older than her twenty-six years. The cracked window near her bed barely kept out the chill. Doubtless Mr. Tavish's grand house had unbroken windows, nice feather beds, and a fire in every room.

She thought of his lecture, dull and empty, and his domestic rituals, obsessive and inflexible. But she also recalled how his legs, swift and deadly, had lashed out at her assailants using a fighting maneuver unfamiliar to her.

Who was the man behind that impenetrable gaze?

Robert awoke to find the bird perched on his chest, studying him from beady black eyes.

"Go away," he growled.

It did not.

He sat up with a jerk, prompting the creature to flee to the bedside table. There, with relentless cheer, the canary chirped a morning greeting.

The clock on the wall said eight o'clock. Unbelievably, he'd overslept. With a muttered curse, Robert swung his feet over the side of the bed and plunged them into the bucket of ice water he ordered placed there every morning.

Frissons of cold shot up his legs, sped through his chest, and settled somewhere in the vicinity of his heart. He stood for a moment in the water, savoring its bite. Thomas Jefferson had had the right of it: A bucket of ice water was a fine start to the day. It awakened the brain. His grandfather—as stoic and stern a military man as there was—would have approved.

His grandfather. Gone these five years. Not a single year had passed without Robert wishing he'd been less rebellious as a youth and tried to understand that behind John Campbell's relentless demands lay a bone-deep love for the heritage that was his birthright.

Back then, Robert wanted no part of either side of the family. He set out, as youth does, to find his own way. What he found were rocks and fragments of ancient creatures, tantalizing clues of bygone worlds. Uncovering bits of the past sometimes made him wonder about pieces of his own past. But self-reflection was not a skill he cared to cultivate.

Reaching for a towel, Robert resolved to finish his paper today. He'd be too busy to call on Mrs. Stanhope and sign that contract.

The woman was a dilemma. George suspected her of treason, even murder. Robert thought her only real crime was being a charlatan and cheat. She had probably bilked dozens of victims through fortune-telling and the matrimonial agency.

It was her fault he overslept. He'd lain awake recalling how that gown showed her form to advantage. Then that teacher who'd been Father Hell's disciple marched through his dreams, put him mercilessly through his lessons, sent him spiraling into the past.

"Contrition," he whispered. "C-o-n-t-r-i-t-i-o-n. You can spell that, can't you, boy?"

Robert opened the wardrobe, where clothes hung in orderly rows. Browns together, fawn trousers separate from buff. Alongside hung abominations like his father's bright yellow waistcoat and pink satin shirt. He had asked Gibbons to get rid of them, but the man turned a deaf ear. With a resigned sigh, Robert selected a pair of brown trousers and a beige muslin shirt.

During a breakfast of kidneys and coddled eggs, he perused the *Times and* its dispatch from the peninsula suggesting Wellington had matters in hand. Still, the report was weeks old and, like all reports intended for the British populace, slanted positive. As Robert knew from serving with

Nelson in the Caribbean, the actual state of war might be vastly different.

When at last he settled in at his desk and began to write, the words flowed.

The Cornwall bone may derive from a massive elephant-like creature. Comparison with known skeletons of Asian and African elephants reveals sufficient differences, however, to suggest it is not from any species that survives today.

This was what he loved. Fossils and rocks, no untidy emotions obscuring facts.

The study door opened. Gibbons appeared, holding some ugly, formless thing.

"Madam left her cloak."

Robert stared at the garment Gibbons held gingerly. Even at a distance, he detected the distasteful odor of the street. "Burn it."

He scribbled a few more words before he realized Gibbons hadn't moved.

"I doubt madam would approve," Gibbons said.

Robert frowned. "Cloak's ruined."

"Perhaps she does not have another."

He did not miss the man's reproachful tone. "Gibbons, try to remember that you work for me, not the other way round."

"That fact is always uppermost in my mind, Your Lordship."

Gibbons betrayed not a hint of insolence. To the eye, he appeared a dutiful and masterful man of affairs, an image abetted by his upright posture and distinguished silver hair.

As a child, Robert hardly noticed his father's major domo. After Portia moved them to

Scotland, years passed without encountering the man. But Gibbons kept track of his whereabouts. After Robert enrolled at Oxford, the man would appear every few months to see if he needed anything. Robert usually managed a half-hour of stilted conversation before inventing an excuse to flee. It was the same after university. Whether Robert was off on digs or teaching, Gibbons always found him.

Robert never understood the purpose of those visits. Perhaps his father had ordered Gibbons to keep an eye on him, but not out of benevolent intent. The earl liked to know the whereabouts of his enemies, and Robert supposed he was one.

Then, two months ago, Gibbons appeared at the Cornwall dig to inform Robert that urgent matters required his attention in town. By then, his father and brother had been dead for several months, due to their refusal to take the pox vaccine that might have saved them. Robert had already seen to their funerals, signed myriad documents, et cetera. The usual process that followed family deaths.

Did he grieve? If so, it was a dulled grief. Robert hadn't seen them in years. His father hadn't bothered to try to retrieve him from Scotland years ago. He had his heir in Neville.

Consequently, their deaths resonated as a piece of a long-ago past. Waves too distant to fundamentally alter the shoreline. And, in fact, their deaths changed little. Robert had the nuisance of a title but remained a scholar, uninterested in their aristocratic world.

Nevertheless, that world kept finding him. Gibbons had persisted until Robert had no choice but to leave Cornwall and address whatever duties faced him in town. Those largely consisted of signing more papers and establishing a process for handling financial matters when he was not in London. But that took time, and Robert couldn't wait to depart this overstuffed house. Gibbons, meanwhile, was a near-constant presence, smoothly running the household but inserting himself in far too many aspects of Robert's life.

The man possessed uncanny instincts for Robert's weaknesses.

Mrs. Stanhope's cloak, for example.

Robert stared at the ugly brown mass. Gibbons had folded it carefully, as if it were a priceless garment and not a soggy, smelly thing that had spent time in the street.

Perhaps, in fact, she didn't have another. Perhaps the only thing she had to protect her from the cold was that ugly, putrid cloak.

"Very well," Robert said. "Return it to her."

"Unfortunately," Gibbons said, his voice filled with regret, "I have sent the footmen on errands. You requested books from Hookham's."

"Then send—"

"After you complained about last night's burned dinner," Gibbons went on, "Cook set the new scullery boy to cleaning the stove. He is covered in soot and unfit to leave the house."

"Then—"

"Cook himself has gone to market with a list

of the items you requested for dinner. It will take some doing. The salmon catch is very bad this year."

Robert took a deep breath. "Thus, the fact that no one is available to return Mrs. Stanhope's cloak is entirely my fault?"

Gibbons bowed his head, but not before Robert caught a glimmer of intrigue in his eyes.

"Then see to the matter yourself."

"Certainly," Gibbons said easily.

Robert waited. He sensed the subject was not yet closed.

"My gout is acting up again," Gibbons said. "A man of my years must constantly battle reminders of his human frailties."

He laid the cloak on a small table. "No doubt I will be well enough in a day or so to undertake such an errand. Perhaps Mrs. Stanhope will not need her cloak before then, although my elbow aches uncommonly. Likely a sign bad weather is approaching."

Gibbons slipped from the room with the grace and speed of a man half his age.

Gout, indeed.

Robert stared at the repulsive thing infusing the air with its vile odors. Clearly, Gibbons meant to shame him into returning it himself.

He grabbed the cloak. The coarse wool felt rough against his fingertips. Doubtless it left tiny abrasions on Mrs. Stanhope's ivory skin as the price for shielding her from the chill.

Robert inhaled. Yes, it stank of the gutter. But there was another scent, one not wholly eclipsed by the street. Lavender, perhaps, or violets—he could never distinguish between them.

No doubt she would wash the thing until the mud and street smells vanished, then cast it over her shoulders as she went on her way, seeking her next prey.

Fortune-tellers, seers, mesmerists, marriage brokers—they were all the same, feeding off the human yearning for happiness. Even if Mrs. Stanhope hadn't sent that Burwell fellow to his death, she'd led him to believe that she could find the woman of his dreams.

A nice fire blazed in the hearth. Robert looked down at the cloak. It was an ugly thing, too thin, quite inadequate and undeserving.

⁓

Emmaline paused under the intimidating elephant sculpture above the door of Mr. Tavish's house. Her knock sounded loud to her ears. She pulled her light shawl more tightly around her shoulders, but it was no substitute for the woolen cloak she'd left behind yesterday while in the thrall of that magical dress.

Mr. Gibbons opened the door. To her surprise, he did not look at her with disdain, or hint that a respectable woman did not call at a gentleman's home unescorted.

"Good afternoon, madam. Come in out of the chill."

"Thank you, Mr. Gibbons. That is a very fierce elephant, isn't it?"

"It's a relic from the days of Charles I. The king had those who supported him against Cromwell erect statues of fierce animals at their gates. It's said they signaled a vast network of safe havens and tunnels the king could use if he had to flee."

"My goodness." Emmaline studied the elephant anew.

"Most of the houses had no such escapes—their owners merely put up the statues to mollify the king. But you didn't come for a history lesson. His lord—Mr. Tavish is in the study. Sorry to leave you on your own, but I was on my way out on an urgent errand."

With that, he ushered her into the house and slipped past her outside. As Emmaline stood in the foyer, she detected an odd, unpleasant smell. She followed it to Mr. Tavish's study.

Gingerly, Emmaline pushed the door open.

Smoke shot from the fireplace.

"Close the door!" Mr. Tavish growled.

Realization dawned. He was burning her cloak! Before she could do more than gasp, the fire leapt up violently, threatening to breach the hearth. Smoke filled the study.

Mr. Tavish loosed an oath, then rushed past her out of the room.

Coughing, Emmaline could see nothing for the billowing smoke.

The door crashed open. She heard a splash, then a sizzle.

"Open the windows," he ordered.

Acrid smoke surrounded them as Emmaline groped along the wall toward the nearest window.

But the latch was stuck. It might have to be pried open. Did he have tools?

Then, suddenly, Mr. Tavish was beside her. He scowled. "I asked you to open it."

"It's stuck," Emmaline retorted.

He put a hand on the latch, twisted it open as if it were child's play, and raised the sash.

Slowly, the smoke thinned.

Mr. Tavish trained a disapproving gaze on her. "Have you recently been doused in whale oil, madam? Something on the fabric of your cloak caused the fire to run wild. Then you opened the door and gave the fire all the air it needed to blaze out of control. Have you no understanding of science?"

Emmaline eyed him in astonishment. "You burn my cloak and dare to blame *me*? I don't care if you're rich as Croesus, I will never be able to find a bride for an ogre."

His gaze narrowed to slits. "*Ogre?*"

"What else am I to call a man who destroys my cloak simply because it was left behind?" she demanded. "I'd forgotten it, not consigned it to the devil!"

"It was beyond repair and—"

"No woman wants to marry a churlish man with such a grating nature," Emmaline declared. "If there is any hope for you, you *must* change."

One brow arched.

Emmaline took a calming breath, but it made her cough anew. "I will be frank. My aunt and I are in urgent need of funds. But I won't take your money unless I know I can succeed with you. At the moment you have no chance of making a match."

Mr. Tavish looked taken aback. "None?"

She shook her head. "Worse, you are my only client—Mr. Burwell's sad death has made us pariahs. I must succeed with you, as daunting a prospect as that is."

"You find me daunting?" He looked perversely pleased.

Emmaline leveled a gaze at him. "The women of my acquaintance are genteel, with strong hearts and refined sensibilities. I will not foist upon them some ill-mannered oaf so wealthy that no one has the courage to enumerate his many faults."

For a moment, he almost looked offended.

"Will you cooperate with my efforts to turn you into a presentable marriage prospect?" she demanded. When he didn't reply, she glared at him. "The answer is either yes or no."

Mr. Tavish was silent for so long that Emmaline was certain he would refuse. That high forehead furrowed in displeasure at her hubris. She had pushed him too far.

Then, suddenly, he shrugged. "If I must."

Relief filled her. "Very well. Present yourself at my door at four."

"This afternoon? But I have work—"

"Either you are serious about this endeavor, or you are not," she said sternly. "If you have no intention of learning how to make yourself amenable to a woman, then let us end now—for this is no joke to me. I will need all the time I can get to find another client."

Emmaline hoped he hadn't noticed the quaver in her voice.

It was too bad their fate depended on this man. If he weren't such a disagreeable curmudgeon, he might appeal. Soot limned his high cheekbones, giving him an earthy air. He'd discarded his coat, presumably to fight the fire. His muslin shirt clung to a tautly muscled torso.

So intent was Emmaline's scrutiny that she only belatedly noticed he was studying her just as thoroughly. Was she, too, covered in soot?

Emmaline tried for levity to break the mood. "You'll see, Mr. Tavish: The ladies will fall at your feet. You'll have your pick of brides."

"That," he growled, "is my fondest wish."

Chapter Five

*T*HE YOUNG OF *warm-blooded higher vertebrates require long gestation and considerable care long after birth.*

Rude, was he? Coarse and churlish? Perhaps. But an ogre?

It is unlikely they could survive amid volatile climates over the centuries.

Was she complicit in treason and murder? England no longer burned traitors at the stake, but she might face death, given England was at war. A woman might try to barter her person to save herself.

He would refuse such an offer.

Or not.

Thus, the scientist looks to other species as links to the earliest forms of life.

Robert's pen moved swiftly. Scholarship left no room for half-truths or speculation not grounded in fact. It was the life he had chosen and would continue, earldom or no earldom.

He very much wished it were no earldom. Unlike Neville, he hadn't been trained for it. Mrs. Stanhope's lessons notwithstanding, he had no intention of transforming himself into someone more refined. As soon as he finished this business with her, he'd be off. His simple cottages in Oxford and Cornwall suited him far better than this overwrought monstrosity.

There, nothing threatened his orderly world. No squawking birds upset his sleep. No drunken dandies drove him to violence. No women disordered his carefully constructed universe.

The canary swooped onto Robert's desk. It landed near his water goblet and peered at him through the stem of the glass, which distorted its head into something akin to a large iguana.

Lizards were an adaptable species. Who knew how long they'd been on the planet? Over the centuries they had survived earthquakes and volcanoes, storms and pestilence. That sparked another train of thought, and soon his pen was moving furiously again. Science, not metaphysics. Fact, not illusion. Reason, not fantasy. That was the natural order of things.

The canary let out a squawk, hopped to the center of the desk, and regarded him.

Interesting. The bird was toying with him. It swooped to the mantel and preened at its reflection in the ornate mirror.

"Good. I've caught you at home." His uncle entered, unannounced as usual. "What have you learned about the mysterious Mrs. Stanhope?"

"Little of note," Robert groused, irked at the interruption.

"The woman's nearly destitute." George settled himself into a chair opposite his desk. "I'll wager a dinner at White's—"

"When I was trying to get Parliament to ban mesmerism, Whigs clubbed at Brooks's." Robert hadn't fit in there. Anything was subject to wager. One betting book entry was over who could be first to have sexual relations in a hot air balloon.

"Perceval favors White's," his uncle said. "I'm at both. She's being followed, you know."

Robert frowned. "Impossible. I would have discerned that."

"Apparently not," George said. "I'll wager you didn't even notice *our* man."

"Your man?"

"We're following her, too. Our man saw you rescue her from those foxed imbeciles. Brilliant stroke to gain her confidence."

Followed—by *two* men—and he hadn't even known it.

"After, you brought her here," his uncle went on. "Did you seduce her?"

Robert bristled. "Certainly not."

"The War Office sanctions seduction as means to a worthy end," George said. "Don't take too long. Certain young men in my office are eager to make a name for themselves and don't care how they do so. A treason arrest would be a prized plum."

"You gave *me* this assignment, distasteful as it is."

"And what have you accomplished?"

Robert sighed. "She wants to turn me into a suitable marriage prospect."

"That would take eons. More time than we

have." His uncle glanced at the bird. "How long has it been since you've visited the castle?"

The abrupt change of subject caught him off guard. "Years, as well you know."

"You might drop by sometimes."

"Week's journey." Robert pointed out. "'Dropping by' is scarcely feasible."

"Your grandfather—"

"Was determined to make me a military hero, like him."

"You'd have made a good one," George said. "But that would've required you to interact with your fellow man. Not your strong suit."

Suddenly, the canary gave a warlike squawk and launched himself at George.

"Damn and blast." His uncle flailed at the bird. "Either eat the thing or teach it manners."

Wonder of wonders, his uncle beat a hasty departure.

"What a strange creature you are," Robert mused. Hadn't she called the bird Galahad? His knight and defender.

The canary merely tilted his head.

⚬⚬⚬

"That nice Mr. Tavish is here for his appointment."

Emmaline ran her hand over Thomas's fur. "There is nothing nice about that man."

"Then again, nice men are so uninteresting," her aunt returned.

Emmaline shot her a weak smile. The contract

she had prepared pledged to present him with a candidate within thirty days. That would take a small miracle. The man made no effort to please. On the other hand, Mr. Tavish's wealth was bound to be a powerful draw.

"A king without love is a pauper, Emmy. And love makes the poorest man a king." Long ago words from her father, one of the few times she had asked him about her mother. Did he believe those words? If so, why had he never sought love again?

"Daydreaming?" her aunt teased. "I can guess who has put those fantasies in your head."

"There's not a fanciful bone in my body."

"It's not the bones that decide such things."

Emmaline did not pretend to misunderstand. "Mr. Tavish is well-favored, but I have no interest in him save as a client who can keep the wolf from our door."

"Wolves are fascinating creatures—as long as one remembers they're wolves."

Emmaline envied Aunt Heloise her confidence. She was as devoted to her art as her brother had been to his scholarly work. None could look away when Heloise Alcott inhabited a performance. Even now, battling debilitating fatigue, her violet eyes gleamed with the life force.

As if to prove the point, her aunt struck a pose outside the parlor. "'He's mad that trusts in the tameness of a wolf...or a whore's oath.'" She paused. "Or was that 'whore's honor'?"

Since her aunt could project to the heavens, Emmaline had no doubt Mr. Tavish heard every word. Sure enough, as they entered the parlor his gaze settled on Aunt Heloise.

"Er, 'whore's oath,'" he said, rising.

Aunt Heloise gave a peal of delight. "'Thou, sapient sir, sit here.'" She sat on the sofa and patted the space next to her. "'Now, you she foxes!'"

Mr. Tavish, Emmaline noticed with interest, was not immune to her aunt's charm—as evidenced by an answering smile that seemed quite out of character.

Obediently, he sat. "You are worlds beyond me, ma'am."

Aunt Heloise shook her head. "You merely want study,"

At Emmaline's baffled expression, she laughed. "It's *Lear*, dearest." She regarded Mr. Tavish approvingly. "How did you come by your knowledge of it?"

"During one Oxford term, I was obliged to help tutor younger students in literature. *Lear* was required. Not my field, but I needed the money."

That was odd, Emmaline thought. How had the man ever wanted for funds?

Her aunt smiled wistfully. "I was an actress for almost forty years. The stage was my lifeblood. But I'm out of touch now. It's all in the past." With a parting sigh, she left them.

Emmaline thrust the contract at Mr. Tavish, who skimmed it, then signed.

"The first thing you must learn is conversation," she began.

He frowned. "I converse."

"Not in the way it should be done. Conversation

is like a game of battledore. I speak, then you. I comment, and you speak again. Discourse is essential to a good marriage."

Mr. Tavish crossed his arms. "Can't imagine having anything to say to a wife."

She regarded him sternly. "A woman expects a man to talk to her."

"My father never talked to my mother or anyone else he didn't care to."

"I suppose that explains why *you* turned out so well," Emmaline retorted.

His gaze narrowed. "You ought to leave off the sarcasm. It doesn't become you."

Why could she not stop goading this man? "Apologies. But you must learn to conduct a proper conversation."

"If it's anything like the one we're having now, I'd just as soon not."

Emmaline inhaled. Why did this man bring out the worst in her? "Let's start again."

"I'd say the question of whether we started in the first place is open to debate."

Exasperated, she rose. Mr. Tavish leaned back against the cushions.

"Now *that* is not the thing," she said sternly. "If I rise, you must also."

"Must I?"

"It is proper to rise when a woman does. That shows you respect her. You cannot do that if you are lolling about on the sofa."

Lolling wasn't the right word, however. His pose was one of ease, but that gray gaze remained watchful. His muscled limbs held a tension that suggested he could call upon them in an instant. Rather like a lion in wait.

Slowly, Mr. Tavish got to his feet. He was more than a head taller than she was and stood closer than Emmaline would have liked. Indeed, the parlor suddenly seemed devoid of air.

"Now what?" he said softly.

"I, er, will say that the weather is lovely, and you agree in a pleasant tone."

"If I agree, what is the point of talking about it?"

"The *point,* sir, is that you must say something in response," Emmaline said in exasperation. "Conversation is give and take. You cannot simply stand there, refusing to grant the other person any ground, making her feel like a complete idiot."

"If you are an idiot, I take no responsibility."

Emmaline brought her hand to her throbbing temple. "You are infuriating."

"Aren't you obliged to say something pleasant and meaningless that I can agree with?"

"Let us try again." She took a deep breath. "Lovely weather, don't you think, sir?"

"I don't think about the weather."

She ignored that. "If I had a fan, I might flutter it, so." Emmaline moved her fingers.

"What the devil are you doing with your hands?"

"I am flirting with you."

"And here I thought you were only clawing at the air."

She stamped her foot. "That handsome face of yours will only take you so far."

Handsome face. Had she actually said the words aloud?

To her amazement, he reddened.

She stepped back, putting space between them. But her bad leg faltered, and she wobbled.

Instantly, his steadying hand closed around her upper arm. "Rain likely."

Emmaline blinked. "Rain?"

"Trying to converse. Though as I am leaving, that appears to be unnecessary." He tilted his head. "Good day, Mrs. Stanhope."

He turned toward the door.

"Mr. Tavish?"

He glanced back.

"I will try to begin on a better foot next time. I'm afraid that I—" Moving toward him, Emmaline's actual foot, her bad one, caught the corner of the frayed cotton rug.

To her complete and utter mortification, she toppled forward into his arms.

———⇛———

Robert's senses were awash.

Her hair spilled out of its pins, tumbled over her shoulders like a silken veil, slid over his hand like a caress. Her faint floral scent evoked a field of wildflowers.

Vast, paralyzing sensations swept him. His arms closed around her.

This would not do.

"If this is another lesson," he growled, "I hope you will leave off."

Instantly Mrs. Stanhope righted herself, her

face flaming. "Unfortunately, I am clumsy. You are rude to point that out or suggest insidious intent."

Robert suspected he deserved that. "Plainspoken, madam."

"I can't afford ambiguity." Her gaze held his. "Let us speak frankly—why do you *really* wish to marry? You profess not to want children, love, companionship, or passion. Why put yourself through lessons in which you clearly have no interest?"

"Told you—no skill with women, don't wish to make a fool of myself." Robert hesitated. "Haven't altogether ruled out passion."

New warmth bloomed across her features.

She cleared her throat. "As we work through this process, it is sometimes necessary to speak of rather intimate subjects. But to be clear, ours is a purely professional relationship."

"Never thought otherwise." Hell. He'd almost forgotten the reason he was here. "Do you ever employ unusual means to match your clients?"

Mrs. Stanhope frowned. "Such as?"

"Mesmerism." That was clumsy of him. Obviously, she'd deny it.

"I am very interested in Mr. Mesmer's work," she said, shocking him. "We have exhausted many avenues for my aunt's health, save that. I confess it's an appealing prospect."

"Did you mesmerize your client...the one who died?" he asked softly.

She eyed him in astonishment. "To make him

stand in front of the Mail? Are you accusing me of murder?"

"Might've tried to make him malleable. More forthcoming. Perhaps that went awry."

"Mr. Burwell was quite forthcoming," Mrs. Stanhope said evenly. "Overmuch, in fact."

"Some fortune-tellers are known to practice mesmerism," he persisted.

Mrs. Stanhope stared at him. "You had me investigated."

"Only prudent," Robert conceded.

Her chin rose. "Before we opened Harmonious Matrimony, my aunt offered her services as a fortune-teller. She was too weak to return to the stage and enjoyed playing Madam Flora. Her Tarot readings brought in needed funds. But her illness progressed, and we had to stop." She glared at him. "No one told Mr. Burwell's fortune or mesmerized him. Investigators have pored over our case. You are the only person to suggest foul play."

Mrs. Stanhope strode to the door and flung it open, her message clear.

Making his exit, Robert had a sinking feeling this assignment was going to require work.

Chapter Six

WHAT HAPPENS WHEN you lose that which defined you?

Heloise Elizabeth Alcott burned for the stage. Theater was her calling, her heart's desire. She'd always known it. As a child, she performed for her parents and played all the parts.

With time, she found a broader audience. London welcomed her to the stage, and she threw herself into every performance, playing royalty, angels, oracles, goddesses, saints—though more often sinners. It was a grand, bawdy life.

Now it was gone. An insidious illness left her struggling to get out of bed on some days. Her heart ached from the loss of that which she loved.

Truth be told, it was the sinning she missed most. There was nothing so rewarding as playing the tramp. She liked her bodices tight and low, with little left to the imagination. What was the point of portraying a slut if one didn't look the part?

Her parents never saw *those* performances. It would have been awkward for them to watch the actor playing Marc Antony to her Cleopatra boldly place his hand on her breast and declare,

"New *heaven*." Not exactly how Shakespeare envisioned it, but London impresarios knew which side their bread was buttered on. When the actor tried the same maneuver off stage, Heloise boxed his ears. Even sluts had standards.

Most of her past lovers were married. They complained that their wives had grown cold and avoided marital relations. Heloise suspected the men hadn't bothered to see to their wives' pleasure. She always insisted they see to hers and sent them back to their wives much improved.

Acting had won her modest acclaim. But these days she didn't have the strength to perform.

Without the stage, who was she? Was Heloise Alcott from Cheltenham quite unremarkable after all? Had she simply avoided that truth all these years?

Existential questions, those. And yes, she knew the word. Her brother had been a scholar, but also an academic snob who thought no one else in the family could absorb esoteric concepts.

Heloise didn't write books as Augustus had. But in her hands, stories grew flesh, words spilled blood. She'd put her skill against anyone, her departed brother included.

It was her gift.

Now gone.

Heloise stared at the woman in her mirror, a shadow of her former self. Her hair needed more henna to bolster the fading red. A seam of her lilac dressing gown, chosen because it accentuated the violet of her eyes, had an obvious tear.

Those problems she could fix.

Heloise slipped the dressing gown off and reached for her magenta dress with its deep decolletage trimmed in lace dyed a bright daffodil yellow. Her gloves matched her dress, and Heloise topped the ensemble with a yellow bonnet from which sprouted a dyed purple feather.

Emmaline never seemed to suffer embarrassment at Heloise's flamboyant attire. Thus, Heloise's conscience was clear as she adjusted her bonnet to a more rakish angle for today's tedious and quite hopeless errand.

If the curtain was coming down on her life, Heloise was determined to look her best.

***

"Likely he's a charlatan," Aunt Heloise said.

"Give him a chance," Emmaline pleaded. "Mesmerism is a new therapy."

"It's theater, dear," her aunt said. "All illusion."

Emmaline's spirits sank. She had persuaded her aunt to try this final doctor, but Aunt Heloise was set against him. She'd sworn off doctors after the last one gave her an elixir that turned out to be an especially strong form of laudanum.

Notwithstanding, she'd finished the bottle.

"With Mr. Tavish's fee we can afford this," Emmaline said. "Mesmerism is said to engage the magnetic fields of the brain—"

"I'll tell you what magnetism is," her aunt interjected. "Those who saw my Ophelia wept so at my demise that I extended the death scene. Once, I even repeated it. *That* is magnetism. It can't heal the sick, only fool people into thinking they're cured."

Emmaline held her tongue. No doctor had found the cause of her aunt's illness, much less a cure. Dr. Jacob Black was a noted practitioner of the new therapy. From what she'd read, mesmerism involved putting the patient into a trance, then speaking to the person's mind on a level that's normally inaccessible. The mind would then influence the body.

Or something like that. She didn't fully understand it.

Her brain was in something of a fog due to an odd dream last night. Blue Beard was there, wearing a rakish pirate's hat and a patch over one eye. Emmaline brought him wife after wife, and he killed them all. No woman satisfied him.

Most troubling, he had Mr. Tavish's face.

A dark metaphor, perhaps, for the prospect of pairing an innocent and worthy woman with such a rigid, judgmental, ill-tempered man. People rarely changed. Was it reasonable—nay, ethical—to think he could become someone she could present to a hopeful bride?

"I'd rather see you spend the money on your own health," Aunt Heloise was saying as they crossed the street. "That lift you use in your shoe can't be comfortable."

"It's wrapped in cotton wool. I barely notice," Emmaline murmured.

"I know you don't wish to appear weak, but I would love to see you discard the thing and simply be yourself."

Emmaline eyed her in amusement. "Spoken by someone who's spent a lifetime playing characters far removed from herself."

Her aunt looked wistful. "Without theater, I'm at sea. Immersing myself in a role was escape, but it also gave me power. Now I have none."

"Power?"

"If the performance is good, the audience is captivated—imprisoned, if you will."

Emmaline caught her hand. "When you are on stage, no one can look away. Even when you told fortunes, you gave it your all. I'm hopeful we can fight this illness."

Her aunt merely sighed.

A dingy stone building housed Dr. Black's office. The door bore a tattered paper noting in scrawled letters that the doctor's full fee was to be paid on the first visit. Beyond that door was a dark, cheerless room. A bored clerk pointed them to another door, the doctor's inner sanctum.

They entered a room that felt like a cave. The drapes were closed, and Emmaline could barely make out a bulky figure in a chair. The only light came from a few flickering candles.

As her eyes adjusted, she saw that the doctor's hulking torso was encased in a mustard-colored waistcoat, his neckcloth sculpted in superfluous twists and folds.

Emmaline had no expertise in men's fashions, but Mr. Tavish's plain style was more to her liking. The doctor's garish waistcoat wore him, rather than the other way around. With Mr. Tavish, there was no doubt that man ruled fabric.

Dr. Black's gaze swept over them. It was obvious that he instantly dismissed them as possessing neither fortune nor connections sufficient to advance his stature.

They sat in two chairs opposite his. He listened in apparent boredom as Emmaline recited her aunt's medical history. Aunt Heloise remained silent.

Later, Emmaline wondered why she hadn't paid more attention to that fact. Her aunt usually had quite a lot to say about her condition.

After Emmaline listed the failed treatments of previous physicians, Dr. Black lifted a candlestick and held the wavering light up to her aunt's eyes. He studied her for a moment, moving the candle around to illuminate the whole of her frame. Then he shook his head.

"Mesmerism is your only hope," he said gravely.

Emmaline thought he ought to have taken more than a cursory moment to examine Aunt Heloise. Over the course of seeing various doctors, she learned that they invariably diagnosed their own specialty. A bone doctor would find problems with bones; one who specialized in digestive disorders would diagnose that, and so on.

Naturally, Dr. Black would decide that mesmerism was what she needed. But that was why they were here, after all. They had tried everything else.

"Perhaps you could elaborate?" Emmaline asked politely.

He turned toward her, his eyes—a flat, putrid brown, rather like pigeon droppings—

disapproving. "I see nothing wrong with her. Therefore, the origin of her illness is in her brain."

"It's not my brain that aches," Aunt Heloise grumbled. "I ache all over."

"Perhaps you might examine her more fully," Emmaline said pointedly.

The doctor scowled. Then he gave Aunt Heloise a condescending smile and pulled his chair close to her. "Remove your gloves, madam."

When she did, he took her aunt's hands between his and pressed two fingers to her wrist.

"You have a decent pulse, you are not overweight, your breathing is even. You do not appear to be bilious. You are well beyond the possibility of childbirth, so pregnancy is not the source of your illness. Your back is straight, without obvious misalignment. Your skin is dry and of normal temperature. Your complexion is clear—one might almost say glowing—"

Her aunt trained her violet eyes on him. Rather intently, Emmaline thought.

"You are attractive for your age—"

"How kind," Aunt Heloise murmured sweetly.

Emmaline felt a twinge of foreboding.

"—and there aren't many women your age who would dare flaunt such red hair and deep décolletage," the doctor continued.

Aunt Heloise tilted her head consideringly.

"Numerous doctors have found nothing wrong," Black said. "I can account for your aches and fatigue in no other way, but to say that they are all in your head. It is possible that your imagination has simply run amok."

"Her illness is real," Emmaline insisted. "Some days she cannot even get out of bed."

Dr. Black shot her a pitying look. "I do not doubt her symptoms, but the answer lies in her head. That is why I intend to work on your aunt's mind."

"Rather like casting a spell?" Aunt Heloise offered meekly.

Too meekly.

Dr. Black allowed himself a dry chuckle. "Not exactly. We will put you in a trance and tell your symptoms to disappear. It may not work; even Franz Mesmer does not succeed every time. Often many sessions are needed for a cure."

Emmaline's spirits sank. No doubt those sessions would be just as costly as this one.

"Several of my friends tried something similar to rid themselves of stage fright," Aunt Heloise said. "My friend Sarah developed a particular *regard* for her mesmerist."

Her aunt's husky emphasis on the word suggested a wealth of other possible meanings, none of them proper. Emmaline felt a frisson of unease.

"There can be what we call transference," the doctor acknowledged. "A patient may come to hold the physician in special affection when it's but gratitude for his services. This mainly happens with women. Their minds are weak and easily led."

"Sarah enjoyed her sessions," Aunt Heloise said softly. "I believe she mentioned the laying on of hands."

The doctor shifted in his chair. "The women do like that part of it."

"*Stimulating* was the word she used." Her aunt's expression was thoughtful.

Emmaline frowned.

Dr. Black clasped one of her aunt's hands. That seemed odd. What disturbed Emmaline more was Aunt Heloise's expression of wide-eyed innocence as she leaned toward him.

"Toying with women's minds while they are insensible must require doctors with great integrity," her aunt said. "Patients are at your mercy then, are they not?"

Dr. Black's smile—surely meant to be reassuring—instead reminded Emmaline of a snake mid-bite. "You have the right of it, madam. But I am extremely scrupulous."

"That is as it should be," her aunt agreed. "After all, your patients are defenseless women and usually—I imagine—quite alone during treatments."

"Often alone, yes."

"Still," she said after a moment, "I have heard alarming stories about other practitioners. Sarah said she was put into a trance that was almost—I blush to say it—*erotic.*"

Aunt Heloise never blushed. Emmaline's misgivings grew.

The doctor seemed to redden—it was difficult to discern with the lighting. "My patients would never say such a thing."

"I found Sarah's description riveting." Aunt

Heloise leaned closer, affording him a fuller view of her bodice. "The mesmerist sat facing her, as you are now. He required that their knees touch." She brushed her knees lightly against his.

Dr. Black nodded. "Necessary to establish a flow of energy between patient and doctor."

"Her knees were *between* his, I should have said." Aunt Heloise nudged hers into the space between his legs.

Sudden dread seized Emmaline. Her aunt was fearless when immersed in a role, and this had all the hallmarks of a performance. Her posture—too close to him, yet somehow with an air of innocence—was deliberate. Her eyes radiated a smoldering fire.

Now the doctor rubbed her aunt's hand with a good deal more warmth. His brow wore a thin bead of perspiration. His eyes focused on her aunt's heaving bosom, displayed to fine advantage by the plunging neckline. Aunt Heloise had never been one to hide her gifts.

"Sarah spoke of stroking." Her voice held a husky note. "Deeply *personal* stroking. I believe she used the word *intimate*."

Even in the dim light, Emmaline could see Dr. Black's features had gone florid.

"The m-mind, of course, is the ultimate goal," he managed.

Her aunt ran the tip of her tongue over her bottom lip, then gave a breathy sigh. "Eyes grow moist, as do other…organs."

"Moist," he repeated, dazed.

"Breathing quickens," she purred. "*Faster.*"

"Faster," he groaned, his eyes glassy as he hung on every word.

Aunt Heloise trailed her fingertip around her decolletage. "Breasts rise…in *tumult.*"

Abruptly, Emmaline rose. "Aunt, I believe it is time to go."

Her aunt ignored her. "*Sensitive* areas grow soft"—she paused— "then…*hard.*"

Dr. Black's breathing grew alarmingly labored.

"We *must* go," Emmaline said firmly. She might have been a fly on the wall. Neither of them took notice.

Aunt Heloise snaked one of the doctor's hands around her waist. Her lips grazed his ear. "They breathe the same air, almost as if they are…*joined.*"

Dr. Black's eyes closed. He looked to be in great pain.

"They move as one." She blew lightly on his ear. "Skin to skin, flesh to flesh."

He moaned helplessly.

"They meet *with full* force." Her words, a throaty growl. "Delicious, *pounding* force."

Sweat poured down the doctor's face. He pressed the balls of his feet to the floor and moved his heels up and down as if pumping…an organ? Church organ, that is.

Aunt Heloise squeezed his upper thigh, just below the tented bulge of his trousers.

"Tremors begin," she purred. "Lovely, *uncontrollable* tremors."

The doctor rocked back and forth in his chair.

"Perhaps I should stop," her aunt said softly.

"By *God,* don't stop!" His rocking quickened.

Horrified, Emmaline stood rooted to the spot.

"And then," her aunt declared in a stage whisper that had brought audiences to their feet, "spasms *come*. Erupting, like the crescendo of a storm in *uncontrollable* release."

The doctor stiffened and gave a cry the likes of which Emmaline had never heard. His tongue sagged, and he emitted a loud, animal groan.

Her aunt rose calmly, pulled on her gloves. "Come along, Emmaline."

In the outer office, the doctor's bored assistant glanced up. "The doctor's fee—"

"Has been paid," Aunt Heloise said, not breaking her stride.

———

Out in the street, Emmaline was too stunned to speak.

"Pray, do not look so reproachful," her aunt said. "I told you the man was a charlatan. Can you imagine what he does to unsuspecting women during his 'treatments'?"

"I-I wonder if he will send us a bill."

"He will not. He disgraced himself before not one but two women."

Emmaline's face flamed. "I cannot believe that you—"She halted, lacking words.

"Don't think badly of me, Em, dear. It's no secret I've led a worldly existence."

"I don't think ill of you. It's only that I've never witnessed anything…quite like that."

"Nor should you have," Aunt Heloise replied. "But the odious man deserved to be humiliated.

He was condescending, as if he was doing us a great favor to see us, making us come to him when I'm sure he pays house calls on women of elevated stations. Then he demeans me, implying that I caused my own illness. Does he think me a lunatic?"

She fingered the edges of her burgundy cloak, faded like her riotous mass of once-reddish curls. "Sometimes, I think worldliness is the only asset I possess. I've seen and done things that would put a respectable young woman like you to blush."

Her voice wobbled.

Emmaline enveloped her in a hug. "You are wonderful, and I love you."

Her aunt wiped away a tear. "I shouldn't have exposed you to such a sordid scene. You've no experience with men like that—no experience with *any* man, I'll warrant. You must think—"

"What I think," Emmaline broke in gently, "is that you are a marvelous actress."

Aunt Heloise gave her a watery smile. "I am."

***

"Off for today's appointment, Your Lordship?" Gibbons was cheerful as he helped Robert into his jacket. "I don't like the looks of that sky. Could be a downpour before long."

The man was as solicitous as a mother hen. "Don't hover, Gibbons. I'm quite capable of seeing myself out the door."

"I sent madam a new cloak, so you needn't worry that she'll take cold."

Robert frowned.

"A nice green, with lilac trim," Gibbons added. "It will go well with her coloring, especially her blue eyes. A nice wool, soft but sturdy weave."

"Why the devil did you do that?" Robert demanded.

Gibbons looked surprised. "You ruined hers. We had a responsibility."

"We?" Robert glared at him. "You didn't enclose a card from me, I hope."

"I did."

He took a deep breath. "Stop interfering in my life."

"I would never interfere, Your Lordship."

"How was the card inscribed?"

Gibbons furrowed his brow. "I can't recall. But I made sure to sign your given name to maintain your, ah, masquerade—which, if you don't mind my saying—"

"I do mind."

"—is rather silly. Madam seems possessed of a keen intelligence. You may wish to inform her of your title. I can't think that she would like to discover it on her own."

"Gibbons," Robert said evenly. "Listen to me."

"Always."

"I am seeing Mrs. Stanhope as a favor to my uncle."

"You aren't the sort to do favors, sir, if you don't mind my saying."

"The point, Gibbons, is that I'm not interested in a liaison with the woman. Not now, not ever. I disregard the title because it's not who I am. I study rocks. I wish to be judged on that alone. I have no regard for prancing lords."

"Forgive me, my lord, but it's possible to be a lord and not prance."

"Have you considered seeking other employment, Gibbons?"

The man looked taken aback. "I have always served the earls of Kent, as my father and grandfather before me."

"Surely they couldn't have been like you."

Gibbons stiffened. "No one has ever questioned my loyalty."

"I don't," Robert assured him. "In the time we've been together, I've seen that you have my interests uppermost in your mind."

"It could never be otherwise."

"But damn it, man, you go too far. It's one thing to be a loyal employee and quite another to send women cloaks in my name."

"Madam has fallen on hard times. With all due respect, she needs that cloak."

Robert abandoned the fight. He strode out to the drive and his waiting curricle.

"She will think well of you for sending it," Gibbons called.

Nothing would alter Mrs. Stanhope's dismal opinion of him, Robert suspected. He climbed onto the seat, flicked the reins of the perfectly matched pair of horses Neville had doubtless prized. His late brother had aspired to be among the dandies who dashed around town in many-caped coats meant to signal their driving expertise. Robert, however, felt ridiculous driving something as fashionable as a curricle.

Still, the hood folded back, allowing him to ride in the open air. It was the vehicle's only virtue, but for him that was everything. The wind on his face was a gift.

Robert focused his thoughts on Mrs. Stanhope. Instinct told him she hadn't intended Burwell's death. But could he trust instinct? She left him off balance, spawned unsettling impulses. Yesterday, when she tumbled into his arms—well, that did not bear thinking of.

Yet think of it he had, and for many moments since.

Chapter Seven

"THIS IS NOT a battle, Mr. Tavish," Emmaline admonished. "You are fighting me."

He glared at her. "I'd fight anyone intent on making me look the fool."

"You would not look the fool if you learned the steps."

Mr. Tavish stood stiffly in her parlor, hands fisted at his side. He'd stepped on her feet so many times they ached.

Emmaline knew he wasn't clumsy. She'd seen the swift grace with which he dispatched that drunken dandy. No, he'd simply closed his mind to this. If *she* could dance, with her bad leg, he surely could. "You must learn a dance or two. A woman expects entertainment."

"Can't women entertain themselves without making spectacles of men?"

Emmaline prayed for patience. "Dancing is graceful."

"I don't aspire to grace."

Defeated, she sank onto the divan.

He sat at the other end with such force it rocked. Silence stretched between them.

"Feels like I've just gone several rounds with Gentleman Jackson," he said at last.

"I am simply trying to make you a more appealing marriage prospect," she said.

"I see no need to change for a woman."

"Nor even try to accommodate her wishes." Emmaline eyed him in exasperation. "Very well, sir. Let us forget dancing. Forget the need to make your bride's existence brighter by pretending that you enjoy the social intercourse common to civilized societies."

"Social intercourse?" His tone was dubious. "Sounds…crude."

Unbidden, the scene her aunt staged in Dr. Black's office sprang to mind.

"I refer to civil interaction evidently foreign to your nature," she insisted, willing that image away. "A wife is not a possession to be tucked in a closet and dusted off now and then for public display. She expects to be escorted, danced with, spoken to. Men do these things to show them respect."

"Is that how your husband treated you?"

That took her aback.

"My life has been very different from yours," Emmaline said quietly.

"You refer to my wealth."

"Men have an advantage in this world, Mr. Tavish. Your wife deserves to benefit from your good fortune. You will have access to grand balls and elite salons—"

"Sounds intensely boring," he declared. "Money's not the measure of a man or woman.

You strike me as one who knows that better than most."

Was that a compliment or insult? Unclear, but in her world, it was best not to look for offense. Emmaline turned to him. "What shall it be? Continue dance lessons or abandon hope?"

"No contest: Abandon hope." He shot her a rueful grin.

Pity he didn't smile more often. It transformed his features, made him less like a forbidding giant on her too-small sofa and more like a human being. Warmth crept into that gray gaze, and she felt it down to the tips of her toes.

Emmaline gave herself a mental shake. Mr. Tavish was no better than he seemed: an impossible curmudgeon with a disregard for the niceties a wife had a right to expect. The man had no interest in accommodating a woman's needs.

Another—more alarming—thought suddenly occurred.

"Are you quite certain you are…fond of women?" she ventured.

He frowned. "Fond?"

"What I mean is…are you drawn to them?" Some men weren't, she knew. Her aunt had enlightened her about that. Perhaps Mr. Tavish had other preferences.

Mr. Tavish crossed his arms over his burly chest. "Women are a category."

Emmaline eyed him in bewilderment.

"My work is research," he added. "I categorize everything. Women are in one box."

"I see." But she didn't. They were talking at

cross purposes. "Occasionally you open that metaphorical box and…?" She trailed off, unable to find words.

"Stir things around," he said.

Emmaline mulled that. "Then you simply close that, er, box and go on about your way?"

"Odd way to put it. Makes me sound…"

"Uncaring." Her lips pursed. "Unengaged. Unwilling to see women as actual people."

He shifted uncomfortably. "It is how I organize my life."

"Women do not belong in boxes," she said. "We're human, like you. We deserve to have our opinions considered. We also require kindness. If you can't at least be kind, I won't try to find you a wife. It would be cruel to the woman."

Mr. Tavish glowered. "I am not cruel."

Emmaline sighed. It's not that she hoped to achieve a love match. With his looks and fortune, some women would be willing to overlook the fact he had no heart.

"Let us adjourn," she said wearily. "Tomorrow we'll work on something more pleasant."

He eyed her warily. "Like what?"

"Politics. It is important for a gentleman to be informed—"

"My loathing for dancing is exceeded only by my loathing of Parliament."

Emmaline eyed him curiously. "Why?"

"I tried to persuade politicians to outlaw people such as yourself."

Oh, lovely. Could this get any worse? "On what grounds?"

"They prey on the weak. It didn't work. Parliament pays lip service to the public good but has no abiding interest in protecting it." Mr. Tavish rose to take his leave.

To his other insensitivities, she would add prejudice. And yet...

"Mr. Tavish?"

"Yes?" he growled.

"I ought to have thanked you earlier you for the beautiful cloak. I shouldn't accept it, but I confess I have no other."

He looked as if he would speak. Instead, he strode to the front door and opened it so forcefully she thought he might rip it off its hinges. At the last moment, he turned.

"Care to take a walk?"

Emmaline looked past him to the street. Raindrops danced in puddles that had been pooling since early afternoon. It wasn't a deluge, but neither was it a day for taking the air.

"I'll get my cloak," she heard herself say.

Robert felt like the world's biggest fool. He hadn't bothered to focus on the outdoors before issuing that rash proposal. He'd been intent on leaving the confines of her tiny parlor, where he felt like some great beast taking up far too much space. He was acutely aware of his large size—the first thing people noticed about him—but in her parlor he felt almost deformed.

Rain lent the cobblestones a slippery sheen. Carriages churned up mud that splattered their clothes as he and Mrs. Stanhope picked their way through the street, a stone's throw from the Tyburn tollgate. The heavy scent of manure, newly pungent by the rain, wafted toward them from the stable yard across the road. The sky had darkened, and the wind had picked up. The day was fast deteriorating—by London standards, at least. In Scotland, it would simply be an ordinary day.

Mrs. Stanhope huddled in the folds of her new cloak. Robert had to concede that the green fabric set off her coloring, especially her blue eyes. How did Gibbons know these things?

A nearby copse of trees offered some shelter, and they took refuge under an ancient oak. Withered leaves and peeling bark suggested its health was fragile.

Around them, the ground turned to mud.

"I should like a reading," Robert said.

She eyed him in confusion.

"The Tarot. I wish a reading."

Her brow creased. "I thought you detested such things."

Robert drew in a breath. "Despite my dedication to science, I remain fascinated with otherworldly phenomena." That was quite possibly the most mendacious sentence he'd ever uttered. He loathed false science and the occult. They were anything but benign.

"The cards might give insight into my, er, bride needs," he added to the perfidy.

Her gaze narrowed. "You've expended little effort to become a worthy groom, which suggests you don't really care whom you marry. Why would you seek the counsel of the cards?"

Robert shrugged. "Hypocrisy is one of my many flaws."

Mrs. Stanhope studied him for a long moment. "We can try a reading at our next appointment, but you must be in a receptive frame of mind. I'll not tolerate ridicule."

"I've gotten us off to a bad start, haven't I?"

She grimaced. "This is possibly the worst relationship I've had with any human being."

"Can't be that bad," he protested.

"It is." Was that a faint twinkle in her eyes? Would dimples follow?

Uncanny how those blue eyes evoked Cornwall seas. Robert wrenched his brain away from that thought. "Did you give Burwell a reading?"

Instantly, the spark in her eyes vanished. "No. Perhaps I should have."

"Think you might have foreseen his demise?"

She shook her head. "I learned the basics of the cards when my aunt grew ill, but I was terrible at it. I'd have missed his sad fate entirely."

Strangely, Robert wanted to believe she was a novice at the cards and innocent of treason. He found himself contemplating her mouth and its sheen of moisture from the rain. Alas, dimples had not appeared. He leaned toward her for…better scrutiny?

"Do you feel faint, Mr. Tavish?" Mrs. Stanhope asked sharply.

Robert stiffened. "No."

"For a moment I thought you were about to

topple into that mud puddle." Without warning, she put her hand to his forehead. "Your face is warm."

Blast. This was beyond him. Women were beyond him. Especially this one. He wanted her hand back where it belonged.

Mrs. Stanhope had not donned gloves, and the hand against his forehead was rough. He'd known she had steel in her spine—she'd taken on those foxed dandies, after all. But that chafed skin marked her as a woman who didn't shun hard tasks.

Belatedly, Robert realized he had covered that nicely abraded appendage with his own. Instantly he freed her hand, which she quickly tucked into the folds of her cloak.

An awkward silence settled. It felt heavy and strange—which must be why they failed to notice that the world around them was anything but settled.

Suddenly, the sky flashed. Thunder roared. The very air sizzled with malevolent intent.

Then, an unnatural stillness.

A jagged bolt of lightning flashed so close by that it summoned his every nerve to attention. The ground trembled. The ancient oak swayed.

He swept Mrs. Stanhope down with him just as the oak split with a deadly crack. Acrid smoke assailed his nostrils as a massive branch just missed them. But the tree's savage shudder told him their luck wouldn't last.

Robert rolled them away just as the oak toppled with a violent, futile protest. Even the earth seemed to sizzle, and he propelled them another turn to try to escape the ground charge.

As the storm raged, they lay motionless in the mud, clutching one another.

Finally, he raised his head to look at her. Shock had frozen her features. Mud splattered her cheeks. Her frame was not slight or frail, but under him she felt small and vulnerable.

At length, distant thunder signaled the storm had moved on. The air calmed.

Yet Robert's arms refused to release her. Rain had matted her hair, forced it from those stingy pins. Her lips parted. Her hands pressed his chest as he stared helplessly at her mouth.

"Mr. Tavish." Her breathy gasp sent all sorts of notions spinning in his head.

"Yes?"

"I-I…" Her lips trembled.

Trembled.

"Can you…?"

Robert waited to hear what she wished him to do, tried not to hope it was something carnal.

"I c-can't breathe," she croaked out.

Oh.

Of course. His size, his might. He outweighed her by six or seven stone—his father's dark legacy, with all the terrible consequences. He was a beast. Best to remember that.

Robert shifted his weight off her. Mrs. Stanhope gasped a deep, shuddering breath.

And sent her elbow into his chin with stunning force.

———✦———

"You nearly suffocated me!" Emmaline bit out.

"Not my intent," Mr. Tavish growled. "Do you not see what happened to our tree?"

"*Our* tree? We don't have a tree, you horrible man." She glared at him.

He hauled her to her feet, none too gently. "Look around."

Now she saw. The oak had split top to bottom, its gnarled trunk reduced to black shards. Mr. Tavish had rolled them out of harm's way.

Emmaline realized she was shaking. With dawning awareness, she saw that their very lives had been in danger. Mr. Tavish had saved them. Stunned, she looked at him.

"Cloak's ruined," he said grimly.

Indeed. The green wool was a muddy brown, its delicate lilac edging obliterated. His clothes were also ruined—trousers muddied, boots covered in muck, coat blackened.

"I'll buy you another," he said.

"No." She could scrub out the mud, although the cloak would never look the same. But if it kept her warm, what did that matter?

Mr. Tavish frowned. "I can afford to buy you dozens of cloaks."

Still dazed, Emmaline found her words came slowly: "I do not want…your charity."

"You'll *have* a new cloak," he growled.

She bit her lip. "I ought not have accepted this one, but your note was so kind."

His glower deepened. "Was it?"

"Yes. Not at all like you, now that I think of it," she said. "But I agreed to walk with you in the rain. The damage is my fault, not yours."

"I tossed you into the mud."

"Likely saving my life," Emmaline said. "I owe you that debt. I'll not add another."

Mr. Tavish glared at her. "Quarrelsome woman."

"I am resolved. The matter is settled."

For a long moment they stared at one another.

Then he took her elbow, propelled her to the cottage, flung her a dark gaze, and was off.

Chapter Eight

WHAT DID IT mean to serve an unworthy man? It was a question that had bedeviled John Gibbons for much of his life. That had started on his father's deathbed.

"Service is a trust, my son. Your lot won't be easy. I was fortunate to serve an honorable man, but this one's weak. I'm sorry for you."

John hadn't wanted his father to expend his last breaths telling him the duty he knew all too well. But his father's watery eyes wore the veil of one who knows he will not see the next sunrise and has much yet to say.

"Ours is a duty few understand. Loyalty is required above all," his father went on. "And when your conscience and his diverge, you must find your way through the thicket."

John understood. The man of whom they spoke was pernicious. How to be loyal to such a man, yet not lose one's mortal soul?

His father did not last long enough to explain.

But John remained troubled. Corruption inevitably corrupts those who serve it. And yet, he had no recourse. Service was his duty. He could not betray his father's trust. Was he a lesser man for serving an evil one?

Perhaps the man wasn't truly evil, only misguided. Perhaps he only needed to be steered toward his better angels. But that was wishful thinking. The man abused his servants, his children, his wife—anyone weaker. He was a bully.

To be sure, John found small ways to subvert. He made sure the whipped stable lad got an extra portion at supper and extra wages to bring home to his mother. Cook's plum pie, which his employer denounced as unfit for swine, was in truth quite good. John made sure to praise it. With his access to the accounts, John was able, over time, to pension off the female servants so they could live elsewhere without fear of being assaulted by the brute who held their livelihood.

Children were harder. What they lacked—a father's love—he could not provide. Nor could he mitigate their father's blows. John didn't worry about the elder boy as much as the younger one. He was a sensitive lad, but also a rebel. The father sent him away to have that rebelliousness purged, leaving the lad's mother inconsolable. Her sobs gutted John to the core.

Serving an unworthy man was the worst sort of hell.

When John saw a problem, every instinct demanded he try to rectify it. But these problems were too great: A child in pain, a wife abused, a house that was not a home but a fortress that falsely proclaimed it to belong to a man of worth.

John never put his own interests above those he served. Yet dilemmas did arise. Was it a betrayal of duty to subvert the harm his employer caused? After all, John had the means to do so only because of who he served.

But there was a higher duty. A man with the chance to turn aside evil must heed the call.

Robert shed his boots at the door. His waistcoat next.

Servants scurried past with buckets of hot water. Naturally, Gibbons had already ordered his bath. Robert trudged up the stairs to his chamber.

The dratted curricle was water-logged from the rain. He was too big for such a flimsy vehicle anyway. That problem he could solve by never driving another two-wheeler. About the other problem—his size, which had almost suffocated Mrs. Stanhope—he could do little.

His strength was an asset on digs. And in town, ruffians and thieves gave him a wide berth. Those who didn't Robert easily dispatched. His grandfather had trained him for infantry and on a multitude of weapons, some ancient, along with some esoteric martial arts. He honed his skills at Gentleman Jackson's and the adjacent fencing academy on Old Bond Street.

But women were another matter. For reasons that lived in a dark corner of his brain, Robert was keenly aware he could do harm without meaning to. Today, he'd acted from instinct, let down his guard, failed to see that in protecting Mrs. Stanhope he'd harmed her.

That must never happen again.

Plunging into the steaming water was sheer bliss. Which failed to dispel the fact that he'd made a cake of himself with her. His brain hadn't formed a coherent thought as she lay in the mud under him. He'd been comparing her eyes to Cornwall's seas. Ridiculous.

Then again, he'd never met a woman like Mrs. Stanhope. She did not equivocate. *I am resolved. The matter is settled.*

Robert forced himself to remember he was engaged in this matchmaking charade to discover whether she'd committed dastardly deeds. He mustn't lose his head.

Alas, a scratching at the door shattered that fine moment of clarity. A boy, lugging a bucket of hot water, stood at the door.

"Mr. Gibbons said I was to help you bathe." The lad was too slight to carry his burden easily. When some of the water splashed onto the floor, he looked stricken.

"I don't require help," Robert growled. "Tell Gibbons he's got straw for brains."

The boy's eyes widened in horror.

Robert sighed. "I relieve you of any obligation to attend my bath."

When the boy hesitated, Robert studied him more closely. The lad, probably about ten, was painfully thin. His eyes were unnaturally bright, and the hand holding the bucket trembled from the weight of his burden. He was plainly terrified.

"Set the bucket down," Robert said, more gently.

The lad sighed in relief as he set the bucket on the floor. Those wide eyes—brown, he thought—looked out of a face far too gaunt for a boy of his years.

"Your name, lad?"

"Peter."

"What is your position here?"

The boy drew himself up proudly. "Scullery boy, Yer Lordship. Cook says I do a good day's work, better than the last one."

"What happened to the last one?"

Peter looked uncertain. "Not sure. Mr. Gibbons hired me a fortnight ago. Gave me a shilling to take home to my ma. She's right proud of me."

A shilling—a pittance. Doubtless the boy had a dozen siblings and an invalid mother dependent on his wages. Robert steeled himself for Peter's tale of woe.

But the lad just stood there, staring in that direct and unnerving way children had.

"Can I please help with the bath?" he asked hopefully.

"No."

His face fell.

"But you can fetch me some clean clothes," Robert quickly added.

The lad brightened. He opened the wardrobe and gave a low whistle. "Satin," he said in awe, staring at a shirt of shiny fabric. "You've got satin shirts. In *colors*."

"Not those. The muslin."

"But—"

"The fancy stuff belonged to my father. Mine's the other."

Carefully, Peter took out a plain muslin shirt and a pair of tan trousers. "These do?"

"Yes. Now let me be."

The boy didn't hear the dismissal—or pretended not to. "Ma says this is a strange house."

Robert closed his eyes and tried to concentrate on the water's enveloping warmth.

"She didn't want me to work here," the boy went on. "Said it weren't natural to have no women in a house. She's scared something will happen to me."

Robert's eyes shot open. "Like what?"

Peter looked away. "Not sure. Something."

"Why did she let you work here, if she thought you wouldn't be safe?"

The boy didn't answer.

Likely the family needed the money. No more complicated than that.

"No harm will come to you here," Robert assured him. "I don't know why the house has no females. Likely, it's because my father was… mean." A wholly inadequate word for the man.

The boy was quiet for a moment. Then: "Are you mean, too?"

"No." He wondered what Mrs. Stanhope would have said to that.

"Mayhap you can hire women," Peter ventured. "My ma's a good cook."

"We have a cook." Robert knew enough not to interfere in his kitchen.

"My eldest sister, May, she's got a temper, but you wouldn't be sorry if you hired her."

Robert's bathwater was cooling rapidly.

"Lizzy's the loud one." Peter sighed. "You wouldn't like her."

"Don't like loud," Robert said. "Or temperamental, or—"

"Jenny, though, she's a sweet girl. Even if she is my sister. Then there's Hetty and Betsy. They're only five. Not old enough."

Apparently, Peter *did* have a dozen siblings.

"Sorry, Yer Lordship." The boy looked sheepish. "Ma says I talk too much. Like Prudence—she's twelve. Two years older than me, but thinks she knows everything. You know how it is with sisters."

"No. I had a brother."

"Wouldn't mind a brother or two. But Ma says no more babies."

"What does your father say?"

"Don't have one. Some of us do when they're around. Mostly they ain't."

Robert gave up hope that a soothing bath could help him puzzle out his response to Mrs. Stanhope. In a world of ragged, too-thin boys, absent fathers, and long-suffering mothers, his own troubles paled.

Mrs. Stanhope would have been quick to point that out.

"Don't infer too much from any one card," Emmaline said. "The key is how it lies with the others."

Mr. Tavish looked bored. He arrived for his appointment at four o'clock and to her great relief made no reference to the muddy events of yesterday or the abrupt way they parted. His hair was tied in a queue, which suited him, as did the trousers, beige lawn shirt, and fawn waistcoat. They covered an impressive physique, she now knew, having felt the full weight of the man.

Which made the parlor seem even smaller.

"Some say the cards have an uncanny ability to chart a subject's emotional and moral state," Emmaline said.

Mr. Tavish scoffed. "Absurd."

"Don't demean what you don't understand. If you don't wish a reading, we can turn instead to the lessons you are in sore need of."

"Ah. My deficiencies. I am all ears, madam."

She sighed. "I don't mean to spark hostilities between us. I will try to be more tactful."

"If I had to enumerate the qualities you lack, tact would be at the top," he said.

"Thank you for that," Emmaline snapped.

Mr. Tavish regarded her. "Didn't say you were in need of tact, only that you lacked it. We might debate whether that's a defect or virtue."

"It's a defect," she said. "Women are trained to be polite and malleable."

"To what end?"

"To find husbands, of course. Men don't want wives who are blunt-spoken."

"You had a husband," he pointed out. "And you aren't especially polite or malleable."

Emmaline made a mental note to be more careful about the particulars of her fictional widowhood. "Not all men are the same."

"Exactly. My deficiencies might well be virtues to some."

"Not to a prospective bride. You may wish to write a list of defects to work on: Your conversational skills are absent, your dancing abysmal, your ability to anticipate a woman's needs woeful. You're self-absorbed and don't care about anything except those rocks of yours."

Mr. Tavish sat back in his chair. "Your knowledge of my character is astonishing."

Emmaline flushed. This was not the way to keep a client. "I don't claim to know your character. I speak only of what you present on the surface. You seem ignorant of things women appreciate. A woman likes to be tended to."

"Like a potted plant?"

"A bit more than that," she replied evenly.

He regarded her. "You don't think me capable of this 'tending'?"

"I suppose there's hope." Though in his case, she wasn't sure. "We needn't reform you completely, just so you'll pass muster."

"What a relief."

Oh, she knew that tone. He was toying with her. "May we return to the cards, sir?"

"By all means."

Unlike her aunt, Emmaline wasn't proficient, so she laid out a simple three-card spread. "These represent your past, present, and future." She frowned. "Three court cards—all of Swords. Most unusual."

"Out with it," Mr. Tavish said gravely. "What do you see?"

"The king reveals you to be unaware of the feelings of others and capable of cruelty."

He gave her a mirthless smile.

"You are possessed of an unfortunate rigidity, but the knight also suggests secretiveness, and coming change. The way he is positioned here, next to the queen, suggests—"

"The change will be her doing," Mr. Tavish said in a bored tone. "And though she is intelligent and quick-witted, the question is whether or not she is trustworthy."

Emmaline pushed her chair back from the table. "One might almost think you've done this sort of thing before. But if you had, you would not have allowed me to make a fool of myself by telling you what you already knew."

"You give me too much credit." But he had the grace to look chagrined.

She snatched up the cards and handed them to him. "Perhaps you will return the favor. Pray, tell me what you see in the cards for me."

"Cards can't predict the future. They simply speak to a person through their own fears and desires. That's how fortune-tellers prey on unsuspecting folk."

"My aunt and I do not prey on people, Mr. Tavish. We preface our readings with caveats that they aren't necessarily truth, only a reflection of the moment."

He didn't respond, merely picked up the cards, cut them, and effortlessly laid out a ten-card Celtic cross spread—far too complicated for her meager talents.

The first card he turned over was the Queen of Wands.

"Obstinate," he declared. "Imagines wrongs."

"Independent," she countered. "Practical and kind."

"Demanding," he insisted.

"Willing to fight," she said through gritted teeth.

"But look," he pointed out. "The knight enters. Action. Change. A sudden departure."

Emmaline stared at the card. "A change of residence. How very odd."

"The queen is home-loving," he said. "She'll find another."

Though she didn't believe cards could foretell events, these were unnerving. "How do you know so much about the Tarot?"

Mr. Tavish hesitated. "My father used mystics to try to control my mother. Some employed mesmerism, others the Tarot."

Whatever Emmaline had expected, it was not that.

"I researched their methods, tried to get Parliament to outlaw them," he went on. "Charles Fox wasn't convinced. Whigs lined up behind him. Pitt retreated to his port and wouldn't lift a hand. Had hopes with Grenville, but he had other priorities."

"Mr. Tavish," Emmaline said softly. "I think you are not what you seem."

He eyed her warily.

"You claim you wish to marry, when clearly you do not. You came to me, a woman who lives in a ramshackle cottage on Oxford Street, to find you a bride, when a man of your standing and wealth has every superior avenue. You possess expert knowledge of the cards, and personal experience with the occult. What are you about?"

He hesitated, as if weighing something.

"I have an uncle," he said finally. "Dabbles in War Office matters. Aspires to be prime minister one day."

Emmaline frowned. "I don't understand."

"He's either an idiot or playing a deep game. Are you aware you are being followed?"

Robert saw she didn't fully grasp the point. "You are in danger."

Bewilderment etched a line down the middle of her forehead. "But I am not important or consequential—why would anyone spy on me?"

"Burwell."

"I had nothing to do with his death," she protested. "He was in the street and—"

"He was involved in treason."

Myriad emotions swept her features— confusion, uncertainty, dismay. *Not* guilt. Her aunt might be a fine actress, but Mrs. Stanhope's bewilderment felt genuine. Robert wanted to trust it.

He had a decision to make. His charade wasn't working. Every instinct told him she wasn't a traitor or murderer. Certainly, she was no mystic. Emmaline Stanhope had her feet firmly rooted in reality. Robert had found nothing to back up George's suspicions.

He pulled the handbill from his pocket. "Do you recognize this?"

She stared at it. "Our fortune-telling flyer."

Robert turned it over to reveal the death card drawing. "It was in his possession when he died. Seems a message, and a threatening one at that."

Mrs. Stanhope eyed him in bewilderment. "We had the Tarot death card printed on the back because my aunt thought it added drama. It's from a commonly used deck—my aunt has a different deck she prefers, but we rarely use it. We distributed these flyers all over town. Anyone could have found one—perhaps Mr. Burwell did."

"Burwell worked in the War Office, which suspects he was targeted by fellow conspirators who feared exposure. You were the last person to see him alive. He had your flyer on his person. You are a suspect."

She blinked. "If that's so, why haven't the authorities accused me?"

"Because there's no mark on Burwell that wasn't put there by a coach and four. They've no proof of foul play—yet."

Mrs. Stanhope leveled a gaze at him. "You

came to me pretending to be a client because you thought I murdered him and were looking for evidence."

"My uncle portrayed you as a charlatan. I wondered whether you put Burwell in some sort of trance. But you're no more capable of mesmerism than you are skilled at the Tarot."

"A ringing endorsement," she muttered.

"Fact remains, you're in the War Office crosshairs." Robert decided she could weather the whole: "If Burwell was a traitor, he was conspiring with others, perhaps abroad, perhaps here. They will suspect you know about their plot and can expose them."

"They want to kill me." Stated simply, without fear.

He nodded. "Your clever stick and rocks would be ineffective against that sort."

Mrs. Stanhope gave him a measuring look. "Since you've told me all this, does that mean you trust that I'm neither murderer nor traitor?"

"Trust is hard to quantify. But you don't seem the murdering type."

"And you don't seem the marrying type," she said pointedly.

Robert shrugged. "Apparently, I have defects."

Mrs. Stanhope sighed. "I had arranged to meet tonight with a prospective bride for you."

"Tell her I changed my mind."

"She meets your requirements, assuming those were genuine."

"Genuine enough, had I inclination to marry," Robert said. "Which I don't."

"Perhaps you should reconsider. She might be the answer to your dreams."

"I don't have dreams," he said. "Good day, Mrs. Stanhope. Doubt we'll meet again."

Chapter Nine

THE CARDS HADN'T lied: Mrs. Stanhope was obstinate, independent, and not easily intimidated, even when facing the prospect of murderous spies. From that first night, when she swung her reticule at that drunken idiot, Robert had found her strength fascinating.

He didn't wish to be fascinated.

Congratulating himself on being well out of her orbit, Robert barreled into his study, intent on work. He nearly ran into the lad.

"What the devil are you doing?" Robert demanded.

"Watching Galahad," Peter said quickly. "Mr. Gibbons said I might."

The bird was preening again in front of the mantel mirror.

"I can't work with that bird here, chirping all the time," Robert groused.

"Sorry, Yer Lordship. I was cleaning the cage and he got loose."

The boy was trembling. Did he take him for an ogre? Robert frowned. Where had he heard that term applied to him? Of course: the ever-insightful Mrs. Stanhope.

"He likes it here," Peter added. "It's the mirror."

"A guinea for you, boy, if you can get him to follow you out of the room."

The lad eyed him in amazement. "A *guinea?*"

"If you accomplish the thing in the next minute."

Peter bolted out of the room, and soon was back with a fistful of torn bread. When the bird flew to the lad's shoulder, Peter shot Robert a triumphant look. Was it imagination, or did he stand a little taller, hold his shoulders a little straighter?

Robert reached into his pocket and pulled out a gold coin. "Well done."

Boy and bird sailed out of the room, and it was difficult to tell who flew higher.

A lesson there. Carrot was superior to stick. Which Robert knew, of course. Still, it was worth noting that the title he deemed worthless gave him unearned advantages.

Was Mrs. Stanhope improving his character from afar?

Impossible.

Even as the thought formed, Robert found himself reaching for paper and pen.

Words. She thought he lacked words. Robert wrote hundreds of words in his work. Plans for digs, findings, presentations. But she wanted meaningless conversation about weather, et cetera. He'd tried that and felt idiotic. His writing was a more deliberate process. He took time to find the right words, reject those that didn't serve. For example:

England's weather is influenced by the ocean and wind currents that bring warm air to battle cold air arriving from polar regions.

There. A factual discussion of weather. But somewhat generic. Perhaps this:

Cornwall weather is milder than that of other coastal regions. That allows for more days to study its wealth of rocks and fossils.

Mrs. Stanhope was probably not interested in Cornwall weather. She'd have wanted more personal words. Something to suggest who he was:

I do not seek a bride. But if I did, I would want someone with a brain.

There. It helped to write things down.

⁓

"You say he is wealthy?" Miranda Fitzwilliam eyed her skeptically.

"Quite," Emmaline replied. "But I must confess that when I arranged to see you, I believed he was serious in wanting a bride. Now he says he is not."

Miranda sighed. "The vagaries of men. Do you know that just this morning I found— I am loath to confess it—a *gray* hair?"

Since Miranda's hair was the color of straw, Emmaline did not see how her friend could distinguish a solitary silver strand, but she nodded sympathetically. "At all events, the man has considerable flaws."

"What sort?" Miranda asked.

How to describe Mr. Tavish's character? "Rigid

habits and a withholding nature," Emmaline said. "Yet he has come to my aid several times and protected me from injury."

"I see. He is strong?"

Emmaline contemplated the sturdy arms that rolled them from harm in the thunderstorm. His solid strength, his reassuring robustness.

"Emmaline?" Miranda prodded.

"Er, yes. Very strong. Physically imposing," she said. "Mind you, his appearance is not in the usual way. His hair is long and unfashionable. It gifts him with a degree of…wildness."

Her friend was studying her. "Are you certain you do not envision him for yourself?"

"Gracious, no." Emmaline had worked too hard to become self-sufficient to need—or want—any man, especially not one who put women in boxes.

Yet he disrupted her senses. Not only with his considerable physical attributes, but also with the way his gaze met hers, as if he intended to gain her secrets and other unthinkable things. His very presence warmed her. She had not been warmed in a very long time. Her life was about keeping the roof over their heads and securing treatment for her aunt.

Things in the cottage were always breaking, and sometimes Emmaline thought she was broken too. But they were managing, if only just. She never thought about men.

Except this one. Why?

Somehow, he made her think of her father's moldy fairy tales, even though Mr. Tavish was no prince—or even polite—and she was no princess.

Any bride of his would need to hold few illusions about the marriage. Miranda Fitzwilliam could have been that woman. They'd met at Lady Warwick's when Miranda was a teacher's assistant. She was older than Emmaline, past an age when women had choices. But she possessed a fine, discerning mind, which might have appealed to Mr. Tavish, if he bothered to pay attention.

Even if he didn't, his bride would have freedom and funds to do whatever she wished. Decades would pass in such a fashion. Lifetimes.

How empty that sounded.

Emmaline was glad her friend wouldn't be saddled with such a husband.

"You and I may well see one another into old age," Miranda said with a sigh.

"Not the worst of fates." Emmaline smiled.

They bid adieu, with promises to meet again soon.

Outside, Emmaline stood on the street in lengthening shadows and a light rain. She didn't mind the damp but given the late hour it was wiser to find a hackney. Mr. Tavish had allowed her to keep his deposit, so she would splurge.

As little raindrops turned into big ones, Emmaline told herself she was grateful to be a practical woman who did not cling to foolish yearnings. Her bad leg made her vulnerable, though she'd tried to remedy that. One day at the market, she'd come upon a woodcarver who crafted hidden compartments in his canes— one held a small brush for cleaning men's pipes, another a letter opener. She gave him nearly a month's rent to craft a stick with a hidden stiletto. Adding lead for heft was her idea.

Emmaline had studied other ways to protect herself. One of her father's books depicted sixteenth century soldiers using quarterstaffs in combat. A fencing book detailed strategies for duels. She read them avidly.

But one could only learn so much from books.

Nowadays, bouts were fought for sport, chiefly under the auspices of Gentleman Jackson, whose club was next to Mr. Angelo's fencing academy. Fighting often spilled outside, where obnoxious dandies in top hats claimed the sidewalks, relegating lesser folk like her to the streets.

Posing as a servant—ladies often sent servants on shopping missions there—Emmaline learned to fend off those unruly dandies and picked up enough defensive techniques to wield her walking stick.

Her independence, like Miranda's, was hard won.

Still, what was it worth? What, in the end, did she have? A shabby cottage with vermin despite her best efforts to scrub away the dirt that drew them? Ancient hinges that rebuffed her attempt to soothe their fractious dispositions? Men who only wanted wives who left them alone?

Sadly, she had no talent for the marriage business. She was simply marking time on a path that led…where?

Emmaline took a deep breath. She would not succumb to self-pity.

Luckily, a hackney was idling on the corner. She hailed it with a wave and hurried over.

But as she looked up at the driver to give her destination, something heavy and suffocating was flung over her from behind.

Rough hands tossed her into the vehicle. A foul-smelling rag was shoved into her mouth.

The vehicle started to move. Emmaline heard thunder.

And then, silence.

———— ∾ ————

Robert dreamed of a canary pecking at his nose. He awoke and found it was no dream. Galahad was perched on his chin, squawking loudly.

Moonlight streamed in through his window, scattering shifting shadows over the bed as his gaze locked with the bird's.

"Go away," he growled.

Galahad flew to the table, but even as Robert closed his eyes, he knew sleep wouldn't return. Not because of the bird, but because of a hollow loneliness that gripped him when his thoughts wandered to his family, especially his mother, who had deserved so much more than that troubled, solitary death. The sort of loneliness that engulfs a man late at night when there is no one to blame for his isolation but himself and his dark legacy.

Ironic that his uncle had him pretend to seek a bride. Marriage wasn't for him. Neither was love, whatever that was. Occasionally he indulged in minor couplings, not to be repeated, but never allowed himself to get carried away. Empty experiences, all.

Robert relentlessly avoided introspection, but such thoughts ambushed him when he didn't have the distraction of work. No wonder his dreams were full of torment.

Something else was at work tonight. He stilled, trying to discern the source of unease.

Emmaline Stanhope.

No. It was not possible. He had not been pulled from sleep by a canary trying to tell him something about her. Yet there she was, her image annoyingly clear in his mind's eye.

Galahad circled the room, frantically beating his wings.

Robert threw his pillow across the room, ripped off his covers, and lurched to his feet.

Then he heard the commotion. Gibbons burst into his room.

"You must come, my lord." The man's voice shook. "There is a matter, a *dire* matter. Mrs. Stanhope's aunt is here."

Robert shook the cobwebs from his brain. Dire indeed if her aunt had come at this hour.

"She insists on talking to you. I didn't want to wake you, but she is…compelling."

Robert strode to the hearth and tried for a rushlight, but the thing went out. With a curse he moved to the wardrobe, fumbled blindly in the dark for his clothes and hurriedly donned trousers, shirt, boots. Something tore, but he ignored that.

By the time he reached the parlor, Gibbons was

offering sherry to Miss Alcott, who stood near the hearth, one hand braced on the mantel. She fixed Robert with a commanding gaze. Held that silent, portentous pose for another beat.

Then her gaze sharpened. Had her eyes been daggers, he would have breathed his last.

"You must find her. You must do it *now.*" Uttered in a stentorian tone that could have projected to the Thames.

The women in that family did not cavil at barking orders.

"What has happened?" Robert asked.

Her censorious gaze flicked over him. "Emmaline went to visit an acquaintance—a prospective match for *you.* She has not returned. At this late hour I fear the worst."

Suddenly, her determined mien crumbled. She swayed precariously.

Robert tried to help her into a chair, but she refused.

"I hired a carriage and went round to Miranda's myself," she said weakly. "Emmaline left there at eight o'clock. It is now the dead of night. The very *dead* of night, Mr. Tavish. Something terrible has befallen her."

Miss Alcott put a hand to her forehead. "Go *now,* I beseech you." Her fingertips fluttered as she pointed to the door. "Number Five Guildford Street."

Gibbons was so moved that he rushed over to her. He, too, tried to guide her to a nearby chair, but she stood unrelenting, a tower of determination despite her obviously frail state.

Robert wasn't aware that he'd been holding his breath, but as he finally exhaled, he realized Miss Alcott had held him hostage as if she were Medusa or Circe or some other lethal female. Quite simply, he could not look away.

How strange that he had awakened with Mrs. Stanhope's image fixed in his brain, as if they were connected. Unescorted women did not undertake errands at night, but he'd seen her throw caution to the wind that night at the Argyll Rooms. It was exactly what she would do.

Not ten minutes later, Robert was at the stable, readying an enormous black, which pawed impatiently at the dirt. That he possessed such a beast surprised him. His departed brother, an incautious sort, likely had been in the habit of riding him neck for leather.

That meant the horse hadn't been ridden in earnest in months. No man with sense dashed into the night atop an unfamiliar beast in search of a woman who might be a traitor but more likely was but a pawn in a high-stakes chess game that his uncle—or worse—had set in motion.

Robert gave the horse a moment to adjust. In calmer circumstances, he would have walked the creature and gauged its response. Tonight, there wasn't time.

Fortunately, the horse quickly settled.

And proceeded to gobble up the night with boundless authority.

Chapter Ten

HELOISE SANK INTO the nearest chair. Her legs wobbled. No one understood the demands of a performance. Persuading Mr. Tavish as to the urgency of Emmaline's plight required all the effort of summoning Lady Macbeth importuning her husband to murder.

She could do little now except marshal strength to get herself home.

"Some sherry, madam?"

Heloise eyed the man—Mr. Gibbons, she recalled. "Stronger, if you have it."

"Oh, indeed. Ratafia? Milk posset?"

"God, no."

"Er, claret or port?"

Heloise frowned. "Is that the best you can do?"

He straightened—but not with indignation. No, it was as if he relished the challenge.

"All manner of spirits are at your disposal, madam," he declared. "I have a fine French brandy, with just a hint of orange. Or a lovely apple brandy."

"No fruit. Perish the thought."

His brow furrowed. "I do have whisky—Irish,

not Scots, since the previous earl didn't care for it. The Irish stuff lacks smoke, however."

"That," Heloise said.

While he was off hunting spirits, she tried to gather herself. This was why she was no longer on the stage. Performing sapped the life blood, left her an empty vessel. There was a time when acting filled her with life. This felt like a slow death.

"Here you are." Mr. Gibbons was back with a small glass on a silver tray. "There's cold gammon if you are hungry."

"No food." Heloise took the glass, tossed it back. She held up the glass. "More."

Mr. Gibbons blinked.

She glared at him. "I suppose you think me unrefined."

"Certainly not, madam."

"I am *thoroughly* unrefined," Heloise said. "Beyond redemption. Bring the bottle."

"Right away, madam."

Heloise was beginning to feel better. Mr. Gibbons was as good as his word. He poured her a second glass, set the bottle on a table, and watched attentively.

"Sit," she ordered. "I must compose myself. It's an interior process, and I don't care to be studied like an odd duck who strayed into your path."

Carefully, he lowered himself to the chair opposite hers.

"Do take whisky," Heloise insisted.

Interestingly, he didn't protest. He poured out a glass for himself.

"An interior process," Mr. Gibbons repeated in a musing tone. "That suggests the inner self is different from what one presents to the world."

Goodness. She hadn't expected such a keen observation.

"Yes. For instance, looking at me you might think I am a bawdy former actress with a scandalous past that I regret." Heloise paused for a beat. "Some of that is false."

"Which part?"

"I regret nothing. Now it's your turn. What is your role in this house?"

He hesitated. "My family has always served the earls of Kent."

Heloise frowned. "Mr. Tavish is an earl?"

Mr. Gibbons nodded. "We pretend as if he is not."

"Why?"

He drank from his glass. Happily, the whisky seemed to loosen his tongue.

"He does not wish the burden of the title and prefers to be known as a scientist. But after his father and older brother died, there was no one else to carry the title."

Heloise pondered that. "Why would an earl, a man with all of this, seek help from my Emmaline, a marriage broker so very far removed from his orbit?"

Mr. Gibbons looked surprised. "I did not know he was in search of a bride."

"There is much about Mr. Tavish— Lord Tavish—that doesn't make sense."

"Lord Kent," he corrected politely. "Tavish is his Scottish name. Perhaps I have said too much." He permitted himself a half smile. "I imagine it is the pleasant company."

"And the whisky," she put in.

"Ought we to get you home, madam? You must be eager to learn if there is word of Mrs. Stanhope. I will drive you." Mr. Gibbons rose and offered her his arm.

Heloise looked him up and down. His silver hair was quite lovely. "You are…nice."

Happily, her low, throaty voice—much unused these days—hadn't deserted her.

Indeed, it felt especially well-lubricated.

⚬⚬⚬

"I am in your debt, sir." Emmaline regarded the tall, dark-haired gentleman who had come to her rescue.

As she'd lain helpless on the floor of that musty vehicle, it had rolled forward, then suddenly lurched to a halt. Through the thickness of the horsehair blanket, she heard sounds of a scuffle. Something slammed against the carriage. The door was flung open. A pair of strong arms lifted her out just as the driver cracked the whip and the hackney sped off.

Her rescuer introduced himself as Andrew Maitland. When he offered to drive her home in his own very fine carriage, Emmaline gratefully agreed. He retrieved her walking stick from the street where it had fallen during her assault.

Now they sat alone in her parlor. Was it weak to feel grateful for being rescued like a helpless heroine in one of Mr. Richardson's novels?

Mr. Maitland looked every inch the gentleman, from his impeccable snow-white neckcloth to his black curly beaver chapeau and polished black top boots. His perfectly cut clothing—also black—evinced little disarray, despite his struggle with her assailant.

Did he always wear black? It gave him a mysterious air. His chiseled cheekbones, regal nose, and high forehead put her in mind of classical sculpture. His gaze, so dark as to resist efforts to plumb its depths, conjured the blank eyes of ancient statuary.

"Can you think of any reason someone would wish to abduct you?" he asked. "Beyond your obvious beauty."

Perhaps it was the nature of polished gentlemen to make such remarks, but Emmaline knew she was not beautiful. "I doubt my appearance has anything to do with what happened."

That aristocratic brow furrowed. "Then perhaps something in your past?"

"My past is very ordinary, sir."

"More recent, perhaps. Has anything unusual occurred?"

Before Emmaline could answer, the front door opened. Her aunt stood on the threshold, leaning on Mr. Gibbons's arm. "You are found!" she exclaimed.

Emmaline eyed her in astonishment. She'd thought her asleep upstairs. "I'm afraid someone tried to abduct me, Aunt. Mr. Maitland came to my rescue."

"I knew it was something dreadful!" Aunt Heloise put a hand to her forehead as Mr. Gibbons helped her into the room. "This can be laid at Mr. Tavish's door. And I told him so."

"His lord—er, Mr. Tavish—is searching for you, madam." Mr. Gibbons carefully closed the door. The hinges offered a noisy protest.

Mr. Tavish looking for her? How odd.

Her rescuer had risen and bowed politely. When Emmaline related the events of her kidnapping and rescue, her aunt's gaze shifted to him.

Mr. Maitland cleared his throat. "I asked Mrs. Stanhope whether anything unusual had occurred that would cause her to become a target. Whether anyone might wish her ill."

"A man met his doom at our gate," her aunt said darkly. "Run over by the Mail."

"He made no effort to save himself," Emmaline added.

Mr. Maitland looked thoughtful.

"He was a client of ours." At his questioning look, Emmaline flushed. "We run a matrimonial service. It is quite aboveboard."

"Forgive me, madam. It is none of my business, and yet…" His voice trailed off.

"You fail to understand how a man can stand in the path of certain death?" Emmaline said. "The investigators also seem baffled. He was cheerful when we spoke moments before."

"Most likely tonight's episode was not connected," Mr. Maitland said. "Still, it seems prudent to exercise caution. Tomorrow I will ask Bow Street to investigate."

"Oh, no," Emmaline protested. "The expense—"

"I will take care of that," he said smoothly.

Aunt Heloise's gaze narrowed—likely assessing Mr. Maitland's financial prospects.

"Would you mind if I called on you?" he asked. "To bring news from Bow Street?"

Emmaline's head was spinning. Abduction, rescue, now Bow Street—perhaps it was the lingering effects of whatever was on that smelly rag, but she felt quite divorced from reality.

Before she could answer, the door crashed open. Mr. Tavish filled the doorway, his hair wilder than usual. His gaze registered her presence, shifted to Mr. Maitland.

Hardened.

Her rescuer looked unperturbed. "Your sartorial style has evolved, Tavish."

Mr. Tavish glanced down at his own clothing as if seeing his bright pink satin shirt and purple striped waistcoat for the first time. Then he eyed Emmaline. "What is *he* doing here?"

"Mr. Maitland came to my aid when someone tried to abduct me," she said.

"I see." A wealth of skepticism lay in those two words.

"He risked his life on my account," Emmaline added.

"You won't persuade him," Mr. Maitland said. "Tavish and I are acquainted. Although it's Lord Kent now, isn't it?"

Mr. Tavish regarded him in stony silence.

Her rescuer gave Emmaline a quick bow. "I'll see myself out." He slipped swiftly past Mr. Tavish and out into the night.

"This calls for spirits," Aunt Heloise said. "Will you help me, Mr. Gibbons?"

As they left the room, Emmaline sank wearily onto the sofa.

"You are unharmed?" Mr. Tavish towered over her like a vengeful giant.

"Mr. Maitland—" she began.

"—is not to be trusted." He lowered himself to the sofa next to her.

Emmaline eyed him in surprise. "How do you know him?"

"We served together with Nelson in the Caribbean six years ago. He was eighteen and filled with naked ambition even then. By now, he's picked up more tricks."

"He rescued me," she insisted. "I have no reason to look askance."

"Exactly."

She studied him. "Your clothing is not your usual."

"Grabbed what I could in the dark. My father's things. He was a peacock. Not my style."

"About that. Mr. Maitland called you Lord Kent."

He grimaced. "Earldom. Not fond of it."

Emmaline frowned. "Once more, I find you very secretive, sir."

"Robert Tavish Campbell Wentworth. Didn't care for the last—my father's surname—and the

Campbell part is complicated. Prefer Tavish. I went to your friend's house tonight."

"Miranda's? Why, that's perfect. You and she—"

"Would not suit," he declared. "But she may have seen your abductor. When you arrived, she noticed a man loitering. Couldn't remember much about him. But I found this in the street."

He produced her reticule. "Motive wasn't robbery. Coins still inside." His mouth curved. "Rocks, too."

Emmaline stared at him. "You went to much trouble on my account. I'm in your debt."

"You miss the point. Tonight's attack was bold. Next time will be worse."

Next time. "What do you suggest I do?" she asked.

"Leave. Find some place safer."

Emmaline was incredulous. "We've not a feather to fly with. There is no safer ground. There is no ground at all." To her dismay, her voice broke. "Apologies. Tonight's events have left me overset. I'm not usually—"

"You'll come with me." Mr. Tavish blinked, as if he couldn't quite grasp his own words.

Emmaline stared at him in astonishment. "Where?"

"Scotland."

Had the man lost his mind? "That is…very far."

He rose, as if the matter were settled, but Emmaline caught his sleeve. "Mr. Maitland has pledged to set Bow Street to the matter. That's the sensible course."

"No. Leaves you exposed to danger—including from Maitland. He's not what he seems."

"Neither are you," Emmaline retorted.

Mr. Tavish scowled. "Ask yourself how he happened to be on the scene of your abduction at the exact moment to save you and ingratiate himself."

"I do not ascribe base motives to everyone I meet," she protested.

He strode to the door. "Bring whatever you and your aunt require."

"Wait! I haven't said—"

"We'll leave at noon, after my lecture to the Society."

And that, it seemed was that.

Chapter Eleven

S HE WAS JUST another helpless female in need of masculine rescue.

Emmaline tilted the candle, allowing the melting wax to drip onto the squeaky front door hinge. It would have been better to remove the rusty pin to apply the wax but dislodging it would require help from someone stronger. A man, naturally. She would make do.

What false illusions she had nurtured! Her walking stick and rocks proved useless last night. A woman alone was no match for the rough sort that plied the streets. She'd been living in a dream world—placing her faith in self-reliance, deluding herself that was enough.

Plainly, it was not. Her matrimonial agency was failing. They lived in a sad cottage on a street that hadn't fully shed the aftertaste of celebratory public hangings, no matter that it changed the name from Tyburn and added shops catering to wealthy folk.

Her life felt as dismal as the fog that blanketed London, as grim as each morning's discovery of senseless drunkards who decided in their inebriated haze that the cracked stoop of their little cottage was the perfect place to seek their rest.

Stop it, Emmaline told herself sternly. She wouldn't succumb to pity. Yet the reality was that if anything happened to her, Aunt Heloise would have nowhere to turn. Their survival hung by the slenderest of threads. Mr. Tavish offered them a lifeline. But he'd lied, pretending to seek a bride, hiding the fact he had a title. Could she trust him when their very lives might be at stake?

Testing her handiwork, Emmaline worked the door back and forth. Blessed silence from the hinges. In that, at least, she succeeded. Next was sealing cracks in the wall of her aunt's room. Aunt Heloise hadn't complained, but the gaps let the cold in as well as uninvited pests.

A sudden commotion erupted in the street. A handsome coach drawn by six horses pulled to a stop, followed by a lumbering vehicle. Mr. Tavish rode beside them atop a great black steed.

Dismounting swiftly, he strode up the steps to her—and frowned. "You're not ready."

She shook her head. "I can't uproot our lives simply on your claim that I'm in danger."

"Danger's real," he growled. "Didn't last night show you that?"

"It was unsettling, but I'm not ready to put our fate in your hands." Yet her wavering voice betrayed her.

Mr. Tavish dipped his face close to hers. "Is that a tear?"

Mortifyingly, it was.

"Regrettably, it seems I am *not* strong."

Emmaline sighed. "I must depend on someone like you or Mr. Maitland to save the day. It's quite lowering."

"I've seen your strength," he said, more gently. "You've nothing to be ashamed of. But this isn't a scuffle with drunken dandies on the street. It's bigger than you can manage alone."

Mr. Tavish pointed to the baggage coach, where a young woman sat with a boy. "Engaged a maid for you and your aunt. Though she's mostly here to look after her brother."

Panic swept her. His plan began to seem inevitable. Still, Emmaline resisted. "Why Scotland? It's so very far."

"Only a week, if we make good time."

"But Mr. Maitland—"

"Is attached to the War Office, a fact I learned this morning from my uncle. Maitland orchestrated your abduction and rescue to gain your trust and learn whether you were involved in Burwell's treason. He's not even your biggest threat. That's from Burwell's fellow spies."

"Even if that's so, I don't want to do this," Emmaline protested.

"Neither do I," Mr. Tavish snapped. "You've a half-hour to pack."

As he stomped out toward the carriage, Aunt Heloise came up behind her. "It will be a grand adventure, dear. You could do worse than that one."

"Worse than forced companionship with a man who orders me around? Who—"

"—calls forth every fantasy about how that

ordering would translate in other scenarios," her aunt said with a saucy smile. "There's nothing to keep us here. Look in the street, Em. I see a lovely coach and six, with a baggage coach besides. Wherever he's taking us will be worlds above our current circumstance. Lord Kent—"

"He prefers Tavish."

"—offers a solution. And while chaperoning is not my strong suit, I shall give it a go." Her aunt winked.

"Mr. Maitland—"

"Was too good to be true, was he not? He presents as a rescuing knight, but appearances can be deceiving. You have only to study his eyes. Darkness there, and I don't mean the color."

Emmaline eyed her with concern. "The trip would be an ordeal for you. Your health—"

"Is the same, whether I'm here or elsewhere. A change of scenery will be *divine*."

———◦◦◦———

Robert crossed his arms and leaned back against the carriage, trying to stem his impatience. Would the recalcitrant Mrs. Stanhope cooperate? If so, how long would she keep him waiting? It seemed unlikely that two women could pack in a half-hour.

But wait he would. The situation had only grown more complex with George's visit this morning. His uncle had claimed to be surprised—but not displeased—at Maitland's abduction gambit.

"Bold, but Drew's an ambitious one," George said. "Might help flush out Burwell's fellow conspirators. Puts her in more jeopardy, of course, but that can't be helped."

As for Robert's activities last night, George was delighted. "Well done. Showing up at the last to ensure her safety. She'll trust you now."

"I doubt it. I have a lecture to finish, Uncle."

But after George left, Robert's pen had wandered, along with his thoughts. He wrote:

Taking her to Scotland is idiotic and inconvenient. I do not care what happens to Emmaline Stanhope.

Robert crossed out that last. He did care, in a small and harmless way, about her fate. He bore some responsibility for the fact George's ruse had thrust him into her life. And despite his instinct that Mrs. Stanhope was innocent of treason, she might not be. An extended journey could give him time to find out.

Why, then, hadn't he told George that he was taking her to Scotland?

It wasn't that he didn't trust his uncle, although the man's ethics were malleable. But if George knew of their trip, he might assume something else was in play—romance, perhaps, though that wasn't remotely possible—and conclude that Robert wasn't an impartial investigator.

There was another, even more compelling reason to take her to Scotland: Portia.

Curse his uncle for invoking his mother to begin with. George knew he was tormented by his failure to protect Portia. That he'd been a lad at the time was no excuse in Robert's eyes.

Now another woman was in danger, perhaps through no fault of her own. Dangerous spies were likely targeting her. Maitland was an added complication. In the Royal Navy, he'd always been after the main chance and hadn't scrupled to trample what stood in his way. Robert couldn't leave her to the man's scheming, not if he had the power to keep her safe.

The past could not be undone. Life didn't offer second chances.

But perhaps I can make amends.

Years ago, Portia had somehow mustered the wherewithal to defy her husband, remove Robert from that brutal school, and flee with him to Scotland, her childhood home. Exactly where he was taking Mrs. Stanhope and her aunt.

The Campbell stronghold.

Ah, but Campbells came with baggage: their loyalties were suspect. Campbells fought with Robert the Bruce to win Scottish independence from England, but centuries later allied with Charles I, the Scot on the English throne. Alas, the Campbell chief threw in his lot with Oliver Cromwell during the English civil war, only to reverse himself—too late, for when Charles II took the throne, he was beheaded. On it went through the years, as Campbells fought with England against the Jacobite risings, the Stuart effort to retake the throne.

George, an adept practitioner of the clan tradition of playing all sides, inherited the dukedom with the death of Robert's grandfather, John Campbell, who had led his militia in England's victory at Culloden, the Jacobite death knell. A military hero made of merciless cloth, he was apoplectic when Robert joined the Royal Navy instead of the Fusiliers or Black Watch.

Robert wondered what Mrs. Stanhope would think of Inveraray Castle. He suspected she disdained castles. He wasn't fond of them either, but she'd be protected there.

Colin will take handle that, and I'll wash my hands of her.

With that bolstering if unworthy thought, Robert had marshalled the troops—Gibbons, Peter, his sister Jenny, the bird, and assorted baggage. And now, wonder of wonders, here was Mrs. Stanhope marching toward the carriage—before his deadline—a bandbox under one arm, cat under the other. He relegated the creature to the baggage coach with Peter, idly wondering how the canary would fare with its new travel companion.

She returned to the house and reappeared with two boxes. "My father's papers."

After those went into the baggage coach, Robert held out a woolen cloak for her.

Her jaw set. "I won't accept another cloak."

"Won't manage Scotland without it." He thrust it at her and handed her into the carriage.

<hr>

Emmaline was accustomed to challenges. But she would be days in the company of a man who unsettled her in ways big and small. Worse, she had little say in the matter.

Mr. Tavish had chosen to ride outside. Astride

that enormous black horse, he looked every bit the rescuing knight, underscoring their helplessness.

"Anger," her aunt said softly, "takes a goodly amount of effort to maintain."

Emmaline turned to her. "The man is a liar. He used me to see if I was a traitor."

"And what woman does not use a man, I want to know?"

"I have never done so," Emmaline said stiffly.

Aunt Heloise regarded her pityingly. "You cannot know what you've missed. Some of my most memorable liaisons were well-used."

Across from them, Mr. Gibbons cleared his throat.

"He doesn't even like me," Emmaline pointed out.

Her aunt arched a brow. "Doubtless that is why he is spiriting us away to safety."

"Aunt, I love you dearly, but you see things the way you wish them to be. Life isn't a play, where you can write the ending you choose."

"Neither is it as dreadful as you wish to make it," her aunt said. "I may be an aging actress with a scandalous past, but I know a thing or two about romance. Without it, life would be the dreary existence you seem determined to make it. You should let him make love to you."

Emmaline's face burned. She dared not look at Mr. Gibbons.

"You never told him that you're not a widow, that in fact you've never been married?" Aunt Heloise added sweetly. "That you lied when you said you had?"

Mutely, Emmaline shook her head.

"Oh, dear. I guess that means you are both liars." Aunt Heloise gave an exaggerated sigh.

"Styling myself a widow was for my safety."

Her aunt looked thoughtful. "Therefore, both of you can be angry at the other's lies, each raging away, sublimating carnal desire into hostility. His gaze wide with fury, his lips curled in scorn—then suddenly capturing your mouth for a searing kiss."

Mr. Gibbons had gone quite still.

"Anger is one of the very *best* emotions," Aunt Heloise added serenely.

Chapter Twelve

SERVING AN UNWORTHY man ravaged the soul, but that was not as bad as falling in love with that man's wife.

John had long denied those feelings, telling himself they were idle fantasies, diversions he created to endure service to his employer. But they overtook his dreams, left him shuddering awake at the shame of coveting another man's wife.

She had a kind heart and a voice like an angel. Likely she thought no one heard her sing, for she did it quietly, almost in secret. But John would stop whatever he was doing to catch the faintest of notes, even rooms away.

In the garden, where her husband never went, she gave herself free rein. John would lurk—no other word for it—behind thick shrubs, pretending to prune them, although that was not part of his duties.

For a few years, all was well. On the surface, that is. But he could see—because he had long studied the subtleties of her features—that she was wilting under the cruel dominance of that unworthy man.

He tried to make things better in superficial ways. He would surprise her with a cup of the special tea she loved for its soothing properties. If her husband berated her, loudly and behind closed doors, he would knock to interrupt with some urgent pretense.

But the abuse came more often and worsened. The first time he discovered her sobbing into a handkerchief nearly gutted him. When she removed the cloth, he saw vicious red marks on her face the size of a man's fist. It got worse until that terrible night that was beyond John's ability to fix.

Troubles began a few years after the younger boy was born. A strapping lad, he was intent on protecting her. Once, he jumped between his parents and took the brunt of the man's fists. Thereafter, he was beaten regularly.

The father did not relent, nor did the lad. The boy was sent off to a school known for its harsh discipline based on teachings of an astronomer, Maximilian Hell. John's employer had him make the arrangements.

She stopped eating. She'd long since stopped singing. There was something new in her eyes, a silent defiance that suggested death would be her ultimate victory.

That's when John knew he must act.

Secretly, he packed bandboxes with her things, not enough to attract suspicion. One morning when his employer was out shooting, John persuaded her to come with him in the landau on an errand in the village, saying the air would do her good.

He drove the vehicle himself; he didn't want other servants to pay for his sins.

Perhaps she was lost in thought, for she wore a faraway look and didn't seem to realize when they had gone far beyond the village.

They stopped at an inn, where he hired a driver. By then, she did notice the strangeness of their journey. He bade her to trust him and had the joy of seeing a smile cross her features for the first time in ages. "With my life," she said softly.

They sat facing one another as the driver ferried them deeper into the country, until they stopped at a forbidding building with iron gates. She eyed him in confusion. But trust him, she did. She waited as John went inside.

And returned with her son.

Some lines and boundaries could never be crossed. She was too far above him. Even so, he'd wanted her with every fiber of his being. But more than that, he wanted her protected. He took them to the place that birthed her, the place that was safe.

It was a long journey; he had invented a dying relative to explain his absence to his employer.

She seemed stunned, not fully absorbing her freedom. The boy wore a haunted look. Something had happened to him at the school. He would not soon recover.

About that, John could do nothing. Nor could he linger. His employer would be outraged when he discovered his wife not only gone, but also beyond reach.

John left her at the castle, knowing he would never see her again.

Ever after, Scotland was a land of lost dreams. He vowed never to return.

Yet here he was.

"I may not be up to this walk." Heloise Alcott eyed the steep hill to Edinburgh Castle.

"Take my arm," John offered. "It's worth the effort to see Queen Margaret's chapel. She's a saint now."

She arched a brow. "I'm not one for saints."

"Perhaps history then?" he ventured. "Mary, Queen of Scots, gave birth to James a few miles from here."

At that, her aunt smiled wistfully. "Always wanted to play her. I'm too old now."

"I'll warrant you could play anyone of any age," he said gallantly. "Come. We'll stop whenever you wish. The gunners still use the cannons, and it's a lovely view from up there."

He would never shed the past, but Miss Alcott had a way of commanding the present.

❧

With Aunt Heloise and Mr. Gibbons gone sightseeing, Emmaline and Mr. Tavish were left standing stiffly outside their inn. Five days into their journey, they'd grown no easier with one another. He kept to horseback. At meals, he didn't bother with casual conversation.

Truly, Scotland was the very end of the earth.

At least Edinburgh was near the water, a welcome change since much of their trip had been inland. Tomorrow they would drive through something called the Trossachs, which sounded ominously like the domain of unfriendly trolls.

"Fancy a walk?"

Emmaline eyed Mr. Tavish in surprise. "To the castle?"

He pointed in the opposite direction. "That hill."

In the distance loomed an immense earthen shape. "That…mountain?"

"Volcano. Top blew off millions of years ago, pushed up that ridge."

The craggy knob rolling up toward the clouds looked intimidating. Still, it would be nice to spend time outside after so many days confined to the carriage.

Mr. Tavish took her silence as assent and propelled her toward his horse. "We'll double up. Only three miles, but daylight won't last long enough to get there and back on foot."

Emmaline eyed the horse dubiously. The big black was all muscle and cocky grit.

Mr. Tavish mounted, extended his arm.

She hesitated. "My last mount was a children's pony at Gloucester Green."

That seemed to surprise him. "In Oxford?"

"Yes. My father taught there before we moved to London. I remember little of it because I was very young, but I do remember the fair on the green."

He nodded. "Still there."

When she did not take his arm, Mr. Tavish made an impatient sound, then reached down and pulled her up behind him. Emmaline had to throw her leg over the horse to avoid falling.

"I'm in skirts," she protested. "It's awkward to ride astride."

"Don't be one of those women who insists on riding habits and sidesaddle."

"I haven't the luxury of riding habits." Emmaline tucked her skirt around her. "I walk everywhere in London."

"Walking in Scotland isn't like city walking."

Mr. Tavish set the horse toward the enormous hill at a sedate pace, perhaps in deference to her precarious perch. "Hold on to me. If you fall, I've a mind to leave you in the dirt."

"I have no intention of clinging to your person," Emmaline said crisply. "I am quite secure clutching the fibers of your coat with my fingernails."

His shoulders shook. Was he laughing?

In truth, her hands wanted to glide over the sturdy fabric, which failed to mask the muscled curves of his broad back and shoulders. With her front wedged against his back, it was impossible to ignore his physique.

When they reached the base of the hill, Mr. Tavish dismounted with easy grace and helped her down. Emmaline wobbled—sitting astride called on unused muscles. She was grateful for his steadying arm, but the moment she had her balance, she shook him off.

"Two ways to go," he explained. "Hard path's

well worth it, but the day's gone late. Easier walk along the crags if you don't mind dirt."

"I don't." In London, carriages sped by without regard to pedestrians. Muddy shoes and skirts were a daily occurrence.

Mr. Tavish started up a path, leaving her to follow.

At first, the terrain was gentle as it wound up the hill. His stride was longer than hers, so Emmaline was always behind. That gave her a different angle from which to inspect the man. Those well-made riding breeches—snug by design, so the horse felt the rider's leg movements—outlined sculpted calves that would be the envy of London dandies with their silly padding. Not even the boxers on Bond Street rivaled him.

Distracted, Emmaline failed to notice that their path had taken a steep upturn. She stared at the bluffs ahead in dismay. Her leg had held up so far, but her shoe lift would give her blisters from that climb. She pushed on, determined to give him no reason to judge her weak.

"They call this Arthur's Seat," Mr. Tavish said. "Some say it was the site of King Arthur's Camelot, but I put no stock in that. Others think the hill looks like a dragon."

Emmaline studied the hill's jagged silhouette. "What do you see?"

"Columnar basalt." He pointed to a massive vertical outcropping.

"The columns are oddly precise," she observed. "Almost like…hexagons."

Shockingly, he smiled his approval. "Formed

when lava cooled as it flowed out unevenly. A hollow in the surface caused it to pool and pile up, forming those columns."

The path took them along the spine of the cliff. From here, their horse at the bottom looked no bigger than a bird. Edinburgh's castle rose in the distance, its towers and battlements looming over the town. The sun had drifted lower, bathing the stone fortress in an orange glow.

"How beautiful," Emmaline said.

"Folks say the same about this hill," Mr. Tavish said. "Women come here to wash their faces in the dew to stay young-looking. Scottish weather ages folk."

He lowered himself to a patch of grass. Grateful for the rest, Emmaline joined him. "How is it you know Scotland so well?"

"Grew up here. Not Edinburgh—points north and west."

That was the most information he'd ever provided about himself.

"We're going to your home, then?" Emmaline asked.

"To Inveraray, the family castle. I lived there for a while as a lad, but my mother preferred a smaller place in Oban, so we moved there."

She absorbed that. "Your family has a castle?"

"Came with the territory. My grandfather was Campbell clan chief."

She wanted to know more, but Mr. Tavish didn't seem inclined to volunteer details. So they simply took in the scenery as a quiet peace settled over them.

"No view like this in London." His voice, deeply resonant in the silence, curled around her like a velvet caress.

"If you dislike town, why not live in Scotland?" Emmaline ventured.

Mr. Tavish made a disparaging sound. "There'd be no end to it here."

"End to what?"

He turned to her. "Scots want your soul. Settle for nothing less."

"I don't know what that means."

"Stay here long enough and you will."

Emmaline didn't press him. It was enough to stare at the horizon, absorb its quiet beauty.

And his silent, sturdy presence.

⁓⁓⁓

Robert had forgotten the joys of a Scottish sunset, even over a town as dirty and crowded as Edinburgh. Here, atop the crags, that joy tugged at him. Uncoiled a few knots.

Now and then he heard rustling, foxes beginning to stir or rabbits seeking a hasty last meal before they did.

Something akin to peace seeped into him. He'd spent hours here in his younger days, when he found work in Edinburgh after his mother's death. Back then, he was running from the past, from the Campbells, from his grandfather's determination to decide his future.

Grief and guilt always followed. He could never escape the raw pain of it.

Over time, nature dulled the sharpness of loss.

He hiked Scotland's peaks and valleys, trudged over its scrub moors, swam in its lochs. Finally, when the Royal Navy decided he was old enough, Robert left Scotland for the sea.

Those were glorious days, with Nelson pursuing the French fleet to the Caribbean. It was no small irony that Britain's greatest naval hero suffered seasickness, a malady that, happily, never plagued Robert. But as much as he loved the sea, he ultimately found a truer calling. Scotland's rugged rocks and weathered moors had never loosed their hold. The natural world held secrets, keys to the past and perhaps the future.

Robert discovered he was a scientist at heart. Long days spent digging for clues about ancient worlds humbled him. His fraught childhood was but an imperceptible fluctuation in the overall arc of existence.

He wished Mrs. Stanhope hadn't drawn that soul nonsense from him—though it was true enough. If his family demanded less, he'd have given it. But Campbells always wanted more.

"Is that a star?" she asked. "It's so bright."

"Planet, most likely. Or a comet. Just this year, astronomers sighted one through a telescope, but you can see it with the naked eye at twilight—"

Twilight.

Hell. He'd lost track of time. Darkness was fast descending. They had stayed too long.

Robert rose abruptly.

"My fault," he muttered. "Blacker than pitch before long."

Mrs. Stanhope looked confused, as if she, too,

had been absorbed in the sunset. She allowed him to pull her to her feet, but when she moved to withdraw, he held onto her hand.

"You won't see the path in the dark. I need you to stay close." Bad choice of words. Robert didn't *need* her to do anything. He simply wished to avoid the inconvenience of Mrs. Stanhope breaking her lovely neck.

The path was barely visible, the ground uneven. She stumbled repeatedly and would have fallen had he not held onto her. At this rate, they'd both come to grief.

Robert halted. "Close your eyes."

"What?"

"Close them. Count to ten. Slowly."

As she did, he studied her features, blurred by the darkness that lent her an air of mystery. He watched her for a beat longer than necessary.

"Open them," he said. "Don't look at anything specific. Let the light come in gradually."

They stood silently for a moment.

"Now notice the sliver of moon rising over the castle. The star off to its left, brighter than the others." Robert watched her gaze soften as she absorbed the play of shadow and light.

"It's easier to see now." Her voice held a note of wonder.

He nodded. "People don't have night vision like some animals, but we need less light than we think we do. The key is to recalibrate. Change your notion of seeing."

"You're a good teacher." She smiled, or so he thought. It was too dark to tell.

"Does that mean you've revised your opinion of my lecture?" he couldn't resist asking.

Mrs. Stanhope thought for a minute. "Your words lacked passion."

That confused him. Robert felt quite passionate about his field.

"It was an audience of educated scientists who expected to hear technical material," he said stiffly. "And you know nothing about the field."

"I know something about passion—or, rather, the lack of it. Recall that I am a failed marriage broker. My heart's not in the work, which is likely why I am failing." She extended her hand. "Thank you for showing me how to see the night. Shall we continue?"

Her hand was cold. Robert felt her shiver.

"Change of plans." He put his arm around her shoulder and tucked her next to his body. "Not having you freeze on my watch."

Neither spoke as they made their way down the path.

"What did you mean when you said the Scots want your soul?" she asked at one point.

Robert eyed her warily. "Is this another lesson in conversation?"

"No. But it was a curious comment."

"Clan loyalty. Even if you're half-Scot like me, clan wants your blood, your death if need be."

"Surely that's overstatement in this day and age."

It would take an eon to explain the Campbells and their ways, so Robert said nothing.

"Family—I miss that," she said. "My mother

died when I was born. It's a void my father couldn't fill." She paused. "That was a thought full of self-pity, wasn't it?"

"More a fact, seems like."

Like him, she'd been lonely as a child. In that, Robert supposed they weren't so different. But he didn't remark on it. Enveloped by darkness, with her nestled under his arm, there was already too much intimacy between them.

"No one can claim a person's soul," she said. "It must be given freely, if at all."

Did the woman never let anything go?

Suddenly, she stumbled. Robert pulled her against his chest. "Watch your step."

"You're supposed to be guiding me."

"Doesn't mean you can abdicate," he growled.

Her small laugh filled the night. It was too much. *She* was too much.

Robert started them down the hill again, picked up the pace, prayed she wouldn't stumble. Because then he'd have to throw her over his shoulder and run to the bottom. More intimacy than he could manage.

When they reached the horse without further incident, Robert sighed in relief. As before, Mrs. Stanhope rode behind him. But this time, her arms snugged around his middle.

Robert felt her soft, yielding form every inch of the way.

"I didn't mind the chapel," Heloise said. "Curious mingling of religion and warfare."

"Was it?" Mr. Gibbons asked absently. "Afraid I'm no student of either."

Heloise tucked her hand into the crook of his arm as they made their way down the hill. "You were right. I do believe the exercise helped. I feel better."

At that, he beamed.

Since Heloise had portrayed queens, it had been child's play to persuade the frowning military officer that she and Mr. Gibbons were dispatched by none other than Queen Charlotte to ascertain how his troops were protecting this important landmark from French invaders. That defied logic—no French invaders would venture so far north—but her skill at inducing an audience to suspend disbelief was matchless.

She insisted on inspecting Margaret's chapel—was the officer certain no stone had been left unturned in trying to locate those still-missing Crown Jewels? Heloise declined to see the prisoners in the dungeon; she trusted the military could keep track of men in chains.

"The palace where Mary, Queen of Scots, was born is on our way after we leave Edinburgh," Mr. Gibbons said. "Perhaps we can stop there for a minute."

"Such a tragic figure," Heloise said. "Her womb was not her own."

He coughed delicately.

"Come now, Mr. Gibbons. After five days in a carriage with me, you surely have become more accustomed to blunt talk."

He cleared his throat. "You are always refreshing, Miss Alcott."

"I try to be, Mr. Gibbons."

They walked in companionable silence to the inn.

"It's all very well to appreciate history, but we're also meant to learn from it," Heloise said. "Otherwise, people keep making the same mistakes. One must move on, look for the new."

He didn't respond; he was focused on making sure their trunks went to the correct rooms.

Or was he?

Heloise prided herself on reading people's facades, and what lay beneath. With Mr. Gibbons she wasn't sure. He seemed fully immersed in the major domo role he performed with such efficiency.

Who was the man behind that carefully scripted exterior?

And what did that slight flush across his cheeks signify?

The Trossachs took them back in time. Pristine lakes and forested hills were as unspoiled as they must have been centuries ago. Puffy clouds dipped to kiss the knolls and bathe the valleys in thick mists. Trees rising from the mud angled sharply toward the sparkling water.

Picturesque it might be, but when the mists turned to heavy rain, travel was slow. Mr. Tavish joined them in the carriage. They paused briefly to stare at a castle where Mary Stuart was born. It was sadly neglected, and they didn't linger.

Later, when the rain eased, they stopped at a lake. Emmaline strolled with Mr. Tavish to the lake's edge. She was relieved to no longer be confined with him in the carriage. Whenever he shifted his position, she was keenly aware of it. Sometimes his legs accidentally touched hers.

"You seemed to tolerate the carriage well enough," she said.

He slanted a gaze at her. "Distractions help. Your aunt's a gifted conversationist."

Emmaline hesitated. "In my search for treatments for her, I came across an interesting theory: To conquer a fear, do the thing you fear. The idea is that more exposure disarms it. Might that help you with closed spaces?"

"I don't fear closed spaces. They simply make me uncomfortable." Mr. Tavish studied her. "That you thought of applying that strategy to me shows—"

Emmaline bit her bottom lip, expecting criticism.

"—that you have a lively mind," he finished.

Oh. "If that's a compliment, thank you."

"There's a flaw in that theory, of course," he added gravely. "To overcome a fear of death, one should not try dying."

"A bridge too far," Emmaline agreed, mustering a smile.

Mr. Tavish's gaze roved over her. "That's the same frock that ruffian tore, isn't it?"

Emmaline shifted uncomfortably. Her worn

green dress was near the end of its serviceable lifetime, and it showed. How unkind of him to notice.

"I repaired it," she said stiffly. She noticed a tiny island just offshore. It would provide a much-needed change of subject. "That island has some stone ruins."

"Crannog. Usually, they're wooden, not stone. You'll see more as we head west."

"I wonder what people lived there."

"Hard to know," Mr. Tavish said. "They left no records. All we can do is examine artifacts they left behind. That's why I study rocks. They hold clues to the past."

Emmaline eyed him curiously. "Like that bone?"

"More than that." A curious intensity burned in his eyes. "Footprints, imprints, remnants of creatures. Echoes of what was. Rocks reveal how the planet was shaped. How great plates of the earth crashed into one another, raised mountains, birthed oceans—the very building blocks of life itself. They tell our past and sometimes, our future."

There. There was the passion missing from his lecture.

"Prometheus," Emmaline said softly.

He frowned. "What?"

"Your words made me think of the story of Prometheus stealing fire. He was determined to share the secrets of the universe with humanity."

"And was therefore chained to a rock so eagles could eat his liver," Mr. Tavish said. "A lesson there. Not everyone wants to learn the secrets of the universe. Folks have their own notions about how the Earth was formed, don't necessarily wish to be told differently."

"But if people saw this place and that…crannog, wouldn't they wish to know more?"

"Perhaps." He sighed. "This place will soon be overrun with tourists, thanks to Walter Scott, his sylvan glades, bounding stags, ladies in lochs, and paeans to lost loves."

Emmaline eyed him in amusement. "Have you no sense of romance?"

"Not for that nonsense. The Wordsworths are as bad, tramping about in carts and writing about moonlight like snow on hills, stars like butterflies—feel free to pick the fanciful imagery."

"Yet it's obvious you've read that nonsense," she said.

Mr. Tavish's brows arched. "You thought me an uneducated sloth?"

"Neither uneducated nor sloth, but I wouldn't have guessed that you would ever read a line comparing trees to black skeletons—"

"I never mentioned the skeletons simile."

Emmaline eyed him in mock surprise. "That you used 'simile' in a sentence robs me of speech. I pronounce you a fraud, sir. You present yourself as a solitary, barely sentient troll—"

"*Troll?*" But he didn't look offended, only amused.

"Grump, then," she amended. "You don't show the sensitive, romantic side."

Mr. Tavish eyed her in horror. "There's not a romantic bone in my body."

Emmaline waved a dismissive hand. "And to think I expended such effort when you were my matrimonial client, trying to show you how to please a woman—"

"Is that what you were about with those lessons and harangues? Instructing me in how to pleasure a woman?"

"I said 'please,' not 'pleasure,'" Emmaline said.

Mr. Tavish's mouth broadened in amusement, but his eyes held something more intimate. "Entirely different kettle of fish. Not something I need lessons in, I promise."

Emmaline felt her face flame. "I didn't mean—fiddlesticks."

He regarded her, seemingly enjoying her discomfiture. Then he threw her a lifeline: "Unless you have more words on the subject, I suggest we return to the carriage."

Emmaline spent the rest of the drive contemplating pleasure. She supposed that mothers instructed their daughters in intimate relations, but her father had never broached the subject. Thus, she had been woefully ignorant.

That changed with her aunt's arrival.

"Forewarned is forearmed, dear," Aunt Heloise had declared. "Always insist on being a full partner in intimate matters."

By the end of her aunt's instruction, Emmaline understood such matters quite well but had no wish to put knowledge into practice. That scene in Dr. Black's office was a fine deterrent. People in the throes of passion apparently made fools of themselves.

It was all Emmaline could do to keep them afloat, never mind finding a husband or lover. Nor could she envision giving a man free rein over her body.

Inconveniently, her thoughts went to Mr. Tavish. Her brain hunted reasons not to think of him kindly. Perhaps he truly aimed to protect her by taking them to Scotland. If so, she'd be grateful but wouldn't mistake gratitude for desire.

Nevertheless, he did have presence. And read poetry. Secrets had begun to emerge. More likely resided in that family castle.

The weather brightened. Emmaline assumed he would prefer his horse. Instead, he again joined them in the carriage. He sat back against the squabs, crossed his arms, and managed to steal her breath each time his knees brushed hers.

It took a great deal of effort not to look at him. When she did—surreptitiously, as he spoke to Mr. Gibbons—she studied that wide mouth, surely meant for sensual pursuits. His long hair made her think of the heroes in her father's tales. Not a brute like Blue Beard, but the Beast, more appealing in animal form than as polished prince.

Having witnessed his passion for the physical world, she found herself wondering: What other passions had he hidden?

Chapter Thirteen

THE LOCH SLIPPED into his vision like a shy maiden, veiled by the trees, guarded by the hills on either side. Farther on, Loch Fyne would broaden to become the fat palm of Kilbrannan Sound and the Firth of Clyde. A blue, ethereal haze hung over the loch and its knolls, silent sentries hoarding secrets that had led to war and strife and eternal grudges.

Scotland. Ever his bane.

When he was a boy, Loch Fyne had crooked its fingertip, beckoned him along its remarkably consistent width, teasing him with the promise of more until it finally widened into the sound separating Arran and Kintyre.

It was there, on a trip with his uncle Colin to inspect a distillery on Kintyre, that Robert stood atop Torr Mor and stared across the sound to the far land mass he knew to be Ireland. He yearned to travel beyond Ireland, beyond that horizon to discover whatever the sea had for him.

Cursed Scotland always brought on woolgathering. Shouldn't he have outgrown that? He'd gone to sea, seen the world, tested his mettle in war, found his way to a new calling.

But Scotland reminded him that nothing was ever settled, that men would die for causes no one would understand centuries later. That despite man's constant attempts to spoil this beauty, Scotland would wield its timeless magic and force the universe to take note of that which would not change, save over eons that rendered wars and memory moot.

How much effort had he expended over the years to put Scotland behind him? And still this shock, this keening awareness each time he saw the loch and the hills that guarded it.

Robert wanted to blame Mrs. Stanhope for his unsettled state, for drawing him into such a rousing defense of rocks. And that naughty pleasure bit. She'd left herself open, but he hadn't exactly played the gentleman.

He wished she didn't always discipline that auburn hair into a tidy knot, though he was glad she didn't wear it in ringlets or other silly styles. She had no need for embellishment. It was all he could do to sit across from her and pretend to be unaffected by their earlier conversation.

He ought to have taken the horse. The deluge had subsided to mere mist. But here he was, sitting in this carriage, reflecting on the magic of Scotland.

Trying not to wonder how Emmaline Stanhope took her pleasure.

❧

"Now *that* is a castle," Aunt Heloise exclaimed. They stared at a quintessential fairy tale castle—a stone edifice symmetrical in design, with crenellated towers rising in tiers from the roof's center and rounded towers at the corners. Dozens of chimneys suggested long winters and blazing fires.

Though the castle wore the look of medieval times, it was in fine condition. Mr. Tavish had explained that it was only a few decades old, replacing a smaller and older structure an earlier duke had deemed inadequate for his rank.

Bushes lining the long, stone drive weren't styled like the fussy topiaries in London that proclaimed an owner's wealth and pedigree. Here, green and yellow spikes thrust wildly upward, at odds with that tidy drive. Thistle injected a dash of purple.

"This is very fine, Emmaline," Aunt Heloise said as Mr. Tavish left the carriage and strode toward the entrance. "We'll do nicely here."

"We don't know the arrangements," Emmaline cautioned. "We shouldn't assume—"

"Nonsense. *Always* assume." Her aunt took Mr. Gibbons's arm, though he hadn't offered it. Nevertheless, he gallantly tucked her hand into the crook of his arm.

Suddenly, a large imposing man carrying an enormous broadsword emerged from the castle entrance. He pointed it at Mr. Tavish, who stood immobile, seemingly paralyzed.

The burly stranger, nearly as large as Mr. Tavish and with a distinctive head of red hair, held the sword in a two-handed grip that suggested much practice in wielding it. As Emmaline watched in horror, he swung the sword in a menacing arc, preparing to strike.

She grabbed her walking stick, flipped a compartment open to expose the stiletto, and marched toward them.

"Oh, no, madam," Gibbons called. "It's not—"

Emmaline closed the distance to Mr. Tavish. Why hadn't he moved out of harm's way?

He turned as Emmaline walked past him to face the assailant. She pointed her stiletto at the stranger's midsection. "Drop your sword, brigand."

The assailant eyed her stiletto. "Ye mean to fight me with tha' wee blade, Sassenach?" The unfamiliar word ended with a guttural sound.

He returned his attention to Mr. Tavish. "Saved your *feileadh-mór.*"

"Won't be wearing it," Mr. Tavish growled.

The man sighed. "Waste of a fine tartan."

"As ever."

With that, the man lowered his sword. The two embraced with a force that might have felled lesser men.

Hardly mortal enemies.

Emmaline wanted to slink away in embarrassment.

Mr. Tavish turned to her. "Mrs. Stanhope, this reprobate is my mother's baby brother, Colin Campbell."

Mortified, she managed a nod, then belatedly, a curtsy. Extending a hand, he smiled, as if she hadn't threatened him with a blade moments before. "Lass, ye give me new reason to live."

She eyed him uncertainly. "I hope, sir, that you

have more reasons than that."

He gave a hearty laugh. "That clever cane—how did ye come by it?"

"I had it crafted."

"Fearsome indeed," he said gravely.

When Aunt Heloise and Mr. Gibbons joined them, instantly Mr. Campbell's expression softened. He strode to Mr. Gibbons and put his hand on his shoulder. "John. It's been too long."

Mr. Gibbons nodded. "Thank you, sir."

"Aye, and it's Colin. Had ye forgotten?"

"Some things are beyond forgetting."

Mr. Tavish frowned. "You know each other?"

"A long time ago." His uncle's gaze shifted to Aunt Heloise, who eyed him with interest.

"Miss Alcott is Mrs. Stanhope's aunt," Mr. Tavish said. "Miss Alcott, may I present—"

"Colin Campbell," her aunt said. "We met ages ago, so he will have forgotten." Her mouth curved upward, as if to suggest otherwise.

Emmaline tried not to wonder about their connection, but her aunt's coy expression fueled every unwanted thought.

Mr. Campbell made a courtly bow. "Ye were a right murderous Lady Macbeth. That performance has burned in my brain for more than two decades."

Emmaline relaxed. He'd simply seen her aunt on the stage. That was all.

Aunt Heloise extended her hand. "As I recall, you came up to me afterward. We had a

conversation about Scottish accents. I believe you

thought mine flawed."

"Nae, it was that idiot who played Macbeth. Couldn't manage it. Yours was flawless."

Was the man blushing?

"On stage, our accents are meant to have only a flavor of the language," her aunt said. "Otherwise, an English audience does not understand."

"Wisnae fault in your performance," he said gallantly.

Mr. Tavish cleared his throat. "None of your fulsome blather, Colin. She'll be offended."

"I am rarely offended." Aunt Heloise smiled. "I will gladly accept a compliment, fulsome or otherwise."

Mr. Campbell grinned. "Come inside—all of you. I've been remiss in the welcoming."

"Damned broadsword didn't help," Mr. Tavish muttered.

His uncle gave him an indulgent smile. "One of these days we must cross blades."

"Of course," Mr. Tavish groused. "Fight is what Campbells do."

In the castle, Mr. Campbell ushered them into a large drawing room, its walls adorned with tapestries of country scenes framed by elaborate garlands and pastel bunting. Lambs frolicked and beatific children played across the panoramas in pastoral opulence. Painted wreaths entwined from the fireplace up to the ceiling, which was decorated in gold geometric designs. They sat on giltwood chairs with tapestry seats near a mahogany harp.

"Obscene, isn't it?" Mr. Campbell offered

cheerfully. "Wrought by Robert Adam, God rest his florid soul. Seems the way to showcase English magnificence is to mimic the French."

"It's a damned museum," Mr. Tavish declared. "How do you live this way?"

"Don't. I live in the cottage up the hill."

"I suppose George isn't here much," Mr. Tavish said.

"I've nae seen him in months. Which is more often than we see ye. How long has it been, Robbie? Three years? More?"

Mr. Tavish shifted in his chair.

Emmaline watched their exchange with interest. She saw a resemblance between the men—Mr. Campbell was almost as broad-shouldered as Mr. Tavish, but not as tall. His eyes were green, not gray. Both had high cheekbones, a firm jaw, and a broad mouth.

It was clear that Mr. Campbell regarded his nephew with affection—and just as clear that Mr. Tavish preferred to be elsewhere.

"I'm guessing ye are nae here to rekindle family ties," his uncle said.

"Someone wishes Mrs. Stanhope ill," Mr. Tavish said.

Mr. Campbell eyed Emmaline. "Because she persists in threatening folk with tha' blade?"

"I apologize, sir," she said quickly.

"Colin," he corrected. "Never apologize for defending your own." His speculative gaze shifted to Mr. Tavish, who looked distinctly uncomfortable.

"The blade—in fact, the whole contraption of

that cane—" Mr. Tavish began.

"Walking stick," Emmaline put in.

"—is useless against the people she is up against," he continued. "Spies, traitors, ambitious War Office underlings. One of them abducted her, then staged a rescue to gain her trust. Bad enough, but there are others who mean worse. She and her aunt need protection."

Mr. Campbell's expression grew grave. "They'll be safe here."

"Might be more comfortable in Oban."

"I've men here. None in Oban. You'd be on your own."

"I won't be staying," Mr. Tavish insisted.

His uncle's expression darkened. "I'm certain your mother raised ye better."

The two men glared at one another. Tension spiraled between them.

Emmaline cleared her throat. "Please do not feel obliged—"

"*Gentlemen.*"

That one word, spoken with authority by Aunt Heloise, drew all eyes to her. "We accept your kind offer and rely upon your good judgment."

With a regal smile, she tossed her halo of reddish curls, recently refreshed by henna.

Colin looked awestruck.

It thrilled Emmaline to see her aunt exert her power. It was her gift, and she hadn't deployed it lately, except for that unspeakable time in Dr. Black's office.

Aunt Heloise rose.

Immediately, so did the men. "I hope you will

excuse us, gentlemen, *Colin*"—the name spoken with a velvet touch. "It has been a long journey, and I would like to rest."

Colin bowed. "It will be my pleasure, madam, to see to yours."

Her aunt merely smiled.

Chapter Fourteen

THIS WAS THE last place John wanted to be. He hadn't been here when she died. No, he'd done his duty, returned to his employer, content in the knowledge that Portia was safe and happy. His employer had been furious at his wife's abandonment—though ignorant of John's own role—but the anger faded as the man realized he no longer needed to hide the women he kept on the side.

Several years passed. John was lonely but took satisfaction in the fact he had delivered her safely to her family. He could perform his duties without seething over his employer's abuse of her.

Strangely, his employer never asked about the boy. He had his heir, the older son, and didn't bother about the other.

The younger son had been badly damaged, but John hoped he would flourish in the care of his mother and her family. He worried about the grandfather, an uncompromising sort, though not cruel in the way his employer was.

John only learned of her death when he found her father's note crumpled on the floor in the earl's study. By then it was weeks old. He sat on the floor, absorbing the news. Tears didn't come, for every part of him denied that she no longer walked this earth.

Was he somehow to blame? Should he have stayed with her? Abandoned his post? Or, worst of all, confessed his love to a married woman who neither asked for nor sought his affection?

He yearned to travel there, to learn how she died, as if that knowledge would somehow undo it. But he had no claim on her. He could hardly present himself to her family, heartbroken and raw, without explanation.

At last, though, John had decided he must go. He had to know of her last breaths.

He invented a family emergency to explain his absence to the earl. He came to this place, only to meet a family riven by tragedy. John tried, in his quiet way, to find anyone who would enlighten him about her death. But the lad would speak to no one; neither would his grandfather. Both viewed John with suspicion, an agent of his employer.

Finally, John had found her younger brother Colin, a man with open features but sad eyes, who'd taken time to speak to him.

"John."

A hand touched his shoulder. He turned.

Colin Campbell's eyes filled with compassion. "Walk with me. It's a fine morning."

They walked through the castle gardens, which were laid in a formal cross pattern. Bluebells were in bloom, as were azaleas and rhododendrons. The River Aray could be heard gurgling nearby.

John liked gardens; in another life, he might have been a gardener.

"I wondered," Colin said, "when you came all this way that final time, what you were after. I have pondered that these years since. It has haunted me. *You* haunted me."

John was silent. He had expected this. Colin had a knack for seeing things others didn't.

"I, too, thought you were his emissary," Colin said. "Should've known better. That man didnae care enough to send someone. But you cared."

John did not want to discuss the past. He wanted to flee.

"Then I found the ballad among her things," Colin added.

That startled him. "What ballad?"

"One of the old broadsheets. She brought them with her. Said she had shopped the London fairs for the old music."

John nodded. He had accompanied her on those trips when a footman wasn't available, always keeping a discreet distance. When he brought her here, he had tucked the music into her luggage, thinking it would give her pleasure.

"This ballad had a curious title," Colin went on. "'The Lady who Fell in Love with her Serving-man.' Your face that day is forever etched in my brain. But I couldn't make sense of your sorrow. When I found the ballad, I knew. Did you give it to her?"

John could hardly credit his ears. "No. This is the first I've heard of it."

Colin nodded. "Somehow, I suspected you

wouldn't have crossed that boundary. The lady in the ballad was in love with a man called 'Honest John.'" He paused. "Does it help to know your feelings were reciprocated?"

"I don't believe that. It's impossible."

"Why? You're nae the only man who's loved someone beyond your reach." Colin hesitated. "The ballad doesn't end well. Obstacles stood in their way—her husband, jealous serving girl, and the like. The story ends in misery and death."

John closed his eyes.

"You and Portia were each miserable. Maybe knowing that she returned your love helps."

"Not true." John shook his head. "I never heard a word from her."

"All the time she was here I felt she was missing something," Colin persisted. "I have to believe it was you."

"Then why did she throw herself off that cliff?" John demanded in a ragged voice.

"Did she? I'm nae sure."

"You think she simply fell?"

Colin sighed. "Mayhap she had a low moment, when she felt all was lost, when she decided to end things. I'd lay that at her husband's door. Our father had arranged the marriage, thinking a match with an English earl would be advantageous. Nae the first time the Campbell thirst for power ended badly. By the time you brought her here with Robbie, she was different, withdrawn. I know he mistreated her—mistreated both of them."

"The earl brought in odd folk to try to control her with a new therapy—mesmerism," John said.

"I don't know why, since I never saw her defy him."

"Maybe she was defiant behind closed doors," Colin said softly. "Man like that wouldnae stomach rejection."

A chill shot through John as the ugly memory surfaced. One that had never been very far away. How long had it gone on? If he had known sooner, could he have saved her?

"And what of Robbie?" Colin asked. "He was a withdrawn and angry lad. Did the mesmerists treat him as well?"

"The earl sent him to a special school that used similar methods. They practiced a cruel sort of discipline."

Colin put an arm around his shoulders. "Come. There's something you should see."

⁓

Verdant green rippled across the hills like waves of emerald velvet. But all was not as it appeared. That lovely veneer masked something insidious, Emmaline discovered. Stepping onto what looked like lush grass, her foot sank into thick, oozing muck that sucked at her shoe.

"It's very wet here, Mr. Tavish."

"Scotland," he said, a dozen feet ahead. "Could hardly be otherwise."

Emmaline hadn't foreseen a hilly hike over muck and boulders when he suggested a walk, so she hadn't brought her walking stick. But instead of the flat castle grounds, he led them on a rocky path behind the castle that quickly rose upward.

In Scotland, apparently, if there was a hill, one must climb it.

Mr. Tavish marched ever forward, his footing sure. Emmaline tried to pick her way over the rocks at the edge of the muck, but the terrain was treacherous. Hurrying to keep up, she stumbled a few times. Fortunately, he didn't notice. The man strode like a colossus, as if the land was his to command.

A fine mist accompanied them, and with it, a deepening chill. Mr. Tavish seemed oblivious to the weather as well. Now and then he made a stab at conversation.

"Something's stuck in my brain," he said at one point.

"What's that?" Emmaline tried not to sound as if breathing was an effort.

"You were going to fight Colin for me."

"Ridiculous, I know." Could he slow his pace?

"Think you would have taken him?" he asked.

"Assuredly not," Emmaline said. "I don't know what I was thinking."

Silence.

"I don't fight with broadswords these days, but I would've made do," Mr. Tavish said.

She sighed. "I'm sure you would have. I remain mortified. May we speak no more of it?"

"It's just that—"

Emmaline's foot sank into the muck up to her ankle.

"—you stepped between me and the point of a sword. Why?"

"It's not because I value your life above mine

if that's what you think. I simply reacted." She'd fallen so far behind she had to raise her voice. "Why did he come at you with that sword?"

"Routine family greeting. Every time I come here, Colin chooses a weapon from the weapons room, and we pretend to fight. John Campbell—his father, my grandfather—insisted on training us on all the weapons in the armory, even those not used for centuries."

When she didn't respond, he glanced back. "Are you having difficulty? You managed Arthur's Seat well enough."

"That's because the ground didn't suck at my feet as if they were fish bait."

"Try the rocks. Solid footing."

Emmaline chose the broadest, flattest rock and stepped on it. But it wasn't flat on the bottom and rocked with her weight. She gave a little cry as she lost her footing.

Instantly, Mr. Tavish was at her side. "Take my hand."

"No." Emmaline batted his away.

His mouth twitched. "Only port in a storm, Mrs. Stanhope."

When she grudgingly accepted his hand, he helped her over the next rocks.

"This is embarrassing. I feel like a child." Nevertheless, Emmaline leaned on him and somehow managed to navigate a whole field of boulders. But the lift chafed her foot, and each step brought new pain.

Finally, they gained the hilltop, which was

shrouded in fog that made it difficult to see more than a few feet ahead.

"You did it." Mr. Tavish's pleased smile warmed her.

"Not without your help."

"I would lay odds you'd have managed."

She felt ridiculously pleased. "I don't understand the grass here. It's wet nothingness."

"That's bog moss—peat. We burn it to heat houses, smoke barley over it for our whisky."

Emmaline looked around. "Tell me about this spot. Why are we here?"

"It's where I escaped to as a child."

"Was the weather always like this?"

"Only constant about Scottish weather is that it can change in an instant." Mr. Tavish pointed toward the horizon. "See? Now the skies have decided to bless us."

The fog had lifted. The sparkling, cerulean lake below flowed as far as the eye could see, with emerald hills rising above it and willows bending at the shoreline. In the distance, Emmaline could just make out a pile of stones, perhaps ruins of some ancient castle.

London had no views like this. One had the Thames, but the river was a dumping ground for waste and gave off putrid smells. Scotland felt pristine. Unspoiled. The scent of fir and pine filled the air, bestirred to greater pungency by the retreating mist.

For long minutes, they simply took in the view.

"What were you escaping back then?" Emmaline asked.

"Mean to pry, do you?"

"You don't volunteer much."

His expression darkened. "Turmoil."

"What sort?"

"Family. My mother grew up here. Her father wanted her to marry an English aristocrat. The marriage was disastrous. She finally fled, brought us here. My grandfather wasn't pleased. He disliked failure. But Portia's leaving my father wasn't a failure. She had to."

Emmaline hesitated. "Why?"

Mr. Tavish looked away. "My father was a brute. Used his fists to keep us in line. I fought back, and that's when he sent me to a school to get rid of my rebellion."

"Did it work?"

"No." He met her gaze. "Have you heard of Father Maximilian Hell?"

"A priest?"

"Jesuit. Fancied himself a scientist, but his methods were monstrous. Like Mesmer, Hell believed magnetic force cured illness. He'd induce pain in a victim, then try to draw out the pain with magnets. The school adopted some of his methods."

Emmaline stared at him. "They tortured you?"

"Not physically. Other kinds. One teacher would wake me at night and demand I recite my lessons. When I refused, he locked me in a closet with a stray cat I always fed. Creature didn't want to be there either. Spent the nights howling and clawing at the door."

His jaw hardened. "Must've spent a hundred

nights in that closet. Used the time to plot my revenge. Juvenile stuff—fantasies of gouging out my captor's eyeballs, that sort."

"That's why you loathe closed spaces—and cats," she said.

"I'm trying to rise above that," Mr. Tavish said. "Takes time."

Emmaline almost reached out to comfort him, but the rigid set of his shoulders stopped her. "How long were you at that school?"

"A year. One day my mother came and took me away. That was odd, since she never defied my father. She brought us here, but she wasn't ever happy."

"Why not?"

Mr. Tavish shrugged. "That eluded the understanding of a seven-year-old. We lived at the castle for a while before she moved us to Oban. I left home as soon as I could. Then she… died. Went over the rocky cliffs above Oban."

Went over. A curious choice of words. "It sounds as if you think there's more to it."

"Don't know if she fell or jumped." He gave a heavy sigh. "I was fourteen and long gone by then. Should have stayed, prevented her death."

Emmaline touched his shoulder. "That's beyond a lad's power, isn't it? Besides, how can one know what was in another person's mind? To this day, my own father is a mystery to me."

"The mind still wants answers," he said gruffly.

She nodded. "I think that's why we keep at it, even if there are only ghosts left to ask."

His mouth curved upward. "I'll be talking to

spirits next. You are a disruptive influence, Mrs. Stanhope."

"You are the very definition of disruptive, Mr. Tavish." The words came out more teasingly than Emmaline intended. She quickly withdrew her hand from his shoulder.

"Ah. Common ground at last. Shall we make our way back?" He extended his hand. "There's another way down, rockier but more solid than bog."

"I may be slow," she cautioned. Her foot ached horribly.

"Lean on me. I'll help you."

"I don't like to lean on people, Mr. Tavish."

"We'll keep this just between us."

As they descended the hill, Robert noticed Mrs. Stanhope's gait grew increasingly unsteady. But she brushed off his arm. This was a woman who preferred to fend for herself.

Finally, he stopped at an old tree stump and made her sit. "Are you injured?"

Her gaze fixed on a point over his shoulder. "No."

"You're favoring your left leg," Robert insisted. "Let me examine it."

Now she eyed him directly. "*No.*"

Robert knelt and reached for her foot anyway. Her half-boots had the thinnest of soles. In some places they were worn through. Wholly inadequate for walking over bog and rocks.

Mrs. Stanhope tried to pull her foot back, but

Robert held onto it. He loosened the laces and slipped her shoe off. What he saw astonished him.

The bottom of her foot was red with blood. Inside the shoe was a chunk of wood that had worn through its cotton wool wrapping, torn through her stocking, and dug into her foot.

"Why didn't you say something?" Robert pulled a handkerchief from his pocket and wrapped it around her foot to staunch the bleeding. "There'll be salve back at the castle. I'll—"

"The state of my foot is not your concern. Moreover, this is too—" She broke off.

Robert waited.

Her face flushed. "Too intimate."

She hadn't wanted him to discover the wooden thing.

"It's a lift, isn't it?" he asked. "Why do you wear it?"

Mrs. Stanhope glared at him. "My left leg is shorter than the other. It also has scars from a childhood encounter with scalding water. They're quite ugly. Thank you for forcing that out of me."

Robert stared at her in amazement. All this time, she hadn't said a word about her pain. Suddenly, another thought seized him.

"Adaptive behavior." He felt strangely elated. "It's why we don't see giant creatures running through St. James. Why sharks will outlive us all."

She blinked. "Has the sight of blood addled your wits?"

"It's a theory I'm working on—creatures that became extinct millions of years ago did so because they failed to adapt to changes in their environment. Those that adapted lived. Those that didn't became the last of their breed."

Her mouth pursed. "I struggle to see why my foot made you think of extinct creatures."

"Because that's what you did with your cane, er, stick. You created a way to adapt to your condition. Same with your wooden lift." Robert beamed. "Brilliant adaptations, both."

"Merely pragmatic," Mrs. Stanhope said. "The lift gives me a normal gait. In London, a limp would make me look vulnerable. I'd be a target."

Robert thought. "Perhaps we can devise a method that does not chew your flesh to bits."

"*We* will not devise anything. I am quite capable—"

"It's not wrong to accept help," he insisted. "Besides, you have a, er, nice foot."

She eyed him incredulously. "You are joking."

"Not one to joke about ladies' feet." Robert hesitated. "I didn't think about your comfort when I brought you here. In a way, I caused your injury. I am sorry."

Mrs. Stanhope was silent. Then: "That view was captivating. Worth the price."

"You are quite the stalwart, madam."

She waved a dismissive hand, but Robert saw her almost smile.

A woman who could choose a view over a destroyed foot. Now *that* was captivating.

Chapter Fifteen

JOHN STARED AT the marker.

"I found something else of Portia's with that song sheet," Colin said. "Snippet of a Burns poem—four lines."

Even now, John could scarcely believe his eyes.

"We'd left the stone bare, only her birth and death years," Colin said. "No one could think what to put on it at the time. But when I found the poem, it seemed like her voice beyond the grave telling me what she wanted. I had the stone redone."

John read the lines again:

Fare thee weel, my only luve!
And fare thee weel awhile!
And I will come again, my luve,
Though it were ten thousand mile.

A declaration of love. Had she really nurtured an unspoken love for him? John wanted to believe it. But what did it matter now? She was gone these many years. The fates had not aligned for them and never would, regardless of that tombstone pledge. An empty promise.

Colin left him to his thoughts. What-ifs burned in his brain. No answers came.

Steeped in melancholy, John made his way from the graveyard back to the castle. The pain of Portia's loss had receded over the years. That was the nature of grief. But the thought that she had secretly returned his love forged a new loss.

Even if he'd known, what could he have done differently? His employer was loathsome, but to have transgressed with the man's wife would have corroded John's soul and dishonored Portia. There was nothing for it but what fate had wrought.

And yet, he found himself wanting more. Had he lived his entire life trying to navigate the chasm between right and yearning, with so little reward?

Looking for distraction, John found himself in the castle's majestic weapons room. On the wall in dazzling display from floor to its tall ceiling hung instruments of man's folly. Muskets, broadswords, axes, daggers. Witness to battles won and lost. He fingered an eight-inch-long dagger with deep hatches across the handle.

"I'm told that belonged to Rob Roy."

John turned. Miss Alcott was perched on a chair in the shadows near the fireplace.

"It's a fanciful legend," she said. "Was he a rank thief or an avenger of wrongs committed by the rich on common folk? Or perhaps only a MacGregor with shifting loyalties?"

John noticed the extraordinary violet color of her eyes—and the keen intelligence there.

"They revere him here, not least because he became a Campbell and escaped whenever he was captured," she said.

"I did not know you were a student of history," he said.

"Not history—it's story I love. Wordsworth portrays him as Scotland's Robin Hood, a champion for the oppressed: 'Far and near, through vale and hill are faces that attest the same, and kindle, like a fire new stirred, at sound of Rob Roy's name.'"

Her resonant voice was smoky, like a fine whisky with peat undercurrents.

"His wife was also brave, but Wordsworth ignored her," Miss Alcott added. "Male writers care little for female characters. Even Lady Macbeth is one-dimensional, though I quite enjoyed playing her. Now and then it's quite satisfying to be a manipulating murderess."

And thrilling to watch, John suspected. Miss Alcott exuded magnetism.

"Still, it annoyed me that she had to die offstage. Her sleepwalking scene *almost* made up for it. 'Out, damn'd spot. Out, I say!'" She smiled. "You can be sure I did my best with that."

John found himself enthralled. "You make me reconsider my avoidance of theater."

Miss Alcott looked horrified. "Why would you avoid theater? It's pure escape."

"For that reason, I think. One shouldn't escape life's challenges. One must face reality."

"Reality is the cruelest of fates. One ought to escape whenever the opportunity presents."

John was taken aback. "And that approach has…stood you well? All these years?"

She frowned. "Not *that* many years."

"I didn't mean—"

"Must we plod through life, amid hardships and setbacks, with nothing to leaven the burden?" Miss Alcott rose and strode past the fireplace to a breathtaking array of muskets. She whirled to face him. "If that is your view, life can't have been any fun."

John blinked. "I…what is your definition of 'fun,' madam?"

A slow smile spread over her features. "I fear it would shock you, Mr. Gibbons. Suffice it to say that I do not think life is a cruel march to the grave in which each moment must be endured in the full breadth of its awfulness. When fate offers escape, I take it."

"My life has been one of duty and service," John confessed. "I've never questioned that it was the right choice."

Miss Alcott stepped closer. "Mine has been one of providing pleasure to those who need it as much as they need food and shelter. You cannot claim that your way is superior to mine without concluding that my life has been worthless."

"I meant no disrespect," John said quickly. "I know not how we came by this discussion."

She regarded him steadily. Her eyes seemed to hold a wealth of possibilities. "You appear lonely and beaten down. Perhaps in need of fun, however you define it. I do not minimize your trials, only insist that distraction can be useful, at times even the bread of life."

Miss Alcott tossed her reddish curls, and John's pulse raced alarmingly.

"Do not worry," she said softly. "I won't interfere in your misery if you do not wish it. But if you care to lighten your load, I'm quite good at distraction."

Panic filled him. Was this a proposition? Surely not. They barely knew one another.

"All the world's a stage, Mr. Gibbons." She tilted her head. "We have our entrances and exits, but what matters is the pleasure between. It takes more effort these days to find it, but I'm not ready to cede the stage. And perhaps you are not either."

"Please call me John," he heard himself say. "That would give me great pleasure."

The smile she beamed at him warmed the drafty room. "Heloise."

"You have enlivened my day, Heloise. I was in a fair way toward wallowing in despair."

"If I have helped, even for a moment, I rejoice." Her voice was silken.

John hesitated. "I have lived my life very much *off* stage."

Heloise smiled. Her sleeve brushed him as she walked away. When she turned, her gaze held the heat of a thousand suns. "I do adore a tough audience."

With that, she swept from the room, leaving him quite at sea.

And…intrigued.

Robert was ready to return to England—or so he told himself. He'd been at the castle for several days, far longer than planned.

He knew why: Emmaline Stanhope. He'd thought her pinch-faced and demanding—ordering him to learn conversation, dancing, manners. Then again, he'd been a terrible pupil.

Had he misjudged? What he saw as stubbornness might simply be determination, even stoicism. On their hike, she hadn't even hinted of pain from that lift. He wondered about her leg scars. She sounded ashamed of them, but weren't they testament to all she had overcome?

Then Robert's brain went in a less noble direction. Examining her foot had given him a glimpse of her stocking. How high did those stockings rise? *Above the knee?* How did she secure them? *Hook, ribbon, buckle?* Likely not a ribbon—too insubstantial. And she wouldn't want the nuisance of a buckle. Hooks, then. Less bulky, but secure.

Schoolboy meanderings. Nothing to do with why he had overstayed the castle.

Needing to clear his head, Robert decided to hike to other boyhood haunts—the arched stone bridge north of the castle and the watchtower, where he could see Loch Fyne start to widen into the firth. That view had nurtured his yearning to escape. The sea had given him a chance to remake his life and ultimately led to his true calling—teasing out secrets of the past.

It was a full life. He ached to return to it.

Then why this delay? Why had he allowed himself to be pulled from his routine? And why the devil had he told Mrs. Stanhope about Portia, his father, that school?

She was changing him. Robert was starting to see a difference between who he'd chosen to be and who he was with her.

Had her marriage been happy? She never spoke of her husband. Had she taken lovers since his death? He thought she would sooner stab a man with her clever cane than take a lover. Protectiveness lived in her; it did not permit easy affection. He shared that impulse, but nevertheless wondered why she allowed no one in.

Best not to dwell on that puzzle. The watchtower awaited.

The path led through woods of Scots pine. Robert loved this clean, invigorating air. And the sparkling lochs, ancient hills, and the peat that made for fine whisky.

Yes, Scotland had a piece of his soul, but only a small one. He could live with that.

Emerging from the woods, Robert started up the steep hill to the tower.

Stopped short.

Standing in his way was Andrew Maitland, as unwelcome as ever. Impeccably attired all in black, completely out of place in the country, and the very epitome of dark intent.

"I have a message from your uncle."

As if they were simply resuming a conversation. As if they'd met on any street corner, not here, hundreds of miles from London.

"Since when are you George's message boy?" Robert demanded.

"When it suits me."

"When it will advance your career."

"I am only doing my job." Maitland smirked. "That you and Mrs. Stanhope fled town for this backwater is highly suspicious. Incidentally, she's not Mrs. Stanhope. Her name is Alcott."

Robert hid his surprise, waited. There would be more.

"George wants you to turn her over to me."

"If you knew anything about George," Robert said calmly, "you'd know that he only asks favors of me in person, under specific conditions, and no more than once every five years. That limit, by the way, already has been reached."

He had the pleasure of seeing Maitland's arrogance slip a notch.

"Moreover, he doesn't know we are here," Robert added. "You are simply trying to further your career by undermining him. No Campbell will help you there."

"I've always heard you Campbells are a malleable sort," Maitland said.

"Not when it comes to family. State your business, Drew. I've a hill to climb."

The other man's gaze slid up to the watchtower.

"Glorious view there," Robert said. "Surprised you haven't been up there to spy on us."

"As it happens, I've just come from there. One of those ugly, centuries-old ruins, like everything in this godforsaken country. Doubtless primitive folk hauled its stones over hundreds of miles for some unfathomable purpose. Relics being your thing, I assume you've studied it."

One day Maitland would come into his own, and the world would need to be on its guard. But for now, he lacked seasoning. Time to point that out.

"You're wrong about everything," Robert said. "The black on the stone was caused by lightning strikes, not age. The windows look gothic but aren't old; neither is the tower. It's purely ornamental, a folly Morris and Adam added when they built the castle fifty years ago. The stone's not from afar—it's granite rubble quarried here at Carloonan. Roof is schist—like granite but metamorphic, not igneous. It, too, is local. The earthen mound the tower sits on looks prehistoric, but it's mere landscaping. You see, Drew, things aren't always what they seem."

The other man's gaze narrowed to slits. "How informative."

"There's no muck on your boots," Robert went on. "Nor are you breathing like a man who hiked the switchbacks. You're here to ingratiate yourself. The rest you made up."

Maitland's dark gaze flattened. "You haven't asked about her name. That's curious. One might think you complicit in her schemes." He paused. "Or her lover."

"You've misjudged." A warning, if the man had the sense to take it.

"And you've aligned yourself with a treasonous lightskirt."

Robert's hands clenched at his sides. "Mrs. Stanhope—"

"Emmaline Alcott, daughter of some obscure scholar."

"—did not cause Burwell's death," Robert said. "Nor is she involved in treason."

"What if I can link her to your mother's death?"

Robert stilled. "My mother died sixteen years ago. Mrs. Stanhope was a child."

"But it's curious that she and her aunt recently visited a noted mesmerist, a Dr. Jacob Black." Maitland watched him carefully.

Robert crossed his arms over his chest. "Name means nothing to me."

"Twenty-three years ago, he was a teacher at the school your father banished you to. Name was Jacques Noirseau. Even I can see how one might fashion 'Jacob Black' from that."

Robert forced himself not to react. "What's he to do with my mother?"

"Mrs. Stanhope and her aunt visited the doctor after Burwell's death. Perhaps they had used his techniques on Burwell." Maitland paused. "But you asked about your mother. Noirseau's job was in jeopardy when the school lost your family's patronage. He traveled to this godforsaken place to persuade her to reconsider. Perhaps he plotted her death when she refused."

"My mother died in Oban, six years after I left the school."

"Circumstances unexplained, I've learned. Think on it. The man was a mesmerist."

Robert leveled a gaze at him. "You propose that

he planted a suggestion in her brain to make her go over that cliff years later? Mesmerism doesn't work that way. It's not proven science, only a deceptive art employed by those who manipulate others for gain."

"Ah, yes. You tried to get Parliament to ban mesmerists. Failed, didn't you?"

"Nothing is a failure if it's educational," Robert said. "I researched it to a fare-the-well. No mesmerist has that skill." He made a mental note to make sure Black left London for good.

"Still, it's interesting that your Miss Alcott—er, Mrs. Stanhope—is one of his disciples."

"She's not."

Maitland regarded him. "Perhaps, my dear boy, you aren't an objective observer."

"I have six years on you Maitland, so I'm not your boy. And I'm on to your tricks. No one rises from midshipman to lieutenant as you did without backstabbing or bribery."

"You wound me."

Robert gave him a mirthless smile. "Then come to dinner and show us your true colors."

Maitland looked startled. "Dinner?"

"Campbells welcome anyone at the table. Traitors, schemers, and the like. Mind you, it's best to watch your back. We keep country hours. Half past five."

With that, Robert turned and headed back into the woods. The watchtower would wait.

Robert caught up with Mrs. Stanhope as she was walking in the garden, cane in hand. Her foot was still healing; she couldn't yet use her lift, and her limp was pronounced. That hadn't stopped her from trudging from one end of the garden to the other to regain her strength. The woman refused to grant weakness any quarter.

Strangely, Robert wasn't angry that she lied about her name. Instead, it fed the very dangerous fantasy that she had a secret, intriguing side.

"A word, madam," he said.

Mrs. Stanhope turned. "Mr. Tavish."

"Given name's Robert. Family uses Robbie, but I'd rather you didn't. Robert will do."

Her eyes widened in surprise. "Are we at given names? That seems…familiar."

"Dislike extra syllables," he said. "'Mr. Tavish' is four. 'Robert' only two."

She appeared to consider that. "What about Rob? That's but one."

"Sounds like a pet dog."

"I know of no dogs named Rob," Mrs. Stanhope said gravely.

This give and take was different from their usual disputes. It felt like flirting. "And your given name?" Robert prodded.

"Emmaline. My aunt calls me 'Em,' but I'd rather you didn't."

"You, too, have an aversion to one syllable."

She frowned. "Perhaps we should dispense with the topic of given names."

A perfect opening. "Let's discuss surnames. I'm told yours is Alcott, like your aunt's."

Her sharp intake of breath confirmed it.

"Are you unmarried?" Robert asked.

Mrs. Stanhope's chin rose. "My marital status can be none of your concern."

"We've spent an inordinate amount of time together," he said. "You owe me the truth. After all, I half-carried you down Arthur's Seat—"

"Made me ride double," she put in.

"Protected you from the lightning—"

"Ruined *two* cloaks," she retorted.

"I've told you things about my childhood that I've shared with no one else," Robert said. "Seems I've been talking to someone who doesn't exist. Someone who, in the interest of finding me a bride, asked many personal questions."

"A bride you had no need of," she pointed out. "You weren't honest with me."

"I imagine," Robert said more gently, "the matrimonial business is best if one appears to have had some experience with marriage."

"Indeed. Do you have any idea, Mr. Tavish—"

"Robert."

"—what sort of unwanted attentions a woman receives if she has no man to render her unavailable to men who believe she is more than willing to entertain them?"

He nodded. "You were insulted."

"And more." Her mouth thinned. "It was assumed that because I lived in a shabby cottage in a shabby neighborhood, my character was equally shabby."

"I see."

She shot him a disdainful glare. "You couldn't possibly."

Robert hesitated. "Then you are not—haven't been—married?"

Mrs. Stanhope drew herself up. "You are like the rest. You wish to know whether I am a loose woman or virginal as the driven snow. To what end?"

He cleared his throat. "I didn't intend to be…" He trailed off.

"Impertinent? Insulting? Degrading? All those adjectives that you omit in your disdain of complete sentences?" Her chest heaved with fury, and her eyes filled with icy disdain. As if she were the one wronged, not him.

"Will you answer my question?" About her marital state, Robert told himself, not her virginal or non-virginal condition.

Silence.

"Virginal," she said finally. "Mostly."

Mrs. Stanhope clutched her walking stick— for a moment he thought she might send one of its secret spikes at him—and resumed her determined walk around the garden.

Chapter Sixteen

DINNER WAS STRANGE. First, there was Mr. Maitland, who simply presented himself in the castle's elaborate state dining room as if it were perfectly ordinary for him to come all the way from London for supper.

As usual, Colin presided, and Aunt Heloise sat to his right, which had become her regular place, affording Colin a fine opportunity to flirt with her.

Colin was in many ways the opposite of Mr. Tavish—Emmaline couldn't bring himself to call him Robert—quick with a joke, an easy conversationalist. Her aunt beamed under his attentions; she enjoyed the flirtation game as much as he did. Emmaline wondered if there were anything serious afloat, but knowing her aunt, they were simply playing off one another.

"Glad you joined us, Maitland," Colin said. "Robbie's friends are always welcome here."

"Enemies, too," Mr. Tavish muttered.

Mr. Maitland, who sat next to her aunt, seemed…curated. Every item of his clothing evoked midnight. Even his hair—dark as pitch—and his eyes—impenetrable and opaque.

When he rescued her in London, Emmaline thought him the epitome of a gentleman. Now she saw the hunger in him that had nothing to do with food. He presented as charming and polished, but calculation lurked in the dark depths. She wondered what he was planning.

Emmaline had never eaten in such a grand room and still wasn't used to it. Paintings of cherubs, angels, and icons were so skillfully rendered they appeared to be sculptures. A massive crystal chandelier hung above the table. The centerpiece featured a gold model of a ship at full sail, which Colin said was meant for pouring wine.

Despite the almost oppressive elegance, Emmaline felt at ease in her plain frock. Colin set the tone, and his brown trousers and everyday muslin shirt were little different from the rough wool he wore for manual labor. The man did not put on airs.

Except with women, and it was a different type of air altogether.

"Your Ophelia quite broke my heart," he told Aunt Heloise in a stage whisper audible around the table. "I wanted to leap onto the stage and save such a tender, fragile soul from the cruel finality of death."

While some women might have blushed or turned aside the compliment, Aunt Heloise gave him a provocative smile. "Did you envision what would happen after that?"

"Aye. I would have carted you off stage and—" Here, Colin had the grace to look around the table. "Story for another day. Rest assured, you have lived long in my imagination, Heloise."

Their banter continued throughout the meal. Mr. Maitland added a few words now and then, especially to her aunt, who seemed delighted to have men at each elbow. The only person who didn't participate in conversation was Mr. Gibbons. Perhaps he was not accustomed to dining with his employer, or, for that matter, in a castle. Emmaline tried to engage him, but he seemed troubled. She wondered what had made him so sore of heart.

Others around the table were members of the vast Campbell family, who spoke a combination of Scottish and English. Some had prepared the food; others had duties in the castle or fields. Several of the women tried to draw Mr. Gibbons out, but soon gave up. There were no rules about who could or couldn't sit at the table. Peter's sister Jenny shyly joined them, but her brother preferred to be elsewhere playing with Galahad.

The meal was plain, but delicious. A meat pie of Angus beef was so tasty it nearly brought Emmaline to tears. Oat bread was freshly made; cabbage and kale came from the castle garden. A robust soup featured smoked fish with onions and potatoes. Dessert was something called a clootie dumpling, a fine pudding with treacle, currants, and spices.

Suddenly, Aunt Heloise rose. A signal for the ladies to depart?

But her aunt had no intention of abiding by

town rules. She graciously thanked Colin for the fine supper, then swiftly moved to her real purpose.

"We must play a game," she announced. "Charades, but we'll make it interesting—Greek tragedies. One team acts out the parts. The other guesses the characters and the play."

Colin smiled. "Advantage to your side, I think."

Her aunt merely inclined her head in acknowledgment.

"Let's even out the advantage," he went on. "Your team will have the Greeks. The other side will perform Scottish legends, and you'll guess characters and story. The Scottish team will wear Highland regalia. Plenty of that here in the castle."

Colin's relatives applauded enthusiastically.

"I do love a properly mounted production," Aunt Heloise said approvingly. "I trust that means the men will be wearing…kilts?" Her eyes danced. "This does hold promise."

Mr. Tavish nudged Emmaline's arm. "Not one for kilts. Care to take a turn in the garden?"

She eyed him gratefully. She didn't relish the game. Aunt Heloise would dominate, and while Emmaline admired her aunt's gift, she had no wish to perform alongside her.

Likely, they wouldn't be missed. Colin's relatives were already drawing Mr. Gibbons into the fray. He looked horrified as they swept him into the adjoining weapons room, which had been deemed a fitting backdrop for the game.

"By the time they realize we didn't follow, we'll be away," Mr. Tavish murmured.

Outside, Emmaline took a deep breath of the cool night air, relieved at the silence.

"You've no love of spectacle either?" he asked.

"And share a stage with my aunt? Her light burns so brightly, it casts all else into shade."

"Nicely put."

When Mr. Tavish offered his arm, Emmaline hesitated. Her leg was stronger—she'd kept to a regimen of walking every day since her injury and didn't need his support.

But maybe she did.

Mr. Maitland's arrival had unsettled her. A burgeoning anxiety had taken root. It had started in London with her abduction, then Mr. Tavish's dire warning of danger. Now it felt as if that danger was closing in. She took his arm gratefully.

Simply touching the sturdy fabric that shielded Mr. Tavish's solid muscles calmed her. Robert Tavish was, in surprising ways, a man who could be counted on.

They walked in silence. Darkness was descending. A sliver of moon glowed faintly above them. The night brought a chill, and Emmaline was glad of the warmth of his presence.

"What do you think of Maitland?" he asked.

"He seems all that a gentleman should be."

"Carefully put," Mr. Tavish said. "But I'll have the rest."

Emmaline sighed. "I am mindful of your warning—that he orchestrated my abduction and rescue to learn about my involvement with poor Mr. Burwell."

"Worse than that. He wants to arrest you for treason."

She eyed him in astonishment. "I don't understand."

"Maitland wants to move up in government. A treason arrest would help."

"But arresting someone without proof—wouldn't that tarnish his reputation?"

Mr. Tavish shook his head. "Men like Maitland don't build reputations on honesty, only on results. Your guilt or innocence would be for a court to decide. Do you know a Dr. Black?"

Emmaline frowned. "Jacob Back? I took my aunt to him after hearing of his skill with mesmerism. But he was condescending and offensive, so Aunt Heloise—" she broke off.

"Please continue."

"I couldn't possibly." Her face flamed. "Suffice it to say she put him in his place."

Mr. Tavish arched a brow. "I remain filled with curiosity."

"Which will go unsatisfied," she said firmly. "Trust me when I say that is for the best."

They had reached the far end of the garden, bordered by conical trees. Mr. Tavish halted them near a bench and gestured for her to sit. It wasn't a large bench, and his broad frame took up most of the room.

He turned to face her. "I find that I do trust you."

Emmaline searched his features. "I sense there is a 'but' coming."

He hesitated. "Maitland suggested you learned mesmerism from Black and put Burwell in a trance. I believe he means to claim Burwell's collaborators knew the War Office was on to him and paid you to eliminate him."

She drew in a sharp breath. "Do *you* think me a murderess, Mr. Tavish?"

"Robert," he corrected. "I've seen you wield that stick, and I don't doubt that you are capable of many things. But murder? Hardly."

"Then…you believe me?"

"Maitland senses each person's weakness. For a minute, I considered his story—only because he tried to link Black to my mother's death."

Heavens. "How?"

"He claims Black taught at the school my father sent me to. That when my mother removed me, Black came here to persuade her to reconsider. When that failed, he used mesmerism to plant the seed that eventually led to her suicide. That's preposterous. Mesmerism can't induce people to kill themselves. But with Maitland, cleverly presented absurdities create persuasive narratives. If he arrested you, people might believe them."

Emmaline was horrified. "If he tries, I will fight him with every ounce of my strength."

Mr. Tavish's mouth curved. "That, Mrs. Stanhope, might just see us through."

"Alcott," she said glumly.

"No need to confuse everyone. Stick with the name you've been carrying."

Emmaline hadn't expected that kindness. "It never ends, does it? Keeping one's guard up.

Staying ready to overcome each new obstacle. Whenever I solve one difficulty, another arises."

And now she had a dangerous enemy. A man to whom the authorities would give credence. Who knew his way around government. Who was clever as he was duplicitous.

As Mr. Tavish shifted on the bench, his legs brushed hers. "Maitland hasn't yet learned how to play the long game. He's impatient and makes mistakes. And you aren't in this alone."

Emmaline stiffened. "I am not asking for your help."

"You didn't ask to be spirited away to Scotland, yet here we are."

"Because you left me no time to think," she grumbled.

"Was the best course." Mr. Tavish rose, extended his arm. "In the event we haven't been gone long enough to avoid charades, let's take another turn around the garden."

For a while, they simply strolled and absorbed the night. An owl hooted, claiming its territory. Scotland felt like a place out of time. Here, creatures like owls and the long-haired cows that roamed these hills weren't estranged from their environment. They belonged.

Mr. Tavish might deny it, but he, too, belonged in a place with open skies, verdant hills, and sparkling lakes. Scotland settled easily on those big shoulders.

"Why do you dislike kilts?" Emmaline asked. "Aren't they part of your heritage?"

He scoffed. "Thanks to Walter Scott and his ilk,

most English think Highlanders march around in kilts all day and quote Burns. They've turned us into pipers with bare knees."

She eyed him in amusement. "Do you fear that exposing your knees will detract from your manhood?"

He arched a brow. "Manhood, is it?"

Instantly, Emmaline regretted her boldness.

"If you wish to see my knees, that can be arranged," Mr. Tavish said.

She knew she deserved that. Bantering of that sort was dangerous. "I do not. But I sense that Colin wishes you to wear a kilt now and then."

"Heritage runs deep in him, like most Campbells—save George, who must curry favor with the English. He can't do that marching around Parliament in knee stockings."

"You deflected my question about your heritage."

Mr. Tavish hesitated. Then: "Spent a few years running from it, but it's with me still."

"How?"

"Bucked my grandfather to enter the Royal Navy—he was a military hero, trained me for infantry. I fought him on clan matters, too. Didn't come to clan celebrations. Settled myself in England, for no good reason that he could figure." His voice had roughened. "Last time I wore a kilt was at his funeral five years ago. I'd have given anything if he'd been there to see me in it."

Darkness obscured his expression, but Emmaline felt his sorrow. "People die, and then you wonder why you'd ever been at odds," she said.

He regarded her. "Spoken from experience?"

"There's much I would ask my father now, if he were alive," Emmaline said. "I never understood him. I couldn't bridge the gap between us."

Mr. Tavish nodded. "Hard to outrun regret. When I'm here, Colin tries to bring me back into the fold. So does George, in his way."

"Do you wish it?" Emmaline ventured.

"There's wish and there's want," he said. "Wish is a dream, requires little effort. Want's deeper, cuts to the bone. I'm not looking to repeat that pain. Got a fair dose when I was young."

"But…aren't you denying part of yourself?"

At first, he didn't respond. Then: "You have a way of drawing things out of me. I've never had such an odd conversation."

"Nor I," Emmaline confessed.

They left it at that and strolled silently back to the castle.

***

Astonishingly, John had enjoyed the evening. Dinner was awkward. The Campbells were a formidable lot. But during charades, a strange magic happened.

Heloise Alcott.

He was not one for Greek tragedies. Long habit caused him to silence hard truths. The story their side performed struck uncomfortably close to the darkest thoughts a man could have about love and betrayal and revenge. Not that John had ever been betrayed, unless one counted the betrayal wrought by his own, weary heart.

Clytemnestra was a queen who murdered the king with an ax in his bath and was in turn killed by her son. The queen had been furious with her husband—he'd sacrificed her daughter and was unfaithful. John did not think that justified murder. But when Heloise embodied the queen and offered her excuses, he was more than persuaded.

Her recounting of the killing, delivered with relish, made his flesh crawl: "'Each dying breath flung from his breast swift bubbling jets of gore.'" Her eyes held fire, her face a murderous flame alongside twisted joy as she faced her accusers and denied nothing.

"'Behold the deed!'" Heloise declared, her arms flung wide.

It was a lot to absorb for a man whose moral battles had played out only in his head. John could not help but admire how the playwright Aeschylus—and Heloise, who brought his words to life—glorified transgression.

Afterward, she seemed drained, as if she'd poured all her strength to the part. But she was sporting enough to linger during the Campbells' presentation of a tale about a giant lizard-like creature said to live in a lake near Inverness. "Nessie," as they called it, was hundreds of years old. Now and then it would leap from the lake and eat a human who drew too close.

As the evening wore on, John could see Heloise wilt. Finally, he moved to sit next to her and quietly offered to escort her to her room.

"You are kind, Mr. Gibbons," she said. "I am tired but reluctant to call a halt to the entertainment."

John eyed Colin and his relatives, who showed no sign of flagging. "I expect they will carry on, though their performances won't hold a candle to yours."

Her smile was radiant. "How gallant."

John felt himself blush, though he was too old for that. As he helped her rise, he saw that the effort cost her. Tentatively, he put his arm around her waist, hoping she didn't think him forward. "Lean into me," he whispered.

He helped her up the long staircase and to her room. She turned, her expression grave.

"One fades, John," Heloise said sadly. "It is a loss."

"Nothing could be further from the truth," he assured her. "Your performance tonight was grand. I have never seen the like."

She regarded him. "As long as one person thinks so, I suppose it is enough. I don't know what I would do if I had to give up performing even small bits like tonight. I am perilously close to losing the very thing that drives me. What happens when I do?"

John tried to think what had driven him since Portia's death. Nothing, really. Only the plodding through his duties, the dull march toward death. Oh, he tried to watch over Robert from afar over the years, but the man was so physically imposing that he hardly needed assistance. And while it was satisfying to devote himself to Portia's son, he could only do so much. Robert carried wounds beyond John's ability to heal.

"I suppose one finds new sources of joy," he told Heloise. "But I struggle with that. At times I feel quite faded myself."

Her violet eyes assessed him. "Why?"

"I lack words to describe it," John said. "But when I look at you, I see you embrace life in a way that has always eluded me."

Heloise tilted her head. "When I look at you, I see a man with great potential."

"Alas, I am a creature of habit. It has saved me many times over, but also kept me firmly in its grip." John feared he was babbling. "I do not regret the choices I've made, but it has been a long time since I've had occasion to make new ones."

Heloise reached up and brushed her lips across his cheek. "We will have to remedy that."

With a broad wink, she slipped inside her room and closed the door behind her.

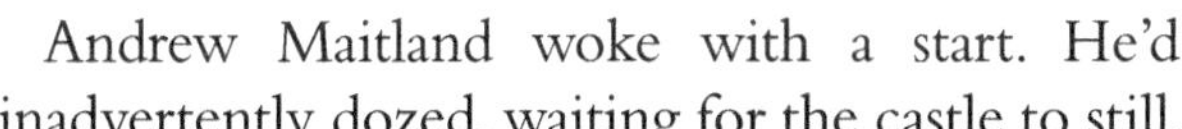

Andrew Maitland woke with a start. He'd inadvertently dozed, waiting for the castle to still.

Judging by the silence, it was the very dead of night. The time when yearning, no longer relegated to shadows, gained substance. When intent need not hide. When a predator could come out and hunt.

Tonight, he sought information. Which room was which, who slept alone, who didn't. He wasn't sure about Colin, who seemed to prefer the cottage rather than this cavernous, musty castle, where the weaponry display and ostentatious furnishings looked to be the point.

Drew edged his way along the blackened corridor, grateful for the night vision the sea had taught him. This wing, where the guests had been put, had wall sconces, but drafts had done them in. Ample cover for his purpose.

Heloise Alcott, he suspected, slept the sleep of the dead. She looked quite tired after pouring herself into that game. Drew was fascinated by her Clytemnestra. Her murder confession lacked contrition; indeed, she relished the crime. A character after his own heart.

He listened at her door—not a sound. Across the hall was another, also silent. He suspected it belonged to the very quiet Mr. Gibbons. The man was troubled, and it looked to be the kind of deeply embedded suffering long nurtured until it becomes a familiar friend.

Drew moved back across the corridor to the chamber next to the aunt. Likely, Mrs. Stanhope would have been put there. Did the two rooms adjoin? He'd have to be careful.

How audacious of Tavish to spirit her away to the wilds of Scotland. Had he meant to play the gallant? Had the woman wormed her way into his affections?

Drew wasn't sure. Tavish kept to himself. Preferred bones to humans. When they served together in the Caribbean, Drew had looked up to him. Tavish was older and easily the best seaman on the ship. Drew hated the sea. Cramped conditions, disease, ghastly food, dangerous and unpredictable weather. Those were bad enough, but battle was far worse.

Wounded men had surgeons digging into their flesh with nothing to ease the pain. Usually, they died anyway. Drew was seventeen when he weathered his first sea battle, and he was scared witless. Tavish, on the other hand, never showed an ounce of fear.

The man remained a puzzle. Drew suspected George had given Tavish some mission with the Stanhope woman. He wouldn't be pleased to learn his nephew had spirited her away to the Campbell stronghold. Sheltering a suspected traitor wouldn't help George's political ambitions.

More importantly, where was Tavish's chamber? Drew had no wish to stumble into a hornets' nest. If Tavish and the woman were lovers, perhaps he bedded with her. Drew put his ear to the door of her room. No sounds that betrayed lovers. He sensed she was alone. Perfect.

He took stock of other nocturnal noises. Occasional scurrying sounds—vermin or other creatures going about their routines—suggested nothing amiss. Vermin kept low, hugged the walls, minimized risk of discovery. The same strategy worked for the human sort, as well.

Drew pulled two vials from his pocket. One held oil, for silencing hinges. The other held a colorless liquid, unstable when exposed to the air. It wasn't ideal—too much could kill; too little had no effect. He wished someone would devise a more reliable product.

It was a Scot who had discovered the stuff. Poetic justice, then, to use it to capture an English rose from under a Scotsman's nose.

With his hand on the knob of Mrs. Stanhope's door, Drew allowed himself a smile.

<hr />

Robert watched Maitland from the shadows. That the man hadn't detected his presence told him all he needed to know. Maitland was sloppy, allowed goal to eclipse means.

Did he intend to capture Mrs. Stanhope and take her back to England? He was a fool to think it would be easy. For now, Robert merely watched, fascinated, as Maitland applied a thin coat of oil to the hinges of Mrs. Stanhope's room. At last, he put his hand on the knob.

"I wouldn't." Robert stepped from the dark.

Maitland jumped.

"Move away from the door," Robert said softly.

Maitland's features arranged themselves into a mask of aplomb, to which he added an extra dash of arrogance. "Or what? You'll challenge me to a duel?"

"Thinking more about tossing you off one of the towers."

The self-assurance slipped a notch. "I suppose you have reinforcements at the ready."

"Don't need them."

"Because you have the advantage in size?"

"Because I'm not sneaking around someone's castle in the middle of the night to slip into a lady's bedchamber uninvited. What were you planning, Maitland? Abduct her like before?"

Drew shrugged. "Might have worked."

"Amusing that you thought it would." Robert closed the distance between them. "Probably ought to return to your room. Think of a better plan."

"Don't be smug, Tavish. You think you know what I'm capable of. You don't."

"I won't let you take an innocent woman into custody to advance your career," he said.

"She's not innocent. You already know she's sailing under false colors. Her name—"

"Irrelevant."

"You make excuses for her." Drew smiled thinly. "That means she has her tentacles in you. Beware, Tavish, that's when men like you are the most vulnerable."

Robert put a heavy hand on Maitland's shoulder. "Back to bed, there's a good lad. Don't abuse Colin's hospitality by trying to kidnap his guests."

Drew's features darkened. But he turned. In a moment the shadows reclaimed him.

———— ∾∾ ————

Despite her exhaustion, Heloise couldn't sleep. She saw a light on in Emmaline's room and knocked gently on the door between their chambers. At her niece's muffled reply, she opened the door.

Emmaline sat on the floor surrounded by papers. "It's no use, Aunt. I cannot finish this. We need the money Father's book will bring, but I am struggling."

"If that's my brother's work, I can see why. He always was disorganized."

"It's not the disorganization of his papers that's the challenge, it's what's in them. Fairy tales. Stories that aren't true and are either ridiculously happy or dark."

Heloise laughed. "Whoever said stories had to be true? That's the joy of them."

"What joy is there in a witch trying to force two children into an oven?"

She sat on Emmaline's bed. "The witch doesn't succeed, and the children cleverly mark their trail with breadcrumbs to find their way home."

"Children shouldn't have to face such things," Emmaline said. "I understand that it's about doing battle with evil. But why must children contemplate evil?"

"Because we all do, dear," Heloise said. "Each of us stares darkness in the face at some time in our lives—often many times. Perhaps it's not a kindness to shield children from that."

Emmaline gathered the papers. "And what are children to take from a tale where a woman falls in love with the beast that imprisons her?"

Heloise considered that. "Perhaps that the beast exists in all of us but can be tamed."

"You are better at this. You instinctively understand."

"Stories embody our dreams and fears," Heloise said. "They're cathartic. I poured my soul into Ophelia. I *want* the audience to be devastated when she dies. I demand they experience emotion to the fullest."

"I can't indulge emotions when I don't know where I will find next month's rent."

"You think you must fix everything, and you put feeling aside to do what must be done," Heloise said. "Too much of that starves the soul, Em. Would it be so terrible if you allowed yourself to, say, contemplate a liaison with the very handsome Mr. Tavish?"

Emmaline flushed. "That's absurd. I'm not beautiful. I have physical defects."

"Mere veneer," Heloise said dismissively. "Worth inheres. *You* determine your worth, no one else. Any man who doesn't see that you are a pearl beyond price isn't worth your time."

"I can't let fantasies get in the way. I need to—" She broke off.

"Take care of me," Heloise finished.

Emmaline caught her hand. "It's no burden, Aunt. But I must be practical."

"Do not dismiss fantasy, Em," Heloise warned. "It's a respite from reality. I wouldn't have had a career if people did not wish to live through the fantasy of my characters."

"I can't live anywhere other than the here and now."

"Perhaps you haven't been paying close attention to the here and now," Heloise said. "I know I'm not imagining that you and Mr. Tavish are becoming closer."

"We have come to tolerate one another," Emmaline conceded. "But I wouldn't know what to do with the man if he suddenly appeared at the door."

A firm knock suddenly sounded, startling them both. They exchanged puzzled glances. Emmaline moved to the door and cautiously opened it.

As if summoned, Mr. Tavish stood there, his expression grim. "You are undisturbed?"

"Why would we be disturbed?" Emmaline asked.

His gaze shifted to the corridor. "Some moving about tonight. You are well?"

Heloise regarded him with amusement. "Come in and tell us about this 'moving about.'"

He looked alarmed. "Not the thing. But you are the chaperone, so—"

"I've never been, nor do I plan to be, a chaperone," Heloise said. "But if it eases your mind, I will try."

Mr. Tavish stepped into the room, closed the door, and faced Emmaline. "I stopped Maitland outside your room. Given that he wants to arrest you for murder, you'd best be wary."

Heloise eyed him sternly. "If Emmaline is in danger, you must keep her safe."

"Aunt," Emmaline protested. "It is not his responsibility."

"It is," Mr. Tavish said gruffly. "It's Colin's castle—actually, George's. But they'd say the same. Our roof, our responsibility."

"Can't you simply tie him up and toss him in that very picturesque lake?" Heloise asked sweetly. "Oh, dear. I suppose that's murder, isn't it?"

"Not unheard of here," Mr. Tavish said darkly.

"Do you have a plan?" Heloise asked.

"I won't run Maitland off—he'd simply resurface. He's determined to boost his career with her arrest, and he's ruthless enough not to let facts get in the way." He looked at Emmaline. "You're not safe until we find a way to stop him."

Heloise eyed Mr. Tavish thoughtfully. "I am known to be quite persuasive."

She didn't miss her niece's look of alarm.

"As Lady Macbeth, I plotted the murder of a king," Heloise said softly. "As Judith, I cut off a general's head and turned the tide of war. As Boadicea, enraged at the rape of my daughters, I led a revolt against the Romans."

Mr. Tavish frowned.

Heloise smiled. "I can certainly manage an ill-seasoned young man with a vaunted sense of his own talents."

For the first time in a while, she felt a burst of energy.

Chapter Seventeen

MR. TAVISH WAS at the table when Emmaline came down for breakfast. That Mr. Maitland had tried to invade her room greatly unsettled her. Mr. Tavish seemed determined to protect her, but what would happen when she returned to London?

She had little appetite, despite the robust meal laid out on the sideboard—square slices of sausage with a mix of beef and spices, oatmeal porridge, eggs, cakes made from barley, and potatoes, or "tatties," as Colin called them.

There was no sign of Mr. Maitland, which was just as well. Emmaline couldn't imagine being cordial to a man who wanted to frame her for murder.

"Taking you to Oban," Mr. Tavish announced. "It will foil Maitland's plan, for now."

Emmaline frowned. "That's not necessary."

"Fearless, are you?"

She bristled. "No, but I could make it difficult for him."

"As in London, when he needed only a horsehair blanket to render you helpless?"

"Now children." Colin entered, Peter in tow.

He often took the boy with him on daily chores chopping wood and other tasks with the tenants. Peter had blossomed under his attention.

"I agree with Robbie," Colin said. "Best to put space between you and the man while we figure out what to do with him."

They had obviously discussed Mr. Maitland's nocturnal escapade. As much as Emmaline appreciated their involvement, she couldn't rely on them forever. "Is Oban far?"

"Three hours," Mr. Tavish said. "We'll stay at my mother's cottage. There's an island offshore I want to study. Rocks of particular interest."

"My aunt wouldn't be up to such a trip," Emmaline cautioned.

He glanced at Peter. "We'll bring Peter and his sister. Gibbons, too."

At that, Peter perked up. "Can I bring Galahad?"

"No," Mr. Tavish said firmly. "He'd end as some eagle's dinner."

"I'd keep him in the cage," Peter insisted.

"Like you don't do now?" Mr. Tavish shook his head. "Not risking it."

An interesting dynamic had developed between Mr. Tavish and the bird, and for that matter, Mr. Tavish and Peter. Galahad was often out of the cage. Sometimes he'd alight on Mr. Tavish's shoulder, which he didn't seem to mind. Peter was fascinated with the castle. Once, Emmaline came upon him and Mr. Tavish in the weapons room. The lad wore a medieval helmet and was brandishing a stick as Mr. Tavish instructed him in stick fighting.

Slowly, an idea began to form.

Emmaline wondered whether her aunt was involved in whatever plan Mr. Tavish and Colin had devised. But after Aunt Heloise's bravura words last night about women warriors turning the tide of battle, she feared her aunt had a plan of her own.

Mr. Tavish rose. "Pack warm clothes."

Apparently, the matter was settled. Emmaline hurried after him. "Wait!"

He turned.

"I wish to bring a weapon—a small knife, one of those Scottish—dirks, is it? The kind you hide in stockings. I want you to teach me to use it."

"Dirk would slice your leg open. *Sgian dubh's* the knife for stockings. Good collection of those in the armory." He frowned. "Why do you want something like that?"

"I need to see to my protection. I was helpless the night I was abducted." She hesitated. "Since you trained on those weapons in the armory, you can teach me."

His brows rose. "Those are battle weapons. For warriors. Not for—"

"Women?" Emmaline glared at him. "Are we not also entitled to defend ourselves?"

"You can't lug a broadsword or crossbow around London."

She smiled. "That is why you'll find something more suitable for me."

Mr. Tavish's jaw set. "No."

"I won't go to Oban with you otherwise."

For a moment they glared at one another.

"Bring your stick," he said gruffly. "We'll work on stick fighting."

For now, she'd settle for that.

As she was packing, Emmaline begged Aunt Heloise to come with her, to no avail.

"The castle has everything I need," her aunt said. "I don't say that Scottish food is easy on the palate—haggis or haggus, or whatever it is, can never be anything but revolting. Still, the place has history and quite a few charms."

"Including Colin Campbell," Emmaline pointed out.

Aunt Heloise dismissed that. "Colin is a flirt. We speak the same language, one you'd do well to learn. I have been with men and without men, dear. *With* men is generally better. You ought to explore what is set on the table in front of you. Namely, Robert Tavish."

"Mr. Tavish is not a beef roast, Aunt."

"But juicy, just the same," her aunt shot back.

"Walk with me, Mr. Maitland. I feel rather weak and could use a sturdy arm."

Drew eyed Miss Alcott glumly. He had wanted a brisk walk, not a stroll in the garden holding up a frail old woman. And where was the niece? He hadn't seen her all day.

Miss Alcott took his arm before he offered it. "I imagine your mother is very proud of you, occupying a position of importance in government."

Drew gritted his teeth. "My mother's been gone a long time, madam."

"Your father then," she said, undaunted. "He must be pleased with your accomplishments."

So very pleased.

"Actually, he prefers that I learn the family business." Drew wondered why he had revealed that.

"Which is?"

"Wealth. Estates. Aristocracy. Idle rich. That sort of thing."

"But you would rather serve the Crown?" she prodded. "Or perhaps have it serve you."

"It is interesting work." And far superior to learning to run the estate with his judgmental father peering over his shoulder. Drew wondered how long he had to endure this inquisition.

"Apologies." Miss Alcott's lashes fluttered. "I was prying. You need not unburden yourself to the likes of me."

Drew tried to be polite—not his usual thing. "I imagine you are a good listener, were I the sort to unburden myself. But I am not."

"You enjoy being secretive, do you not?"

He was taken aback. "I—"

"*Feed* on it, in fact," Miss Alcott added in a steely tone. "I have known the sort."

Hell. This walk could not end soon enough.

"But it's a sort that's often misunderstood, I've found," she continued.

"I never thought of myself as a 'sort,'" Drew said stiffly.

Her mouth curved in a smile. "Nicely said. You put me in my place, dear boy."

Boy? Now *that* grated. He was twenty-four, well into adulthood. But when Drew opened his mouth to object, she pressed her fingers into his arm.

"It's futile to fix you as one particular sort," she said. "Your talent is knowing when to be one thing or another. With that skill, you will build a fine career."

Drew had had enough. "I beg you, madam, leave off."

Miss Alcott gave a weary sigh. "I fear I must sit. Would you mind helping me onto that bench? Pray, do not leave. I feel decidedly faint."

Suppressing a sigh of his own, Drew put a steadying arm under her elbow. She listed alarmingly into his chest, and it took both of his hands gripping her upper arms to help her sit.

"There." Her smile was wan. "I can endure your harangue easier from a sitting position. Join me, please." Miss Alcott patted the space next to her.

"It was not a harangue," Drew protested, even as he sat. "Indeed, the shoe is on the other foot. You were enumerating my faults when you don't even know me."

"You mistook my words. I *admire* a man with the talent to transmogrify."

Drew arched a brow. "Like a butterfly?"

"Or a chameleon," she murmured.

"Madam, I no longer know what this conversation is about. Only that I must ask you to release me from any obligation to ensure your safe passage through this garden."

And if she fell on her face all the better.

Miss Alcott began to laugh.

Drew eyed her in bewilderment.

"I heard your words but read your darker thought: You wish me at Jericho," she said. "I don't blame you. But you need instruction in the art of becoming a chameleon. Because *I* see your true character quite clearly. Surely you do not wish others to."

His gaze darkened. "What I wish is to be instantly transported to Hell, for it cannot hold such tortures as this discourse has wrought."

"Blasphemy is a dangerous art," she warned. "Do you mean to tempt the Fates?"

Drew glowered. "The Fates can offer nothing I have not seen or dreamt of. I do not recoil from darkness. A proper fortune-teller would know that."

"I am not proper," Miss Alcott said. "I am a woman who's seen a great deal of life, and what I see is a young man who will never succeed unless he pays attention to what people like me can teach him."

Drew stared at her. "What deep game is this? You know I mean to arrest your niece at the first opportunity. I would see her hang for her crime."

"There you go, giving away the ending," she admonished. "One must always keep the audience guessing. Besides, Emmaline isn't here. Mr. Tavish took her away. I suspect she will return, but in the meantime, are you not interested in what I have to offer? You would benefit greatly. At the moment, you are simply a rank amateur."

His head had begun to ache. "Am I to understand that you wish to improve my skill at treachery? That won't wash, madam, given that your niece's imprisonment is my aim."

"If you learn from me, you'll have no need to arrest Emmaline."

Not for the first time, Drew regarded her in disbelief.

And yet, the woman had already succeeded in trapping him for a half hour in a conversation he should have fled at the first inkling.

Perhaps this shop-worn thespian could teach him a thing or two.

Robert managed three hours in the closed carriage, despite tight quarters with Peter, his sister Jenny, Gibbons, and Mrs. Stanhope. He spent much of the time counting the minutes.

He also took the opportunity to study Mrs. Stanhope as she watched the passing scenery. Her upright posture and the resolute set of her mouth bespoke determination. She'd hold him to his promise to instruct her in stick fighting.

What sort of female equipped herself with battle weapons? What sort of female didn't retreat into hysterics at the prospect of being framed for murder or targeted by murderous spies?

If, while studying her, Robert decided she was as handsome as any woman he'd seen, it was a harmless thought. Handsome fit her best, though by many measures, including the startling blue eyes and auburn hair, she was beautiful. He suspected she did not think of herself as such.

Beautiful women need not cultivate character or strength; the world catered to them. It did not cater to women like Emmaline Stanhope. Lacking wealth or position, she was left to forge her own way. She found a way to walk without a limp and refused to give in to pain. She held her own, despite her precarious financial state, and took care of her ailing aunt.

For all those reasons, Robert respected her. And so, he would teach her to fight with her clever stick despite his resolve that she would never have to do so on his watch.

Strangely, Gibbons said little during the drive. Perhaps he had no wish to play nursemaid to Peter, who hadn't stopped talking. The lad had seen more travel in the past few weeks than the whole of his young life. The prospect of a seaside town thrilled him.

"I'll miss Galahad," he said. "But Mr. Colin swears he'll take good care of him."

If Gibbons didn't perk up, it would be a dreary trip. Robert missed his good-natured chatter, even his unnecessary mothering.

Mrs. Stanhope was quiet, too. Perhaps she was worried about her aunt, likely with reason. Who knew what she and Colin planned for Maitland? Colin was a bloodthirsty Scot, and the unpredictable Miss Alcott knew no bounds. Robert needed a solution to the Maitland problem far better than anything they would devise. For now, Mrs. Stanhope was safe in his care.

He hadn't been to Oban in years. It's where he spent the best of his childhood, learning to sail and fish. On the water, pitting himself against the elements, he'd imagine some great sea creature, hitherto unknown, rising from the sea. The image ultimately inspired his study of rocks, essentially a treasure hunt for ancient beasts and the paths they trod.

Now he was returning to his childhood home, the site of his mother's death, and pieces of a fraught past Robert had never managed to outrun.

Was that what life was about? Finding—and reckoning with—beasts?

Why did that always lead him to Scotland?

After a carriage ride filled with Peter's chatter—and unaccustomed silence from Mr. Gibbons—Emmaline was relieved to arrive at the cottage in Oban. "Cottage" was a misnomer. It was a stone manor house perched on a hill above the bay near cliffs that towered over the harbor.

She loved it instantly.

Brown stone formed the façade in an uneven pattern that nevertheless looked deliberate.

"My grandfather built it as a sanctuary when he wasn't at war or in the castle," Mr. Tavish explained. "The stones look chaotic, but all comes right in the end."

Two large stone chimneys rose at either end

of the gray slate roof. Judging by the number of chimney pots, each encompassed a half dozen fireplaces. A climbing hedge angled upward to encircle a dormer window. Even with two symmetrical wings, the house exuded warmth.

Yet inside, Emmaline saw no portraits or personal items. Servants obviously kept the place in order, but the house felt empty. "How long did your mother live here?"

"Seven years." A deep furrow bisected Mr. Tavish's forehead. He seemed ill at ease.

He wasn't the only one. While Peter raced through the house exclaiming over each room, Mr. Gibbons was oddly quiet.

"Are you well, Mr. Gibbons?" Emmaline asked.

He cleared his throat. "Quite, madam. Glad to be done with the journey."

She and Mr. Tavish went outside to the rear of the house. Here, fields sloped away from the cottage, then swept up into rolling hills. The air felt brisk and clean, faintly tinged with salt.

What would it be like to live in such a place? Emmaline wondered.

Mr. Tavish was staring at the cliffs. "My mother walked there in the evenings. It's where she died."

Emmaline put her hand on his arm. "I'm sorry."

"Seems strange to speak of it." He wore a faraway look. "I ought to have been here. But I'd left home, with the carelessness of untested youth, to forge my own course. She was alone."

"You aren't to blame, surely," Emmaline said.

"She'd been beaten down by life, by my father,

by those he hired to try to control her." Mr. Tavish shook his head, as if trying to banish the image. "I thought that since we escaped him, she would heal. But she didn't. She had secrets, a darkness she never shared."

A strangled sound came from behind them. Mr. Gibbons strode past, as if the devil was at his heels. He marched off toward the cliffs.

They watched in baffled silence as he grew ever smaller against the horizon. Soon he was but a shadow, quickly subsumed in the first signs of dusk.

⚬⚬⚬

Portia had walked these cliffs, staring out at the sea, perhaps imagining a different life.

Certainly, the life she had was painful. John had done his best to ease things, but in the end she was alone, and he was hundreds of miles away.

Likely, she'd never thought of him.

But what Colin said pulled at him. Had his feelings been reciprocated? Would that have mattered? They had been bound by the same code and borders that couldn't be crossed.

Yet she'd treasured a ballad about love between a titled lady and a servant.

Would Portia's fate have been different if she had known she was loved? Would that have saved her? Would it have saved *him* from a life of futile regret?

Hubris to think it. *And yet.*

Had she slipped while walking on the cliffs? Or was death her final act of defiance to a marriage filled with abuse? Or had she simply come to care less about living and ended it?

None of it mattered now. Yet it did, terribly.

John was weary of living in the past, of mourning what might have been. Sorrow's weight had become oppressive. He loved her, but even that was in the past. His life yet remained.

What would he do with it?

<hr>

"Naked ambition," Miss Alcott declared. "It's written on your features. One suspects that you are always calculating your next move, judging the weaknesses of others."

"Because I am," Drew said simply.

She shook her head. "Ambition is no good if it's naked and obvious. That puts people on their guard. You'll never succeed that way."

What did she know? She was just an actress at the end of a not-illustrious career. In her day, perhaps she was something. But that was a long time ago.

"You have to work on two levels," she said. "What you wish people to see and what you do not wish them to see. And there's a third level, which allows you to calibrate your performance even as you act."

"Too complicated," Drew said.

Miss Alcott gave him a pitying look. "Yes, I imagine it's beyond you."

They were in the garden, but at some distance from the castle. She had seated herself on a bench.

Now she rose, as if to abandon him. "Pity. You had promise."

She was bluffing, Drew thought. Toying with him, trying to undercut his confidence.

"Wait," he heard himself say.

She turned, her gaze hard. "Only if you pay attention."

Damned if he would take marching orders from this woman. He wanted to tell her so, but the taunting look in her eyes stopped him. She didn't think he was up to the task.

Drew muttered something about trying again.

She arched a brow. He felt like a schoolboy under a teacher's withering gaze.

Miss Alcott condescended to sit once more. Drew joined her.

They were quite close, which unsettled him. The woman had to be nearly sixty but commanded a raw magnetism she could deploy at will. She favored frocks with deep necklines and in gauzy fabrics suitable for something other than a daytime stroll through a formal garden. Today's gown was a shade of purple trimmed in a putrid shade of yellow. In softer shades the colors would complement, but now they fought for attention. Silvery beads woven into her bodice caught the light each time breathing caused her ample chest to rise.

"Let us suppose," she began, "you want something from me quite badly. Imagine, if you will, that I am a faded actress, ever more insecure in her gifts. How would you try to obtain it?"

Easy, that. "I would try to gain your favor."

"Ah. How?"

"Flattery, I suppose."

"*Sincere* flattery," she corrected. "Falseness would betray you. Go ahead, Mr. Maitland. Flatter me. See if you can seem sincere."

This was deuced awkward. "Your, er, hair is a nice color."

"Owing entirely to henna," she said, leaving him exactly nowhere. "Praising my artifice does you no good. Women want more. They've gone to the trouble of achieving a pleasing appearance, but most do not wish to be admired for superficiality."

"Ironic," he scoffed.

"That does not change the truth of what I said."

Drew rolled his eyes.

"Remember that this exercise is about getting what you want from one woman—me. A woman who knows that her beauty is years behind her, a woman who knows her looks have faded. Thus, such praise can only ring false. Try again."

He thought hard. "It's clever of you to resort to henna."

Miss Alcott clapped her hands. "Much better. One might even think you see me as a person with a brain, rather than a means to an end."

"Damning by faint praise," he murmured. "But I will take it."

Abruptly, she reached over and put her fingertips on his temples, nearly causing him to jump from his seat. But he could not—dared not—move.

Her fingers massaged his temples, then moved to his forehead.

"That creased brow won't do," she said. "The deep crevice makes you look angry. Not the way to persuade your target to let down her guard."

The cool of her fingertips was not unpleasant. Drew began to relax.

"Open your mouth," she said softly.

Terror filled him. "Madam—"

"As wide as possible. Unhinge your jaw."

Unhinged precisely described his condition, but Drew opened his mouth like a great crocodile, to what purpose he dared not imagine.

Miss Alcott's clever fingertips went to the outside of his jawbone, just below his ears. She pressed firmly against each joint, then trailed her fingers along the length of his jaw until they met in the middle, just below his mouth.

The tip of one finger brushed his lower lip.

"How does that feel?" she whispered.

"Absurd."

She gave him a slow smile. "You may close your mouth."

Thank God.

Drew stared at her, trying to get his bearings. "I was beginning to feel—"

"Exposed?" she purred. "That was not my intent. It was to ease that angry brow and tight jaw, so that you don't look so duplicitous. One must begin any masquerade anew, with a clean slate. Who you were in the last masquerade must be purged so you can recreate yourself."

Miss Alcott paused. "Now: Who must you be to win my favor, to plumb my deepest, darkest secrets, to get what you want? Think on that."

Bewildered, Drew stared into violet eyes that liquified to bottomless depths. Her mouth curved, whether in provocation or pique or pleasure, he could not tell.

He shook his head. "I'm utterly off balance."

"Don't retreat at the first sign of difficulty," she admonished. "Put aside confusion, arrogance, all that stands in your way. Immerse yourself in the role. Become who I need. Who I *want*. The person to whom I wish to unburden myself of exactly what you seek."

Drew eyed her blankly.

She rose. "That's the end of today's lesson. Perhaps if you sleep on it, enlightenment will come."

He was aware of a profound sense of failure.

⸻ ∿ ⸻

Colin was bored. Normally, his small cabin suited him after a day of robust activity. Riding the estates, meeting with tenants, helping families thrive. It was what he loved.

George, though duke and clan chief, never bothered. His preferred territory was London, the drawing rooms and salons British aristocracy wielded to feather their status and power.

Colin didn't mind not being chief—it was George's birthright, after all. But keeping to town, never bothering with the folk who needed him, was not Colin's idea of proper chiefdom. And so, he filled the breach.

George had no idea of the difficulties tenants faced farming in thin soil and a short growing season or raising livestock on rough moors and inhospitable hills. Colin had earned their respect. They knew he would do what needed to be done.

Today had been long and filled with backbreaking work. He helped McNair with butchering, Alastair with blacksmithing, and Widow Barrie with fence repair. After chores, Colin usually returned to his cabin, its cozy fire and warmth far superior to the drafty castle.

Tonight, that wasn't quite enough.

Colin told himself he had no specific destination, that when his feet took him down the slope to the castle it was by happenstance.

It was not. In the absence of his nephew and Emmaline, it had become his habit to discover Miss Alcott in the garden in time for her nightly stroll.

She wasn't always alone. Sometimes that miscreant Maitland was with her. Colin knew Heloise was playing a deep game—thrilling thought, that—but it wasn't why he sought her out.

Long-ago memories of a heady trip to London and nights spent agog at the city's pleasures flooded his brain. Though he was too old to put stock in youthful memories, they nevertheless seduced him. For it was in London that he first laid eyes on Heloise Alcott.

Colin was in the box at Drury Lane with George and their father, who did not much care for frivolity. But this play was anything but frivolous. It was one of Shakespeare's best, about the Scottish general Macbeth, whose power-hungry wife manipulated him into killing the king and assuming the throne.

Most in the audience were there to see John Kemble, then at the peak of his powers. Colin hadn't cared for Kemble's interpretation of Macbeth. The man could declaim to the rafters, but his style was artificial and self-reverential. He did not express emotion so much as pronounce it. Nuance was a foreign language.

Miss Alcott, on the other hand, commanded the stage effortlessly as Lady Macbeth. Her power drew from a different source than Kemble's. She did not declaim. Rather, she inhabited the character. Each word came not from a script, but from within. She stalked the stage like a cat hunting its prey—the audience.

From her first words, she had held Colin and the theater in her palm, her voice low but with a raw edge as mad intent threatened to burst free. Her green velvet gown, trimmed in brown at the tantalizingly low neckline, brought out the startling color of her eyes—deep blue or violet, he thought. The fabric swirled around her lush form with stylish elegance, as befit a general's wife; yet her features sharpened with the calculation of a woman who aimed far higher.

When she tossed her red hair and uttered the words "unsex me here"—the lament of a woman who knows her path would be far easier were she a man—it was all Colin could do not to rise in protest. Nothing could erode that feminine power, the provocative tilt of her head, and the sway of her hips as the seductive fabric flowed around her.

Lo, these many years later, she was still a bird of paradise.

Tonight, the stars were out, and Colin found her alone in the garden on a bench. Happily, Maitland was nowhere to be seen.

She wasn't surprised to see him and moved over so that he might join her.

Rarely at a loss for words or confidence, Colin felt strangely shy. "It's gracious of you to make room for a Scotsman who's spent the day in hard labor. I'm a bit ripe."

Heloise smiled. He was reminded of that first night, when he dared to wait for her outside the theater, much to his father's disgust. When Colin refused to leave, his father and George took themselves off.

"You have an admirable work ethic, Colin," Heloise said softly. "It makes for a good life. I can't imagine you have many regrets."

"Oh, I do," he protested. "Not the least of which is not staying longer in London that week you were at the Drury Lane."

She laughed. "Did you not get your fill of *Macbeth*? You came to see it every night."

"I came to see *you*, as you well know. And, no, I didnae get my fill." Colin hesitated. "You were kind enough to keep me company, and yet we didnae…" He trailed off.

"No, we did not." She didn't mistake his meaning.

"I have always wondered why," he said. "Suppose I was lacking, somehow."

Heloise tucked her hand in the crook of his arm. "You lacked nothing. You were—are—a handsome, robust man and, I suspect, an uncommonly generous lover. That red hair alone could seduce. Even now, I yearn to run my fingers through it."

Colin felt himself blush to its very roots.

"I was honored that you chose to escort me around town," Heloise added. "Many women were envious, I assure you."

"But?" He waited.

"But you had stars in your eyes."

"I confess to being blinded by your loveliness, your talent—all of you, really."

Heloise sighed. "I welcome adoration from my audience. It means I succeeded in my craft. But I am not the person you see on stage. What you saw was artifice. Not real."

"I know that," he insisted.

"I am sure you do—now." Heloise turned to face him. "Back then, I had a noble streak. I didn't want to break your heart. The men I chose had no expectations, so that was not a danger."

"I had nae expectations," he protested. "How could I? You were so far above me."

"But I wasn't, don't you see? I was an actress. Deception and artifice were my tools. I lived a very different life than you, Colin. You reek with authenticity."

He gave a rough laugh. "Reek, is it?"

"You have ever only been yourself. You take care of others, labor tirelessly to keep this vast estate in shape, and do not shirk that responsibility."

"You make me out a boring drudge," Colin grumbled.

"I know you are not." Heloise regarded him. "I can't help but notice there's no lady by your side. Is there no woman lucky enough to gain your regard?"

"Not one who stuck."

"Why not?" she asked.

"Shakespearean stuff."

Heloise tilted her head, and Colin was reminded of Lady Macbeth's assessing gaze. He sighed. "There was one lass, Annise. I thought we'd suit. But she was a MacDonald. She couldnae get over that bit of history."

"A clan feud?"

Colin gave a ragged laugh. "Bit more than that. A Campbell led government troops in the massacre of MacDonald Jacobites, including some who were unarmed. Took their land, too. Over a century ago, but people here have long memories. Some got over it—some haven't."

"Did she marry someone else?"

"Aye. Another MacDonald. Lost his life in a pub fight several years ago."

Heloise studied him. "That means she's free. Will you try again?"

Colin shook his head. "If she cared for me, old grudges wouldnae matter."

"That sort of thinking did not help Romeo and Juliet," she murmured.

"Fact is, she made her choice. Now she has to live with it."

"And you are not in the least interested?" she prodded.

Colin's face warmed. "I've contented myself with observing from afar, doing what I can to see she has what she needs, without her knowing."

"I knew you were a romantic." Heloise smiled. "A secret benefactor who pines for her. There have been worse plots, I assure you."

He scowled. "I'm nae the pining sort. And nae looking for more rejection."

"Perhaps her heart has changed."

"And mayhap yours has," he parried.

Heloise eyed him in surprise. "So that's what this is? An attempt to rekindle our past? I'll put it bluntly, Colin: I have no heart. Comes from cheapening it all these years. You do not want a woman like me."

"I'll be the judge of that," he said.

"You are rooted here," she said. "Scotland is beautiful, but it's not for me. I like my creature comforts, and though I can't afford them anymore, I still yearn for them. And I fear my health would be compromised. The weather—"

"Is not for the faint of heart. Which you aren't." Colin made a sweeping gesture that encompassed the terrain. "Green hills, dancing brooks, the loch flowing to the sea—they're life-giving. I've seen the color come into your cheeks as you walk these paths."

She shook her head. "I'm no intrepid Scotswoman. I'm faded and jaded. I can't change."

"No one's a prisoner of their history," Colin protested.

"Aren't they? You pine for the MacDonald lass, who's a prisoner of her family's history." Heloise patted his arm. "I lost my vitality courting dissolution. I've nothing left to give, save whatever artifice I can employ to save Emmaline from the clutches of that dreadful man."

"Ah, I knew you had a plan."

"Plan would be overstatement," she said. "I've created a path. We'll see where it leads. It's all I have energy for, Colin. Let us bow to that reality."

"Not until I can kiss you," he murmured, his voice low. "Thought of it for decades."

Heloise arched a brow. "How very bold."

Colin knew a challenge when he heard one. When he brought his face to hers, he had the satisfaction of seeing her eyes widen.

Her mouth tasted as delicious as he imagined all these years. Her pillowy lips yielded to his pressure—and returned it, to his delight. Colin's arm slid along the back of the bench, grazed her nape. He felt her little shiver. Perhaps she wasn't as jaded as she claimed.

And then Colin was lost, robbed of all thought as Heloise Alcott swept him into her magic. He was no longer that green youth, but a man of years and substance willing to give her as much or little as she would take. He yearned to carry her back to his cabin and sink into her.

Her kisses left him reeling, desperate to capture her power and return it full measure.

But at length she pulled back to study him.

"Dear Colin." Her breathy voice had him hoping she was as affected as he was. "You still have stars in your eyes."

Then she put a hand to his chest and gently pushed him away.

Colin covered her hand with his much larger one. "I see you as you are, Heloise. Not with the eyes of a twenty-two-year-old. You are the most vital woman I know."

She gave him a sad smile. "I cannot keep up with a man of your vigor. And you would tire of having to modulate all that pent-up masculinity."

When he started to speak, Heloise put her fingertip to his lips. "Your heart was broken once. I refuse to be the next woman who does so. And truthfully, I have grown bitter. It is a battle to keep that from coloring the days I have left on this earth. It would poison us."

She rose. "A few stolen hours with you would take my breath away. But there would be an 'after' that I'm not up to. Let us agree to take this no farther."

"Take your breath away, would I?" Despite the wound she'd opened, Colin managed a smile.

Heloise planted a soft kiss on his cheek. "Of that, my dear, I have no doubt."

Chapter Eighteen

MR. TAVISH EYED Emmaline's walking stick. "Lead gives it weight. Helped with those drunken sots in London, but you needed both hands. Can you wield it with only one hand?"

They stood in the field behind the cottage, with Peter an eager onlooker for her first training session. Mr. Tavish had found her breeches and a shirt so she could move more freely. They were a welcome change from her limited wardrobe.

Emmaline held her stick with one hand above her head. To her chagrin, it wobbled. "But I can manage with two hands," she insisted.

He shook his head. "One hand will be occupied with fending off your assailant, who will not stand idly by and wait for you to fit two hands to the thing. Ludicrous notion."

Emmaline glared at him. "You might be kinder in pointing out my follies."

"Kindness never defeated any attacker, Mrs. Stanhope."

"Emmaline," she corrected. "We're at the point, I think, where you must use my given name.

Don't worry. I shan't return the favor." He was an earl, after all.

He shot her a fulminating look. "Let us have done. You are Emmaline and I am Robert. No need to go on about it."

Robert appeared to be in a volatile mood. Perhaps it was the setting—his mother's home. But Emmaline suspected another reason. "It's clear you don't wish to train me. Why?"

Crossing his arms over his chest, he regarded her with a mulish expression. "There's no need. *I* will see to your protection."

"I see. You will rush to my aid if I'm abducted, robbed, or otherwise insulted?" Emmaline gave him a measuring look. "Always? Or only when delusions of grandeur strike?"

"I have an idea," Robert growled. "Lacerate your assailant with that sharp tongue of yours. That will send him fleeing into the Thames."

Emmaline supposed she deserved that. Bitterness had seeped in as she sensed Mr. Maitland's net closing around her. "I know you mean well, but—"

"What I *mean* is that a woman shouldn't fight criminals, especially alone."

"In an ideal world, perhaps," she said. "But that's not the world I live in. I've a hobbled leg and no way to travel the city other than by foot. I must be prepared to defend myself."

For a moment he was silent. Then, gently, he took the walking stick from her.

"Keep the stick down, pointed and angled in

front of you." He demonstrated. "Difficult for an opponent to seize, and you won't appear threatening."

"But…doesn't lowering my stick expose the rest of me to attack?"

"You'll *look* vulnerable," he said. "An attacker is thrown off guard. When he moves in, you react, and this way you'll need but one hand to do so. Go ahead. Try to attack me."

Emmaline lunged. He brought the stick up, stopping a hair's breadth from hitting her.

"Now you try." Robert handed the stick to her.

With that, he rushed her.

She wasn't ready. Momentum carried him into her with a force that robbed her of breath. His big, burly arms wrapped around her.

Robert was a mountain of a man. His rock-hard torso was an unbreachable wall. And this full-on contact felt…overwhelming. Emmaline caught the scents of leather and sturdy wool. Her hands, the only part of her not imprisoned, curled around his forearms.

Abruptly, he released her. "You didn't follow directions."

"You gave me no time to prepare," Emmaline said.

"Neither will an attacker."

This time as he rushed at her, she brought the stick up fast—inadvertently delivering a blow to an intimate part of his anatomy. Robert reeled backward and doubled over in pain.

Horrified, Emmaline rushed to him. "I didn't intend—"

"Next time, can you simply *pretend* to hit me?" He grimaced. "Let's go again."

She hesitated. "You are recovered?"

"Enough not to want to belabor the matter."

For the next hour, they worked on moves that jammed the stick under the attacker's chin or at his eyes. They also practiced counterattacks and shifting it from one hand to the other.

"Remember: You can't match an attacker's strength," he told her. "Be clever instead. When he lunges, move your feet to catch him off balance. Opposite of what he expects."

Peter, watching avidly, applauded every joust. "Can I be next? I want to learn, too!"

"After she gets this right," Robert said.

By the time they were done, Emmaline was tired, and her leg ached. Would she remember her training in a real attack? How would she manage in skirts?

Robert read her doubts. "Don't underestimate yourself. Everyone has a fight reflex. When the time comes, you'll be fierce as any warrior."

"Fierce?" With a weary sigh, she sat on the grass. "Hardly."

He knelt, his face inches from hers. "You are the fiercest person I know."

She blinked. "You give me too much credit."

"Not enough." Robert shook his head. "All this time, not nearly enough."

Heat bloomed in his gaze—and in the space between them.

"You don't give up," he said gruffly. "You try,

and when you fail you try again. Fierce resolve, I'd call it."

He rose, extended a hand and pulled her to her feet. Emmaline was tempted to lean into that solid chest, sink into his strength. What it would be like to rely on this man, to have him protect her? To trust in someone other than herself?

For a moment their gazes locked in wordless dialog. His eyes searched her features. Settled on her mouth, sharpened with intent. A magnetic force pulled Emmaline into that gray gaze and set off a fluttering deep inside.

Robert's hands slid to her waist.

"My turn!" Peter tugged on Robert's sleeve.

He released her. His gaze was hooded, as if he regretted what he'd let her see. Then he turned to Peter.

But Emmaline had seen.

Something fundamental had changed. Some hitherto unknown chord lurking silently within her suddenly sounded in full, unadulterated glory.

⸻❦⸻

"Come walk with me, Mr. Maitland."

Drew eyed Miss Alcott warily. "Is this another lesson?"

She laughed softly, melodically.

Quite beautifully, really.

"I am intent on a walk," she said. "Exercise seems to help my condition."

She took his arm. "If you wish to continue our *instruction*"—she drew the word out, so it held a world of promise— "I am not averse."

When she raised her eyes to his, they held a beguiling twinkle—which left Drew oddly willing to escort her over hill and dale. He shook his head to clear the cobwebs and reminded himself not to be fooled by her tricks.

They walked in silence for a few minutes. He let her set the pace while he tried to recover his equilibrium. Her breathing had gone more rapid with the exertion, and he found himself listening to each soft intake.

What was her "condition," anyway? He knew she wasn't entirely well, but his knowledge of female miseries was nonexistent. Ought they to stop and rest?

Drew opened his mouth to suggest it. She forestalled him. "Let us get to the matter at hand. The information you seek from me. What is it?"

"How your niece killed Burwell," he stated bluntly.

There. That ought to give her pause.

Miss Alcott smiled. "If Emmaline killed Mr. Burwell, why would I tell you?"

"I have no idea. Why are you helping me now?" he demanded.

"Am I?" Her look was coy.

Drew sighed. "I do not know what you are about, madam."

"I believe you suffer from a failure of imagination, Mr. Maitland."

They walked for a few more minutes as Drew pondered that.

"If your niece is innocent," he said at last, "you may have information that would exonerate her.

Therefore, it is in your interest—and hers—to tell me what you know."

She patted his arm. "Clever. You used the fact that I can only have Emmaline's welfare in mind. You are making progress."

Drew felt unaccountably pleased at her praise.

"Suppose I told you that it was not Emmaline, but I who was responsible for that man's death?"

He frowned. "You'd have to persuade me. You are by your own admission frail. I can't see how you could force a man to stand immobile in the face of certain death."

Her gaze narrowed. "But you can imagine Emmaline could? A woman who has only ever brought dedication and diligence and honor to every task she takes on?"

"Smokescreen," he said dismissively. "It brings me no closer to the truth."

"I wasn't aware you were seeking truth. You've decided that Emmaline is your killer. You need an arrest to help your career. It doesn't matter whether she is innocent or no."

"Stop protecting her," he growled.

Miss Alcott leveled a gaze at him. "Here is truth: Emmaline's father was a noted scholar but an idiot in many ways. Her mother died in childbirth, so she grew up under the burden of her father's guilt and benign neglect. Upon his death, she found he left such debts that she had to sell his house to pay them and move into a ramshackle cottage on Oxford Street. It was her fondest wish to live on such a street, with the Mail kicking up its filth, drunkards using her stoop for rest and the discharge of bodily fluids, and the vermin who view themselves as rightful tenants."

Drew took a deep breath. The woman was skilled with a story; he'd give her that.

"Do not try to play on my heartstrings," he warned.

"Certainly not," she said easily. "Let us suppose that in these penurious circumstances, Emmaline became aware that her aunt, who had never been one to honor family ties—she was too busy in her scandalous life on stage and off—was forced by illness to leave her lively life and desperately needed a home. Let us suppose that Emmaline took her in and that the two women, to keep a roof over their heads, turned to the usual sewing and the like. And when that was not enough, they took up fortunetelling and eventually formed a matrimonial agency to profit from the human craving for wedded bliss."

"Not everyone has such cravings," Drew pointed out.

"What you mean is that you do not."

He did not disagree.

"Let us suppose," she went on, "that Emmaline sought unusual treatments for her aunt, the usual ones having failed. She found a physician known for mesmerism. She visited the man, persuaded him to teach her his skill. Thus armed, she waited for the next lonely bachelor to engage our bottom-drawer matrimonial services, mesmerized him, forced him to turn over his funds and, to forestall the possibility of his coming to his senses, induced him to stand in the path of the Mail and die."

Miss Alcott gifted him a beatific smile.

"That's what happened, isn't it?" Drew eyed her hopefully.

"I thought you were smarter than that, Mr. Maitland. But it seems you are no less willing to swallow a shaggy tale than my audiences at Covent Garden."

"But I know you visited that physician—Dr. Black."

"A charlatan. He is incapable of teaching anything. Much puffed up about his own importance." She shot him a secretive smile. "Perhaps less so after our visit."

Her violet gaze, less charitable now, bored into his. "I could spin you another tale. One where your Mr. Burwell, desperate as he felt the government close in on his treasonous activities, decides to take his own way out. So desperate, in fact, that he stands in the path of the Mail and watches his destiny approach with a thundering of hooves and the trumpeting of a horn."

"Though if *I* decided to end it all," she added. "I would choose something less painful. An excess of laudanum, coupled with a spirited toast to my full but fading life."

Her eyes grew watery. "If I can even find someone to toast me these days. I fear I am close to being forgotten."

Drew was pulled into her limpid gaze. Maybe *she* had learned Black's skills.

But no, it was simply the way her body inhabited

her words. A tear so small he could have missed it welled in the corner of one eye. Her bottom lip trembled so imperceptibly he might have missed that as well. Her shoulders slumped. He watched as she retreated into herself, into a place so bleak it threatened to destroy her.

Drew felt her overwhelming grief, her regret for mistakes too numerous to count. Her deep and abiding self-loathing, as if her life had been for naught. As if she were ready, finally, to fade away for all time.

He leaned toward her, wanting to offer comfort—anything to ease her pain.

Except: He *never* offered comfort.

He'd been had.

"Miss Alcott." Drew was so shaken that he barely recognized his own voice.

Slowly, she raised her violet gaze to his. Sly amusement lurked there.

"I do not think anything about you has faded," Drew said. "Indeed, I deeply regret never having seen the full glory of your talent on the stage."

He caught her hand and brought it to his lips in tribute.

Chapter Nineteen

"ONE OR TWO of you can sail with me to Staffa tomorrow," Robert said.

"I'll come!" Peter said.

Robert kept his expression neutral. But an overenthusiastic lad could get into much trouble on Staffa. "In that case, Gibbons will come to supervise."

Gibbons looked dubious. "I am not a sailor."

"It's not far out—Inner Hebrides."

"Open water, nevertheless." Gibbons coughed. "I'm prone to seasickness."

"You'd miss an extraordinary sight," Robert persisted. "Volcanic columns the likes of which you'll not see again."

Gibbons remained silent. Not budging.

"I will come," Emmaline said.

Robert suppressed a sigh. He ought to have said he'd take anyone *but* Emmaline. After their stick-fighting session, he feared his grudging admiration of her pluck and determination had surpassed "grudging." Not to mention that odd moment—had he almost kissed her?

"Have you ever been sailing?" he asked her gruffly.

"No. My familiarity with water is limited to the wafting odors of the Thames."

Robert frowned. "I suppose neither of you swim?"

Peter shook his head. "But I'm not afraid."

"I don't swim," Emmaline said. "That doesn't dissuade me."

Of course not. *Fierce resolve.*

Still, he'd be fine with one non-swimmer. Not two—especially if one was a boy in need of close supervision.

"No sailing until you learn to swim," he told Peter.

The lad looked crestfallen.

"Perhaps while we're away, Mr. Gibbons can teach you," Robert said. Might give the man something to erase that dejected look he'd worn since they arrived in Oban.

***

Emmaline had never been on a boat. Which might seem odd, since she lived on an island. But she never thought of England as such. And the Thames bore no resemblance to the bobbing seas she faced this morning.

Tentatively, she put a foot onto the boat Robert had hired. The thing dipped alarmingly. He put out a hand to steady her, and she managed an inelegant lurch onto the little craft.

"Might be bumpy," he warned as she perched on the bench. "You'll need to hold on."

He had other instructions—watch out for the

boom during a turn, the boom being the big horizontal pole attached to the mast and a sail. She was to sit where he told her and wear an odd collar made of cork, which would float if they capsized—though he assured her they would not.

As the craft made its way from Oban's harbor into the sound, noisy gulls flew above, and sunlight danced across the sparkling waves. Emmaline was eager for this new adventure. There was a lightness to the day, as if her cares were left onshore. For once, she could put worry aside.

Robert busied himself with the ropes and lines that controlled the two sails. He had tied his hair back, but some of it escaped, and the wind whipped it around his head like a sandy halo.

Mindful of his warning, Emmaline kept a tight grip on her seat. She wore yesterday's breeches, enjoying the ease of movement they afforded.

Robert balanced easily on the balls of his feet and seemed not to notice the rocking. When he turned and gifted her with a smile, it nearly took her breath away.

"After Mull, we'll have open water," he said. "From there Staffa isn't far."

Staffa had hexagonal rocks, he explained, as on Arthur's Seat but more spectacular. They must be a wonder to put such a look on his face, Emmaline thought. She'd never seen him so content. She found her own excitement building and barely noticed the occasional spray of water as they sailed toward the little island.

"Tide will be out," Robert said. "We'll get to see the cave. Haven't been there in years. It's where I first grew fascinated by rocks and their secrets."

She smiled. "You found your passion. I'm envious."

He tilted his head and regarded her. "Is there nothing that rises to a passion for you? Your marriage business or…something else?"

Emmaline shook her head. "My father's passion was my mother, and he lost her when I was born. I've taken that lesson to heart. I don't have passions. I do what I must to survive."

How sad that sounded. But it was the truth. Passion was a luxury she could not afford.

"As for the marriage agency," she went on, "I had the naïve notion we would unite couples in a love match. But most weren't looking for that. They simply wanted resolution."

"Resolution—settling the matter, you mean?"

"Yes. To be done with the chore of finding a spouse. And sadly, men don't view wives as equals. Wives are simply ballast that allows them to go about their lives without bothering with details like the house, food, and a warm bed." Emmaline hesitated. "That was you, I thought."

Robert sat next to her. "Not looking for ballast. But it's an interesting concept."

"Women like Miranda Fitzwilliam—she'd have been an excellent wife for you, by the way— face hard choices," she said. "To avoid becoming penniless spinsters, they must settle for an indifferent husband with no thought of attending to her needs or opinions."

"Miss Fitzwilliam seemed pleasant, aside from

her distress at your abduction," Robert said. "But even if I'd been looking for a bride, she wouldn't suit."

"Why not? She's quite agreeable."

His free and easy smile surprised her. Perhaps he, too, had left some cares onshore. "If the rocks on Staffa were merely 'agreeable,' we wouldn't be on this boat heading toward them."

Then he fell silent. They sat side by side watching the sunlight glance off the waves. Doubtless his thoughts were on the rocks they were soon to see.

"Tide's favorable," he said finally. "Be there in no time."

———

With Staffa's crosswind, bringing in the boat required all of Robert's attention. There was no dock, only a short pier and pilings. That would soon change. Walter Scott and his ilk had sung the uninhabited island's praises. It was only a matter of time before tourists descended.

Today, happily, they had the place to themselves. After Robert moored the boat and helped Emmaline disembark, she eyed the steep hill of jumbled rocks.

"Oh." Then: "It's quite high, isn't it?"

He had forgotten about the climbing.

The tiny island was only a half mile long, but much of it was straight up. A thin metal handrail had been hammered into the rocks, but it stopped halfway to the top. Even with railing, the climb was precarious.

"I've been an idiot," Robert said. "Didn't think about footing."

"You're here to study rocks," Emmaline said. "I insist you do so. I will manage."

Once more, her determination captivated him. The cave was at sea level, so perhaps that was possible. But they'd have to navigate jagged stone pillars on the way.

"Cave's what most people come to see," Robert said. "We'll start there."

Emmaline tucked her hand into the crook of his arm. He moved slowly, making sure her balance was solid before progressing to the next rock. They used the shorter columns as steppingstones, the rock wall to their right as an anchor.

As they neared the cave, the path grew harder. Emmaline held his arm more tightly, leaning into him as they picked their way across the stones.

Unfamiliar longing seeped into Robert. Beyond physical work at digs, he'd never felt his size and strength served any purpose. Now, somehow, it did. With Emmaline's hand locked around his arm, he felt he could move mountains—if it meant keeping her safe.

At last, they stood at the cave's arched entry, carved by the sea over millions of years.

"Fingal's Cave," Robert said. "Legend says it belonged to a giant, Fingal, whose bridge connected this part of Scotland with Ireland. The same hexagonal rocks—columnar basalt—lie directly across in Ireland. Like those we saw at Arthur's Seat, but more precise."

"I've never seen anything like this." Emmaline's voice was hushed.

"Peek in. I'll hold you." Robert put his arms around her waist as she leaned over the rushing waters and peered into the massive cavity.

Waves smashed against the columns, creating echoes, seemingly in harmony. The sound never failed to thrill him. "That's the sea rushing in," he said. "Some say it sounds like—"

"Singing," Emmaline said in wonder. "The cave is singing!"

She felt the cave's magic. That surprised him. He'd have bet Emmaline Stanhope hadn't a fanciful bone in her body. It struck him that although they had spent much time in one another's company, they didn't really know each other.

He had secrets that would never see the light of day. Perhaps she did, too.

They listened to the cave's sea song for a long time. Robert kept his arm around Emmaline—so she wouldn't fall, he told himself. Her delight was obvious—he caught a glimpse of those dimples. After a while, bigger waves began to narrow the passage. It was time to leave. He kept a firm grip on her hand as they retraced their steps over the stones.

Emmaline was fascinated by the six-sided rocks. "I didn't know nature was capable of such precision. It's as if the whole island is devoted to symmetry."

Robert told her about volcanoes and lava edges cooling faster than the molten center. He blathered on about the bottom and top of the flow cooling at different rates, about contraction and fractures and columnar jointing.

Then he realized how pedantic he sounded. "This must be boring for you."

"No." She smiled. "May we sit here for a while? I want to imprint this on my brain."

They sat on some flat rocks with the rock wall behind them for support. A few curious gulls hovered nearby. The breeze disrupted her tight bun, and as Robert watched those errant tendrils, he was in no hurry to leave.

"Thank you for showing me this," Emmaline said. "For telling me about the giant. I wonder how the story came to be?"

"Humans want to understand their world, especially odd bits like hexagonal rocks. A giant's bridge appeals because it's fanciful." He hesitated. "Also strikes a deeper chord."

"How?"

"Land's where roots lie," Robert said. "The notion that Scotland and Ireland once were joined speaks to a longing for…wholeness, I suppose. Welsh have a name for it—*hiraeth*. It's a longing for a home that maybe never was. Ancient places to which we can't return. It is in the wind, the rocks, the waves. Nowhere and everywhere."

Emmaline was staring at him. Was that a tear in her eye?

"Sorry. That was bleak," he said.

She was quiet. Then: "Is Scotland that place for you? It calls you still?"

"No—that is, I don't think so." And yet, a kernel

of truth lay in those words. Robert cleared his throat. "We should return to Oban."

"But you came here to study rocks," she protested. "You've not done that."

He hadn't. But as he stared into that blue gaze, Robert realized he could happily sit with her for hours. He leaned back against the rock wall and allowed himself to savor the sun's benevolent warmth and a moment out of time.

A quiet peace flowed over him. For the first time in a long time, he felt content.

———✍———

"Hell."

The growl made Emmaline bolt upright. She must have dozed. Evidently, both of them had. Robert stood looking out to sea. A scowl swept his features.

"Should've left an hour ago. That dark out there is a squall, moving fast. We won't make Oban. Might manage Iona."

She followed his gaze. Menacing clouds bathed the sky in shadow and gloom. The sun had vanished. The sea had kicked up, and an ominous gray column connected sky and water where the horizon ought to have been. Rain, she thought. Or worse.

They needed to hurry. But Emmaline couldn't. Not over those rocks.

Without a word, Robert lifted her into his arms and swiftly covered the distance to the boat. As the storm rushed furiously toward them, he launched the little craft. The turbulent seas bore no resemblance to the calm waters that had brought them here.

"Watch the boom," Robert shouted over the wind. "Have to put the squall at our back."

Emmaline ducked as the pole came at her and the boat lurched violently.

Moments later, she was curled at the bottom of the craft, clutching the bench and praying for solid ground. The boat pitched angrily; her stomach heaved with it.

Robert worked the rigging in some incomprehensible fashion she desperately hoped would get them to land fast and in one piece. The violent tossing didn't seem to faze him. Emmaline knew he'd served in the Navy, but how in the world did one get used to this?

He moved fluidly between lines and tiller, his muscled limbs managing both against the tempest. Should she offer to help? But she wouldn't know what to do. Trying to stand would court disaster. Even now, clinging to the bench, she might be flung overboard at any moment.

The sea swept in, drenching them. Emmaline fought her rebelling innards. She lost all sense of time. Were they making any progress? She saw nothing beyond the dark and angry sea.

When at last the boat slowed, she dared a peek. A shoreline loomed. But her relief was short-lived. The storm pummeled them anew with a ferocity Zeus himself might have unleashed.

"Can't put in here," Robert shouted. "We'll make for the sound."

It took another half hour before he brought the boat to where the water, if not calm, was less violent. As he heaved the craft onto land, Emmaline clawed her way to a sitting position.

Suddenly the storm erupted with new fury over them. They'd outrun it, but only just.

Robert bent his face to hers. "Are you well?"

Emmaline's rueful laugh came out a sob.

He put his arms under her and lifted her out of the boat.

"I-I can walk," Emmaline protested.

But when Robert set her on her feet, her knees buckled.

This time, he ignored her protests and swept her up as if she were a defeated toddler.

"Don't worry," he murmured. "I have you."

Emmaline didn't even try to fight him.

***

"Where are we?" she asked.

Robert glanced down at her. "Iona. Street of the Dead."

She eyed the sea of flat stones and the upright ones beyond them. "It's a…graveyard?"

"Yes."

"Put me down, please. If I am to pass among the dead, I prefer to be upright."

Robert set her on the path. "Can you walk?"

"I think so." She shivered. "Is there shelter?"

"Here. St. Oran's Chapel." He pulled her through an arched opening into a small stone structure. It was derelict and crumbling, but the roof and walls were intact.

Emmaline shot him a game smile. "At least we are out of the storm."

"My fault. Ought to have left Staffa—"

"Staffa was a wonder," she said. "I will remember it always."

Robert felt the same. Something had happened to him there. Though they hadn't explored the island, he'd been utterly captivated—by his companion, not the rocks.

But he'd nearly brought them to disaster, falling asleep and failing to take note of the coming storm. They'd had to flee for their lives, but their little craft wasn't equipped to ride out twenty-footers. He had tried to run downwind, but the storm constantly changed on him. They'd barely made Iona before nightfall.

Emmaline sank to the chapel floor, clearly exhausted. Dusk sent only feeble light into the ancient chapel through two windows on either side of the tiny altar and from the arched entry, which had no door and was open to the elements.

Robert sat beside her. "Iona has better accommodations. The abbey is nearby. There's even an inn on the other side of the island."

She shook her head. "I am too tired to walk. My legs are like jelly."

"I'd carry—"

"No," Emmaline said. "It's lowering to be carted about like a newborn lamb."

Robert hesitated. "We're here for the night then."

She looked around. "Those flat slabs on the floor could serve as a pallet."

"They are graves."

She blinked. "Oh."

"Scottish kings and clan chiefs are buried here," Robert said. "More lie outside. Iona is hallowed ground for centuries of powerful rulers, many of them barbarians and murderers."

Emmaline bit her bottom lip. "Then I suppose the chapel is haunted."

"Depends on whether you believe in ghosts."

"I don't—though this place might change that."

Robert nodded. "At least one soul was sacrificed here—Oran. Volunteered to be buried alive to sanctify the place and prevent the walls from falling down."

"They haven't fallen, so I'd say he managed it." She studied the stones. "It's too dim to read the inscriptions."

"None legible now, though a few symbols survive. The ship on that one, for example"—Robert pointed to a slab angled against the wall— "likely one of the MacDonalds. They controlled these islands hundreds of years ago. Clan Donald, it was then."

"That arched recess near the altar looks like a crown," Emmaline said.

"Tomb, likely more than one. Macbeth's one of the kings here. Other kings go back to the beginning of Scotland. Their coffins would have been carried along the Street of the Dead."

Emmaline was studying him. "Why go elsewhere for digs when you can work closer to home in places like this?"

"Scotland's not home." Despite that *hiraeth*

nonsense. "Oxford is where I teach, prepare research." He hesitated. "But I've had another site in mind—Skye, an island to the north. Cornwall can be overrun with researchers...." He halted. "This can't interest you."

Her hand touched his arm. "On the contrary. It's intensely interesting."

Talking was better than not, Robert thought. Otherwise, they had only descending darkness and the chapel's centuries of gloom.

"A type of limestone seems to correlate with fossils," he said. "Specifically, carbonate deposits in the Jura Mountains along the French–Swiss border. Rock strata suggest that area was once a vast desert. Then something changed, created a more favorable environment for living creatures. You can see that change in the Jura deposits."

"But we don't have those mountains here."

"That is what's interesting," he said. "The same limestone is found on Skye. No researchers are working there."

"Then perhaps you should be," Emmaline said.

Robert shrugged. "Studying fossils is a new field. Not even a name for it. And if there's no name, scholars tend not to recognize it."

"You do not strike me as a man who readily accepts such limitations."

He could no longer see her features. But they sat so close that when she suddenly yawned, Robert felt it to his bones. "You're exhausted."

"And wet," she agreed. They both were.

Emmaline put her head on his shoulder. "I'll just rest my eyes for a moment."

Within seconds, she was asleep.

For a long time, Robert dared not move. Then, carefully, he eased her down in what he hoped was a more comfortable position with her head pillowed on his thigh.

Her hair had long since come loose, and it splayed out in a tangle around her head. Absently, Robert began to toy with it. That had him running his fingers through the strands, which turned into something very like caresses.

Thank God she was asleep, for his willful hand brushed across her forehead. His fingers feathered over her cheeks. His thumb grazed her lip.

Suddenly, her eyes opened. He froze.

"Robert," she murmured sleepily, "did we almost capsize?"

"No." He hesitated. "But it was a near thing."

"Thank you for saving us." Her hand caught his, pressed his rough palm to her lips. "I didn't want to die today."

Her eyes closed. She drifted off once more.

Robert's world tilted on its axis.

Chapter Twenty

"TOO COLD!" PETER shrieked.

"Think of it as invigorating," John admonished.

"I want to go home!"

John sighed. "You wanted to learn to swim."

"He's very grateful, Mr. Gibbons," Jenny put in quickly. She turned to her brother. "You could do with manners. Mr. Gibbons has better things to do."

The truth was that he didn't. Unless brooding and moping about and dwelling on might-have-beens and lost love counted.

After Robert and Mrs. Stanhope departed for that island, Peter's disappointment at not being allowed to go sailing settled over the lad like a dark cloud.

That tugged at John's heartstrings. And he'd had quite enough tugging at heartstrings to last a lifetime. When he asked Jenny for permission to teach Peter to swim, she looked doubtful.

"He won't come to harm," he assured her. "I am a good swimmer."

"It's not you I'm worried about," Jenny said. "He's a reckless sort."

"You won't always be able to keep him safe," John said gently. "There's no end to trouble he can get into on his own. Wouldn't it be best to give him a lifelong skill to protect himself? If he learns, perhaps Lord Kent will take him sailing the next time."

"I don't see why a toff like that—or you, for that matter—wants to help the likes of us."

He hesitated. "When the earl was near Peter's age, he faced difficult circumstances that shadow him to this day. I've come to think there's a window in a boy's life when light can come in. It closes as he hardens into manhood. Peter's ready to learn. He won't always be."

Jenny was silent for a moment. Then: "I'd want to watch."

John smiled. "Of course."

He chose the small Oban marina, where the water was calm. Peter was persuaded to put his toe in, then his legs, but balked at total immersion.

"You'll get used to it," John said. "The water will hold you up if you stop fighting it."

Peter glared at him.

"Do what Mr. Gibbons says," Jenny said. "He wants to help you."

The lad shot his sister an even darker gaze. But John saw what lurked there: fear.

"I was once afraid, too. But do you want to master the water, or let it master you?"

Peter's chin rose. Challenge registered.

"Lean back," John said. "My arm is under you. I won't let you sink."

That vow he could uphold. Others he'd failed.

Here, near the site of Portia's lonely last breaths, John felt his failure acutely. But maybe he was being too hard on himself. He'd done what he could to protect her. Perhaps it was time to accept that.

Slowly, Peter leaned back.

"That's it," John said encouragingly. "Try to relax. Let your feet come up. I'll keep my arms under you, but the water will support you."

Peter closed his eyes tightly, fearfully. But John saw the moment he decided to let go. The lad's feet floated free.

John kept his arms where they were, not really holding him up as much as reassuring the lad of his presence. He held his breath, waiting to see if Peter would panic.

But the lad was made of stronger stuff. He floated.

Peter let out a whoop of joy. "I did it!"

"Indeed, you did. Let's learn some strokes and see how far you can go."

"To forever!" Peter vowed.

Such enthusiasm, such confidence, such faith.

Had he ever been so young?

***

"It's dreary out. Pull up a chair, Mr. Maitland. Let's engage with the cards."

Drew sighed. It was indeed a drenching day, as if the lake had decided to empty itself into the clouds, which in turn unleashed all that water back on them. He joined Miss Alcott on a long sofa near a cozy fire.

He had no wish to play at cards. Cards were mindless games. More than once he witnessed some young blood, addicted to the thrill of risking all, obliterate his inheritance by foolishly staying the course when the cards were plainly against him.

Ah, but this was not to be any ordinary game. Drew watched, fascinated, as Miss Alcott pulled out a Tarot deck. Perhaps now he would learn the deceit behind her art. Still, it was strange that she offered, given the investigation.

"If you meant to put me off the scent, you're all out," Drew said. "You must know that your handbill with the Tarot death card drawing was found in Burwell's pocket."

Miss Alcott arched her brows—and exquisite they were, he couldn't help but notice. Seemed to match her hennaed hair, which was an unusual shade of—

"The death card is much misunderstood," she said gravely. "Like you."

Drew stiffened. "You know nothing about me."

She tilted her head. "Perhaps not. But the death card is about transformation. It can signal an end to something, but that doesn't mean death awaits. No more than it does for all of us."

"Grim, madam. Very grim."

She smiled. "The card signifies a new beginning. Ending the old, starting the new."

"Balderdash," he said. "It's a skeleton in black armor on horseback, skull and crossbones on the bridle. He tramples people, uncaring of their fate. That river is likely the Styx."

"Did you miss the image of the small child, offering him a flower without fear? Dawn breaking between the pillars of life? And that river—perhaps it leads not to the underworld but to the promised land."

"Metaphysical nonsense," Drew said.

Miss Alcott arched a brow. "That discomforts you, I see. Perhaps you are at a turning point in your own life, Mr. Maitland. One that could lead to the highest peaks or the bowels of Hell. Change is inevitable. Resist at your peril."

Drew scowled. "You can't make the card about me. It's but a card."

"On the contrary. The Tarot is always personal. It's a mirror of your soul. Are you afraid of what you might see?" Without waiting for his response, she picked up the deck. "Since you are impatient, we'll start with a simple three-card spread."

As Miss Alcott started to lay out the cards on the sofa between them, Drew reached over and stilled her hand. "How do I know you haven't already ordered them?"

She offered him the deck. "Shuffle and cut them yourself."

He did, feeling like a fool.

When he returned the deck to her, she laid out three cards, then turned them over from their sides. "To keep their orientation as they were dealt," she explained. "Whether the card is upright or reversed is important."

Drew feigned boredom as Miss Alcott studied the first card.

"Three of Pentacles, upright. You think of

yourself as masterful." She eyed him slyly. "I wonder if that is warranted."

She moved to the next card, which depicted some old English chap in leggings and a cap. "Page of Pentacles. Change indeed. There will be a test, to see if you are worthy."

Then she shook her head mournfully. "Alas, the final card—the star—is reversed."

To Drew, it simply showed a naked woman kneeling. "A tragedy involving a woman who lacks sense to clothe herself?"

Miss Alcott's violet eyes held pity. "It's a sign of despair. Loss of hope."

"Perhaps it's your performance that is lacking."

Drew thought she might take that bait, but Miss Alcott merely regarded him calmly. "You are out of balance. Missing opportunities. Not the sort that further your career, but those that nourish the soul. I fear for your future if you remain on this course."

"Dear God, woman. You produce no evidence—"

"You abducted my niece," Miss Alcott said in a steely tone.

"She was unharmed."

"You pretended to rescue her."

"I was trying to solve a murder," he protested.

"You were trying to advance your career at the expense of an innocent woman."

Drew scoffed. "Innocent? I think not."

Shards glinted amid the violet gaze. "I have lived quite a tawdry existence, Mr. Maitland. I've seen life from all sides, including some you cannot imagine, even at your jaded young age. I know what innocence looks like. For all her grit, Emmaline is the merest babe."

That gave him pause. Then he reminded himself that Mrs. Stanhope's guilt or innocence was a matter for the courts—not him—to decide.

"I have not wronged your niece," Drew insisted. "If the evidence warrants, she'll be arrested. I'll have merely played a part."

"There is a world of difference between playing a part and living it."

"Pithy, perhaps even poetic, but irrelevant," he said disdainfully.

She leaned forward, granting him a tantalizing glimpse of her considerable charms. Drew was not unaffected. Which, he told himself, was absurd.

"What I see in these cards is that you are at a turning point," Miss Alcott said. "Will you be a man of courage? Or one who seals his fate as hopeless and empty?"

Drew rose abruptly. "As ever, madam, you have proved entertaining."

He strode away without a backward glance.

But he felt a stabbing pain, like a knife embedded between his shoulder blades.

Robert barely slept. He dared not move for fear of waking Emmaline, or worse, having her slide onto the rough stone floor. And the unforgiving wall behind him didn't encourage sleep.

Night enshrouded them, as thick as whatever mysteries lurked in those long-dead bones.

He had plumbed the secrets of the earth long enough to know that truth could be pried from even the most inanimate stone. He spent some of the long night imagining the history of the kings and chiefs who rested here, and he did not delude himself that they were all heroes.

Perhaps they were laughing at him for the odd vigil he kept over the sleeping form of Emmaline Stanhope. In the impenetrable dark, the sensation of her head pillowed on his thigh threatened to banish rational thought, no matter that he tried to contemplate the Jura strata.

Alas, his thoughts strayed to the feel of her mouth against his palm. Her tangled hair slipping through his fingers. The softening of her blue gaze as sleep summoned her.

Inevitably, fatigue won out. Deep into the night Robert slid to the floor without resolving the inconvenient complexity of his relationship with Emmaline. And if he dreamed of a time when kisses were real instead of illusory, he knew better than to mistake dream for reality.

Dawn nudged him awake. Emmaline was sprawled atop him, her slow, even breathing the only sound besides his own thundering pulse. Her dark eyelashes fluttered. Opened.

Confusion, then awareness, bloomed in those sapphire depths.

Gingerly, she pushed herself to a sitting position. She looked flushed, though perhaps that was the rosy blush of dawn. Robert tried to gauge whether she had recovered from their ordeal. He'd failed her profoundly, savoring those sun-dappled moments on Staffa until it was nearly too late. Would she loathe him for that and for the night passed in macabre ruins?

Remarkably, she seemed unfazed. Those blue eyes were as direct and intelligent as ever. From what he could see, the damage was superficial. Her hair was gloriously disheveled. Her breeches were beyond saving, as were his clothes. Minor stuff.

"Are you well?" Robert asked.

"Yes." She smiled. "Since it seems you served as my pillow, I might ask you the same."

"Other than guilt at nearly getting you killed, I am remarkably well," he said.

"Let's dispense with guilt. It was a lovely afternoon, and we are unharmed." She hesitated. "I suppose some may draw conclusions from the fact we passed the night together."

That hadn't occurred to him. But she was right.

"Despite the fact," she added, "that we weren't together in a...fuller sense."

Robert tried to banish thoughts of what a "fuller sense" might be.

"If I continue my abysmal failure of a marriage agency"—Emmaline shot him a self-deprecating smile— "people may form an entirely different idea of what I am brokering."

Ah. This was about her business. Or partly about that. He both burned and dreaded to know what her kiss on his palm meant. Likely she'd been half-asleep and didn't recall it.

"No one will learn of this," Robert assured her.

"Scotland is not London. We're hundreds of miles from that world."

"Yes." Emmaline looked pensive. "I…have made some discoveries on this trip."

Robert held his breath. Had she, too, felt the universe shift?

"You've shown me your country. I very much like the view."

Of Scotland, surely. Or Staffa.

"Leaving London was a drastic change, but I've come to see that change can be rewarding," she added. "I've been rigid. Perhaps not as much as you, but rigid nevertheless."

Robert did not pretend to misunderstand. "My rituals. Brandy and the like."

She nodded. "I resolved to finish my father's work, when I've no skill at it, no grasp of his stories, or even of who he was. It's the same with the marriage agency. I'm hopeless at it."

"Don't blame yourself. I wasn't a good client."

Emmaline studied him. "It occurs to me that you probably needed no lessons in wooing a bride. It's true you aren't skilled in social niceties. But some women have no use for those."

Some women—her?

"I came to you under false pretenses," Robert said gruffly. "Made matters worse."

Emmaline smiled. "Stepped on my feet."

"Pushed you into the mud."

"Ruined two cloaks."

Their gazes held.

"I was rude that night at the Argyle Rooms," she said. "I thought your lecture boring."

"And said so," Robert groused.

"I was wrong to do so," Emmaline conceded. "But I also wonder if the problem was that your heart wasn't in it. Yesterday, when you spoke of Skye, I sensed a new spark. Perhaps that could lead to exciting new research."

Robert shook his head. "One day, perhaps. Skye, like much of the Highlands, has unpredictable weather, much of it punishing. Cornwall has a more temperate climate that allows me to keep to a schedule."

Perhaps it was lack of sleep or being surrounded by bones of ancient titans, but Robert suddenly felt drained. It was one thing to grasp that their trip to Staffa and their night together had altered something between them, quite another to reorient his life's work.

"Science is method, facts," he said stiffly. "Digs are planned months and sometimes years in advance. Changing on a whim could be cataclysmic."

As cataclysmic as the world reshaping itself around Emmaline Stanhope.

What had he been thinking? Life must be ordered around realities, not dreams or fantasies. Emmaline wasn't aware of all that stood between them. Though he might nurture tender feelings for her, it could go no further. If she knew the truth, she'd agree.

His path was set, his legacy inescapable. Robert would not wish for more. Emmaline Stanhope was an extraordinary woman. Strong, not given to hysterics. Forthright and principled. If he ever decided to fix his attentions on a woman, it would be someone like her.

Fortunately, he was a master at keeping people at arm's length.

It was time to return them to safer waters.

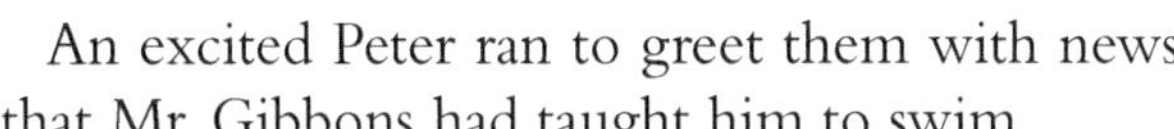

An excited Peter ran to greet them with news that Mr. Gibbons had taught him to swim.

Indeed, Mr. Gibbons looked rather pleased, Emmaline thought. The dark cloud that had followed him on this trip evidently had lifted. He seemed his usual cheerful self.

Alas, the brooding had shifted to Robert. He'd said little since they left Iona. Perhaps it was too much, that intimacy in the chapel. Moreover, she'd overstepped by suggesting he conduct research on Skye instead of Cornwall. No wonder he was irked.

Emmaline changed out of the torn and filthy breeches into her green frock. She wanted a bath but made do with a washbasin, then hurried to look for Robert. She found him in a stall in the stables grooming a horse for tomorrow's return journey.

He didn't acknowledge her, though she knew he felt her presence.

"You are angry," she said.

His attention remained on the horse. "No."

"You've scarcely spoken since Iona. You're as silent as the graves around us last night."

When Robert didn't reply, Emmaline's temper flared. "This works best if you respond when I speak. That creates the possibility of meaningful conversation."

"Not looking for meaningful conversation." Still, he did not look at her.

Emmaline stepped closer. "Is it because we passed the night together? It's left us uncomfortable and strange. I have no…expectations if that worries you."

His brows knit together. "Expectations?"

"No claim on you." Why was he making her spell it out? "I thought we had gained a measure of trust and harmony between us. But now you've shut me out."

Robert made an exasperated sound. Turned to face her. "Why must you push?"

"Because I have a *vocabulary*. Words. Civilized folk use them, Mr. Tavish."

"Robert," he growled.

Emmaline bristled. "Back to given names? But we're not friends. We're not anything."

He tossed the curry comb onto the straw. "You thought we got to harmony? Barriers falling and all that? Those barriers, madam, are there to keep you safe."

"What went wrong?" Emmaline persisted. "It was a fine trip, even with the storm, and now it seems we are farther apart than ever."

"Far apart suits me," he snapped. "You want to talk everything to death. But you wouldn't understand—"

"Your refusal to explain gives me no chance to understand." Almost, she reached for him. But his rigid bearing and stern jaw sent an unmistakable message.

Emmaline refused to let him retreat into stony silence. She drew closer. "You showed me Staffa, saved our lives in the storm, and watched over me in the chapel. Now you're angry and can no longer abide my presence. Why?"

"Not angry at you. At myself. The trip upset the equilibrium. Made me forget…things."

"What things?"

Robert ran his hand through his hair. "That it's my legacy to hurt people."

Emmaline eyed him in surprise. "I've never seen you hurt a soul."

"Because I take precautions."

What did that mean? Perhaps she should stop pushing for answers and accept that Robert Tavish was an impenetrable mystery, locked inside some box in his brain. She ought to let him be.

But she couldn't. They'd come a long way since that first day he had sat in her parlor and pretended to be in search of a wife. That man was impenetrable and cold. This man was in pain.

"The legacy," Emmaline said. "Tell me about that."

For a minute he didn't speak. A heavy silence descended. Even the horse was quiet.

This was beyond him, she thought. Whatever caused his anguish would stay buried. After all, why should he open himself to her? She was only some middling female whom circumstances had brought into his orbit. She'd made too much of a relationship founded on happenstance.

Then Robert proved her wrong.

"My father was a large man," he said. "Stood against all takers at Jackson's. Drink got in the way, and he grew mean. Used his fists against those who couldn't fight back, like my mother."

Emmaline's breath caught. "And you."

Robert nodded. "I fought him. But a lad had no chance against a man of his size. All I could do was to resolve never to be like him. My father ruined lives. I won't."

"But you aren't—"

"I am even bigger than he was." His jaw hardened. "I can never forget that."

Emmaline knew in her bones that Robert wasn't a brute. He might look strong enough to move mountains, but he used that strength for good—carefully tending her injured foot, patiently instructing Peter in weaponry, carrying her over treacherous rocks, safeguarding her from nefarious spies and even a ferocious storm.

Studying him, she saw that while the anger in his gaze had faded, stormy seas remained. Robert Tavish looked to be a man at war with himself.

She touched his arm. Willed him to remember what they had shared yesterday. "Robert."

Their gazes met.

He reached out, and his thumb brushed her cheek. "Don't know what to do with you."

Emmaline caught his hand, traced the calluses roughened by the ropes he wrangled in the storm. "These hands are for good, not ill."

She brought his palm to her lips, kissed it gently.

Robert inhaled sharply.

"You turned back into a grump, keeping me distant," Emmaline said softly.

"Keeping you distant is the only way." But he put the lie to those words as his hand slid around the nape of her neck and brought her closer still. "My legacy is to cause pain, Emmaline. I can't—won't—allow myself to lose control."

Emmaline saw his anguish, felt an answering sorrow in her own heart. She put her fingertip to his lips, silencing him. "You're strong, not mean. And you've forgotten one thing."

"What?" His voice sounded strained.

"I'm not weak," she said. "You can't hurt me."

Robert's gaze darkened. "You have a reckless streak, Emmaline Stanhope."

"Perhaps I'm only a good judge of character."

For a long, wordless moment, they stared at one another.

Then Robert lowered his mouth to hers.

His lips felt like rough silk. Abrasive. Seductive. *Magical.*

As if some silly chit's daydream of the perfect hero—a man out of time and fashion but utterly in harmony with her secret longings—had gifted her with a kiss beyond all imagining.

Robert's unshaven chin abraded her skin, awakened her every nerve. The warmth of his mouth drew from her a primitive groan. Here, amid scents of stable and horse, Emmaline understood for the first time what it was to be swept by an inexorable wave of longing.

Did he know it would be like this? Did he guess that his kiss would kindle a deep, nigh-unquenchable yearning? That she would rise on her toes so she could fling her arms around his neck and return his kiss with wild, insatiable hunger? That her pulse would stampede beyond all reason as her fingers slipped through his thick, gloriously unruly hair?

Robert's arms slid around her, but with restraint, as if she were glass.

"I want…more," Emmaline pleaded, as if that made any sense.

With a low growl, he locked her in his arms. His scent—sea brine and leather—flooded her senses as his mouth plundered hers. When she gasped for breath, his tongue demanded entry. Emmaline readily granted it. She wanted the full measure of him.

Their heights were a mismatch. She couldn't stand on her toes forever. "Robert—"

He lifted her off her feet as if she were the merest feather. Held her there—chest to chest, heart to heart. Then, slowly, he turned them around, pinning her against the wall of the stall, keeping her there with his body.

This was Robert not keeping her distant. Defying his rules.

Emmaline's spirits soared.

His big hands slid under her thighs, elevating them so her knees straddled his torso. He stepped between them, wedging their bodies even closer.

Emmaline nipped his bottom lip—softly enough not to draw blood, hard enough to let him know she could.

"It's a battle you're wanting?" Robert growled.

"Only if you're up to it." A bold doxy had taken residence in her brain.

With one hand, Robert imprisoned her hands above her head. The other skimmed up her ankles and her calves, sliding like silk until his fingers found her stocking fasteners.

"Hooks," he murmured, sounding oddly exuberant.

Some brazen instinct made Emmaline cinch her legs tightly around him. With a moan, he cupped her bare backside. She'd been in too much of a hurry to bother with a shift. Now she was glad. But his hand still held hers immobile.

"I want to touch you," she pleaded.

Instantly, Robert freed her hands. Emmaline tore at the front of his shirt, hungry to feel the hard curves of his chest under her palms—and more. Her aunt, thank the stars, had enlightened her about all manner of masculine anatomy. She wanted to learn all of him.

Emmaline arched into him with unseemly enthusiasm. Begging, as it were.

Alas, that proved too much. Robert swayed— and she with him.

Backward they tumbled into the straw, landing mere inches from the horse.

The creature snorted, gave a little stutter-step. Which brought them both to their senses.

"Dear God," he muttered. Spikes of straw stuck in his hair like a disheveled crown.

Emmaline tried to push herself upright, but his arms lingered.

"Release me," she pleaded, "before I make a greater fool of myself."

She had thrown herself at him like some shameless lightskirt. But he'd been reckless, too. And now they had only embarrassment between them.

With a wary eye at the horse, Robert eased them to a sitting position. Finally, his arms fell away from her.

"Were you harmed?" His voice was rough, ravaged.

An odd question.

"I suffered no injury unless you count *my* equilibrium," Emmaline croaked out.

Robert helped her stand. They stood there awkwardly, brushing off bits of straw. Then there was nothing to do but end this mortifying ordeal.

She turned to flee.

"Emmaline."

She halted. Met his anguished gaze.

"I didn't intend…this," Robert said.

"Nor did I." But she wasn't truly sorry.

Was he?

Silence.

Chapter Twenty-One

JOHN FELT LIGHTER than he had in years. Seeing Portia's house had removed a weight. Could he have prevented her death if he'd been there? Fate had not permitted him that, and he accepted that the answer was lost to the ages.

He mourned her still. That would never change.

Nevertheless, this new lightness gave him hope that he could yet forge a life not centered on the past. That although love was lost, life went on. It didn't have to be merely a march to that dark end they all faced.

A day after they returned to the castle, John found himself in the garden, trying to decide if any of the delightful blooms might flourish in indifferent London soil.

Heloise Alcott was sitting on one of the benches.

When she greeted him, it seemed only natural to offer his arm and take a turn around the grounds with her. They were becoming friends, he realized. John found himself confessing that he hoped to turn a new page in his life's journey, though he didn't know exactly how. For now, perhaps it was sufficient simply to plant a garden in town.

"No, you must do more," she said. "Speaking as one who has created many lives for herself out of necessity, you can't stop with simply a garden."

John eyed her uncertainly. "You refer to the many roles you've played."

"More than that. There are times when one's support dissolves." She smiled. "I do not refer to my various body parts—though age has eroded them as well—but to the men I've known. Liaisons. For one reason or another, they do not last."

His face warmed. "I see."

"I knew I liked you, John. There was not a shred of judgment in those two words."

John found himself laughing—*laughing*—at her sly tone. "You are a wonder, Miss Alcott. I only wish I had seen you perform."

"I've implored you to call me Heloise. And isn't every day a performance? It might be an easy and superficial one like a game of charades, or deeper, aimed at, say, masking grief." She studied him. "I sense that you know about that sort of performance."

Something lodged in John's throat, making it hard to swallow.

She saw. "I thought so. You mustn't think you're the only one. We all have our masquerades. If you feel the need to unburden yourself, I would be honored to hear your story."

And so, John told her the whole.

They sat on a bench. He might have shed a tear or two—but without embarrassment, thanks to her intent absorption of his tale.

An hour passed—or was it two? At the end, he felt utterly depleted.

That disappointed him—had he not convinced himself he was strong enough to start a new life, beginning with flowers? But he hadn't been ready. Something had to come first—this unburdening. *Purging.* How embarrassing.

John eyed her helplessly. What must she think of him?

"Dear John," she said softly. "You have a beautiful soul."

He eyed her uncertainly. "All these years…I have been weak."

Heloise shook her head. "The very opposite. You have strength the rest of us can only dream of having. Would you forgive a highly personal question?"

"Yes, of course."

"Portia, the woman you devoted your life to— you didn't *have* her? I mean that in the fullest, Biblical sense of the word."

John colored. "That would have dishonored both of us."

She looked him up and down. "That's noble, I suppose."

"How is it anything but unacceptable to be with another man's wife?"

"From what you have said, the man did not deserve the wife."

"That changed nothing. Principle is not malleable."

Heloise sighed. "What would you think of my life, I wonder? I have been all kinds of malleable.

I wouldn't have been drawn to acting if I viewed life as you do."

"I don't mean to judge," John said quickly.

She arched a brow. "It seems to me your principles allow for nothing but judging."

"I judge only myself," he said. "My duty to serve warred with the reality of serving an unworthy man. I tried to straddle that divide, but conscience plagued me. It is another reason I could not add another sin to the long list of ills that came with that duty."

"Ah." Her lips pursed. "You have been tormented. That changes things."

He frowned. "I do not follow you."

"Torture. Torment. Fault lines, John. They build character. We think principles are writ in stone, but they rarely are. Instead, we compromise." She smiled. "I have spent my entire life compromised, in every sense of the word. In truth, I've been a bit of a slut. Had I been born wealthy, I'd have had more choices. But I don't regret the ones I have made."

John was amazed at her frankness—and inexplicably drawn to it.

"I honor you for what you did, for taking care of her and the son who was precious to her," Heloise went on. "But would Portia want your life to end there?"

"At times *I* have wished Puhat."

"No more, I hope," she said. "Now is the time to spread your wings. Fly. Take risks. You may crash and burn like one of those new hot air balloons, but you'd have tried. That's everything.

However arduous, it's no worse than what you have lived these many years."

John cleared his throat. "I had only gotten as far as planning a new garden."

Heloise smiled. "A start."

"What about you?" he dared to ask. "Is there a new beginning in your future?"

She sighed. "One fades. Sluttery is a younger woman's game. Emmaline has been kind enough to take me in, and I fear she's determined to fix what ails me. I suspect that is holding her back from fulfilling her own dreams."

Then Heloise rose, a bit shakily. "Forgive me. I feel the need to rest."

Instantly, John was on his feet. "Will you permit me to escort you to your room?"

"Dear John. You are determined to be gallant. It's almost annoying. But I remind myself that you have unimagined depths, and that your gallantry comes from a deep well of torment and pain. And I find I tolerate that very well."

Unbidden, a smile spread across John's features.

He offered her his arm, and she took it.

❧

Drew had searched Mrs. Stanhope's room while she was in Oban. He found nothing incriminating. He also examined the two boxes, thinking they might contain information about Burwell and his treasonous activities.

Alas, they held fairy tales. Quite a lot of them. Those he *really* didn't want to read, but perhaps they held some sort of code.

"Blue Beard." A wolf masquerading as a girl's grandmother. A prince turned into a beast.

How tedious. Drew tried to remember if his parents had read such stories to him. Certainly not his father, who disdained the trappings of childhood and whose chief interest was in turning him into a masterful steward of his vast estate.

He had higher aims. The War Office held a world of opportunities for adventure and power. He meant to make it his fiefdom. Solving this case would catapult him over the laggards.

Disappointingly, a shred of doubt nagged at him. Mrs. Stanhope was the last person to see Burwell alive, but it was indisputably the Mail that killed him. Instinct argued for something nefarious but Drew lacked evidence to arrest the woman.

Heloise Alcott had dangled other possible scenarios. Was she somehow involved in the plot? Each time Drew got a fix on her, she led him in a different direction. She was toying with him, but always came back to the lack of proof against her niece.

Now the niece was back, along with Tavish and assorted other protectors. Drew was beginning to feel as if the trip to Scotland was useless. But returning empty-handed would only lower his stock. He needed a win.

Instead, he had harmless fairy tales.

<hr>

Robert eyed the various implements of war hanging on the wall in the weapons room, wondering whether Emmaline had designs on any of them. Some, like the small *sgian dubh*, perhaps ought to be put out of reach.

Just then Peter raced into the room, worry etched on his features. "Mr. Gibbons says canaries are songbirds. But Galahad doesn't sing. Is it because he's sad?"

Robert shifted his attention to the lad. "I'm no expert on birds. Likely they sing to attract a mate."

"He's lonely, then," Peter said. "What do we do?"

"Haven't seen any other canaries about, so I'm afraid he's out of luck," Robert said.

"If he could sing, others would come," Peter insisted. "Can you fix him? What about mesmer—whatever that is?"

Robert eyed him in surprise. "How do you know that word?"

"Heard you talking to Mrs. Stanhope the night of the acting-out games. She put someone in a trance. He did what she wanted and got run over by the Mail."

"You only heard part of the conversation," Robert said sternly. "No one knows why the man didn't save himself. She didn't mesmerize anyone."

"But mesmer-ing can put someone in a trance," Peter persisted. "Can you put Galahad in a trance and make him sing?"

Robert's expression softened. Franz Mesmer himself had put animals in trances. "I will look into the matter. Can't promise anything."

The lad brightened, and Robert felt guilty for

raising his hopes. The odds weren't in his favor. How did one persuade a bird to do what it should already know?

"I have a plan." Aunt Heloise swept into Emmaline's room. "Rather, it is mine and Colin's."

Emmaline eyed her warily. "A plan for what, Aunt?"

"To get rid of Mr. Maitland. Metaphorically speaking. We won't actually harm him. Do you wish to hear it?"

"I fear I am not good company just now," she said. "I've been spending far too much time in my own head. I made a fool of myself with Mr. Tavish during our trip. It's made being in his company quite awkward."

Her aunt sat on the bed. "What happened?"

"We ran into a storm on Staffa and by the time we got to Iona, it was raging in a way that prevented further travel. We were forced to pass the night in an ancient chapel."

"I see."

"It was unavoidable. Nothing untoward happened. But after, in Oban, he was angry and withdrawn." Emmaline hesitated. "Then he kissed me and made it worse."

Aunt Heloise arched a brow. "My dear, a kiss has never made anything worse."

"The kiss went wrong—well, better. Harder. Deeper." Emmaline closed her eyes in mortification. "We fell into the straw. Next to a horse."

Her aunt clapped her hands. "And were overcome with passion!"

"With *regret*," Emmaline corrected. "Before, we had achieved a camaraderie of sorts. I'd give anything to go back in time and not make a fool of myself."

"There are all kinds of foolishness in this world, Em," Aunt Heloise said. "The only real fools are those who close their eyes to truth."

"The truth is that my behavior was shameful."

Her aunt frowned. "Do not let your character be judged by someone else's rules, Em. The only rules that matter are those you choose to live by."

"Even by my own standards, I was an idiot. Brazen. Out of control. I didn't know I had such yearnings. It was dreadful."

Aunt Heloise studied her. "Was it, though? So very dreadful?"

Emmaline sighed. "Not at the time. Only after. We were both mortified."

"Following your instincts isn't a mistake. People who ignore them are as good as dead inside. They never challenge or redefine themselves."

"I haven't the luxury of redefining myself," Emmaline said.

Aunt Heloise touched her arm. "It saddens me for you to deny yourself pleasure to take care of me. I will survive. And if not, I have lived an interesting life. I don't ask more."

Emmaline pulled her into a hug. "You are no burden, Aunt. And pleasure is an extravagance for others, not me."

"Pleasure is for those with the courage and

sense to take it. A man like Mr. Tavish is a *world* of pleasure. Do not deny yourself that, dear. Or his kisses."

"I have little experience in kisses," Emmaline said. "One or two of Father's students, but theirs were wet and disgusting. A teacher at Miss Warwick's, a lecherous roué. His kiss was dry and disgusting. Kissing Robert was not like those."

"I should think not," Aunt Heloise murmured. "Desire will out, dear."

Emmaline sighed. "I doubt he truly desires me. I'm not beautiful or worthy or—"

"Nonsense. How *you* determine your worth is the only measure that matters." Aunt Heloise looked thoughtful. "Nevertheless, the relationship has been altered. What to do?"

"Avoid one another."

Her aunt rolled her eyes. "Avoidance never solved a thing. Women ought to know what they want and take it. Meanwhile, would you like to be the witches?"

"Witches?"

Her aunt smiled. "The play's the thing wherein we'll catch the conscience of the king."

Emmaline eyed her in alarm. "You know I am not good at performing."

"I need women, dear," Aunt Heloise said impatiently. "I can't play all the female parts."

<hr>

Emmaline's aunt decreed at dinner that they were to mount *Macbeth*. Robert was appalled to learn he was expected to play a part. What he wanted was to return to England and prepare for his next dig.

No, there was one thing he wanted more: to turn back time and undo that ill-fated trip with Emmaline. He had failed her on two fronts: when that storm nearly doomed them in Staffa, and in Oban, when he abandoned every principle he held dear.

To make matters worse, he'd babbled on about his brute of a father. A grown man ought to be able to put the past behind him. But as much as Robert tried not to dwell on the past, it was embedded in him like a wound that festered until it was beyond hope of healing.

He knew the harm brute strength could do. He shuddered to think what might have happened if they hadn't lost their balance and tumbled into the straw. Discovering that Emmaline, who claimed she lacked passions, possessed a hidden erotic nature, nearly caused him to lose all control. What if he had harmed her?

But while the trip had been a disaster, Robert did learn a few tantalizing facts: Emmaline made soft sounds as she slept. And apparently, she could sleep anywhere—in a rotting chapel, her head pillowed on his thigh, and even atop his large form. That, too, aroused him.

Clearly, he'd been in Scotland too long. Its beauty beguiled, then turned on you with raw ferocity. It was ever uncivilized, no matter how poets tried to soften its edges. Even now, Scotland's romanticism seduced him. How else to explain this alarming conviction that Emmaline

Stanhope was the most interesting and alluring woman he'd ever known?

And completely out of bounds. He'd brought her here to protect her. Only a cad would turn that to advantage.

Strangely, she'd wrought changes in him. Perhaps because words were important to her, Robert had started to write. At first, they were just snippets he put down on a piece of foolscap he'd found in the castle library. But sometimes snippets grew into a longer examination of the confusing feelings that threatened his carefully ordered universe.

He longed to return to his prison of predictability: Sherry at dusk. Dinner at eight. Brandy after. His morning ice water bucket. He could only imagine what Emmaline would say to that.

What mad introspection was this?

They'd spoken little since returning from Oban. That interlude in the stable hung heavy between them. But because Emmaline faced challenges head-on—be they daunting hills, a ghostly chapel, or a looming murder arrest—Robert suspected she'd insist on discussing it.

After dinner, Colin and Miss Alcott led the way to the weapons room, where the play was to be staged. Robert held back to speak to Emmaline.

"I apologize for my behavior in Oban," he said. "It was unacceptable."

Emmaline tilted her head. "Kissing me was unacceptable?"

"It was an unwarranted intrusion on your…" He trailed off hopelessly.

"On my mouth?" Her lips pursed.

Which made Robert's gaze lock there.

Then she sighed. "My behavior was also inappropriate. And I made you fall."

"It was the…hooks." Even now, the fantasy of unhooking those cotton stockings, sliding them down those firm calves, and exploring her mysteries was intensely arousing.

She frowned. Clearly wanted more words.

"I couldn't sort my thoughts about that night on Iona," Robert said. "Instead, I let impulse rule. And when I discovered your stocking hooks, reason eluded me. I apologize."

Emmaline studied him. "Very well. What next? Do we return to bristling at one another?"

"Might be beyond that," Robert conceded.

"Perhaps we can simply agree that we shared an irrational moment—"

"Not to be repeated," he finished.

She nodded. "Where would the world be if people gave in to irrational impulses?"

Robert tried to ignore an irrational impulse insisting that what he most needed was *her*.

So, he reverted to form. Shot her a fulminating look and growled, "*Macbeth*."

As if that made any sense.

Robert took her arm and nearly dragged her to the weapons room.

Colin assigned Drew the part of Macbeth. Heloise was Lady Macbeth. Mrs. Stanhope would be the witches, all three of them. Tavish was Macduff, Macbeth's antagonist. Gibbons was to play Banquo and assorted other male characters.

Drew bore this in resignation. So far, he had accomplished nothing. Unless Mrs. Stanhope burst out with a confession, this trip would go down as a failure—underscored by the ignominy of playing the general who murders the king.

Ah, well. He was not unfamiliar with murder; one did what one must for king and country. He wasn't a born killer; he simply couldn't stomach running his father's estates when war and intrigue were infinitely more alluring.

Someone passed around the text of the play so they could see their roles. Heloise had everyone's part memorized, of course, and was happy to criticize performances she found lacking. Her niece, for instance, wasn't in the least compelling as she practiced the witches' role.

"More menace, dear," Heloise urged.

"'Fair is foul, and foul is fair: Hover through the fog and filthy air,'" Mrs. Stanhope read, without an ounce of passion. Did she even realize the couplets rhymed?

Heloise decreed that they would not perform the entire play, which Drew suspected was a ploy to claim for herself the most and best lines. They began with a section in which various nobles praised Macbeth as a valiant warrior.

Then it was time for Drew's entrance. He dutifully proclaimed his loyalty to King Duncan—

played by Colin. That set up Heloise's entrance as Lady Macbeth.

"'Come, you spirits that tend on mortal thoughts, unsex me here, and fill me from the crown to the toe top-full of direst cruelty! Make thick my blood,'" she demanded.

Drew rarely got to the theater, but when he did it was to hear the likes of Kemble and Sarah Siddons, who eschewed any hint of licentiousness in her roles.

Heloise eschewed nothing. All possible meanings of "unsex me here" hovered in the air.

Drew couldn't help but stare. How strange to feel attraction for a woman twice his age.

"'Come to my woman's breasts, and take my milk for gall, you murdering ministers,'" she declared.

Another image to ponder.

Finally, it was Drew's turn to greet her. Her features transformed to delight as she declared with warmth, "'My *dearest* love.'"

But the dratted king arrived, and after some flattering words, took Lady Macbeth's hand, which Drew thought Colin fondled overmuch.

There followed a private moment between Heloise and Macbeth. She spoke of nipples and blood, and it was all an incoherent mix because Drew was fixated on her heaving breasts.

Someone handed him a dagger, and Drew had to babble about it at length but was denied the satisfaction of plunging it into the king's chest. That was meant to take place off stage.

The rest of the play was a blur. The witch

stirred her caldron, chanting something about dragon's scale and wolf's tooth. Mrs. Stanhope was right to avoid the stage. Her performance held no conviction, and her words were anything but ominous.

Heloise, though, was riveting as she tried to wash off the king's blood that stained her hands. Her desperation rose to a frantic pitch as she descended into madness, her bosom rising, her breath quickening.

Passion lived in her, fairly bursting at the seams.

Drew's role was not yet done. Macbeth, now king, learns of his wife's suicide—that, too, occurred offstage, which must have irked Heloise—and gives a speech about candles being doused. Finally, he fights Macduff, who severs Macbeth's head to carry around as trophy. They had few props, so Tavish toted a bust from the mantle.

Gibbons then denounced "'this dead butcher and his fiend-like queen,'" and all was finally brought to a close.

Drew made his way to Heloise. She was surrounded by the others and beaming at their praise for her performance. He felt like a green lad waiting for an audience with the queen.

Before he could talk to her, Colin came up to shake his hand. "You were an excellent Macbeth."

Drew managed a tepid smile.

"We have a tradition that every Macbeth must sign the book." Colin pulled him over to the tattered Shakespeare volume. There was a long list of names and dates, such that Colin had to turn to a new page for Drew to sign.

"You've been performing the play for generations, it seems," Drew observed.

"Macbeth was King of Scots," Colin said. "Done in by ambition, a treacherous wife, and witches. Eternally interesting." He dipped a quill in ink and handed it to Drew.

Drew scrawled his name.

"The date also," Colin said. "Important for posterity."

Rolling his eyes, Drew obliged.

By the time he wrangled a private moment with Heloise, she looked exhausted. He offered to escort her to her chamber—a chaste offer, even though he inadvertently uttered the word bed—but she demurred.

With that, he had to be content. But her performance lingered. He would not soon forget the image of her heaving breasts. Or her acting skill, in stark contrast to her niece's lack of it.

Another nail in the coffin of his theory that Mrs. Stanhope had killed Burwell and lied about it continually since. Apparently, menace didn't live in her, nor did deceit.

Ah, well. He would think of something.

⁓

Heloise looked as if a feather would blow her over. John waited at a discreet distance as she accepted accolades. She'd been magnificent, but the performance had taken a toll.

Finally, she saw him. John thought he saw relief

in her eyes, so he made his way to her. "May I escort you to your chamber?" he said quietly.

She nodded and at first had no trouble walking, but once they were out of sight of the others, she leaned more heavily on him.

John was alarmed. "I could carry you."

She looked horrified. "I leave a performance under my own power."

"Yet I see what it does to you. Is it not time, perhaps, to stop taxing yourself?"

Heloise shook her head. "Performing animates me, John. It's what I live for. It's the thing that makes me myself. To stop would destroy who I am."

"I understand some of that," he acknowledged. "Serving others has been my life. But that may be changing."

She eyed him curiously. "How?"

They reached the stairs. John helped her ascend, one arm under her elbow, the other around her shoulders. She didn't object, which told him how very tired she must be.

"As you know, I served a corrupt man who neither cared nor noticed. My sense of duty also kept me from the woman I loved."

Heloise paused to study him. "What would you have done differently?"

"With respect to Portia, probably nothing. The barriers between our stations were too great. But I might have opened myself to the fact that duty isn't the highest—or only—master."

"I don't have your insight." She started up the stairs again. "I cannot bear to face my limitations, or the possibility fate may have something different in store for me."

They were almost at the top. John kept his arms around her for support.

Heloise smiled. "You are a good anchor."

At the door of her chamber, he hesitated. "Do you need help? I will summon a maid."

Heloise shook her head. "I might sleep in my clothes. Does that shock you?"

"Not at all, mad—" He broke off.

She laughed. "You almost called me 'madam.' But I am not that. Indeed, you and I may be kindred souls, John."

"Er, how?"

"Each of us followed our natural path, and bore the burdens that came with it," she said. "Mine has nearly burned me out, like a star that blazed too hot until it used up its fire. Your path kept you from the fire. Either way, we are each a little lost, are we not?"

"But perhaps finding our way," John put in.

Heloise sighed. "Do not take this for an untoward invitation, but I fear I do need help with the most basic things. Like removing some of my clothes. Would you mind?"

Mutely, he shook his head.

"I find I need you with me tonight," she added softly.

⚬⚬⚬

Now that *Macbeth* was out of the way, Emmaline found herself preoccupied by her earlier conversation with Robert. Could they return to the relative equanimity they achieved before the boat trip? Did she wish to?

She saw that Mr. Gibbons was helping her aunt, who looked drained. He was solicitous and kind, everything her aunt needed. Colin had gone, presumably to his cottage. Mr. Maitland had vanished, likely to continue plotting her arrest.

That left Emmaline and Robert alone in the weapons room, surrounded by instruments of war and destruction, an apt metaphor for the new, combustible turn in their relationship.

He was studying her. "You enjoyed that play about as much as I did."

"I am no good at pretense," Emmaline said. "Whereas my aunt—"

"Fully embodies her characters."

She nodded. "She lives every role. She can give no less than her all."

Robert didn't respond. He simply stood there, silhouetted against the fading fire and the old muskets artfully mounted on the wall. Emmaline pretended to study the pole arms that stood like sentries near the door, as well as smaller daggers like the *sgian dubh*.

Awkward silence stretched between them.

"What I didn't say earlier about my behavior in Oban," she began, "is that it's not in my nature. I don't want you to think I'm, er—" She halted.

"Overly passionate?" Robert offered.

"Yes. Not normally that. Women alone must be careful."

"Not be vulnerable, not lose control, that sort of thing."

Emmaline nodded in relief. This was turning into a reasoned discussion. "You seem quite careful as well."

"Not an ounce of passion in me," Robert deadpanned.

She managed a smile. "You are passionate about your work."

"But we weren't speaking about that sort of passion, were we?"

Back to awkwardness then. Was he trying to unnerve her? Two could play at that. "I imagine you, too, are rarely given to that sort of passion," Emmaline challenged.

"It's rocks or nothing," he said. "How could you think otherwise?"

She hadn't missed the spark in that gray gaze. "You are a terrible man."

"A terrible, unpassionate one, you mean."

Flustered, Emmaline gave up. "Truthfully, I completely abandoned myself in Oban."

Robert drew closer. "What if it's the opposite?" he said softly. "You gave impulse free rein. Perhaps that's your true self."

"I'm no more given to impulse than you," Emmaline insisted.

"You don't know my impulses." He paused. "But I think I would like to know yours."

How had the conversation ventured into such dangerous territory? Emmaline searched for something lighthearted to break the tension. But his next words scuttled that.

"Some men," Robert said softly, "would die for such a kiss."

She covered her face with her hands. "Talking of it makes it worse."

Gently, he pulled her hands away. "Says the woman who insisted I learn conversation."

"Not *this* kind." This felt like flirting, a skill beyond her. Robert brushed his thumb along her jaw. Suddenly, Emmaline was back in that horse stall, desperately needing what he offered.

"Good night, Emmaline." His low murmur, rich with undercurrents, kindled new heat. "Sweet dreams."

He left her in the weapons room by herself.

Drew was impatient. He had to arrest the woman or retreat. Retreat amounted to conceding that the time he'd spent on this case had gone to waste. Winning was worth everything. It was his path to greatness.

And he intended to be great. A high government position, head of the War Office at the very least. Even his father would have to acknowledge the achievement, although this was emphatically not about his father. It was about making his mark, his own way. Andrew Maitland would be accorded his due. His brilliance would be recognized.

Which is why, when he came upon Emmaline Stanhope staring intently at the weapons on the wall—and at an hour when the rest of the castle had retired—Drew saw opportunity.

"Most women would find those weapons of war unsettling."

She turned, fixed him with a steely gaze. "You are kind to consider my sensibilities."

Her tone did not suggest that she thought him kind.

"I am taken with the pole arms," she added. "One or two of them would be suitable."

Drew frowned. "Suitable for…?"

"Combat." Her gaze hardened. "If that becomes necessary."

Was the woman threatening him? How ridiculous. She'd be no match for him. She was taller than most and her frame looked sturdy, but she was a mere woman. This was some scheme to throw him off. Did she not know her freedom was in his hands?

Mrs. Stanhope took one of the smaller poles and studied its spear-like tip. "This will do."

Then she favored him with a thin smile. "Did you wish to discuss something, Mr. Maitland? Please speak frankly, as I have no patience these days with pretense or lies, such as those you perpetrated the night when you claimed to rescue me."

Drew scowled. "If you mean to use that weapon against me, madam—"

"Dear heavens, no." Her blue eyes widened.

"Let us be done with these games," Drew snapped. "The only thing that matters is whether you killed the man and betrayed your country."

Mrs. Stanhope regarded him steadily. "What have you concluded?"

"You make no case for your innocence."

"And you make no case for my guilt," she said. "Are we at stalemate?"

That was exactly where they were. He had no evidence, only the handbill's death card drawing, which proved exactly nothing.

But he could not return to London empty-handed. His colleagues would pounce. George would spread the word among the political cognoscenti, ensuring a mortal wound to Drew's promising career.

Perhaps another approach.

"You cannot stay in Scotland indefinitely," he pointed out. "I would be happy to escort you to London and help you clear your name."

Her brows arched. "Once, I might have been taken in by such an offer. But now I understand better who you are, Mr. Maitland. I do not wish to go anywhere with you."

"Then I have no choice but to arrest you and let the legal system decide your fate."

"On what grounds?" she demanded. "That I waved to Mr. Burwell as he stood in the street? I tried to warn him. I had no reason to end Mr. Burwell's life. He was a paying client. More funds would come to us when I found him a wife."

"Perhaps those involved in his treasonous activities paid you to see to his demise so he could not implicate them."

She laughed. "You have seen our cottage. Can you believe I am flush with cash?"

Drew stepped toward her. "I suspect, Mrs. Stanhope—Alcott, rather—that you are not the innocent you claim."

"I *know* that you are not who you claim," she retorted. "You look every inch the gentleman, yet you cloak yourself in the stench of falseness. You have one goal only: to advance your career. I will not be your instrument."

Drew used his superior height to loom over her. "How do you mean to stop me?"

Suddenly, the point of that spear pressed under his chin.

Drew put his finger on the tip. When she didn't press her advantage, he dared to guide it away from his throat. He wondered if it had drawn blood. Ruined his neckcloth.

"That was unwise," he snarled. "You have no idea who you are dealing with."

She smiled. "Neither do you."

Mrs. Stanhope strode from the room, toting that pole arm as if she was born to it.

Chapter Twenty-Two

HELOISE HADN'T AWAKENED with a man in her room in a very long time.

Too long.

Alas, this man wasn't in her bed, but sprawled on a divan across the room.

She sat up and studied John, who was curled in an awkward position that would doubtless cause a cramp in that long neck and sturdy shoulders. She remembered how he had helped her into bed, turning away as he removed her dress, leaving her in her shift. He tucked her in and pulled the covers up to her neck, as if she were a child.

He was such a modest man, a puzzle still. Heloise wondered whether unburdening himself about his past love had truly lifted the load. Perhaps he would always bear the weight.

She pulled her dressing gown around her and walked over to the divan.

"John," she said softly.

He stirred. Stretched. Then recalled his surroundings and bolted upright. "Madam?"

"You do not work for me," she snapped. "I've asked you to use my given name."

"Apologies…Heloise. Habit of a lifetime, I'm

afraid." He looked so contrite as he rose and politely bowed that she instantly regretted her tone.

She softened. "I am grateful for your assistance last night."

"Happy to help, mad—Heloise." He flushed.

"The problem, John, is that you are too nice. I am not accustomed to nice men."

He regarded her. "Are you not?"

"A woman with my history rarely encounters men who aren't self-inflated and weak of character. Thankfully, you are not that."

"I should hope not."

Heloise sat on the divan. "Sit, John. I cannot talk with you towering over me."

He perched stiffly next to her.

"I know it is in your nature to take care of people," she said. "But I don't need a caretaker. At least not yet. I may feel poorly now and then, but I hold my own."

He nodded, but Heloise knew he did not yet see her point. She hated to be blunt, but what was the point of dancing around?

"I cannot be a substitute for Portia," she said.

John colored. "I never thought so."

"Perhaps not in the fore of your mind, but I suspect it is there, even so. You must think of yourself and the new life you are forming. Just because you spent the night here—"

"I wanted to make sure you were well," he interjected.

She patted his hand. "I know. But you must forget this night and move on."

He looked confused. "Did something…happen between us?"

Heloise laughed, though it felt hollow. "You were the perfect gentleman. I only warn you against making too much of it. You are moving past your long devotion to Portia. Don't transfer that devotion to me. It will hold you back from becoming the man you are meant to be."

John stiffened. "You make too much of a night spent on the sofa."

There. He was pushing back, beginning to reclaim himself.

"And you aren't really my type," Heloise added, for good measure.

"You're more Colin's type, I suppose," John said.

"A man like Colin has many types. But it's true that I've always drawn men who drink life's pleasures in full but prefer their devotion in fleeting bites." Bitterness crept into the words.

John held her gaze. "I cannot imagine being satisfied with half-measures of you."

"Dear John, you make me blush, and I have not done so in years. You'd best leave."

He stood and gave her a little bow. With that silver hair and erect posture, he cut quite a distinguished figure. He opened the door and—always discreet—surveyed the hall before making his exit.

Heloise touched her cheeks. They felt warm, as if she possessed the sensibilities of an innocent schoolgirl.

A pall had settled over the castle, perhaps the after-effects of *Macbeth* or the dreary weather. Whatever the cause, Emmaline was restless. The turn in her relationship with Robert provoked some unpleasant soul-searching.

"Why should he affect me so?" she asked her aunt. "I have been content on my own."

"Don't let independence get in the way of happiness, Em. Men can be difficult. But we need them."

"I don't," Emmaline declared. "Neither do you."

Aunt Heloise gave a bitter laugh. "You think I've chosen my solitary state? No matter what we tell ourselves, no one chooses to be alone when the curtain falls. I enjoyed many men, all unfit as life companions. Perhaps I chose them for that very reason. I wanted to be free. And here I am, quite free. It's not an ideal vantage point from which to close out my days."

Emmaline pulled her into a hug. "You are not alone, nor shall you close out your days any time soon. I will take care of you."

Her aunt's eyes misted. "Look to your own happiness, dear. Life with the right man need not be a prison. I shunned permanence and chose men who fit that life. But the narrative plays out, and one is left with consequences. I'm no example. Indeed, I am a cautionary tale."

"You are not!"

"I told myself I was following my heart, but in truth I was looking for thrills to affirm I was alive—pleasure, joy, delight. But from this vantage point, those look ephemeral. I chose to pour my heart out on the stage, to *live* there. It wasn't enough. Don't make that mistake, Em."

Emmaline sighed. "I'm such a poor performer, there's no danger of that."

"You are too literal, dear. I only mean that you ought to take the blinders off. See what's in front of you. Perhaps you'll see a strong, worthy man who can give you what I never had."

"I don't believe in fantasy."

"It's as necessary as breathing," Aunt Heloise insisted. "We're meant to be inspired and dazzled by imagination. We're not meant to drag ourselves through each day, merely surviving."

"Survival is necessary," Emmaline protested.

"Yes, but if I had only that to direct my days, I'd just as soon exit the stage." Aunt Heloise caught her hand. "Leave room for surprises, Em. Don't miss your life."

⸻ ❧ ⸻

She was an early riser. With luck, Robert would find her in the breakfast room.

Then what?

They would converse.

About?

The weather.

Boring.

But far preferrable to dissecting their trip again. Now, finally, he understood what that trip had brought to light: the desperate, damnable desire he'd formed for Emmaline Stanhope. He couldn't act on it. But every time he saw her, he wanted her more.

She was already at the table. To his amazement, she smiled. "I have a proposition."

Robert tried not to look eager. He took time to fill his plate and help himself to *cofaidh,* the stout concoction Colin enjoyed that was more like mud. He took a sip of thick brew and tried not to choke on the stuff. Colin said one cup saw him through morning chores, and Robert could see why. Already, his heart was racing.

That had nothing to do with the woman across from him, whose avid expression should have given him pause.

She laid something on the table.

Robert stared at the thing, a lance with a narrow, axe-like top. "What is that?"

"Colin called it a voulge. But it's too long for me to manage easily." She reached under the table and came up with another. "This one is shorter, but the blade's too big."

Then she produced *another* weapon—did she have an armory at her feet?

"This has a shorter staff and simple spear tip, and it's light enough that I can maneuver it with one hand," Emmaline said. "It is quite suitable."

Robert frowned. "Are we preparing for war?"

"I'm broadening my combat skills. Thanks to your instruction, I've learned how to better wield my walking stick. But this weapon is more powerful. I'd like you to teach me to use it."

Incredulous, Robert stared at her. "You cannot carry that around London."

"Only at night, or when I need more protection than my walking stick affords," Emmaline said. "This is small enough to hide under my cloak."

"It's a medieval weapon," he protested. "No one fights with those now."

Emmaline nodded. "Which is why I'll have the element of surprise."

"If that spear hits its mark, you'll be in worse trouble. Besides, you are safe here."

"You do realize I don't live in Scotland? I'm a woman alone in the city, with an ailing aunt to provide for. This—" her sweeping motion encompassed the castle and likely all of Scotland—"is not my real life. I need to see to my own protection more effectively, as my abduction proved. That's if Mr. Maitland doesn't arrest me first."

Robert shook his head. "I can manage Maitland."

"That's kind of you but—"

"I am *not* kind," he growled. He had stayed up half the night writing his thoughts pertaining to their…situation. And gotten exactly nowhere. He couldn't stop thinking of her, couldn't stop wanting to touch her—he'd nearly done so last night in the weapons room.

Emmaline's chin rose. "It's time I stand on my own, Robert. With proper weapons. I know you've been trained in these. I will look elsewhere if you refuse to teach me."

Robert took another robust shot of Colin's deadly coffee. It didn't help.

——⚒——

Emmaline watched as Robert fashioned a protective tip for the end of the spear, akin to what she had seen on the points of fencing blades at Mr. Angelo's academy on Bond Street.

"To prevent you from accidentally stabbing me to death," he muttered.

First, they worked on posture—feet apart and balanced, as in fencing. It was a challenge; without her lift, her legs weren't even. Robert didn't remark on it, though he surely noticed.

"Grip the upper part of the pole with your strong hand," he said. "Your right, isn't it?"

She complied, but Robert shook his head. "Overarm, not underarm, which relies on the wrist. Wrist is weaker and limits your range of motion."

Emmaline tried again.

"Good. Move your left hand farther back on the pole. Now the strong hand can direct the spear to the target, either by thrusting out, or upward toward the throat. Like a bayonet."

Emmaline tried both ways. "Up is better."

He nodded. "Gives you more power. An assailant may block your thrust by turning the pole off to the side, but that leaves his body exposed. Your recourse is to move the pole down in a diagonal slashing swing." He demonstrated.

Emmaline frowned. "What if I panic and forget?"

"Then he turns the spear back on you and you'll be quite dead." Robert gave a heavy sigh.

"Suppose your assailant is a former military man? A thug with street-fighting skills? A fencing expert. Medieval enthusiast. I could go on."

"Your point?" she demanded.

"That it's one thing to have a clever cane. Quite another to pretend to be some female warrior with no chance in hell against the experts."

Her gaze narrowed. "I am not pretending. You think I'm not up to it?"

"What I think is that you possess a strong will that doesn't always lead you wisely. To think you can outmaneuver an assailant with this is sheer folly. A joke—" He broke off.

Looked down at her.

At her spear, rather. The tip of which was pressed against his throat.

"You're right," Emmaline said softly. "I don't have a man's fighting skills. But men always underestimate women, as Mr. Maitland—and now you—have demonstrated. And yes, you could use your strength to turn this pole back on me."

She lowered the spear. "But by then it will be too late. You'll be bleeding profusely from the hole in your gullet. And I will stand by and calmly watch the life seep out of your big, strong, masculine body."

With that, she stomped off, leaving Robert to make of that what he might.

⁓

"Ah, a warrior."

Emmaline jumped. Colin stepped from the

shadows of the pine woods, where she had retreated after the frustrating session with Robert.

"Apologies, lass. I was patching some stones at the tower and saw you tearing through the woods like a wulvor."

She eyed him in confusion.

"Werewolf. Not that ye resemble such." His eyes focused on her pole. "I see you settled on that one. Are ye thinking to fight someone?"

"I need to be better prepared for my defense when I return to London. Your nephew doesn't think this suitable."

Colin regarded her. "Reason being?"

"Some outdated notion of what women are capable of."

He gave a hearty laugh. "Didnae know Robbie had notions about that one way or another. But have you considered that he might simply want to do the fighting for you?"

"That's not possible. I need to return to my life, Colin. I'm grateful for your shelter, but I must manage on my own. I *was* managing, up until the abduction attempt. My leg makes me vulnerable. I can't walk around London with a limp."

"Or with that weapon, I imagine."

"Only at night, and I'll keep it under my cloak," she said. "I can't let fear imprison me. My aunt needs doctors. We need provisions and income. Robert's life is very different from mine. I have no expectation that he will protect me. Nor do I wish it."

Colin stroked his chin. "You're an independent lass, and a fighter besides. I know the sort. We've females here that would sooner put out a man's eye as look at him."

"I would never harm Robert. I wish him well."

"Wish him well?" He regarded her closely. "Seems more than that if you ask me."

Emmaline flushed. "We are friends. No more than that."

"If ye say so. But dinnae fault him for wanting to protect you, especially with that Maitland fellow's scheming." Colin looked around. "In fact, I dinnae like the notion of you walking through these woods alone. Why don't we return to the castle?"

"I was trying to find a place to calm my thoughts," she said. "Somewhere peaceful."

"It's peace ye want, I've just the place." Colin took her arm and turned her around.

For a few minutes they walked through the woods, but at the clearing they didn't turn toward the castle. Instead, he led her to a path that veered off to an old cemetery.

"I've a fondness for places of the dead," he said. "But if ye feel it's too morbid—"

"Not at all. On Iona, we took shelter in an old chapel by a graveyard."

"Ah. St. Oran's. Ye didnae mind it?"

Emmaline shook her head. "Robert told me about the kings and clan chiefs buried there. It felt oddly comforting to be surrounded by so much history."

"'Tis a holy place," Colin said. "I've nae been there in years. Maybe it's time I went back.

There's an ancient peace there. It's a place for pondering—nae that I'm any good at that."

She smiled. "Maybe you only need practice. Will you show me this place?"

"Aye. Generations of Campbells rest here—not all of us, but enough so one's not lonely."

Emmaline wondered what Colin had to feel lonely about. The man was warm and gregarious, and seemed to enjoy being with people. Perhaps that hid some inner turmoil.

He held the old iron gate open for her, and they entered. Some markers looked as old as those on the Street of the Dead. In the center of the cemetery stood a grand mausoleum.

"For important folk," Colin said. "Dukes and the like. Maintains the fiction that they were somehow more worthy than the folks over in the corners."

He opened the granite structure's enormous bronze door.

"Now Archibald, here"—he pointed to a crypt—"lost his head—literally, as did his father before him. Fine examples of Campbells switching loyalties. It's what we're good at."

"Sounds like a fascinating story," Emmaline said.

"This Archibald's father—also named Archibald—was the eighth earl. A powerful politician with a fine head of red hair."

"Like yours?" she ventured.

Colin grinned. "Aye. The father was a Covenanter—religious folk who broke with the Catholics. He supported Oliver Cromwell against

Charles I, but later switched sides and supported Charles II's restoration. In the new king's eyes, the damage was already done. Archibald was executed, his head displayed on a prison spike. We eventually got it back. Head and the rest of him are interred here."

"The son suffered the same fate?" Emmaline asked.

Colin nodded. "Claimed to be a royalist but he had known protestant sympathies. Charles II tried him for treason, but Archibald escaped and, like a good Campbell, threw in his lot with the Whigs, no friends of the Stuarts."

"How did he lose his head?"

"Led a rising against James, who succeeded Charles II. Had the bad luck to be captured. Like his father, he was fated to the Maiden."

"The Maiden?"

"Guillotine. Not as fancy as what the French had but served the purpose. Defiant to the end, he gave a speech against 'Popery' before they lopped his head off."

Emmaline blinked. "That was brave."

Colin shrugged. "He was going to die anyway, so it was no great stand. But you're right. He did keep to his principles. Each duke has a story, but I'll nae bore ye further. There's another grave that might interest you. Outside the mausoleum."

Emmaline was filled with curiosity as Colin led her to a corner of the graveyard and a solitary stone marker. It bore the name "Portia." Lines from a poem were carved under her name.

"My sister—Robbie's mother," Colin said softly. "Stone was bare for years, but I found a poem that spoke more to the truth of her and added some lines."

"Robert spoke of her in Oban," Emmaline said. "He regretted not being there when she died and not knowing how or why she ended at those cliffs."

Colin regarded her closely. "He never speaks of it. That he did to you says something about the two of you."

Emmaline shook her head. "You read too much into that."

"And ye not enough," Colin said. "Ye heard his regret, but missed what was unsaid—Robbie's abiding guilt at not protecting her from his father, an English blackguard rotting in hell if there's justice. Pardon my language."

"But Robert would have been a boy," she said. "How could he have protected her?"

"Guilt is guilt. Campbells have a fair amount, Robbie more than most." He put a fatherly hand on her shoulder. "Don't ye see, lass? The need to protect his own runs deep in him."

His own. The words hung there.

"Might be why he opposes you learning weaponry," Colin added. "He'd want to protect you himself, the way he couldn't protect Portia. Doubt he'll be dissuaded."

"But—he's never said so," Emmaline protested.

Colin laughed softly. "Robbie's a man of few words."

Emmaline pondered that. "It's been a rocky

path to friendship between us, but it's no more than that. I am resolved to see to my protection."

Colin sighed. "Two more stubborn folk I've yet to meet."

⁓

Gardening offered a multitude of pleasures, John decided as he knelt amid the castle's patch of ornamental onions. Tending such beautiful purple flowers would be richly rewarding.

That was enough, wasn't it? Creating beauty, admiring his handiwork—such a future would be fine. He wouldn't ask for more.

Don't transfer that devotion to me.

He would not. He wasn't worthy of Heloise in any case. She was an orchid of rare beauty. He was a crowberry shrub, best kept to the undergrowth.

Yet he couldn't help but compare the two women. Portia had been quiet and tormented, an abused and desperate soul. Heloise was loud and bawdy, willing to say what others would not. She would never be—nor did she wish to be—accepted in polite society.

Through long habit, John had kept much of himself hidden throughout his years of service. Denial was its own curse, but frankness was an unfamiliar state. His nature and hers were at opposite ends of the universe.

Or so he thought—until the moment he felt her standing over him.

Heloise's hand pressed his shoulder, and his world started to spin.

"Dear John," she murmured. "You are where

I thought to find you, tending to the things that need you."

John rose carefully. "Do you have need of me, Heloise?"

She sighed. "I fear I've come up against a hard truth. It plagues me."

He frowned. "You speak in riddles."

"I'm wondering how I can prove my worth when I am declining in every way."

"Why should you need to prove anything?" he asked.

"When I look in the mirror, I can't help but see that I am not the woman I once was," she said mournfully. "My looks, my abilities, are in desperate retreat."

"Heloise," John said sternly. "Are you fishing for compliments?"

Heavens, he thought. Where had those words come from?

She looked startled. "Was I?"

"Tending that way."

Heloise regarded him closely. "Are you quite well, John?"

"I can find no fault with my wellness." Indeed, he felt a new exhilaration now that grief had finally released its tentacles.

"You seem…not yourself," she observed. "Rather cheeky."

"Because I interrupted your soliloquy on fading?"

Her gaze narrowed. "Fading is no small thing. John. It can bring one low. So low that one cannot see how to raise oneself up again."

"Thus, you come to me, angling for compliments." Egad. How *bold*.

Heloise frowned. "I've a notion to box your ears."

John took her hand and raised it to his lips, his heart in his throat. "If you wish, but first allow me to tell you what I see: a woman with fire in her eyes, possessed of the power to put every other woman to shame."

Her lovely eyes widened.

"Perhaps you aren't the woman you once were," he said softly. "Perhaps you are *more*."

"I need to sit," Heloise said faintly. "You've taken my breath away."

John put his hand under her elbow and guided her to a nearby bench. Then, when he might have looked away, or down at his feet, or anywhere but directly into that violet gaze, he faced her. He saw a woman full of life and spirit and beauty and creativity that would never leave her, no matter how many years she had on her plate.

"I wish you could see what I see," he said quietly.

She blinked. "John?"

"Heloise." He said no more.

Uncertainty swept her features. Then, a shy smile.

"One day I shall punish you for this," she said softly.

"I hope so," he murmured.

"You wish me to beg." She leaned toward him.

"Never. You are a queen."

Heloise brought her mouth close to his. "One

who is *very* willing to beg. Will you kiss me, John? I would grovel on my knees for you—if I thought I could get to my feet again."

"The woman I see grovels to no one."

Her lips parted on a smile. "You *do* see me."

"You may kiss me," John said. Would she box his ears instead? Truly, he deserved it.

"Wretch." But Heloise pressed her lips to his.

John nearly forgot to breathe.

What was this madness?

Robert inspected the wedge he'd fashioned. It was like the lift that ravaged her foot but tapered. Leather, not wood. Wrapped in soft but sturdy fabric. Crafting it was simple. He often adapted trowels, sieves, picks, and other tools for digs. He ought to have done this sooner.

If he couldn't act on the desire he felt for her, he could at least do this simple thing to make her life easier. Alas, he was under no illusion that Emmaline would welcome his offering. She was probably still angry that he predicted the pole arm would bring disaster.

"Whatever's causing that scowl 'tis likely your own fault."

Colin tossed something on the worktable Robert had set up in a room off the armory.

His kilt.

"I'm tired of keeping it, so it's yours, whether ye wear the thing or nae."

Robert eyed the blue, green, and black plaid.

Mere fabric, yet his grandfather, a military man through and through, never stood as proud as when he wore the Black Watch, the ancient Campbell plaid.

He ran his palm over the wool, traced the right angles the colors formed with their crossing patterns. Kilts were back in favor, thanks to romanticized portrayals of Highlanders. The Crown had banned Highland dress more than half a century ago to suppress the Jacobites. The army had been exempted, but his grandfather wouldn't have obeyed the restriction anyway. John Campbell had fought in Falkirk Muir and Culloden. No one dictated his attire.

Colin was watching him closely.

"Is that a wee dram of understanding I see in your face, Robbie? Do you ken that it's more than a length of cloth? That it's worthy of respect, even from a rebellious young lad who lacked the sense to look beyond his nose? You've never understood that you belong to us, Robbie, whether you wish it or nae. You can leave us, but we will never leave you."

"You're plainspoken when you're not trying to charm the ladies," Robert muttered.

"When the Almighty was doling out charm, he gave it to those best suited," Colin said. "Skipped you altogether. Don't blame Him. You'd have no idea what to do with it."

"What's this about?" Robert demanded. "I never laid claim to charm, and I'll own every youthful mistake. But I've long since left youth behind."

"You're acting like an idiot with my dear Emmaline."

"Your dear? Can you never leave the ladies alone?" At Colin's grin, Robert broke off. "You said that to bait me."

"I've just spent a nice hour with the young lady, and I can report that she wishes you well. Is that what you want, Robbie? To be wished well?"

Robert didn't reply.

"I see it's not," Colin said. "I thought so. What's your plan?"

"No plan. But if I had one, it would have logical steps. Like a dig."

Colin laughed. "The only steps you need worry about are those she'll be taking away from you. Make no mistake: Emmaline's a strong woman. She's planning for an independent life. You've got a long way to go in the matter of charm."

"She's practical," Robert insisted. "Doesn't want to be charmed."

"Mother of God," Colin muttered. "How are you of my blood? Or even a Campbell? I know your brute of a father had no kind bone in his body, but that's a poor excuse. Portia would have taught you better. Her voice could charm any beast."

Robert sighed. "You didn't see her all those years. He'd beaten her down. She retreated into silence."

"And never was herself again," Colin said softly. "That much I bore witness to."

"I still don't understand how she mustered strength to take me out of that school and bring me here," Robert said. "I'd have thought it was beyond her. I should have stayed here longer to know her better, to have her explain. But she was lost, Colin, so very lost."

His uncle was silent for a long time.

"Aye," Colin said finally. "But she couldnae have explained how she took you out of that school, Robbie. She didn't."

Robert frowned. "I don't understand."

"It wasn't her," Colin said. "You were right. It was beyond her."

He eyed his uncle in bewilderment. "Then how?"

"Who else was on that trip?" Colin asked.

"I don't know. I was seven, for God's sake. A driver, I suppose. I don't remember a maid. Only Gibbons." Robert had tried to forget everything about that period.

Yet a few images tugged at him, even now: Gibbons with the luggage. Paying the drivers. Arranging the change of horses. Seeing to the food, the accommodations. Watching him and Portia to gauge when they were too tired to continue.

His mother's dazed expression. With every mile that took them deeper into Scotland, her countenance grew lighter.

Gradually, Robert, too, had come more alive. He'd peppered Gibbons with questions about their new home, one where cruelty was not the coin of the realm. His grandfather, stern but welcoming. And finally, Gibbons leaving them, his sad expression visible in the carriage window as the vehicle turned back toward England.

Truth dawned.

"Gibbons," Robert said in wonder. "It was him. He made everything happen."

Colin nodded. But there was an odd tension about his jaw.

"There's more, isn't there? What are you not telling me?" Robert demanded.

"What's not mine to tell. May we return to the matter of Mrs. Stanhope?"

Robert rose. "Damnation, Colin. I want the whole."

"You'll have to ask the man himself."

Impossible. He and Gibbons didn't share confidences. But maybe that long-ago memory was incomplete. Maybe it merited revisiting.

The set of Colin's shoulders told him the subject was closed.

"Very well." Robert sighed. "Give me your pearls of wisdom about Emmaline."

Colin's gaze was stern. "First off, let's agree the aim isn't seduction."

"You surprise me. I would have thought a man like you—"

"You have no understanding of a man like me, Robbie. Let me be plain: I admire Emmaline. Won't be a partner in anything sordid."

Robert scowled. "Not my plan."

Colin's features relaxed. "That's settled, then. Have you thought of forgetting about steps and simply leading with your feelings?"

"Flowery declarations? That's not me, Uncle."

Colin made an impatient sound. "What is it that draws you to her, Robbie?"

Robert considered. "She's strong. Brilliant. Beautiful without artifice. Brave. Doesn't flinch from hard things."

"Then that's how you come to her— unflinching. Not roundabout, nor in mincing, orderly steps. Get to the point, and quickly. You need to be as brave as her." Colin paused. "There's more, though. The other that makes her…shiver."

Robert blinked. "Take her someplace cold?"

His uncle muttered a curse. "A more ignorant Scot, I've yet to see."

"I'm not a Scot."

"Ye will be when I'm done," Colin declared. "The key to wooing a woman is understanding what women want. Scotswomen are not unlike your Emmaline. They want a man who's up to the task. Who can shoulder burdens. Fight enemies, to the death, if need be. Not worried about you there."

"Grateful for that, I suppose," Robert muttered.

"But women want more. The stuff that fires the flesh and inspires poetry."

Robert waved a dismissive hand. "Don't tell me to quote Burns at her. I won't."

"Most folk don't understand Burns," Colin said. "He wisnae only about red roses and larking about Highland meadows with his heart on his sleeve."

"Uncle…"

Colin cleared his throat. "'What length o' graith, when weel ca'd hame, Will ser'e a woman duly?

The carlin clew her wanton tail, Her wanton tail sae ready; I learn't a sang in Annandale, Nine inch will please a lady.'"

Robert stilled. "I understood enough of that Scots to want to strangle you."

"Burns wasn't above bawdy."

"I'll not ply her with crudeness." As it was, he'd taken untoward liberties in Oban.

"Wouldnae hurt to introduce her to the terrain," Colin retorted.

"This conversation is ended."

Colin's sly smile told him the opposite. "I've embarrassed ye by insinuating that such a manly specimen as yourself has nae notion of how to kindle a fire in a female. Prove me wrong."

"Emmaline isn't any female," Robert insisted. "She's above all that."

Colin was incredulous. "Ye have no idea what she is above, or below. Are ye not drawn to her? Do ye not lay awake at night thinking of her in all the ways she might be *above* or *below?* Ye might discover that she does the same."

For a moment Robert was silent. Then a confession: "I might…harm her."

Colin stared at him. His features softened. "You're taking care. I commend ye for that. Men of your size can easily hurt a woman. Your father deserved to hang for what he did to Portia, and ye saw it all as a lad."

"When ye and Portia arrived here," he went on, "I wanted to set out straightaway and kill the man myself. Our da forbade it. Said she was safe with us and the past would catch up to the man.

But I hate that we had to wait until the pox took him."

Colin put his arm around Robert's shoulder. "You're not like him, Robbie. Ye have the strength of ten men, but you'd never use it against any woman. For God's sake—have you killed any women ye've been with?"

Robert drew in a breath. "No."

"Likely never allowed feelings for them, either."

He shook his head.

"I want to weep for that," Colin said quietly. "For the man ye are, for the abuse that made ye so careful. Only a true man takes that sort of care."

"I don't want praise for being civilized."

"If ye don't try with her, your father will have won," Colin said. "Branded ye forever with his cruelty. Don't let him keep ye from the woman you deserve. Emmaline's made of strong stuff. It's time ye discovered that."

Robert exhaled. "Damned Scots. You always want my soul."

Colin grinned. "Only thing worth having, my boy."

⚬⚬⚬

The talk with Colin unsettled him but crystallized a truth: He and Emmaline couldn't go back, couldn't retreat into friendship. Another truth: In Oban, Emmaline hadn't seemed repulsed by those liberties, even urged him on before the interlude ended in mutual mortification. And last night, when he almost kissed her, Robert knew he hadn't misread her interest.

Yet he still couldn't risk harming her. Colin believed he wasn't like his father, but Robert hadn't been tested in that way with women. He'd always held himself apart during intimate relations, never risked losing control.

Perhaps a more cerebral, dispassionate approach?

Colin had laughed at his reference to digs, but the process was a proven strategy for accomplishing challenging tasks. One did not simply set out with a shovel and hope for luck. Purpose must be stated, a site surveyed, images drawn, test samples collected, significance assessed, excavation plans drafted. Only then did work proceed. Robert meticulously filled dozens of notebooks with such details. He was a planner through and through.

Robert pulled out a blank page and began to write. Preliminary evidence gave him hope. But like any expedition, success was not guaranteed. He needed to think more precisely about the goal. What, really, did he want?

To be her lover, certainly. But more. The whole. No barriers between them.

There: The true objective.

Terrifying thought, that.

Did he really mean to take this on? Was he a thousand times a fool?

Chapter Twenty-Three

ROBERT FOUND HER in the garden doing her exercises. Her leg must be hurting, for her limp was pronounced. Likely she intended to push through the pain until she could return to London and get another lift just as punishing as that horrendous block of wood.

Did she think she deserved to suffer for the disability fate had dealt? That by refusing to grant pain purchase she could negate it?

A stoic after his own heart.

Emmaline must have felt his presence, for she turned. Another woman might have offered a polite greeting, but she regarded him silently, waiting for him to speak. When had *he* become the lugubrious one?

"I have something for you." Robert began. "Will you sit on that bench?"

She regarded him curiously but sat.

"Extend your foot." He knelt, hoping she would comply. She did, giving no hint that it was an odd request. "May I, er, remove your left shoe?"

"This grows interesting," Emmaline said. But she offered no objection.

Robert worked the laces of her worn half-boot,

its leather so thin as to provide little protection for her foot. Before Emmaline, he recalled only one other time he'd removed a woman's shoe. A hazy image floated through his brain of an evening spent in his cups with a very willing companion.

This, of course, was not that. But thanks to that disastrous interlude in the horse stall, he now knew she preferred hooks for stocking fasteners.

A *horse stall*, for God's sake.

Ah, but he had wandered far afield—not as far as he wished, perhaps, but too far for the task at hand. How long had he been holding her foot?

Robert looked up. Her blue eyes danced with amusement.

"I burn to know what is next," she murmured.

He pulled the lift from his pocket. "It's this. I hope it fits."

Emmaline stared at it in wonder. "You made this?"

Robert nodded. "Leather's more forgiving than wood. It's wrapped in—"

"Plaid." Emmaline stared at it. "Never say you cut up a lovely kilt."

"Only an old scrap," Robert assured her. "You'll find the fabric's soft."

She ran her hand over the fine worsted wool. "This is lovely."

Their gazes met. Held.

Robert cleared his throat. "May I fit it to your shoe? Or would you prefer to?"

"You crafted it," Emmaline said softly. "Proceed."

"This is longer than the other, and I've tapered it toward the toe to prevent it from slipping and provide a more stable base." Robert inserted the lift into her boot, making sure it was seated. He looked at her for guidance. Did she wish to put the boot on herself?

"You do it," she said, reading his question. "I won't deprive you of the chance to test your invention first-hand."

"It should be more comfortable than the other. Whoever made that ought to be shot."

Emmaline smiled mischievously. "I readily admit to lacking your skill."

Of course. *She* had crafted it. He should have guessed. Ignoring her sly smile, Robert curved his hand around her heel to guide her foot into the shoe. Alas, the act of holding her foot made him yearn to slide his hand upward, to roam higher as he had in Oban.

Resolutely, he willed his thoughts elsewhere and seated her foot. "Shall I do the laces?"

She nodded. He worked them slowly—only because he wanted to get the fit right, no other reason—moving upward until he secured the top one. "Not too tight?"

"It's perfect." Her expression was unreadable. Was she, too, thinking of Oban?

"Shall we try it out?" Robert extended his hand, fought an urge to pull her into his arms.

Emmaline took a step. Another. Then she smiled and tucked her hand into the crook of his arm. They walked the length of the garden. She moved easily, without a limp.

"It's wonderful," she said, beaming. "It doesn't dig into my foot. Thank you."

Her smile eased the strain that had festered between them since the pole arm session.

But she had not forgotten.

"Colin said you didn't want to teach me the pole arm because you wished to fight my battles for me," Emmaline said. "Is that true?"

Robert hitched in a breath. Colin had advised honesty. "The thought of you using it to fight street thugs or worse—a seasoned spy with means to kill you—is abhorrent to me."

She studied him. "I'm sorry for that, but you are not in my life, Robert. I will return to my ramshackle cottage and you to your digs. I must see to see to my own protection."

You are not in my life. The words landed in his brain with a deafening thud.

"If I have overstepped with the lift, please say so," Robert said stiffly.

"You did not. I don't mean to look askance at your kindness, but—" She broke off.

"But what?"

"Why, really, did you do this for me?"

Now it was his turn to take offense. "You suspect me of ulterior motives?"

"I find it's important to examine things."

In truth, he did have ulterior motives. He knew what Colin would say: *Woo the lass.*

But Robert wasn't Colin. Words stuck in his throat. And when Emmaline murmured something about retiring, he let her go.

Scotland's problem, Drew decided, was its women. The culture put men atop the clan pyramid, but in practice women ruled. Case in point: Colin's two comely cousins, strapping specimens who worked alongside him in the fields repairing fences, shearing sheep, herding those odd-looking cows. Neither woman looked the least biddable.

Likely, they'd be energetic bed partners—if a man could forget that they hid sharp knives in the pockets of those long skirts. One of the women had shown hers to Heloise during rehearsal for one of those dratted skits. She claimed it was for skinning animals, but Drew suspected it had darker possibilities. A man would do well to be wary.

Worse, the female militancy was contagious. Mrs. Stanhope had taken to practicing moves with a medieval pole weapon. He intended to take her away from this place tomorrow. He might have to reckon with Tavish, an unpleasant prospect.

But Drew was more worried about Heloise, whose weapon of choice was feminine wiles. More than three decades older, she was one of the most seductive women he'd met. To his embarrassment, Drew found himself drawn to her.

A woman old enough to be his mother.

The sooner he left Scotland, the better. Which is why he followed Mrs. Stanhope outside for her morning walk. He'd finally hit on something she wouldn't turn down.

Faith in the justice system? His assurances she would be treated fairly? She wouldn't believe those—Tavish had forever tarnished him in her eyes by exposing that staged abduction. No chance to recover lost ground there. Mrs. Stanhope neither trusted nor liked him.

There was, however, someone she did care about.

"Good morning, madam," Drew said.

She glanced at him, no charity in that icy gaze.

"I plan to leave tomorrow," he said.

"Did you expect mourning, sir? You won't get it here."

"'Tis a pity you and I have come to this pass," Drew said. "Nevertheless, I offer you a proposition."

Mrs. Stanhope's brows arched. "Let us be frank, Mr. Maitland. You are well-favored and to all appearances a gentleman. Some women will take that as evidence of good character. I cannot. Nor can I imagine accepting any proposition from you."

"You wound me, madam," he protested.

Her gaze narrowed. "I think not." She resumed her walk.

"If I must be resigned to your low opinion of me, pray do not let that obscure what I can offer your aunt," Drew said.

Mrs. Stanhope turned. "And what is that?"

"I hold Heloise in some affection, as perhaps you have seen," he said. "I cannot help but notice she is not in the best of health."

Her features hardened. "Are you threatening to harm my aunt?"

"The very opposite," Drew assured her. "If you return with me to London, I will have her seen by the best physicians. I will also pay for her treatment."

Her quick intake of breath told him more than words that he'd hit the mark at last.

She said nothing at first. Then: "We have seen many doctors. None have answers to what ails her. Some were charlatans."

Drew nodded. "But I don't imagine you've been able to afford the top medics. And by that, I refer to those trusted by members of Parliament, even the king."

"If those doctors helped the king, why do we have the Regent?" she challenged. "One hears stories of King George growing worse by the day."

"They are making headway," Drew improvised. "At all events, your aunt's malady, whatever it is, has nothing to do with old George."

"*Mad* George," Mrs. Stanhope corrected.

"Who is in his *eighth* decade," Drew pointed out. "Do you think your aunt would fare as well under the care of some Fleet Street apothecary?"

"Likely not. But you can't promise that your physicians will cure her. If there were easy answers, we would have had them."

"The courts will deal with you fairly. In the meantime, your aunt will have the best of medical care." Drew paused for effect. "If there is a chance to cure her, should we not try?"

Mrs. Stanhope regarded him. She looked troubled. But he noticed a glimmer of something else in her eyes: hope.

⁓

Emmaline marched up the path to the viewpoint where Robert took them weeks ago. The new lift provided solid support without pain. Her leg felt strong enough to tackle this hill, even the rocks.

She needed to put distance between her and the distasteful Mr. Maitland. Yet she couldn't escape the logic of his proposition. He could provide her aunt with better doctors. Perhaps they, too, wouldn't be able to treat her illness, but one fact was inescapable: It was wrong not to try.

Oh, she was wary. A man who could so shamelessly use her aunt's illness as currency would not be bound by his promises. The justice system had little interest in proving her innocence. She might languish in prison, leaving Aunt Heloise alone and destitute.

That wouldn't do. Emmaline had one thing to bargain—her freedom. Before she agreed to his proposition, she would demand that Mr. Maitland not only pay Aunt Heloise's medical bills, but also provide a companion and a living allowance for the rest of her days.

It was time to settle things. Robert wouldn't be obliged to protect her any longer. She was leaving in the morning and would likely never see him again. Instead, she was forced to put her faith in Andrew Maitland, which was no faith at all.

But she would manage. Even if she were dealt a long prison sentence, she'd survive. Like the cottage vermin, she would carve out a life amid the dregs of what remained.

⸺〰⸺

Robert leaned back against a tree, letting his eyes absorb the hills and lake below. It was a view that never disappointed, even when clouds rolled in to obscure the valley.

Years ago, he stood here, pondering his future with all the feckless wisdom of an impatient adolescent with physical strength beyond his years, desperate to set a course far from those who would control him. He spared no thought for how his strength might have been a balm to Portia had he remained in Scotland.

Who would he have been if he had stayed? A more worthy son?

A man who knew how to love?

Because he was failing now. The preliminary findings were dismal: Emmaline refused to let him take on her burdens or fight her battles. A more polished man—one who didn't need lessons in love—might have persuaded her. That man would know how to speak unflinchingly the things a woman needed to hear.

Was he in love with this brave, fearless woman? If so, how to tell her? She prized communication, the very skill he lacked, though he was making progress with his journal. Writing seemed to clarify things. Perhaps the right words would come.

Robert turned to leave, only to come face to face with the very person who'd commandeered his thoughts. Emmaline had trekked up the path that had given her such trouble earlier and bloodied her foot. He hoped his lift helped this time.

She looked surprised to see him. And not particularly pleased. As they regarded one another, the moment felt heavy with thoughts unsaid.

Suddenly, Emmaline burst into tears.

Instantly, Robert went to her. "Whatever it is, I—"

"This can't be fixed." Her shoulders shook with her sobs.

Bewildered, he pulled her against his chest. His hand stroked her hair. He'd have sworn that Emmaline Stanhope never cried. This was not a woman given to vapors.

Her arms went around his middle, and she buried her face in his coat. Robert's chin came to rest on the top of her head, and his arms closed around her, securing her against his heart.

Something in him shifted, as if a missing piece had been found and fitted to the very place it belonged. Robert wanted to claim it for all time. Never let it go.

Not it. *Her.*

Slowly, Emmaline pulled back to look at him. "Embarrassingly, I've turned into a watering pot. Apologies. The lift is wonderful. You've been more than kind. I'm grateful for all you have done for us."

Robert didn't want her gratitude. He wanted…

but words failed. Instead, he said this: "Have you ever been to Cornwall?"

Her forehead furrowed. "No."

"You'd like it." Truly, was that the best he could do?

She stepped away from him. "Undoubtedly. Just as I'd like Paris. Rome. Greece. I've as much chance of seeing those as Cornwall. I'm a city dweller, Robert. The sort London makes room for, but grants little purchase. I don't belong in those places, just as I don't belong here in Scotland. It's time I was home, living the life I have, not dreaming of places I'll never go."

Robert burned to know what troubled her. "Cornwall's not exotic in the way you mean. But it's perfect."

Emmaline mustered a smile. "Because it has those rocks you love?"

"The granite is fascinating," he confirmed. "Embedded with lilac lepidolite and black tourmaline, red and green serpentine—although that last isn't true granite."

He was babbling. But like an idiot, he kept on: "It's created when water is introduced as molten rock cools. Similar to Staffa. My theory is that Staffa is the earth in microcosm."

Undoubtedly bored her with that.

"Microcosm?" Emmaline repeated. "I don't know that word."

Ah. She was interested.

"Little world," Robert explained. "Small bits of the universe that give us truths about the whole. But I've digressed."

"I find your theories fascinating."

He hesitated. "Not boring, nor dry as dust?"

Emmaline shook her head. "I see the fire in your eyes. I hear the enthusiasm in your voice. You weren't like that addressing your society in London."

Robert shrugged. "Never liked declaiming before a group."

She sat on a rock, hands on her knees, her gaze fixed on him. "Tell me about Cornwall."

"You'd expect the cliffs to be brown and rugged. They are, but what captivates are the colors— red, green, lilac with gold mixed in. The sea is a brilliant turquoise. The green turf is so saturated in color that it takes your breath away."

"Like Scotland," Emmaline said.

Robert nodded. "Rain's the reason here, but in Cornwall it's the easier climate. The land doesn't have to work so hard to grow lush. It's almost healing."

She was studying him. Was she intrigued?

"I want you to come with me on a dig." The words were out before he could stop them.

Emmaline blinked. "What?"

"It would be strange not having you around," he added. "I'm accustomed to you."

Her gaze narrowed. "Like a comfortable old chair?"

"I, too, am ready to leave Scotland," Robert said. "Thought you'd like to see Cornwall."

"My geography is in no way deficient. Cornwall is far from here."

"Two weeks. Less, with favorable weather."

"What about Aunt Heloise?" Emmaline asked.

Robert smiled. "She'd come, too."

Her lips pursed. "How long did you imagine we'd be in Cornwall?"

"Month or two," Robert said. "I've a cottage there. Plenty of room."

"A month or two. In your cottage."

He felt hopeful.

But the lovely blue eyes so reminiscent of Cornish seas had hardened to icy slits.

"There's a word for women who depend upon the largesse of men for the roof over their heads and the food on their table," Emmaline said, her tone stiletto sharp. "I do not care to have it applied to me. So, no, I will not go with you to Cornwall."

Robert frowned. "You mistake my meaning."

"I think not. You are offering me *carte blanche*."

"You—and your aunt—would like it there," he persisted, with the last effort of a dying man. "You'd be well provided for."

She arched a brow. "We'd all be friends, is that it? Gather 'round the table for meals *en famille,* walk out to your digs to watch you chip away at those *strata*—"

"Not what I envisioned," Robert protested.

"At night, I'd be all yours, I suppose, like other women who are *well provided for*." Her gaze was withering. "Anyway, my plans have changed. My aunt and I leave tomorrow to return to London with Mr. Maitland."

Robert stared at her, uncomprehending. "Why the devil would you do that?"

She looked away. "He says the courts will be open-minded about my case."

"He will present you to the War Office as a presumed murderess and traitor. Why would you agree to such a thing?"

"Mr. Maitland promised to pay for the best doctors for my aunt."

Robert eyed her incredulously. "You believed him?"

"I don't have the luxury of doing otherwise. My aunt needs care."

"I will pay for her medical care," he nearly shouted.

Emmaline shook her head. "I won't be beholden to you any more than I already am."

"But you'd let yourself be beholden to Maitland? A man without honor or honesty?"

"Your *carte blanche* would make me a kept woman. Mr. Maitland simply views me as the means for feathering his career."

"You'd choose that over Cornwall?" Robert demanded.

"What I'm *choosing* is to return to London and see to my aunt's care," Emmaline said. "I've done everything for her within my power, but it's not enough. I see Mr. Maitland's character quite clearly, but I also see that he's my best chance to provide for her."

"I've already said I will pay—"

"I have responsibilities, Robert. I'm not someone who can dash off to Cornwall, even if I had the means. And certainly not with a man who..." She halted.

He closed the distance between them again. "A man who…?"

"Who wants to keep me around because he's *accustomed* to me."

"I never said that." Or perhaps he had, but not with that intent.

Emmaline's chin rose. "If you mean to stand there like some great towering bully and try to stop me from going with Mr. Maitland, know that I won't be cowed."

That hit too close to the bone. "Is that what you think—that I use my strength to bully women?" Robert growled. "When have you ever seen me do so?"

She flushed. "Perhaps that was unfair."

"Tell me that you know I would never try to bully or harm you," he insisted.

"I…do."

That she hesitated, if only slightly, gutted him.

"I will take you to London," Robert declared. "I'll see to your aunt's medical care. Unlike Maitland, I care what happens to both of you. That's worth more than the empty promises of a man you don't trust."

"And your terms?" Emmaline demanded. "You'll do this if I come to Cornwall?"

"No terms," he snapped. "I leave at first light. Maitland's carriage or mine. Your choice."

⁓

"You'd put your fate in Drew's hands?" Aunt Heloise eyed her in alarm as they prepared to go into dinner. "Have I taught you nothing, child?"

Emmaline sighed. "You've taught me a great deal, Aunt. But I don't think Mr. Maitland will let this go if I refuse. And he did promise to provide for you."

"The promises of a man like that are worthless."

"So Robert tells me. He's also offered to do so. But he's little different." Even as she spoke the bitter words, Emmaline knew they were untrue.

"Let's examine that," her aunt said. "Take honor. Does Mr. Maitland possess a shred of it? How about honesty? Trust? Sincerity? No need to answer. We can see plainly. Whereas Robert has moved heaven and earth to protect you—taking us to Scotland and under the wing of his family. He's demanded nothing in return."

"That's not entirely true," Emmaline said. "He wants to me to come to Cornwall for a month or two during his dig. I—we—would live in his house, eat his food—"

"Never say you told him no!" Her aunt looked horrified. "Cornwall is lovely. There's a theater by the sea, an amphitheater built into the rocks, down at the southwest tip. It's a majestical backdrop. I played there back in my youth. I would love to see it again."

"He as good as offered me *carte blanche*," Emmaline insisted. "We'd be his dependents."

"And what, pray, are we now?" Aunt Heloise demanded.

"If that is so, then it's time to end it. I want to return to London, find you new doctors. Good ones. End this legal morass that has ensnared us."

Aunt Heloise shook her head. "I can't let you sacrifice yourself."

"Mr. Maitland is not a man who gives up easily."

"Neither do I," her aunt said firmly. "I need to settle a few things with Colin tonight, but I believe there's a way to keep you out of Drew's clutches. I thought we had more time, but apparently that is not to be. Meanwhile, pack for tomorrow."

Emmaline was puzzled. "We're going with Mr. Maitland?"

"Didn't you say Robert has offered to take us to London?"

"Yes, but—"

"His carriage is *infinitely* more comfortable."

⚬⚬⚬

"It's time, Colin," Heloise said. "Drew leaves for London tomorrow. He wants Emmaline to accompany him and face whatever twisted justice he arranges, but I hope I have persuaded her to go with Robert instead."

Colin poured out a glass of whisky for her. He'd been lazily contemplating the next day's chores from the doorway of his cottage when she greeted him. He poured out a glass for himself, forced himself to abandon the hope that Heloise had come with a different intent. "I suppose that means ye'll be leaving as well. Stealing the joy from a poor man's tattered heart."

Heloise laughed. "Whatever tatters exist in your heart are none of my doing."

He eyed her mournfully. "Nay, there's a piece of

ye here, Heloise, always will be." Which was true for every woman he'd loved. Between infatuation and love, of course, lay a vast in-between, and sometimes it was hard to tell the difference. Pain was the key. If he pined for years, smoldered like stealthy peat fire, likely it was love.

Not that he'd ever been able to fix that.

She waved a dismissive hand. "We must act now. Have you the letters?"

"Aye. When do ye wish me to post them?"

"At first light. With any luck, they arrive in London before Drew."

"If you and Emmaline go with Robbie, Maitland will travel alone and faster. But he won't seek out George straightaway. He'll ponder his next move. There's only one, but it'll take him time to fix on it. The man's a bowfin conniver but still green around the edges."

Heloise took a swallow of whisky, then sputtered. "I've tried to like this, but it's like drinking dirt."

"That's the peat. Wealth of history and culture in it—land, loyalty, family. A reminder that those abide no matter what power-hungry Englishman proclaims himself king."

Heloise studied him. "Isn't that same history keeping you from the MacDonald woman?"

That took him aback.

"She's not the only woman in Scotland, Colin," she went on. "You're a romantic. Why keep to your solitary cottage?"

Colin caught her hand, raised it to his lips. "The memory of you."

"Balderdash. We had a minute in one another's

orbit. If you truly carried a torch all these years, you'd have done something about it. Admit it. We are alike, you and I."

He frowned. "How?"

"Flirting in the shallows, never daring the deep," she said. "That fleeting, early excitement grabs us. When it passes, we're on to the next. It's no way to live, but by the time one realizes that fact, it's too late. Youth has fled and options are few."

Heloise drained her glass. "The peat doesn't put me off so much now. I'll have more, please."

She leaned close to him. As Colin inhaled her scent, he felt a stab of desire. Heloise Alcott was as riveting now as she'd ever been. "It's not too late for us, Heloise. Say the word, and I will prove it to you."

Her easy laugh was answer enough, and he supposed she was right. He was still about the shallows, and perhaps, at this time of her life, she wanted more.

"I treasure our friendship, dear," Heloise said softly.

Colin sighed. "Can I convince you to stay?"

"No. Emmaline thinks I need her help. In some ways she's right, but she also needs mine. I'd like to see her settled, not struggling for each penny, not always in search of quacks for me."

"If you're hoping it's my nephew who'll win the day with her, I can't vouch for that," Colin said. "Robbie had a hard upbringing. Wears that like a hair shirt."

Heloise tilted head. "It burdens him still?"

"His father was cruel. Talked with his fists.

Seems Robbie's had no reason to think he's other than a big brute like his father."

"I've known cruel men," Heloise said. "Robert isn't one."

Colin eyed her darkly. "Aye. But love's a foreign language to him. If anyone could succeed with him, it's Emmaline. She's strong, that one."

Heloise sighed. "Alas, she's not looking for a husband. Nor even a lover."

"Hopeless, both of them." Colin drained his glass.

"Like you, if you let history stand between you and love."

"And that's why you're in the theater," he said. "Always hoping for another plot twist. Real life is different."

"Yet where would we be without inspiration?" Heloise shot him a sly smile. "I do believe the whisky's growing on me."

———∿∿———

With growing dismay, Heloise eyed the staircase that led to the bedchambers. Was it two or three glasses she and Colin had shared? Fatigue had seeped into her bones. She could go no farther. She sat on the bottom step. Perhaps someone would come along.

Midnight used to signal the beginning of her night—after the show, after the bouquets and accolades, her time was her own.

Except it never was hers. Gentlemen always wanted something, and not all of them were gentlemen about it. Time was, she could pick and choose. Those times were long gone. And so, it had come to this: sitting at the foot of the stairs, hoping for rescue.

Emmaline believed women should not wait for men to rescue them, that women were more resourceful than the world gave them credit for. But she never had to contend with the theater milieu, where men dangled lavish presents in exchange for favors, where beauty was the only currency because wages didn't cover living expenses.

Heloise enjoyed being courted. Theater life was exciting. When the lights went down, audiences never saw the threadbare costumes, the set's peeling paint, the flooring's rotting boards. They wanted only to be transported into a world where dreams came true or were dashed, where love was requited or rejected. Then they returned home and resumed their lives.

For performers, it was the opposite. Onstage, they had power. They lived in the world of imagination, far removed from demands of angry landlords and tradesmen and the money that was never enough. Colin was right. Heloise had lived in a world divorced from real life.

They'd soon be back in Oxford Street. This castle would be only a memory, like the roles she played. Colin, Robert, and John would no longer be part of their world. She would miss John the most. He'd given her hope that she might have someone real in her life at last.

John was a fine person, a worthy one. He'd lost

someone dear and needed to heal. She'd seen the promise in his eyes. It would be interesting to see where that led. But he deserved better.

Exhaustion clouded her senses. Heloise leaned against the wall, papered with colorful flowers and birds. She could pretend she lived among them, if only for a minute.

"Heloise."

A hand touched her shoulder.

John stood over her, concern etched on his features.

"Don't tower, John," Heloise grumbled.

He sank onto the step beside her. "Are you ill?"

"It's only life, dear." She gave a rough laugh. "Survivable, until it isn't."

"What did Colin do to you?" he demanded.

Heloise eyed him in surprise. "Nothing. Were you spying on me?"

"I saw you set off toward his cottage."

She blinked in surprise. "Are you jealous, John?"

He looked away.

Tempting as it was to flirt with him, she wouldn't take advantage. "Open your eyes and look around, John. The world's a cruel place, full of heartbreak. But that's not all there is. I'm the very least of what the world has to offer." Her voice cracked on that last.

As Heloise struggled to her feet, his arm went around her. "I'll help you to your room."

She wanted to refuse, but she couldn't manage alone. Slowly, they made their way up the stairs to her bedchamber. At her door, he hesitated. "May I come in?"

"I don't think that's wise," she said. "Temptation is an old friend."

He frowned. The dear man needed everything spelled out, didn't he? With a sigh, Heloise walked into the room, sat on the edge of the bed. He followed her.

"I could help you with your things," he said softly. "As I did that first night."

Heloise shook her head. "That was chaste. I don't feel chaste anymore. You bring out what little altruism is left in me, but it's finite. That's why you must leave."

"I don't understand."

She sighed. "You've spent decades caring for people, John, including a woman you couldn't be with. It's splendid that you are that kind of person. I'm not. I don't put others' interests above mine. I'm selfish."

John sat next to her. "Stop, Heloise. I'm no saint."

Heloise gave a rough laugh. "I can't be someone you tend like a dried-up plant left out in the sun too long. I don't want your charity. Put yourself first for a change."

"Perhaps I am. Perhaps you're what I need." He brushed a strand of hair from her face.

Heloise leaned into his touch, wanting what she could not have.

"I'm not what you need." She made her voice hard. "I'm not worthy. I hope there's life in me yet, but I know there is in you. Go and find it,

John. Find someone better, someone who doesn't need you like—" She broke off. "Go, John. Just… go."

John gave her a long look. Then he rose. "I am going. But I'm not gone, Heloise."

When at last he closed the door and the brush of his hand on her cheek was but a gossamer memory, Heloise fell back against the pillows, exhausted. Her conscience, starved for attention these many years, had picked a fine time to make itself known.

Being noble in real life was harder than it was on stage.

Chapter Twenty-Four

DREW WAS NOT expecting Heloise Alcott to present herself at his door before breakfast. She was not, as far as he knew, an early riser. But here she was, looking alarmingly alert.

"A letter has been posted to the duke," she said.

He eyed her blankly. "The duke?"

"Your superior in the War Office. Colin's brother George. The Duke of Argyll."

A twinge of alarm shot through him. "What letter?"

"Your confession to planting evidence in our cottage so that you could arrest Emmaline for murder and convict an innocent woman to further your career."

His jaw hardened. "You wouldn't dare."

"My dear Drew, it's no more than truth," Heloise said. "You planted the Tarot deck matching the death card from poor Mr. Burwell's flyer."

"I wasn't in your cottage until much later—the night of your niece's abduction," he protested. "And I planted nothing. That would be—"

"Reprehensible?" Heloise smiled. "That a part of you recognizes that fact gives me hope.

Nevertheless, that is what you admitted to in your confession."

He stared at her.

"The thing is, that death card does not conform with our Tarot," she went on. "Even someone unfamiliar with the Tarot must realize that decks can be different. One may feature witches, another animals, stars, elves—you take my point."

"I'm beginning to," Drew said grimly.

"The deck you planted is a standard one, used all over London, but our Tarot is unique. It depicts only women. Its death card is a winged woman bathed in fire. We didn't put that image on the flyer lest it be mistaken for some extreme female cause. The world isn't kind to those who envision a society not based on patriarchy."

Heloise smiled. "You recall I told you the death card symbolizes transformation. In ours, the woman is reborn in fire, rising in flames to overcome her suppression by men."

Drew stilled. "Your ridiculous philosophy aside, that isn't the deck you used when you read the Tarot for me just days ago at the castle. That deck matched the flyer."

"You are mistaken," Heloise said. "We have used a female-only deck for some time. It is quite subversive, but subversion is its own reward."

"What have you done, Heloise?"

"Saved you from the great embarrassment of putting your career on the line with faulty evidence," she said. "I believe Robert's uncle— the duke—will find your confession persuasive. Admit it, dear, you were out of options. No evidence ties my niece to his death."

"*Someone* killed him," Drew insisted.

"Can you be sure? It may help to know that a letter from poor Mr. Burwell—"

"Stop calling him that," Drew said through gritted teeth. "He was a traitor."

"Exactly what he wrote to your superiors," she agreed. "He confessed the whole in a separate letter that arrived posthumously at the War Office. The man was overcome with guilt and needed to unburden himself of the matter. The letter makes quite clear that he intended to end his own life to avoid the consequences of his treachery."

Dazed, Drew lowered himself into a chair. "The handwriting will be analyzed. If it's fake—"

"It will withstand scrutiny."

"Did you have one of your theater types forge the thing?"

Heloise regarded him pityingly. "That begins to sound like a man who sees his career slipping away. With *poor* Mr. Burwell's confession, and your own admission to planting the Tarot deck, you'll have your hands full explaining why you targeted our family as the means for boosting your career."

Drew was silent.

Heloise smiled. "There is one other, small thing."

His gaze narrowed.

"In your letter, you acknowledge a romantic obsession with a relative of Emmaline's. Sadly, the woman rejected your attentions, which angered you. As such, you could not be an unbiased investigator and worse, sought revenge on

Emmaline and her family."

Drew eyed her in bewilderment. "A woman? Who?"

"Why, me, dear."

He gaped at her. "No one will believe that."

"It's in your letter. The letter you signed and dated confessing to your mistakes."

Drew blinked. He thought for a long minute. Then it came to him.

"The Shakespeare volume I signed after *Macbeth*." Colin started a new page, had Drew date his signature. He'd made a novice's mistake, failed to pay attention to what he signed. "It was a separate document, wasn't it? Not part of the book."

Heloise ignored his question. "For all these reasons, you will find it best to drop this investigation. My niece is incapable of murder. I think you realize that in your heart of hearts."

"I have no heart of hearts," Drew growled.

She smiled. "You do, but I worry that it gets little nourishment. You will have to watch that as time goes by. Give *Macbeth* a deeper reading, Drew. Unchecked ambition corrupts, even kills. It's a lesson that has stood the test of time."

Drew put his hand on the door, barely restraining himself from strangling her. "What I vow to watch out for is conniving actresses."

Heloise's gaze softened. "If it helps, our liaison brought me great pleasure. It is not often that a woman of my age commands the interest of a younger, virile gentleman."

"Next you will fool me into thinking it was

real," he said gruffly.

Heloise trailed a fingertip over his shoulder.

"It's men like you, Drew, who keep me young."

Robert wanted to sabotage Drew's carriage. Fiddle with the axle, remove a spring. The vehicle would be undriveable. Emmaline would have no choice but to return to London with him, instead of Drew. She'd be furious if she knew he'd taken the decision out of her hands, but after his clumsy Cornwall invitation, Robert had little to lose.

It would be easy.

And unworthy. Only cowards took the easy way out.

Which is why he knocked at Drew's chamber before breakfast.

Drew opened the door. His neckcloth was askew, his shirt laces undone. His pantaloons looked as if he'd slept in them. His eyes were bloodshot, as if he had rubbed them raw.

"Rough night?" Robert queried.

"Rougher morning," Drew snarled. "What do you want, Tavish?"

Robert stepped past him into the room. "Drop your investigation of Emmaline."

Drew rolled his eyes. "Is everyone in the castle intent on defeating me today? You're the second person to try. I'm not taking her with me this morning. Intervening factors."

"You will end your investigation?"

"I'm leaving without her," Drew said. "That's

all I can promise."

Robert closed the distance between them. "To be clear: I want you out of her life. If you harass her, arrest her, or in any way harm her, you'll answer to me."

"Even you aren't above the law, Tavish," Drew snapped.

"And you've been acting like you are the law. But you're only a scheming bastard who prizes career over justice. Not sure the War Office will tolerate that kind of blackguard."

"I'm not afraid of your empty threats."

Robert gave a rough laugh. "Nothing empty about them. I may not be good with words, but I'm more than decent at combat. Fisticuffs would suit—unless you prefer something fancier, in which case the castle's armory has some tempting weapons."

Drew was incredulous. "Are you challenging me to a duel?"

"Only if you cross me in the matter of Mrs. Stanhope," Robert said.

"Does anyone ever refuse you, Tavish? What's it like to be the biggest man in the room? The one everyone fears. The brute."

Robert had worked most of his life not to let his size define him, but people always saw that before anything else. Naturally, Drew homed in on it. It's what the man did—picked at weakness, until it festered into abscess.

"That's your definition of a man?" Robert challenged. "A brute who intimidates and threatens?"

"You just threatened me with a duel," Drew pointed out.

Robert's mouth thinned. "I'm not above threats, Maitland, but it's not a way of life. That's the difference between us. You seize advantage by exploiting people's weaknesses, pretending to be honorable when you are anything but. I don't pretend to be something I'm not."

That never worked out. Case in point, his failed lessons with Emmaline.

Drew had been given fair warning. The man's fate was in his own hands.

Now it was time to head to London.

Colin sent them off with hearty embraces. Emmaline didn't miss the knowing look he and her aunt exchanged or the fact Mr. Maitland's absence went unmentioned by everyone.

Boxes of her father's papers went into the baggage coach; the work remained unfinished. The boxes offered such silent reproach that Emmaline hadn't even written in her diary for days.

"Because you are not Augustus," her aunt said as they climbed into Robert's carriage. "You can't know his mind, so you don't know what to write."

"The publisher wants a finished book," Emmaline said.

"Then finish it in your own way, with your

own voice," Aunt Heloise said.

"They aren't paying for my voice. They want Augustus Alcott."

"I never knew what was in the playwright's mind when he wrote the words I spoke on stage," her aunt said. "I simply made them my own. Each of us interprets art through her own prism. The goal isn't to mimic the writer, but to make the words authentic. Don't be the actor who merely recites words. Pour them from your soul. Let the world hear you, Em."

Emmaline was silent as Mr. Gibbons joined them, then Robert, who took a seat opposite her. That surprised her. The weather was fine, and she thought he would have preferred to ride.

"I don't understand why Father collected tales that portrayed love in such fantastical terms," Emmaline said, picking up the thread. "In 'Beauty and the Beast,' she loved him as Beast. Yet the story turns him back into a prince. Are we not entitled to be loved as ourselves?"

Mr. Gibbons spoke. "Perhaps the Beast, knowing he was loved, came to see himself in a better light. Shedding his beastly nature enabled him to become who he was meant to be."

Aunt Heloise regarded him. "You suggest love makes us better than we are?"

"No one falls in love and remains unchanged," he said.

Sensing undercurrents, Emmaline glanced from Mr. Gibbons to her aunt. "If Father thought love

transformative, it's odd that he never sought love

again after my mother's death."

"Are you sure of that, dear?" Aunt Heloise said.

Emmaline sighed. "I'm sure of nothing. It's as if I'm shadow boxing with his ghost, never finding the real person."

Mr. Gibbons's gaze fixed on his employer. "It is difficult to know what is in another person's mind unless they tell you."

Robert, who had remained silent, merely crossed his arms and closed his eyes.

———⚬⚬⚬———

Bad decision to ride in the carriage. Close quarters, awkward talk about love and the like. Emmaline looking stiff and remote, Gibbons staring at him—how did the man sense everything?

Secrets abounded. Gibbons owed him an explanation about Portia. Robert suspected that Heloise, along with Colin, had something to do with the fact Maitland had found *intervening factors* and abandoned his plan to take Emmaline to London. Which is why Robert elected to ride in a closed carriage, if only to take the temperature of everyone's secrets.

He, too, had a secret. When he thought of Cornwall's lush cliffs and turquoise seas, he saw only one woman at his side. He'd failed to adequately convey that and insulted her instead.

And so, Robert had poured his heart out on the page. The journal snippets he had dashed off

here and there in recent days had primed the

pump. Writing had gotten easier, more personal. Last night, his pen had unleashed a storm:

Dear Emmaline: I apologize for inviting you to Cornwall. I did not intend to insult you.

Robert had almost stopped there, but he pressed on.

Cornwall is so exquisite, so unlike any other place on earth, that when I picture it in my mind's eye, I see you there. Indeed, you might be a selkie born from its waters, for your eyes hold its aquamarine seas, and your hair the warm mahogany of its cliffs. Like Cornwall's colorful granite, you give no quarter. My strength is nothing to yours. You can gut me to the marrow with only a look. A word. A sigh.

Embarrassingly florid. But he persevered.

I could not say these words today. My thoughts muddle when I'm around you.

An unflinching admission of weakness.

I hope you will not be offended by this letter's personal tone. We have been together in exigent and varied circumstances, but I do not assume that you have granted me the liberty of thinking of you in such terms. (Perhaps you will take exigent *as a small sendup of my pedantic tendencies, exhibited to my detriment at that lecture.)*

Would she smile at that?

Will you grant me the privilege of calling on you properly? As you've noted, I lack skills for winning a bride. Nevertheless, I have decided to try again. If I have offended you beyond redemption, I nevertheless

beg your indulgence that I may make a proper apology

in person.

Yours,

Robert Tavish

He had sailed under cannon fire, bested all challengers in fight. But this was the battle of his life. Always he'd protected his heart, kept it under lock and key. Doubtless it had shriveled nigh to nothingness.

Yet something lived still, demanded to break free. Demanded that he set down those words. Find courage to give them to her. Wait while she determined his fate.

Robert was prepared for defeat, prayed for victory.

"Robert doesn't speak to me," Emmaline told her aunt. "It's as if I don't exist."

Aunt Heloise smoothed her hair in the mirror. She'd taken a nap before dinner at their inn in Stirling. "Silence can have a multitude of meanings, dear. Why choose a negative one?"

"We ought to be comfortable with one another by now. Yet he avoids me."

Her aunt regarded her closely. "Do you not find that telling?"

"Indeed," Emmaline said. "It tells me that he does not wish for my company."

"Or that he wishes for it more than he can say. Ask him, for heaven's sake."

Aunt Heloise smiled as she surveyed her reflection. Emmaline thought she looked radiant. Not for the first time, she wondered whether Mr.

Gibbons was the cause.

"I have no appetite," Emmaline said. "I am going for a walk."

Stirling was their return journey's midpoint. Its centerpiece was Stirling Castle, a massive fortress that for centuries was a Stuart stronghold. Perched on the plateau of a hill, the castle afforded majestic views. Yet it was the cemetery and ancient monuments that drew Emmaline.

Ever since Iona, she'd been fascinated by gravestones, their clues about the dead and their lives. Here, too, words on most stones had eroded. Carvings that survived offered clues to the deceased's trade. A pick, mallet, and chisel suggested the person was a quarryman. Another stone bore carvings of gardening tools, another a plough, another loom and shuttle. One elaborate monument portrayed cherubs guarding the family plot. Its base was carved to resemble a coffin with a plaque admonishing, "Remember death."

"If you don't get enough death here, there's a nearby hill with a beheading stone."

Robert stood watching her.

Ask him.

She faced him, took a deep breath. "Why are you avoiding me? It's as if I don't exist—"

"I wrote you a letter," he said.

"A…letter?"

"Can't remember a word now," he added. "Gist is I've decided to take a bride after all. I need lessons—conversation, dancing, and the like."

"But…why did you change your mind?"

A muscle moved in his jaw. "You found me

lacking. I need to not be lacking."

"I was unkind," Emmaline said quickly. "What one woman abhors, another may adore."

"Like Beast in the fairy tale."

So he *had* been listening in the carriage.

"Yes," Emmaline said. "One person's flowers may be another's weeds."

"You've put me in with the weeds, I suppose," Robert said.

She smiled. "Wildflower at worst. Or dandelion. A moment of splendor, then lost to the wind."

"If there was a moment of splendor between us, I missed it."

Emmaline felt her face warm. "You don't need my help finding a bride. Scores of women will wish to marry you." Why did that prospect dismay her?

"Not looking for scores," Robert said.

"The truth is that I have decided to abandon my marriage agency," she said. "You'll find suitable matches on the Marriage Mart. All you need do is appear at Almack's…"

"No!"

His vehemence took her aback.

"I wish to work with you," Robert said, more calmly. "You know my…peculiarities." He cleared his throat. "Moreover, it seems that in the right circumstances, I am quite biddable."

———※———

"The hinges are back to their old tricks," Aunt

Heloise said as they stepped over the usual street rubbish and entered the cottage.

Robert had insisted on carrying their luggage and boxes into the cottage himself, and Emmaline cringed as she imagined their surroundings through his eyes. Compared to the castle and the Oban manor, it was humble indeed, never mind how it compared to his Mayfair mansion.

He propped her pole arm and walking stick in a corner near the front door and promised to call tomorrow. Apparently, he truly intended for her to find him a bride.

"He still hasn't apologized for offering me *carte blanche*," Emmaline said after he left.

Her aunt frowned. "Being a man's mistress is not the worst thing in the world, Em."

Emmaline wanted to claw back the words. "I did not mean to suggest—"

"That I've done anything tawdry? Well, it's the truth. I don't fit anyone's idea of a lady. I've had a full life, and if it were to end tomorrow, the only thing I'd regret is leaving you alone."

Emmaline wrapped her in a hug. "Nothing will happen to you. I swear it."

"Tsk-tsk. Ladies do not swear." Aunt Heloise gave her a mischievous smile. "They make promises, which they sometimes break."

"I won't break mine," Emmaline insisted.

"Not the one you've made to me. But perhaps you'll struggle to find Robert a bride. Perhaps you might instead claim him for yourself."

Emmaline stared at her. "He's an earl, for

heaven's sake."

"But a diamond in the rough," Aunt Heloise said. "He'll be devastating when he gains a little polish. Already, he makes your heart flutter wildly."

"Robert is nothing to me." But heat washed over her.

"He's everything you've ever wanted," her aunt said. "The prince come to claim you."

Emmaline sighed in resignation. She was done arguing with her aunt over fairy tales.

An hour later, she was in her room, poring over her father's papers, determined to finish at last. His introduction to *Intimations of Romantic Love in Selected Fairie-Tales* was too brief. Usually, he wrote a longer, deeper analysis. Perhaps time robbed him of that.

Still, his words riveted her.

"Romantic love, a concept foreign to Perrault's time, nevertheless is given voice by the mysterious, undeniable power that transforms beasts into princes and scullery maids into princesses. These tales offer proof of the human need for love—even when they did not know its name."

Oh, Papa. If love was an essential need, he'd been bereft since her mother's death. Perhaps, in these fantasies, he'd found a measure of joy. But princes, knights, queens, kings, and imaginary creatures stood as ridiculous counterpoint to real life. It was no kindness to make readers think fantasy could ease their trials.

Yet was that so terrible?

Emmaline began to write. For all the princes who never followed her to the ends of the earth, for all the knights who slew her no dragons. Something persevered still, and she was determined to find it.

Chapter Twenty-Five

"I SENT YOU TO investigate the woman, not take her to Scotland." George stared at his nephew. Something was different. Robbie seemed more...human. Less cold, but more volatile. Perhaps it had something to do with that canary, which perched on the desk as if it was his right.

"Her name is Mrs. Stanhope," Robert snapped.

"No, it isn't, I've learned," George said.

His nephew's jaw hardened. "She's committed no crime."

"If she is innocent, show me the proof."

Robert's glare held daggers. "Even Maitland found no evidence of her guilt."

"His investigation is suspect. You saw the letters." George pointed to the documents on his nephew's desk. "I'd like to know what trick Colin pulled to get him to sign that confession."

"I suspect Colin had help. Heloise Alcott is a formidable talent."

George began to pace. "Bad business for the War Office. We're supposed to accept that Burwell committed suicide because he felt guilty for betraying his country, and that Maitland's investigation is tainted because he planted evidence and had a dalliance with the suspect's aunt, a woman more than twice his age? It's preposterous."

"It serves," Robert pointed out. "No one is falsely accused. The only blame attaches to Maitland. But he will rebound. That sort does."

George's gaze narrowed. "Might personal considerations have colored your view about Mrs. Stanhope's guilt or innocence?"

Abruptly his nephew rose. "You believe I'd cover up murder and treason to shield someone I care about?"

George eyed him in astonishment.

"What?" Robert growled.

"I am mulling your words," George said. "Specifically, 'someone I care about.' I've never heard you admit to caring about a woman. Has the universe turned upside down?"

Robert didn't bat an eye. "Only righted itself."

***

Baskets of flowers, enough to open a florist shop, came in the morning. Two hours later, the turquoise dress that had belonged to Robert's mother was delivered to their cottage, along with a pair of evening slippers made of soft kid.

"What is this?" Emmaline asked when Robert arrived for their appointment.

"I am practicing," he said. "Prospective husbands are supposed to send flowers."

"Not a garden's worth," she protested.

Robert ignored that. "I sent our acceptances to the Marquess of Ainsford's party tonight."

"*Our* acceptances?" She eyed him in bewilderment. "But I wasn't invited."

Thomas was nuzzling Robert's leg. After a moment's hesitation, he bent down to pet the cat. "No matter. I sent word you'd attend. Your aunt and Gibbons, too. Chance for me to work on social niceties. Train for my eventual, er, groomhood."

Emmaline sat on the sofa, the only furniture not covered with flowers. "Surely your invitation does not entitle you to bring a horde of uninvited guests."

"Ainsford's been inviting me to parties for weeks. He'll be pleased."

As Robert claimed the remaining space on the sofa, her pulse quickened. If she'd ever been indifferent to the man's considerable physical attributes, that time had passed.

"Gibbons knows what to do at these events," he added. "He'll smooth things over."

"But my aunt—"

"Will sail through. You cannot doubt her skill."

Emmaline stared at him. "Why are you doing this?"

"You once called me an ogre." That gray gaze held an odd vulnerability. "Maybe I want to prove you wrong."

"I'm sorry," she said. "I was frustrated because you weren't trying."

Robert regarded her. "Now I am."

"I don't belong at a marquess's party. I don't know how to do my hair or—"

"*I* do." Aunt Heloise struck a pose in the doorway. "Never fear, dear. You will look every inch a princess. Mr. Tavish—Lord Kent—will be your prince and I will be…well, I'll think on it. By the time tonight arrives, I'll be an exotic something-or-other."

Emmaline's spirits sank. "Will there be dancing? My leg will make me clumsy."

"Any clumsiness will be on my part," Robert said gallantly. "I am a terrible dancer."

"I, on the other hand, am an excellent one," Aunt Heloise said. "John—Mr. Gibbons—and I can give you lessons."

Emmaline eyed Robert in dismay. "If it's a salon, there will be witty intellectuals and if there is dancing there will be graceful debutantes and grand ladies. You can attend such events on your own when you are ready."

"I am ready. And I want you"—his mouth curved in an enigmatic smile— "to be there."

⌘

Robert knew Emmaline was nervous, but she looked regal in that dress, even in the gilded monstrosity of Ainsford's home. He, on the other hand, detested the confines of breeches and a snug waistcoat. Who decreed these uniforms?

The house was as absurdly ornate as his own, absent the elephant sculpture. The first-floor ballroom had all the usual folderols, wide moldings, tall ceilings, inlaid flooring, gilded columns. Furniture was arrayed around the perimeter, as if to emphasize that the room was for dancing and that those who did not would be viewed, quite literally, as wallflowers.

Emmaline hadn't brought her cane. Perhaps she feared it would make her stand out.

Heloise, on the other hand, had no intention of blending in. Her pink and purple gown blinded in its intensity, and her matching turban added bright green and blue peacock feathers. Gibbons, in contrast, wore a staid black topcoat and gray trousers.

The marquess and his wife greeted their party effusively.

"What a rare privilege!" Lady Ainsford exclaimed. "It is an honor to welcome the reclusive Lord Kent to our humble home."

Robert bowed politely but did not offer a response. He was only here to show Emmaline that he could conduct himself like a worthy groom. He was about to present Heloise when she pushed forward and introduced herself as "Lady Featheringill."

Ainsford bowed and allowed that he was charmed to meet her.

"Oh, we have met," Heloise said, "though so long ago one struggles to recall."

The marquess smiled politely. Clearly, he did not remember.

But Heloise was not done. "I do recall that it was in Covent Garden, just before it burned, so it must have been in '07, about four years ago. A *Hamlet* performance."

"Ah." Ainsford looked confused.

"You were in good company, as was I," she went on. "It was a jolly evening."

The marquess frowned.

"What I recall most particularly was that the actress portraying Ophelia was in excellent form," Heloise added. "There wasn't a dry eye in the house during her pond scene. You felt so moved that you introduced yourself to her following the performance."

Lady Ainsford looked at her husband, who had paled. Apparently, his recollection had improved, and it was not a memory he cared to acknowledge.

Gibbons took Heloise's elbow and gently guided her away from the marquess, but Robert did not miss her parting shot—a mischievous expression that spoke volumes.

Emmaline had spotted a bevy of young ladies in the corner. She propelled him in their direction. "These are the very sort of women you should meet. Try to manage a conversation. When the musicians start, ask one of them to dance."

With that, she pushed him forward and took herself off.

Robert stood stiffly facing the group. There were five of them, all wearing variations on insipid pastel gowns. "Er, greetings."

As one, they curtsied. One giggled. Robert couldn't think of anything to say. Weren't they supposed to speak now, so he could reply and keep things going?

Thankfully, one did. A lady in pale pink said her name was Analiese. The giggling one in lightest blue was Jaqueline. Others chimed in. Robert lost the thread, wondered where Emmaline had gone.

Fortunately, the ladies started chattering like magpies. He pasted a frozen smile on his face and pretended to listen.

⁂

Emmaline made her way through the crowd and escaped to the quiet of the terrace. At least Robert was talking to the debutantes. They looked dull and uninteresting but more suitable than any bridal prospects she could find for him. Women at such parties married for money or title but hoped for both, which made Robert a prized catch. It might take him time to learn this world, but as a wealthy earl he'd be granted all leeway.

The thought of him with another woman made her heart ache. Yet he was worlds above her touch. Her practical nature nurtured no fairy tale illusions of him as her prince.

But perhaps…she had? She rode here in Robert's fine carriage and wore a lovely gown that might have been conjured by magic. All that was missing were glass slippers.

"May I join you?"

An elegant man in a dark-blue tailcoat and buff breeches stood several feet away.

"I've no claim on this terrace." Her thin smile failed to soften the edge in her words.

He did not betray by so much as an eyelash that he found her rude. Instead, he strolled easily toward her and bowed politely. "Forgive my manners, madam. I am George Campbell."

Robert's uncle. Colin's brother. The duke.

Tall like Robert but not as broad-shouldered, he was polished in the way of men who moved in powerful circles. His hair had a touch of Colin's red, but his face lacked his brother's amiable, open expression.

Emmaline curtsied. "Emmaline Stanhope, Your Grace. I'm acquainted with your family. Robert is here, in fact, if you—"

"It's you who hold my interest. I imagine you know why."

Of course. He oversaw the War Office.

Her gaze narrowed. "And it is you I have to thank for sending Andrew Maitland to me."

"I didn't. He took the initiative." The duke smiled. "A most enterprising young man."

"Conniving, I would say."

He regarded her. "Perhaps we can agree on inventive."

Emmaline's chin rose. "We cannot. He sought to arrest me for murder and treason without a scintilla of evidence. I'd wonder at a man who could sanction that."

"Point taken. I do not condone arresting the innocent. Neither do I approve of a fiction that applies a fanciful whitewash to serious crimes."

What was he suggesting?

"I did not murder Mr. Burwell or know of his treasonous activities," Emmaline said. "You have no evidence against me."

"That is why we are at *point non plus*. Officially,

the crime remains unsolved, which is very much not ideal at a time of war. Our men are dying. Spies like those working with Burwell cause more deaths. I won't apologize for the fact that our methods can be unorthodox."

"Neither will I apologize for condemning them."

"Perhaps we can turn to the subject of Robbie," the duke said lightly. "I confess to being astonished that he has found someone. He is not an easy man to abide."

Emmaline frowned. "Found someone?"

"Ah. He has not communicated that. Not surprising." He hesitated. "For some context, allow me to bore you with a bit of my background. As a young man, I gambled irresponsibly. I was given to bad hours and worse habits. My father rescued me from debt numerous times. He thought marriage would settle me, but I resisted. After his death I did marry my best friend's former wife— they were divorced, you see—which my father would have viewed as scandalous."

Emmaline was struck by the nonchalant tone in which he related such intimate details.

"Society did not care, however," he continued. "When one is a duke, much is forgiven."

"And your friend?" she couldn't resist asking. "Did he not mind as well?"

The duke laughed. "A fair question. Lord Paget, my friend, says often and publicly that I'm 'the best creature in the world.' He gives no sign that he thinks otherwise, and I am content with that.

There are other sordid details I probably shouldn't share with you."

"On the other hand, you've come this far," Emmaline said.

"You are unflinching, I see. Now I understand why Robbie likes you. Paget had an affair, which is why my bride had divorced him. His affair was with the wife of Henry Wellesley, brother of Arthur Wellesley, our esteemed commander of the peninsula war. No one wished to cast aspersions there, and that benign approach extended to us. Alas, we are accepted everywhere, for I would dearly like to avoid parties such as this."

Emmaline studied him. "Why are you telling me this?"

The duke put a hand on the railing and looked out over the gardens, where roses were beginning to bloom. "I've led a life of carefree decadence, with distasteful details all too common among the nobility. I'm the rule, you see, rather than the exception."

He turned to her. "My nephew and I have nothing in common. He does not accumulate gambling debts, nor angle for other men's wives. I'm astonished to find him at this gathering, because he avoids frivolity, and to Robbie, all *ton* parties are frivolous. He is a brilliant scholar who does nothing by halves. You ask why I share my sordid story? It's a warning. There is no check on my power in this world, and I've been known to retaliate."

Emmaline heard the threat but refused to be cowed. "What is it you want from me?"

"I do not wish to see Robbie hurt," the duke said. "If you sought his protection in hopes of eluding criminal charges, leave off. Robbie has no sway with the War Office or the courts."

Her gaze hardened. "I seek no man's protection."

"You have it, nevertheless. Robbie's protective instincts run deep. He did not take you to Scotland merely to breathe the fine Highland air."

Emmaline glared at him. "Is that all?"

"No. You must withdraw Maitland's absurd confession."

Emmaline frowned. "What confession?"

"She doesn't know." Robert stood at the edge of the terrace. "Stop meddling, Uncle. She had no part in the letter. It was Colin and her aunt."

Emmaline looked from him to the duke. "What did they do? The truth, please. Don't try to keep it from me." She gave them a thin smile. "That's *my* warning, Your Grace."

The duke's brows rose in amusement. Robert was not amused, however. He closed the distance between them. His gaze raked over her. "Hand over the weapon."

"No."

The duke looked puzzled.

"George isn't your enemy," Robert insisted. "He's not going to clap you in irons. You don't need to protect yourself from him."

"It is beyond annoying that I keep being asked to prove I am neither murderess nor traitor." Emmaline glanced at the duke. "If I were a criminal, I'd already have used this on you."

She reached under her gown and pulled out

the knife secured in her stocking. The blade of the *sgian dubh* was as sharp as the day it was forged centuries ago.

His Grace eyed her in astonishment.

"Now," Emmaline said softly, testing its tip. "Tell me about the confession."

———

Heloise had not danced this much in a very long time. John was an able partner, but by no means her only one. Indeed, she was much sought after. It felt like the days when she was a desirable and fascinating woman at the peak of her power.

Back then, she knew who she was. Now she was devoid of definition. Still, it didn't hurt to pretend for a little while. But the days when she could dance all night were gone, and when John finally reclaimed her for a final dance, Heloise was spent.

Nevertheless, the aura of desirability seduced her; she wanted to feel that once more.

"You know, John," she said in a husky voice, "you could have me for a song."

He regarded her for a long moment. "I've never been able to carry a tune, Heloise. Leastwise not a fancy one."

"Perhaps you only want coaching."

John shook his head. "I'm too old to learn new ways. And perhaps we are past our dancing days."

"Nonsense. I still dance as well as I ever did."

"You know what I mean."

Almost, Heloise could believe that he held her in affection. But John was only just tasting freedom after a life of pain. He deserved to sample a smorgasbord of delights. She didn't want to be the first he tasted. And it was too much to hope she'd be the last.

Time passes so quickly. Heloise could not help but wonder how much time was left her.

Would there ever be a man who wished to keep her? Not for a week or a month or even a year, but for all time? Had those performances she'd thrown herself into meant anything when all was said and done? Her memories would die with her. Had it all been a waste?

Suddenly, her eyes filled with tears. She would not turn John into one in a long line of conquests who helped her pass the time until her time came to an end. Back then, she pretended it didn't matter, because she was using them as much as they used her.

Now she found it mattered very much.

"I'm sorry," Heloise whispered. "For thinking you would wish to have anything to do with me. You are too fine, John, much too fine."

His finger brushed a tear from her cheek. "You are a shameless flirt, Heloise, and I love your spirit. You bring light to my darkness."

"Could you come to care for me? After you've gone out and had your smorgasbord—"

"My what?"

"Of women. All the women who will rush to your door once you are ready to open it. You deserve freedom to sow your wild oats." Heloise sighed. "I suppose it's a futile hope that you will one day find your way back to me."

John pulled her away from the dance floor. "I don't have to find my way to you, Heloise. I am already here. Come. It's time we went home."

⚈⚈⚈

Nothing could be done about Colin's and Heloise's trickery, as each was ungovernable. George conceded the War Office had no choice but to stop focusing on Emmaline. Robert doubted Maitland would drop the matter, but for now he lacked standing. Emmaline refused to relinquish the *sgian dubh* on grounds the party might yet get out of hand.

As the evening wore on, Robert forced himself to ask ladies to dance. He endured the silly affectation of signing their dance cards, stepped on a few toes, and was fatally bored. He soon ran out of inane topics like the weather and quickly concluded that none of those women would try to understand rocks or be persuaded to sail to Staffa.

George led out Emmaline for the cotillion, which put her instantly in demand as a dance partner. She managed without limping, which he knew must please her. Robert couldn't help but stare as she moved. She was a vision in that blue gown. His mother would have been charmed.

As one man after another claimed Emmaline for a dance, her eyes sparkled, and she smiled often. One man sought her out for a waltz, but she demurred with an appealing blush.

Parties like this were a waste. Superficiality reigned. He was never doing this again.

Somehow, another hour passed. Was it not time to leave? He had played the gentleman, danced clumsily, and conversed meaninglessly. But just when Robert thought the wretched evening was done, Emmaline presented herself to demand a dance.

Was this some new test? Wasn't she tired from all that cavorting with others?

But when she gave him a playful curtsy and offered her hand, every thought fled. Robert found himself staring into those sapphire eyes as if they held the secret to life. His life, anyway.

He was past pretending otherwise. Did she feel that, too?

Their dance was some baroque thing requiring the lady to execute a turn under his arm, followed by the man turning under hers. Robert tried to fit under Emmaline's arm, but it was impossible. They stumbled, laughed, and finally ceded the floor to more experienced dancers.

Robert breathed a sigh of relief. "I am ready to leave."

"I daresay no one will miss us," Emmaline agreed.

"George left long ago," he said. "He pretends to like these events but secretly prefers to be home with his wife."

"He seems every inch the duke," she observed.

"George wears the title well, but at heart he's a Scot longing for home. He could choose another path, but the politician in him won't allow it." Robert helped her into her cloak. "Gibbons ferried your aunt home. He'll be back with the carriage."

"He is very attentive," Emmaline said. "She must be exhausted."

Robert regarded her. "Are you not? You danced every dance after George anointed you with the aura of his dukedom."

She smiled. "Strangely, no. Your lift did not trouble me and for that I am most grateful."

They left the marquess's house and walked toward a street corner where carriages waited for their owners. Robert wondered why he suddenly felt unsettled and not a little glum, especially since Maitland was disarmed and his shoe lift was a success.

Ah. Now he had it.

"I don't want your gratitude." Spoken more harshly than he intended.

Emmaline turned to him. "What *do* you want, Robert? At first you claimed you wanted a bride, but that was a ruse. Now you say you do, and I don't know what to make of that. Did any of the ladies you met tonight take your fancy?"

"One."

"Oh?" She looked taken aback. Almost… dejected?

That gave Robert hope.

They stood in silence for a few minutes. Pretended to watch for the carriage.

Finally, Emmaline pressed his arm. "Who is she?"

He didn't respond.

"If you have fixed on someone, tell me, so I may celebrate your success," she prodded.

Robert studied her. "Would you? Celebrate?"

"Of course." Emmaline looked away. "We're friends… aren't we?"

If they were simply friends, he didn't have a prayer. Robert was tired of wondering about her feelings. He wouldn't let her hide behind gratitude and nonsense about celebrating his success. He wanted the Emmaline who faced truth.

"What if the only woman I want is you?"

Her little gasp thrilled him. But her eyes were daggers. "This is about Cornwall, isn't it? Let me be clear, Robert: My frocks may be threadbare and my cottage crumbling, but I will never be any man's mistress."

Emmaline pointed to Ainsford's townhouse. "I don't belong in that world. You do. Any of those ladies will be a suitable bride. They won't complain when you leave for digs. They'll ensure you get sherry and brandy on schedule."

"Don't want them," he said mulishly. "I want you." Where the devil was that note he'd written? Words looked better on the page.

She shook her head. "You're simply *accustomed* to me."

Panic filled him. Hadn't he passed her tests? Flowers, conversation, dancing? But something was still lacking. *He* was lacking. Her words felt heavy. Like goodbye.

No—*farewell.*

Robert crossed his arms over his chest. "What about marriage?"

Was that a proposal? If so, it, too, was lacking.

Emmaline gave a ragged laugh. "Those ladies are what you want—a wife who isn't a bother. I, on the other hand, would be a *complete* bother as a wife."

She turned away, her shoulders set.

Robert understood, finally, that he'd failed. No organized plan, testing, or analysis could deliver what he wanted—the woman of his dreams. Dreams he hadn't even known he had.

Why had he let himself believe he could have her? Why had he gone to such lengths to prove himself a worthy groom? It wasn't enough. Moreover, Emmaline would only come to grief at his hands. She deserved someone civilized, who wasn't fated to cause pain.

All his false hopes shattered. There was only a bottomless chasm of despair.

Ah. There was the carriage. Gibbons, always sensing when he was needed.

Chapter Twenty-Six

"ARE YOU MISS Emmaline Alcott?" Emmaline stared at the tall, slender woman on their stoop. She wore a gray frock with lavender pelisse, buff gloves, and a plain brown bonnet. Fashionable, but not opulent.

"Stanhope is my name now." Emmaline eyed the woman in confusion. Her brain was thick. She'd scarcely slept after last night's parting with Robert. The brash words she'd flung at him in Oban haunted her: *"I'm not weak. You can't hurt me."*

But he *had* hurt her with that offer of *carte blanche.* And made it worse with that half-hearted proposal—if that's what his words last night meant. The notion was laughable. If that party showed her anything, it was that she didn't belong in his world.

"You are Augustus Alcott's daughter, are you not?" the woman asked.

"Yes." Was this about yet another of her father's debts?

The woman studied her intently. "May we talk?"

Puzzled, Emmaline led her into the parlor. The

visitor looked to be a few years younger than Aunt Heloise. She seemed ill at ease and refused an offer of tea. "I ought to have introduced myself. I am Sarah Manchester. I knew your father."

Did she want money? Surely not. That their resources were meager must be obvious.

"Are you aware he died two years ago?" Emmaline asked.

Miss Manchester nodded. "I dithered about this a long time before deciding to find you. It wasn't easy. I didn't know you used a different name. I have followed your aunt's career, however. When she retired from the stage, I went to the theaters asking for her until someone said I might find you both here. I came a few weeks ago, but you were away."

"We've been in Scotland," Emmaline said warily.

Miss Manchester pulled a packet from her bag. "Augustus was working on this before he died. It's the forward to his final book."

Emmaline knew her father often used students to help with his work. But women weren't permitted at Oxford, and she was much older than his students. "You were his assistant?"

She nodded. "We met at one of his public lectures. I was fascinated by his work. He translated tales from many cultures and demonstrated how they share common themes."

Miss Manchester grew animated. "Often, lovers must prove their worthiness. Cinderella, for example, had to fit into a glass slipper to win her prince. Thousands of Cinderella stories exist. It's thought the original came from China. That was to be Augustus's next project."

Her voice wavered on that last; she took a moment to compose herself.

"There are no opportunities for women to pursue studies, so I asked him if he needed an assistant," she went on. "At first, he resisted. Said he had others, as well as a daughter who tried to help him get organized."

Emmaline smiled wistfully. "I don't think I ever succeeded in that."

"Augustus's process was chaotic," Miss Manchester conceded. "I only wanted to learn from him, but I fell in love. He was the most romantic man I've ever known."

Emmaline blinked. "That does not seem like my father."

The other woman smiled. "Not on the surface, but he had the mind of a romantic. He often sent me flowers. Once, for my birthday, he commissioned an ice sculpture."

Finally, that bill from the ice sculptor made sense.

"I know that you sold his house. I assume that was to cover his debts." Miss Manchester looked apologetic. "I'm afraid he was a spendthrift in affairs of the heart."

"How long were you and my father together?"

"Five years," Miss Manchester said. "The very blink of an eye."

Emmaline was astonished. "He never mentioned you."

"He insisted on secrecy. I believe he was

worried about your reaction. He never intended to marry again. For years he was content to live the life of an ascetic."

"And to collect stories with happy endings," Emmaline said softly.

"Vicarious happiness," Miss Manchester agreed. "After he hired me, it was months before he was easy in my company. I fell in love long before he acknowledged his feelings."

How wonderful it would have been to know he found love, Emmaline thought sadly.

"This must come as a shock," Miss Manchester said. "Neither of us were seeking romance. I couldn't take your mother's place, but I hope I offered him some comfort."

"I wish I had known," Emmaline said. "We could have met under other circumstances. I would have thanked you for persevering with him. It could not have been easy."

"At times I despaired," the other woman conceded. "Caring for a man who pushed away every opportunity for caring was maddening."

Her father had indeed been such a man. And— the thought suddenly landed with startling clarity—so was Robert, in his way. "How did you manage?"

"I allowed him to push me away many times." She smiled. "And then one day, I didn't."

Miss Manchester rose. "Thank you for hearing me out. I simply wanted to meet you and deliver Augustus's last writing."

"I am very grateful," Emmaline said.

Her visitor hesitated. "To the polite world,

I suppose I'm a fallen woman. But I have no regrets. I was with the man I loved for as long as he drew breath. That is a glorious privilege."

After she left, Emmaline stared at the envelope. Hands shaking, she pulled out five pages scrawled in her father's slanted script. He'd rewritten the earlier, truncated introduction and singled out three tales: "Blue Beard," the wolf and the little girl, and "Beauty and the Beast."

Because Blue Beard's bride defied him by venturing into a forbidden chamber that held corpses of previous wives, the tale seemed to warn against female curiosity. But Augustus saw it differently. Because the bride survives Blue Beard and inherits his wealth, the story "opens the door, literally and figuratively, to greater power for women," he wrote.

In the tale of the wolf, the girl lies in bed with the wolf, who's masquerading as her grandmother, and is eaten. Augustus again rejected the obvious interpretation that the story warns of danger from strangers. Instead, he saw a metaphor for sexual awakening: "Drawn by the wolf's animalistic nature, the girl goes with the wolf and she, too, becomes wild."

That left the Beast. Her father argued that Beast "was capable of love all along, or he wouldn't have fallen in love with Beauty. Who is to say he did not save himself in the end?" The Beast, he wrote, "lives among us—indeed, it may *be* us. Love requires a leap into the unknown, sometimes by loving a beast who fits no idealized notion of love, sometimes by banishing the beast in ourselves."

Augustus added a personal aside: "Love eluded me for years because of barriers I erected in despair after my wife's death. Happily, those were felled by a heroic lady. While I don't expect to live much longer, I take heart in finally understanding that love will always triumph."

Tears ran down Emmaline's face. The code of silence, finally broken.

⌁

Robert had found a 1680 publication that described efforts by Athanasius Kircher, a German Jesuit whose work presaged Mesmer's, to put a chicken into a trance. Whether the method would work with a canary was uncertain. Privately, Robert thought Galahad would sing when he was ready. Nevertheless, he would try to mesmerize the bird.

Kircher's chickens weren't harmed when he held them upside down to immobilize them. That wouldn't work with Galahad, who was small and not very robust. They'd need another way.

"Birds don't move much when it's dark," he told Peter. Galahad was in his cage in Robert's study. "Put a blanket over him, let him get used to that."

As Peter laid a cloth over the cage, the bird squawked an objection. He didn't like to be confined and preferred to perch on a shoulder. But after a while, Galahad quieted.

"Now remove him gently and lay him on his

side," Robert told Peter. "Take care not to press on his chest. Hold his head lightly with your thumb and first finger."

The lad's hands shook, but he managed it. Robert held his breath, knowing that they'd likely only get one chance at this. Kircher had used his finger to draw an imaginary line from the chicken's beak to a spot just beyond its eyes, slowly repeating the movement until the creature was in a trance.

Neither of them spoke as Robert tried the maneuver. At length the bird grew motionless, his eye membranes slightly opaque.

Peter's eyes widened in alarm. "Is he dead?"

"Merely waiting for your command," Robert said softly. "Tell him to sing."

The lad looked terrified. "What if I kill him?"

"You won't." At least Robert hoped not. There was less science to this than wishful thinking. "Go ahead."

Peter put his mouth near Galahad's head. "Please sing," he whispered. "Ye were born to."

A lump formed in Robert's throat. They could do no more than this. And the less time the bird was senseless, the better. "Now put him back in the cage, and we'll rouse him."

Once Galahad was safely in his cage, Robert clapped his hands softly. But the bird remained motionless. For a long, agonizing minute they watched his seemingly lifeless form.

"It was your words he heard in the trance. He may be more responsive to your voice," Robert said. "Try to wake him."

Peter clapped his hands. "Galahad. Wake up." His voice broke on the last.

The canary stirred. He stood on one leg, then the other. Then he squawked.

Robert breathed a sigh of relief.

"When will he sing?" Peter asked.

"We don't know that he will," he said gently. The boy put too much faith in what might be nonsense perpetrated by a seventeenth-century trickster. But Robert found himself hoping against hope that their rudimentary attempt worked. "I suppose we wait."

———

Robert stared at the fireplace mantel, seeing in its protruding carved rams a willful ignorance of the woman in placid cameo between them. Likely she'd prefer to be more than a passive vessel for their acquisitive arrogance.

How many epiphanies could a man have? Today's, coming on the heels of their tenuous experiment with Galahad, offered similarly dubious prospects.

Nonetheless, he now understood that every judgment Emmaline had uttered against him, starting with those first days, proved true. He'd been rigid and graceless, unwilling to make himself amenable. When he asked her to come with him to Cornwall, he thought of himself, not the damage to her reputation and self-esteem. And last night, he congratulated himself for dancing and conversing with the debutantes but gave her no credit for teaching him the skills.

To be sure, he remained clueless about something she said at one of their painful early sessions: *A woman likes to be tended to.* One day, that epiphany might come.

Too late, like all of them. Emmaline would never be his.

Ah, but here was Gibbons, invading his study, interrupting his self-flagellation.

The man presented him with a list. First was a demand that Robert hire a dozen female servants. And by that, he meant Peter's large family.

"This house has been too long without women. There's ample room should they wish to live here," Gibbons said. "The timing is fortuitous, for I have decided I can no longer remain in your employ. Peter's mother will make a fine housekeeper."

Robert stared at him. "Your family has served mine for generations."

"Yes, and I'd thought to remain, watching you find the happiness that has eluded you since childhood. But I need to look to my own happiness."

His childhood. That conversation was overdue.

Robert cleared his throat. "I've meant to ask about the time I was pulled from school and taken to Scotland. I didn't grasp then that it was your doing. But Portia never would have found the strength to defy my father. I should have realized it was you all along."

Gibbons merely stood there, dignified and attentive.

"I know you didn't do it only for me," Robert said.

"No," he said after a moment.

"You protected her. I'm sorry I didn't know that before. We owed our lives to you."

Gibbons looked taken aback. "It was my responsibility."

"But it was more than that, wasn't it?" Robert persisted. This was unfamiliar ground. He and Gibbons never spoke about such personal matters.

"Yes."

"I want to know the whole."

Gibbons nodded. "Second thing on my list."

Robert poured a glass of whisky, handed it to him, and took a glass for himself.

Waited.

"Your parents' wedding was the event of the season." Gibbons wore a distant look. "King George himself sat in the royal pew."

"Your father lived for the hunt," he went on. "After your mother gave him an heir—your brother Neville—the earl began to neglect her and surrounded himself with fellow hunters. They were a coarse and unruly lot, much fond of drink."

Gibbons hesitated. "One night, the earl drank too much and came to Portia's door, which she'd taken to locking against such a possibility."

Robert stilled.

"He was not kind with women. It's why I had found the female servants posts elsewhere. By then he'd begun his slow descent into spirits that would rule him ever after. That night, after an especially rowdy party, he broke down her door. Easy for a man of his strength."

Robert's innards constricted.

"I found her the next morning huddled in the garden, bleeding and bruised and weeping," Gibbons said. "If I'd been any kind of a man, I'd have killed him. But it wasn't in me to harm my employer. I sent the servants home—all men, by then. I wanted no one to see her in that condition. I prepared her bath, washed away the blood as if I could somehow wash away his cruelty. It was an unthinkable intimacy, but I helped in the only way I knew—by serving her."

Robert kept silent. Instinct told him there was more.

"She was never the same after that night," Gibbons said. "She shut herself into a chamber of her mind and never fully came out of it. He had destroyed her spirit."

"Did you…did the two of you—" Robert paused. "Hell. You know what I'm asking."

Gibbons shook his head. "The idea of breaching the boundaries of my class was abhorrent. I was a servant. She was far above me."

Robert studied him. Gibbons displayed no outward hint of the anguish he surely felt. "It cannot have been easy for you to tell me this. I suppose the truth does not like to stay hidden."

"It does not." Gibbons held his gaze. "I am not done with the story."

Ah. The worst was yet to come. Robert could not imagine what it might be.

"The day after the assault your father took himself off to the Continent with his friends. Said he was after bigger and better game. He did not return for several months." Gibbons paused for a heartbeat. "A few weeks after he left, your mother discovered she was with child."

Truth landed on Robert like a stone. He was conceived during that assault. That *rape*.

No wonder his mother had been so fragile. And tried for the rest of her life to rid herself of the stain of his violent conception. The mesmerists his father brought in weren't to blame for her frailty—and certainly not her death. She had other demons, ones that left her broken and locked away from everyone. She'd been damaged irreparably the night he was conceived.

It had never been within Robert's power to save her. He hadn't failed, so much as tried the impossible. A mere youth had lacked power to help a woman so profoundly wronged. But he might have stayed to offer comfort, instead of fleeing Scotland to forge his own way.

How he longed to turn back the clock, to be there when Portia needed him. To denounce his father as the criminal he was. To renounce his blood legacy.

"Robert."

He felt Gibbons's hand on his shoulder. The man had never used his given name.

"You are not your father," he said quietly. "You are ten times the man he was. His violence does not run in you. I have watched you from near and far, and I stake my life on that."

Robert hitched in a breath. Speech was beyond him.

"I fell in love with her," Gibbons went on. "I

didn't want to—there's no future for a countess and a servant. But while I never breached our boundaries, after that night we grew closer. I looked after her, tended her."

A woman likes to be tended to. The elusive notion finally crystallized: put her needs first, safeguard her, help her thrive.

"You protected her," Robert said softly.

"To the extent I could. It was easier once the earl sank into spirits and his health diminished. Even so, not until I took her to Scotland was I sure she could no longer be harmed." Gibbons paused. "I'd have died for her. And for you."

Silence stretched between them.

"Do not perpetuate your father's legacy by letting it haunt you," he added. "Don't fear the power of your strength. Redeem it. Use it for good."

Again, Gibbons touched his shoulder. "Fate did not give you a worthy father, but you desperately needed and deserved one. No one can take the place of family, but I've thought of you as my own. I've tried to be there…" He trailed off.

"When I needed you," Robert finished. All this time, he thought Gibbons's mothering was merely a result of the man's fussy nature. How wrong he'd been.

All these years, he hadn't known that Gibbons had loved Portia. That he sacrificed that love in the service of honor. That his soul held unimaginable depths.

Gibbons straightened, then retreated to the doorway.

In two strides, Robert was at the door. Barring his flight.

Gibbons froze.

"Damn it, man, look at me," Robert growled.

Slowly, Gibbons turned. Steeled himself.

"If I must choose between the brute who called himself my father and the man who was there when I needed him…" Robert cleared his throat.

Gibbons waited.

"I choose you," Robert said, his voice rough. "If you'll have me."

Whatever Gibbons might have replied was lost as Robert enfolded him in a violent hug.

⚬⚬⚬

Several hours later, Heloise squinted out the carriage window at the elegant landaus and dashing curricles in the park. A coachman drove them in Robert's stately town coach, but she would have preferred an open vehicle.

"No one can see my peach bonnet," she groused.

"I can," John said. "It looks lovely on you, Heloise."

She beamed. "That was exactly the right thing to say."

"I am just a humble servant who aims to please." He smiled.

"Coming it too brown, dear. I am glad you and Robert had that talk. But it's too bad you are leaving. I…will miss you." She injected a note of wistful sorrow into the words.

John regarded her. "I am leaving his employ,

not the universe. There is a house in town I've had my eye on. Robert offered to buy it for me, but I don't think I will let him. I must get used to this new world and its possibilities. I'd like to meet it on my own terms."

"What possibilities?" Heloise adjusted the brim of her bonnet to a more rakish angle.

"The chance to plant a garden."

Heloise frowned. "How...nice."

"Take in the theater, too. Perhaps you'd be kind enough to accompany me."

She sighed. "Yes, of course."

John eyed her with concern. "What is amiss, Heloise?"

"I am glad you have plans for your new life. Is there anything else you desire beyond pulling weeds and watching costumed actors spout lines on a stage? Something...deeper?"

"Such as?"

Heloise's gaze narrowed. "You are toying with me, John. Don't deny it."

"I could deny you nothing," he murmured. "I daresay no man can."

That pleased her. Enough to say what was on her mind. "I know Portia is still uppermost in your thoughts..."

"Do you?" His gaze was unreadable. And Heloise prided herself on reading gazes.

"That is understandable. You've gone through a long, painful ordeal, and I know you are not recovered, not ready to, er..." She trailed off, suddenly unable to say more.

"To love another woman?"

Trepidation filled her. She wanted him to begin his new life and discover all he'd missed.

Just not without her.

"Perhaps you are wrong," John said. "Perhaps that is what I am most ready for."

Heloise decided to risk it. "And that woman might be…me?"

"Time has a way of sorting things. That can take a long while, as with my feelings for Portia, or be blazingly quick." He reached for her. "How have I managed to live without you?"

She gave a ragged laugh. "You've no idea how many men have managed to live without me."

"They were fools," John said softly.

Tears sprang to her eyes. "Don't be misled, John. I am a bawdy woman who's led a bawdy life. There is nothing in this world I've said and done that is anything but tawdry. I am unworthy. And faded. And old."

"You are a flower, Heloise. A bird of paradise. Beautiful and rare."

Heloise shook her head in disbelief. "Where do you get these notions?"

"It is I who am unworthy," John said. "But if I had the courage…"

"What, John? What would you do?"

"Insist that you marry me."

Heloise blinked. Those words had never been addressed to her. "Was that a…proposal?"

"Not a graceful one. Should I have first declared my love? I love you with all my heart."

Her pulse raced. "I'm afraid you've fallen in love with a peacock, not a pigeon. I require embellishment. I apologize if that is inconvenient."

"It is I who must apologize. You deserve to be courted, surrounded with flowers, and serenaded with sonnets." He hesitated.

"Go on," Heloise prodded.

"I've wanted to make love to you, Heloise. I've wanted to stand beneath your window at night and sing hymns to your exuberance. You live life to the fullest."

"Yes," she acknowledged. "But I have a past. You cannot wish to saddle yourself with a soiled dove."

"Peacock," he corrected gently. "Gloriously painted in the colors of life. May I hope that you care for me a little?"

Heloise covered his hand with hers. "You bring me joy, John. And peace unlike any I've known. I can be myself with you and know that you accept me fully. After all this time, and all the years I have on my plate, I've fallen in love for the very first time."

John beamed. "That makes me the happiest man on earth. May I kiss you?"

"My dear, that is the very *least* of what you may do."

"But..." He hesitated.

She frowned. "But?"

"You are not well, Heloise. I shall understand if you do not wish to consummate our marriage. It may be too taxing for you, too uncouth."

"Uncouth?" Heloise stared at him.

John shifted awkwardly on the seat. "Perhaps that was not the best word—"

"'Tis true my health is indifferent, but I'm by no means at death's door." She smiled. "Meanwhile, another treatment comes to mind. An actress I knew swore by it. May I show you?"

"Show me?" He looked puzzled.

Heloise glanced out the window, then returned her attention to him. "No one can see us in here. We face each other like so. I bring my knees close and push them between yours."

John regarded her warily as she inserted her knees between his.

"A bit closer, John. Yes, that's right." She caught his hand and placed his palm over her abdominal region. "Put your hand here. Energy must flow between us."

His face went scarlet.

"It helps if you move your hand lower like this. Try a stroking movement as I move my knees further apart." Suddenly, she inhaled sharply. "Yes, that's quite acceptable."

"Is there no end to what you can teach me, Heloise?" he asked softly.

"Probably not," she murmured. "Put your other hand here, around my body. Lean forward. Closer. Yes, like that. We are close enough to kiss, aren't we?"

John needed no further invitation. A long moment later, Heloise looked up at him through the fringe of her lashes. "Do you wish to try the rest, John? This is very daring, isn't it? It is not even dark, and we are only a stone's throw from the nearest carriage."

"I would like to try the rest."

Heloise shivered. "John, you make me tremble with excitement."

"I can't begin to describe what you do to me, Heloise."

"The stroking should be lower," she said, her voice sultry. "In the region of my ovaries."

"I haven't the faintest idea where a lady's ovaries are, but I think I can take it from here."

As he did, Heloise gave a little gasp. "Oh, John."

<hr>

Would she lose all self-respect if she went with Robert to Cornwall? Emmaline knew what Aunt Heloise would say: Plunge in, embrace the possibilities, even the fairy tale. Still, a mistress was at the mercy of her keeper. Not her own person. Not independent.

Emmaline prided herself on facing obstacles. But what if her stubbornness was itself such an obstacle? After all, what did she have to show for her grim embrace of reality? For her refusal to compromise? For her rejection of even a faint hope that love might one day find her.

And there it was—the beast inside her. It wanted to stay in splendid isolation, hold fast to principles and independence, reject anything that risked heartache. Was her father right—that the Beast had been capable of love all along? Had even yearned for it?

Oh. She had fallen in love with Robert Tavish.

And pushed him away. A man so unsuitable that he spirited her away to Scotland to protect her from an unprincipled knave. A man so selfish that he saved her life at sea, watched over her in a derelict chapel, fashioned a clever lift that eased her pain. A man so uncouth that he sent her flowers and an elegant gown, then escorted her to a ball she was certain he loathed.

A man who had gotten quite good at complete sentences.

Who, despite his professed change of heart, hadn't really wanted her to find him a bride.

Because he was courting…*her.* The flowers, the dancing, even the complete sentences—had they all been for her? *"You found me lacking. I need to not be lacking."*

Emmaline would not let her beast hold her back. She would not grant it the power to rob her of happiness. *She* determined her own worth, as Aunt Heloise often declared, and if her choice was to become Robert's mistress, so be it. Love was what mattered.

Propriety was a silly reason to refuse the man she loved.

On her way out, Emmaline seized her stick. Because she intended to walk very fast.

Nearly ripping the door off its hinges, she marched out to Oxford Street.

Gibbons's revelations hit Robert with seismic force. He hadn't understood love. Hadn't understood the tending. Hadn't allowed himself to get close enough even to glimpse the territory.

Whereas Gibbons, with his unselfish caring and courtly honor, embodied the concept.

Love didn't come with power to undo the wrongs that had forged a damaged life. About some things, nothing could be done. But avoiding love only guaranteed emptiness. Life was more than moving in orderly fashion from one paper to another, one dig to the next, marking time in measured tasks, controlling his world by closing himself off from it.

Emmaline made him yearn to reach for something that endured, that transcended time. Robert knew now that he could never hurt her. Love didn't work that way. His father's brutal legacy was his to reject. Gibbons had given him answers, just when he needed them.

Did fools get a second chance?

Robert intended to find out. He grabbed his coat just as a loud knock sounded at the door. With an impatient growl, he flung it open.

Emmaline stood there. With her pole arm, pointed at his heart.

⚬⚬⚬

Emmaline froze, realizing how silly she looked. She didn't belong here, on the stoop of this very fine Mayfair mansion, below a magnificent elephant trumpeting in permanent pantomime. Its faux ferocity felt as useless as her ancient spear.

Gingerly Robert took the pole arm and leaned it against the iron railing. "What were you going to do with that?"

"I meant to grab my walking stick, not this," she said apologetically. "I was in a hurry." Judging by

Robert's coat, he, too, was hurrying somewhere. Her timing was abysmal.

Emmaline took a deep breath, fought for courage. "I'm sorry for your past, for the cruel childhood that left such a mark. For the boy who was too young to protect his mother. I'm sorry for the pain you suffered."

Now she couldn't stem the rush of words. "You've held back, tried not to care. But I've seen you with Mr. Gibbons, with Peter, with my aunt. You care, no matter what you say."

"Might I get a word in?" Robert began.

But Emmaline pressed on. "Above all, you are *not* lacking. I tried to make you into something you're not—a 'proper' groom, and a shallow one at that."

"Talking about the weather isn't obligatory? Such a relief." Robert pulled a piece of paper from his coat pocket. "I was coming to give this to you. Easier than saying the words."

Emmaline stared at him. "You wrote something?"

"Right. Used words. Strung them into sentences." His mouth curved.

Something was different. *He* was different. Lighter somehow. Was he glad to be free of her? Was she too late to change his mind? If so, her next words would be a terrible risk.

"I will come to Cornwall if you still wish it," Emmaline said. "Even as your mistress. I hate that word, but I don't fit in your world any other way. The party last night—"

"Was an abomination." Robert bent his face to hers. "I'll have you no other way than as my bride."

The blazing heat in his eyes left her weak with need.

"You shoulder burdens with the nobility of a warrior," he said. "You meet life head-on with no expectation it should be otherwise. You take care of your own. Your heart is precious and true. It would be the greatest honor of my life if you consent to be my bride."

Robert drew in a breath. "Complete sentences, all."

He caught her hand, brought it to his lips. "I will work to win your love. Try to be better at conversation or dancing or whatever—"

"No," Emmaline said. "I was wrong to try to change you."

"But I *have* changed. It's as if something inside has finally broken free. I love you, Emmaline. Dare I hope you feel the same?"

This wasn't possible. The love of one's life did not suddenly make her believe in fairy tales. Yet this was no fantasy. Emmaline let her eyes drink in the man, from his unruly mane to the granite jaw, robust torso, and powerful limbs. Her strength was nothing to his.

She knew that worried him. "I'm not fragile, Robert. I want the full measure of your passion. You mustn't hold back. I have many ideas about carnal conduct, thanks to my aunt."

"I can well imagine," he murmured.

"I do love you, Robert, but—"

His gaze faltered. "*But*? Dear God, Emmaline, what is it?"

"I won't let you fight my battles."

Robert crossed his arms, regarded her with a mulish expression. "Not agreeing to that."

Her chin rose. "The Queen of Wands fights alongside her partner."

"She is stubborn," he pointed out.

"Independent," Emmaline countered.

Their gazes locked. His mouth twitched. "It's a battle you're wanting?"

"Only if you're up to it."

Suddenly, he pulled her against his chest with a force that robbed her of breath. Gave her a taste of his power.

Exactly what she wanted.

"It's yes, then, to marriage?" Robert murmured in her ear.

She pulled back to regard him. "Are you sure? Your wife deserves—"

"Everything that is within my power to give her," he said softly.

Then Robert dropped to one knee. "Will you marry me, Emmaline? All the words in my vocabulary begin and end with that question."

It was then Emmaline knew: If he'd held a glass slipper, it would fit her foot perfectly.

"Yes," she whispered. "With all my heart."

Above them, the elephant roared in triumph.

Epilogue

Two months later

THE DOUBLE WEDDING ceremony at Grosvenor Chapel was attended by a small and bizarrely amicable group.

Among them were Wellesleys—not Arthur, as he was busy waging the Peninsula War, or his brother Henry, Britain's wartime ambassador to Spain. But juicy complications lurked: Henry had divorced his wife Charlotte for her adultery with Lord Paget, to whom she was now married. And it was just as well that Charlotte's brother—also named Henry, who challenged Paget to a duel—was fighting abroad and unable to attend. Paget himself attended the nuptials with his new wife (Charlotte), as did his former wife Caroline, who had sued him for adultery (with Charlotte) and was now married to Paget's best friend George, the Duke of Argyll.

Perhaps not the greatest recommendation for marital bliss—but then again, why not?

George was all ducal elegance as he walked Emmaline down the aisle, bordered by rows of staid brown pews. Two tiers of arched windows lent charm to the chapel's simple rectangular layout. Arthur Wellesley's father, Garret, was interred in a vault beneath the chapel, with space saved for his wife, whenever she departed her mortal coil.

Death, however, was on no one's mind this day.

Colin served as best man for both Robert and John. Emmaline's friend Miranda was her attendant, and Heloise had summoned an array of colorfully attired actors and actresses for hers.

The ceremony was uneventful. The drama came after, during the party at Robert's house.

Galahad, granted attendance privileges, landed on George's shoulder, which greatly displeased the duke. Peter, attempting to cajole the bird elsewhere, accidentally knocked the elegant hat of (Paget's former wife, now George's wife) Caroline from her head—which she bore with equanimity, as she had weathered far worse crises.

But then, wonder of wonders, Galahad unleashed a long and melodious series of chirps.

"He's singing!" Peter exclaimed. Caroline's hat was forgotten as the boy captured the bird in a joyous embrace. Galahad, seemingly enamored with his newfound voice, began an even louder song.

"Can't you do something about that bird?" George asked Robert.

Alas, his nephew's gaze was fixed on Emmaline.

Then Andrew Maitland, who emphatically had not been invited, arrived to speak to George on an urgent matter. The two men conversed, to the disapprobation of those who held Maitland in dislike—basically, the entire wedding party.

"Our friend Maitland has news," George told them.

"Not my friend," Robert growled.

"Figure of speech," George amended. "Maitland has dug up a chemist."

Robert frowned. "And?"

"Nitrous oxide," Maitland explained. "A gas created by heating ammonium nitrate. Not yet in general use, except for a few idiots who amuse themselves with it at parties. Inhalation can induce laughter. More often, it puts the victim into a stupor and robs him of motor control."

"Like Mr. Burwell." Emmaline's gaze sharpened.

"Surely you don't suggest that Emmaline used it on him," Robert challenged.

"No," George said. "But nitrous oxide could explain why he remained in the path of the Mail and failed to save himself. The chemist recalls selling it to someone."

"Who?" This, from Colin.

"He claims not to remember," Maitland said. "But he was quite proud of his invention—a small bellows attached to a rubber tube sprays the gas from a canister. The device can be hidden up a sleeve or under a cloak and activated by compressing the arm against the bellows."

"Burwell stopped to give an old woman direction," Robert said. "Someone in disguise?"

George nodded. "I've given Drew the task of improving the chemist's memory as to who purchased the device, and he need not be polite about it."

Maitland's jaw tensed, but he said nothing.

George fixed a stern gaze on Colin, then Heloise. "Obviously, this raises questions about the validity of Mr. Burwell's purported suicide note. It would be highly unusual for the man to have been both a murder victim *and* a suicide victim."

His brother merely returned him a bland gaze. Heloise stifled a yawn.

"Even if Burwell's assailant used the device, there's still the question of whether his conspirators might target Emmaline," Robert said.

"Since we haven't come after them, I imagine they realize she didn't learn anything from Burwell that might expose them," George said. "Moreover, now that she's married, I doubt any of them would be fool to take you on."

Then George noticed his wife, Caroline, looking daggers at her former husband's new wife (and adultery partner), Charlotte. His brain immediately shunted the Burwell matter off to the side. He strolled toward the women with every expectation of making each believe she was in the right and had his wholehearted support. It was what Campbells did.

Robert pulled Emmaline away from the others. His fingers stroked the inside of her wrist, then trailed up to the sensitive inner part of her elbow. "Can't wait to see more of you."

"I already see more of you," she teased, glancing

at his legs. "Exposing your knees does not detract from your manhood in the least."

"And here I'd thought my blushing days were behind me," he said.

Emmaline caught his hand. "Your grandfather would be proud. I'm glad you wore it."

"More exposure than I'm used to, but it is my wedding day." Perhaps somewhere, John Campbell knew his reprobate grandson had finally conceded that the kilt was more than a length of cloth. And not just any cloth: the Black Watch.

Life with Emmaline had enlightened Robert. He was devoted to science but discovered that heart and mind could exist in balance. He was thinking of last night's spirited debate on the proposed Corn Laws, which ignited a long night of lovemaking. She and Heloise had moved into his home weeks ago, and neither pretended to keep separate bedchambers from their lovers.

Emmaline embraced lovemaking the way she did everything—with fierce resolve. At first, she was embarrassed to show her leg scars, but to Robert they were marks of her courage in overcoming physical challenges—he delighted in kissing them.

"Did I tell you I've found a husband for Miranda?" Emmaline said. "It's that nice professor who visited last week to discuss the dig. He'll be perfect for her."

A few feet away, Heloise beamed. "You see, John? All's well that ends well. I have several women in mind for Colin. The man needs a wife."

"Shouldn't he find her himself?" John asked.

Heloise sighed, which John mistook for sadness. "It must be difficult to be surrounded by your fellow thespians," he said quickly. "I know you miss the theater."

"Not so much these days." She shot him a saucy look. "I've come around to another view: I got to do the thing I burned for. It was a privilege. I am not the lesser for it. I am *more*."

"Indeed." John kissed her cheek.

Heloise held out her glass for a refill of whisky— she no longer minded the earthy peat undertone. "Colin bollixed things with that Scottish lass over an old clan dispute. Women here in town will find him fascinating. That Scottish accent, his looks, the small fortune—"

"What if he doesn't want a wife?" John brought her free hand to his lips.

"It is universally acknowledged that a single man in possession of a good fortune must be in want of a wife," Heloise said.

John eyed her curiously. "Where did you hear such a thing?"

"I met a clever woman from Chawton at the theater last week. She's written a novel to be published in January. We had a lovely talk about matchmaking and obstacles like pride and prejudice."

"I will buy it for you on your next birthday," he pledged gallantly.

"Thank you, dearest. Who knows? It might be a great piece of theater one day."

From a distance, Andrew Maitland surveyed them all with disgust. He'd learned much over the last few months. Heloise had been right when she said he was at a turning point.

Would it be the highest peaks of power for him or the bowels of Hell?

He knew precisely which.

END

AUTHORS LOVE REVIEWS! Please leave them on whatever platform you prefer. To keep up to date on new releases, subscribe to my newsletter @ https://www.eileenputman.com/newsletter/

Author's Note

THE DUKES OF Argyll aren't buried at Inveraray Castle. Most repose in the family mausoleum at Kilmun Village. (I moved it so Emmaline didn't have to take a long carriage ride.) One noteworthy denizen is Archibald Campbell, beheaded in 1661 for treason—collaborating with Oliver Cromwell's government, among other acts. His head was stuck on a spike in Edinburgh and was interred three years later. Son Archibald met a similar fate in 1685.

Franz Mesmer's hypnotic trance was considered highly erotic in its day; patients sometimes fell into convulsions or screams of ecstasy. Mesmer liked to hypnotize animals, including his pet canary. The canary slept in an open cage and woke him every morning by landing on his head. When Mesmer died in 1815, the bird would neither eat nor sleep and was soon found dead in its cage. I've shamelessly stolen the loyal creature as the model for Galahad.

As to the other bits of history woven into this book, I'll mention dinosaurs, my son's first love as a toddler. Englishman Robert Plot is believed to have discovered the first dinosaur fossil, a large bone, from a Cornwall quarry in 1676. It wasn't until England's Regency period (1811–1820) that scientists documented fossils linked to an ancient order of giant lizards.

And although this work is entirely fictitious, the tangled romantic history of George William Campbell, sixth Duke of Argyll, is well-documented. The duke did indeed marry his friend Lord Paget's ex-wife Caroline, who had divorced Paget over his affair with Lady Charlotte Wellesley. *The History of Parliament: the House of Commons 1790-1820* notes that Paget publicly called George "the best creature in the world." More telling, perhaps, was Caroline's opinion of George, whom she married in 1810, three weeks after her divorce from Paget. The duchess is said to have told Paget's brother that she had never known "the superlative degree of bliss which she was now enjoying" with George. (I found no record of Paget's reaction to that.) Perhaps it's relevant that Caroline had eight children with Paget during their fifteen-year marriage, none with George.

Acknowledgments

I AM INDEBTED TO John W. Griffith and Charles H. Frey, editors of *Classics of Children's Literature* (Macmillan Publishing Company, New York, 1992), for their provocative anthology of fairy tales, including French author Charles Perrault's 17th century versions: "Le Petit Chaperon Rouge" ("Little Red Riding Hood"), "Cendrillon" ("Cinderella"), "La Belle au bois dormant" ("Sleeping Beauty"), and "Barbe Bleue" ("Blue Beard"). They are in no way to blame for the fact that I infused this book with my own irrational ideas on the subject. The reader will also recognize Heloise's reference to the opening line of Jane Austen's *Pride and Prejudice;* Clytemnestra from Aeschylus's *Agamemnon;* and, of course, *The Tragedie of Macbeth* by William Shakespeare. I have referenced Robert Burns' bawdy poem, "Nine Inch Will Please a Lady," in an earlier work. The poem remains endlessly inspiring.

Thanks also to Georgetown University Professor Emeritus Leona M. Fisher, whose work on the male gaze, fairy tales, and women's studies proved revelatory.

Eileen Putman
eileenputman.com

Excerpt

Read on for a sample of *King of Hearts*, the first book in the Maitland's Rogues series.

Prologue

Spring 1815
London

HE WASN'T ABOUT to traipse all over London looking for virgins.

Not as long as Our Lady of Mercy convent lay cheek by jowl with the Market Street dock, where his newly acquired boat bobbed in waters swollen by high tide. With any luck, he could be on his way before the tide went out.

Like most of the ladies Gabriel Sinclair met, luck danced to his tune. This very night, luck had dealt him a perfect vingt-et-un, while the Earl of Sedbury had gone bust trying to improve on his puny pair of sevens — thereby gifting Gabriel with the earl's trim little yacht. Luck had not given him the courage to sneak into a convent full of sleeping nuns, but Gabriel had found that in the earl's wine.

The gnarled gypsy who had emerged from the midnight shadows as a glum Sedbury was showing him around the boat would have given any man pause. An ageless wisdom inhabited her wrinkled face, and her eyes gleamed with fury.

"Death," she intoned, pointing her bony finger at them. "Death seeks to bring you into his bosom. Bring me a lock of hair from a virgin's head, taken without harm, given without regret. Only then will death loose his grip on your soul."

Sedbury had shooed the woman away. "They haunt the docks," he grumbled. "It's that new prison hulk. Too close by half. Draws the riff-raff." He eyed the yacht wistfully. "Always meant to move her upriver."

They had shared a laugh at the old woman's attempt to scare them. Then a strange light had come into Sedbury's eyes, and the wine had flowed anew, and the gypsy's words became a reckless new bet that sent each man reeling drunkenly into the night in search of a lock of hair from a virgin, one of the scarcest commodities in all London.

The gypsy's curse hadn't bothered Gabriel. He was not afraid of death. In the years since leaving England for Jamaica, he had beaten that black angel more times than he could count. Boredom alone unsettled him, for it left him face to face with a man he did not care to visit long.

Besides, the gypsy had it wrong. Luck, not death, embraced him tonight. Luck had caused him to wander past this convent, thereby showing him the means of winning the new wager and depriving the earl of his London townhouse, the stakes Sedbury had put up in his desperate bid to regain his boat. But desperate men made unwise bets. The earl would never find a virgin at this hour, when chaste women slept peacefully in their own beds.

Gabriel suppressed a yawn. What did he need with Sedbury's house, anyway? He didn't intend to remain in England, though it might be diverting to sample the life he could have had if he'd been dealt a different hand years ago. A boat was all he needed. With it, he could bid the past farewell as sweetly as these sleeping maidens had said their evening prayers.

In the darkened convent bedchamber, he surveyed them. They were young — novitiates, perhaps. A veritable bevy of virgins. And none of them had thought to latch the front door. A trusting group, indeed.

Which would he choose? Gabriel studied their sleeping forms, forever removed from the world of men. He imagined them in the secular world, dressed in fine gowns and jewels, their hair piled high atop their heads and secured with combs of finest ivory. They would fan themselves coyly, each daring him to choose her. Would he select the blonde, the chestnut-haired, or the chit with the riot of auburn curls?

He usually had his pick, for women adored him. They were all alike: vain and prideful and needy. Even nuns, he suspected, had their vanity.

Gabriel slipped his knife from the slim leather holder he always wore under his waistcoat. He moved quickly past the bed of one young woman whose breathing was shallow and uneven — much too light a sleeper. He passed two others whose nightcaps obscured their hair. At last, he came to a young woman whose single blonde braid lay invitingly on the pillow. She snored so loudly that nothing short of cannon fire would wake her.

He stared at the knife and briefly wondered whether he'd lost his mind. A lock of hair from a virgin's head, taken without harm, given without regret. He didn't believe in the gypsy's words, but he did believe in fate that masqueraded as luck. For the moment, he would be its pawn.

Gingerly, he lifted the braid, feeling its weight, judging its substance. He could certainly take it without harm; he wasn't sure about the regret part. Then again, the girl could hardly regret what she didn't know. He shifted the knife to his right hand and bent over her.

"What are you doing?"

Gabriel froze. Carefully, he turned toward the voice. The girl he had pegged as a light sleeper sat upright, staring at him. "What are you doing to Mary?"

She looked just groggy enough that sleep still had a few tentacles in her. He pitched his voice low, so as not to wake the others. "Blessing her, of course." He was surprised that his words sounded slurred. Perhaps he should have left the cork in that second bottle.

"But —"

"Keep your voice down." He tried for a note of command, but a whisper had its limitations. "It is forbidden to speak," he improvised.

The girl hesitated. "Who are you?"

"Gabriel." Here, of all places, that name should carry weight.

Apparently, it did. She stared. "The...angel?"

"Archangel," he recklessly volunteered.

"You do not look like an angel."

Insolent chit. "Appearances can be deceiving." He still held the sleeping girl's braid. If his annoyingly persistent questioner would just look the other way...

"What is that thing in your hand?" Her gaze was riveted on the knife, though the room was dark enough he doubted she could make it out distinctly.

"It's a, er, wand." Did angels carry wands? No, that was fairies. Hell.

The girl stared at him in stunned silence. Suddenly, her eyes widened.

"A knife! You've got a knife!"

"Quiet, brat," he growled. That did not sound very angelic. Well, he might as well have something to show for this night's labors. In one swift movement, he sliced off the sleeping Mary's braid. She never stopped snoring.

"Murderer!" the other girl shrieked.

Even as he dashed down the stairs, Gabriel heard footsteps on the landing.

"Mother Dolores! Help! Come quickly!" The answering screams of the others as they awoke rose in a jarring harmony that would have waked the dead.

When he gained the street, Gabriel looked wildly around. He had not planned for this. Sedbury's carriage was long gone, the traitor.

Gabriel had no means of escape except his own two feet, and they were looking strangely blurred at the moment.

Suddenly, his gaze lit on a dray cart and horse standing placidly across the way. No sign of a driver. Once again, luck had intervened. He sprinted across the street, took a moment to tuck the braid safely into his pocket, and grabbed the reins.

But as he flicked them smartly on the horse's rump, a flock of nightgown-clad young women and one fire-breathing dragon of a Mother Superior in a hideous red nightcap streamed into the street. They threw themselves in front of the horse.

"Stop!" shrieked the dragon lady — the worthy Mother Dolores, no doubt. She clutched a chamber pot and waved it wildly at the horse. Like baby chicks following the mother hen, the novitiates raised their arms, too. And just like that, the street was filled with a mob of flailing, screaming females in high-necked night-rails.

Gabriel had a sinking feeling his luck had turned.

The horse did a nervous sideways dance and tried to rear, something no self-respecting dray nag would do. The women ran toward him — didn't they have better sense than to race into the path of a thrashing horse?

He jerked on the reins, forcing the horse to still. The horse shuffled backward, trying to ease the pressure of the bit. Gabriel bent forward just as the nag's tail whipped up and caught the corner of his eye. The searing pain brought tears to his eyes.

"My hair! He cut off my hair!" cried a young woman he took to be Mary, awake at last.

"Quiet, child!" cried Mother Dolores, whose nightcap dipped perilously low over one eye. She turned to Gabriel. "You shall die for this, you scoundrel. They will hang you forthwith, and I shall be among the spectators."

"Now, now," Gabriel warned. His eye hurt like hell, and he was in no mood for vengeful nuns. "You must set a proper example, Mother. Charity and forgiveness and all that."

Mother Dolores stared at him. "What sort of monster are you?"

"He claimed he was an angel," said the girl who had first discovered him.

"I see." Her face was grim. "Matilde, fetch the Watch."

"That is not necessary," Gabriel assured her. "I was on the point of leaving." Shielding his injured eye, he jumped down, squinting as he searched for a path through the sea of women. But their flailing forms pressed against him, forming a human wall.

Imprisoned by virgins. Was there anything more lowering?

"Ladies, step aside," he thundered, trying his best to sound archangelic. "My work here is done. The, er, heavens demand my return." He saw the indecision in their eyes. Almost, he had them. Then the dragon lady intervened.

"Sit on him, girls!" she commanded.

As one, the young women wrestled him to the cobblestones and planted themselves on him.

"Now, angel," she scoffed, waving the chamber pot at him. "Let's see you fly away."

"Alas, 'tis the molting season," Gabriel managed, forcing air through his badly compressed lungs. "My wings have been clipped."

"More than clipped, you heartless villain. Your goose, sir, is cooked!" With that, Mother Dolores brought the chamber pot down on his head.

Yes, virgins were nothing but trouble. He would never go near one again.

Chapter One

"THE HANGING IS at noon," said a gruff masculine voice.

"I do hope Miss Wentworth will be brave." Louisa Peabody tied a black scarf over her hair, obscuring flaxen gold so gleaming it could be seen from a distance. She shrugged into a man's dark jacket several sizes too large. Then she placed a cap over the scarf and checked her appearance in the dingy tack room mirror. "I am afraid this is the best I can do."

The man at her side inspected her dark breeches, boots, and coat. When his gaze reached her head covering, he frowned uncertainly.

"Do not worry, David," she said. "I have tied the scarf tight. Not a strand of my hair is visible. Besides, I will be inside the carriage."

David Ferguson was a man of considerable size but few words. Although he did not reply, the tension in his jaw was answer enough. Louisa made one last effort to assuage his doubts. "Alice Wentworth has no one, David. All she did was steal a loaf of bread to feed her child. We must help her."

Their gazes met in pain shared and remembered.

Then, without a word, David walked out to the carriage.

"Be careful," warned the only other occupant of the stable, a boy of about twelve. Holding the halter of a big black stallion, he regarded Louisa with a mixture of determination and doubt. The weight of nascent masculinity sat uncertainly upon his slender shoulders. "I still say you ought to let me go. Midnight and I could cut through a crowd like a knife through butter."

Louisa shook her head. "Midnight is too high-strung, and he is not yet ready to be ridden again. Besides," she added gently, "you are too young, Sam."

"If you got caught..." His voice, straddling the cusp of manhood, wavered.

"We will not."

"The last time —"

"Was unfortunate. But we learn from our mistakes. Do not worry. David will take care of me." She gave him a quick smile, then followed David out to the carriage.

⌇⌇

His head was in the noose. Any moment, now, the executioner would release the lever on the scaffold and send him on a permanent trip to the Great Beyond. He supposed he should be filled with despair, but he felt nothing. Only a vast emptiness, far more desolate than the possibility of death.

The crowd was enormous, no doubt due to that nun's embellishments at his brief trial, which had been reported in all the newspapers. "Fallen Angel," the headlines had called him. It wouldn't surprise him if she was out there somewhere, waiting for him to die.

Through his suffocating hood, he could hear the impatient shouts, the jeers. A great clamoring mass of humanity had gathered outside Newgate to watch the life jerked out of him in the gruesome satisfaction of justice.

If there was any real justice in the world, those nuns would pay for their lies. They had made him out to be a rapist and attempted murderer. No wonder his trial had taken less than an hour.

Ah, well. The life of a scoundrel was mercifully short. And the life of a clumsy drunk with the stupidity to invade a convent armed with a knife even shorter.

In truth, many of the details of that night eluded him. He remembered the chamber pot being brought down on his head, then darkness. Still, a blow like that would not account for the gaps in his memory. He'd awoken in pain, chained to a wall in a dark cell crawling with vermin. He must have been beaten, for the darkness and pain entwined in him, leaving shadowy images of a thick beam brought down across his shoulders and many fists and implements applied to his person.

One day they had cleaned him up and brought him to the Old Bailey, where he could not summon enough brainpower even to speak his name or account for the circumstances that brought him there. Only after he saw the head nun — Mother Dolores, she styled herself — and listened to her vivid testimony had shreds of memories returned. Pieces were still missing, for a well-dressed Lord Something-or-other testified about events for which he similarly had no recollection. Apparently, he'd tried to steal his lordship's yacht.

Surely, the witnesses had exaggerated. Whatever his crimes, they could not be so heinous as attempted murder, rape, fraudulent taking of his lordship's yacht, and the theft of a cart and horse. He might be a scoundrel, but he was fairly certain he had no taste for crimes such as those.

Justice being what it was, his protestations of innocence mattered not. With no recollection of his actions, he could not supply a convincing alibi; nor could he summon character witnesses, having no memory even of his own name.

So he was here on the scaffold, a mere two days after his trial, wishing he could recall whatever it was he should know to prevent his imminent journey into Hell.

"Save yerself, angel!" jeered a voice.

"Fly away, angel," ridiculed another. "Fly on to heaven."

A chorus of laughter rose from the crowd. He felt the executioner check the ropes that bound his hands. Snug and tight. No way out there. He heard the man speak to the magistrate. He couldn't make out the words, but his imagination easily supplied them:

I'll let him swing long enough to please the crowds, then hand him over to that surgeon who's been after me to give him something for that anatomy class of his. Did you want him to suffer a bit first, my lord? Those nuns seemed awfully upset.

By all means, Executioner, let the bugger suffer. I've seen the way you snap that platform down, and if you do it just right, their necks don't break right away and they hang there reaching with their toes, trying to gain a purchase as the air sucks out of them. The crowd loves that.

Well, he was always one to please the crowds. And this was better than that new treadmill invention he had been threatened with, the cylinder of steps that had to be walked until one dropped. Better to die from hanging than boredom.

He supposed he should say a few words to his Maker, but he doubted anyone up there would hear him. Still, it was worth a shot.

I was looking forward to taking up residence at Sedbury's townhouse. Might have turned respectable, made something of my life, taken a seat in Parliament

Sedbury's townhouse? Parliament? Where had those thoughts come from?

Could've turned all those lords against slavery, told them about Jamaica and the plantations.

Jamaica. Another memory teased his brain.

What's that? Yes, I know it's late to make promises. No, I don't mean a word of them. Hell, the last thing I want is a home.

He knew in his bones that last was true. No home, no family. Never again.

More memories seeped from the recesses of his mind. Perhaps his own name would join them.

Surely, he was someone. Surely, he knew people who could vouch for him.

Abruptly, the floor beneath him shuddered. No time, then. Apparently, there was no one Up There to hear the ramblings of a doomed man. He tried to swallow, but the noose cinched him, closing his throat. *I wouldn't have minded one last chance…*

A cheer went up from the crowd. Bloodthirsty buggers. He'd barely formed the thought when his feet left the ground.

Excited shrieks came from somewhere, probably the vicinity of Mother Dolores. The rope cut into his neck, shooting dizzying pain through him. He could not breathe. His hands wanted to claw at the thing that was choking the life out of him. But they were bound, and it was only in his dreams that he grabbed the rope and flung it off, restoring blessed air to his lungs.

Soon he would slip the knot of his human misery.

The cheers of the crowd faded into oblivion. He heard a strange slashing noise. Felt a jerk. The noose released its hold, and he floated heavenward to his final reward.

Heaven was deuced uncomfortable, though. Heaven felt like a man's strong arms pulling him through the air, depositing him unceremoniously on his head on the floor of a carriage. Heaven sounded like a man's confused curse and a woman's urgent admonition as a blanket was flung over him and the vehicle lurched forward with angry shouts in pursuit.

He should have known he would go straight to Hell. How else to describe the sensation of being slammed about, blind to his surroundings save for the pain? His neck felt as if it had been seared by flames. His air-deprived lungs struggled for breath.

Every time he tried to right his bruised body, a booted foot pushed firmly on his posterior and a woman's sharp voice cut through his misery. "Stay down!"

He stayed down. He would not risk the ire of this Mistress of Hell. But he longed to remove the oppressive hood, to take in enough air to banish the dizziness that threatened his mind's thin hold on the events around him. The jostling of the carriage and the burning in his lungs and neck were his only reality.

Was this Heaven or Hell? Maybe there was no difference, after all.

At last, the carriage rolled to a stop, and someone lifted the blanket that covered him. He heard the woman gasp as her hands removed his hood.

"You are not Miss Wentworth!" She turned to the Goliath who suddenly appeared outside the carriage door. "It is a man, David, a man!"

She removed the cap from her head and a black scarf that had hidden hair the color of spun gold. But that was not what rendered him speechless. It was her eyes, which regarded him with a mixture of fury and confusion, and which were as deep and bottomless and blue as the sea on a cloudless day. A tiny birthmark sat between her upper lip and the tip of her nose.

Hair kissed by the sun. Eyes bluer than blue. A small, tantalizing mark above her lip. If Heaven had angels like this, he had come to the right place.

"Madam," he rasped, his voice all but destroyed by the hangman's noose, "will you marry me?" He gave a wild, mirthless laugh as the world around him faded to black.

***

Louisa stared at the limp form at her feet. "What in the name of all that is holy am I to do?"

David shrugged. "Take him home, I suppose." He climbed back up to his perch and with a flick of the reins sent the team of horses barreling down the road.

Louisa crossed her arms and stared out the window, trying to look anywhere except at the motionless man on the floor. But outside held only trees and grass and the occasional cow. At her feet was the scourge of her sex.

A man. And from the look and sound of him, an insolent, puffed-up, arrogant, shameless example of the breed. *Madam, will you marry me?* Mad hubris, indeed. Facing death had not humbled him. Doubtless he had deserved his death sentence.

And she, of all people, had saved him.

He lay on his side, filling the floor space between the seats and then some. Louisa curled her legs under her to avoid touching him and then decided that in his current state he would scarcely know if she rested her feet on his back.

His hands were still bound, and his body jostled roughly as the carriage raced over the road. Senseless, he was hardly a danger to her, so she reached down and tried to loosen his stiff bindings. At last she freed his hands, and they flopped limply at his sides. There was nothing harmless about their size, however. They were of a piece with that broad back; his shirt fabric strained across the wide expanse of muscle and bone.

The man they had saved was strong and dangerous. A criminal, likely a killer. Yet even if he had been none of those things, Louisa would have hated him on sight.

***

Gabriel awoke to find the giant towering over him. The man was six and a half feet, if he was an inch. His face bore deep, irregular scars, as if unskilled hands had chipped his features out of stubborn granite. His hair was dark, his chin bearded, and he resembled a savage ogre who feasted on naughty children and wayward princesses in fearsome fables. The man studied him from his impossible height, his face as expressive as stone.

His angel sat in a chair beside a hearth with a blazing fire. Her hands were crossed primly in her lap. She held herself stiffly and regarded him with an icy gaze. That long, golden hair flowed around her like a halo.

"Who are you?" Her voice was as dry and brittle as dead leaves.

He was lying on the floor. Not the way to meet an angel. It put him at a distinct disadvantage, for though he was not as tall as the giant, he could certainly stand as straight. And a man on his feet thought better than a man on his posterior.

Gabriel tried to rise. He struggled to his knees, pushed off from his hands, and tried to heave himself up. But he was weaker than he thought. Like a babe whose reach exceeds his grasp, he fell backward onto the floor.

He ached all over. His neck felt as if it was belted in edged steel. His lungs could not take in enough air. His stomach lurched queasily.

An encroaching blackness clawed at him, narrowing his sight to a pinpoint of light, pulling him into the blessedness of oblivion. And though he fought it, his brain felt fuzzy, as if it was packed in cotton wool.

"Name," he murmured, fighting off the blackness. He had to know her name.

"I am Louisa Peabody," she said crisply.

"Lu-we-sa Pe-body." He tried to say it, but his tongue seemed twisted. He must be hallucinating.

"Who are you?" she demanded.

"King," he managed.

"King?" He heard the note of puzzlement in her tone. "Mr. King?"

"Not mister," he said thickly. "King — Majesty."

He grinned. It was a little joke — bitter as sin, and too much work to explain, even if he could recall the details. Perhaps his joke would drive that chill from her voice.

"You are a king?"

He nodded, pleased that she understood. Too bad her features kept blurring around the edges. His eyes must be crossed, for her nose kept moving around on her face. It would be difficult to rivet her with one of his meaningful stares. Mistresses of Hell were probably impervious to masculine charm anyway.

Frowning, he tried to conjure the elusive memory at the edge of his awareness. He vaguely remembered talking to someone — or something — about mending his ways.

Where was he now? Among the living or the dead?

"The only king we have is old George," she said. "You do not look anything like him."

Mad George in Hell, too? He hadn't heard that the king had cocked up his toes, but then Newgate prisoners led a sheltered existence.

"Not George." His voice slurred. "Gabriel." That much had come back to him. Perhaps, there would be more.

"King Gabriel." She rolled the words around on her tongue. "Pray, what are you king of?"

He heard the derision in her tone. Gabriel looked up at her from his lowly position on the floor. She was studying him, her head tilted to one side, waiting. The firelight caught the lights in her hair and sent their shimmering warmth straight to his gut, a spear of heat that threatened a mortal wound. He tried to say the words that burned in his befogged brain.

"Take you there," he vowed.

A large, booted toe nudged him in the ribs. He

had forgotten about the giant. Gabriel ignored the man and smiled at her.

Her eyes filled with uncertainty. Good. He had her interest — much better than her contempt. Conquest would be his. Unless she really was an angel.

She turned toward the giant. "You had best fetch the doctor."

No doctor, Gabriel wanted to say. He was better now. He might even be alive. He raised his head, tried to speak.

"Island. King of island," he said weakly.

Lu-we-sa Pe-body eyed him in disgust, then rose and left the room. The monster lifted him off the floor as if he were a sack of feathers, carted him up some stairs, and tossed him onto a soft feather bed. As Gabriel sank gratefully into it, letting the darkness take him, the man bent down close to his ear.

"And I," the giant snarled contemptuously, "am Queen Charlotte."

Books by Eileen Putman

MAITLAND'S ROGUES:

Andrew Maitland's extraordinary group of daring rogues who worked clandestinely for England during the Napoleonic Wars. Hardened and deadly, they have no use for love—until it ensnares them:

King of Hearts (Book 1)
Lord Shallow (Book 2)
Lord Difficult (Book 3)

LOVE IN DISGUISE:

In these tales of Regency intrigue, nothing is as it seems: A street wench masquerades as a debutante to fulfill a rake's wager; an actress pretends to be a vengeful lord's mistress to catch a killer. A noble war hero disguises himself as a much older man to woo an on-the-shelf spinster. An independent widow forces her disapproving business partner to pretend to be her fiancé— and teach her about passion. All are daring masquerades, with love as the prize.

The Perfect Bride (Book 1)
The Dastardly Duke (Book 2)

A Passionate Performance (Book 3)
Reforming Harriet (Book 4)
Words of Love (Book 5) Coming soon!

Join my Mailing List!
https://www.eileenputman.com/newsletter/